I Say No

Wilkie Collins

TABLE OF CONTENTS

BOOK THE FIRST—AT SCHOOL.

CHAPTER I. THE SMUGGLED SUPPER.

Outside the bedroom the night was black and still. The small rain fell too softly to be heard in the garden; not a leaf stirred in the airless calm; the watch-dog was asleep, the cats were indoors; far or near, under the murky heaven, not a sound was stirring.

Inside the bedroom the night was black and still.

Miss Ladd knew her business as a schoolmistress too well to allow night-lights; and Miss Ladd's young ladies were supposed to be fast asleep, in accordance with the rules of the house. Only at intervals the silence was faintly disturbed, when the restless turning of one of the girls in her bed betrayed itself by a gentle rustling between the sheets. In the long intervals of stillness, not even the softly audible breathing of young creatures asleep was to be heard.

The first sound that told of life and movement revealed the mechanical movement of the clock. Speaking from the lower regions, the tongue of Father Time told the hour before midnight.

A soft voice rose wearily near the door of the room. It counted the strokes of the clock— and reminded one of the girls of the lapse of time.

"Emily! eleven o'clock."

There was no reply. After an interval the weary voice tried again, in louder tones:

"Emily!"

A girl, whose bed was at the inner end of the room, sighed under the heavy heat of the night—and said, in peremptory tones, "Is that Cecilia?"

"Yes."

"What do you want?"

"I'm getting hungry, Emily. Is the new girl asleep?"

The new girl answered promptly and spitefully, "No, she isn't."

Having a private object of their own in view, the five wise virgins of Miss Ladd's first class had waited an hour, in wakeful anticipation of the falling asleep of the stranger—and it had ended in this way! A ripple of laughter ran round the room. The new girl, mortified and offended, entered her protest in plain words.

"You are treating me shamefully! You all distrust me, because I am a stranger."

"Say we don't understand you," Emily answered, speaking for her schoolfellows; "and you will be nearer the truth."

"Who expected you to understand me, when I only came here to-day? I have told you already my name is Francine de Sor. If want to know more, I'm nineteen years old, and I come from the West Indies."

Emily still took the lead. "Why do you come here?" she asked. "Who ever heard of a girl joining a new school just before the holidays? You are nineteen years old, are you? I'm a year younger than you—and I have finished my education. The next big girl in the room is a year younger than me—and she has finished her education. What can you possibly have left to learn at your age?"

"Everything!" cried the stranger from the West Indies, with an outburst of tears. "I'm a poor ignorant creature. Your education ought to have taught you to pity me instead of making fun of me. I hate you all. For shame, for shame!"

Some of the girls laughed. One of them—the hungry girl who had counted the strokes of the clock—took Francine's part.

"Never mind their laughing, Miss de Sor. You are quite right, you have good reason to complain of us."

Miss de Sor dried her eyes. "Thank you—whoever you are," she answered briskly.

"My name is Cecilia Wyvil," the other proceeded. "It was not, perhaps, quite nice of you to say you hated us all. At the same time we have forgotten our good breeding—and the least we can do is to beg your pardon."

This expression of generous sentiment appeared to have an irritating effect on the peremptory young person who took the lead in the room. Perhaps she disapproved of free trade in generous sentiment.

"I can tell you one thing, Cecilia," she said; "you shan't beat ME in generosity. Strike a light, one of you, and lay the blame on me if Miss Ladd finds us out. I mean to shake hands with the new girl—and how can I do it in the dark? Miss de Sor, my name's Brown, and I'm queen of the bedroom. I—not Cecilia—offer our apologies if we have offended you. Cecilia is my dearest friend, but I don't allow her to take the lead in the room. Oh, what a lovely nightgown!"

The sudden flow of candle-light had revealed Francine, sitting up in her bed, and displaying such treasures of real lace over her bosom that the queen lost all sense of royal dignity in irrepressible admiration. "Seven and sixpence," Emily remarked, looking at her own night-gown and despising it. One after another, the girls yielded to the attraction of the wonderful lace. Slim and plump, fair and dark, they circled round the new pupil in their flowing white robes, and arrived by common consent at one and the same conclusion: "How rich her father must be!"

Favored by fortune in the matter of money, was this enviable person possessed of beauty as well?

In the disposition of the beds, Miss de Sor was placed between Cecilia on the right hand, and Emily on the left. If, by some fantastic turn of events, a man—say in the interests of propriety, a married doctor, with Miss Ladd to look after him—had been permitted to enter the room, and had been asked what he thought of the girls when he came out, he would not even have mentioned Francine. Blind to the beauties of the expensive night-gown, he would have noticed her long upper lip, her obstinate chin, her sallow complexion, her eyes placed too close together—and would have turned his attention to her nearest neighbors. On one side his languid interest would have been instantly roused by Cecilia's glowing auburn hair, her exquisitely pure skin, and her tender blue eyes. On the other, he would have discovered a bright little creature, who would have fascinated and perplexed him at one and the same time. If he had been questioned about her by a stranger, he would have been at a loss to say positively whether she was dark or light: he would have remembered how her eyes had held him, but he would not have known of what color they were. And yet, she would have remained a vivid picture in his memory when other impressions, derived at the same time, had vanished. "There was one little witch among them, who was worth all the rest put together; and I can't tell you why. They called her Emily. If I wasn't a married man—" There he would have thought of his wife, and would have sighed and said no more.

While the girls were still admiring Francine, the clock struck the half-hour past eleven.

Cecilia stole on tiptoe to the door—looked out, and listened—closed the door again—and addressed the meeting with the irresistible charm of her sweet voice and her persuasive smile.

"Are none of you hungry yet?" she inquired. "The teachers are safe in their rooms; we have set ourselves right with Francine. Why keep the supper waiting under Emily's bed?"

Such reasoning as this, with such personal attractions to recommend it, admitted of but one reply. The queen waved her hand graciously, and said, "Pull it out."

Is a lovely girl—whose face possesses the crowning charm of expression, whose slightest movement reveals the supple symmetry of her figure—less lovely because she is blessed with a good appetite, and is not ashamed to acknowledge it? With a grace all her own, Cecilia dived under the bed, and produced a basket of jam tarts, a basket of fruit and sweetmeats, a basket of sparkling lemonade, and a superb cake—all paid for by general subscriptions, and smuggled into the room by kind connivance of the servants. On this occasion, the feast was especially plentiful and expensive, in commemoration not only of the arrival of the Midsummer holidays, but of the coming freedom of Miss Ladd's two leading young ladies. With widely different destinies before them, Emily and Cecilia had completed their school life, and were now to go out into the world.

The contrast in the characters of the two girls showed itself, even in such a trifle as the preparations for supper.

Gentle Cecilia, sitting on the floor surrounded by good things, left it to the ingenuity of others to decide whether the baskets should be all emptied at once, or handed round from bed to bed, one at a time. In the meanwhile, her lovely blue eyes rested tenderly on the tarts.

Emily's commanding spirit seized on the reins of government, and employed each of her schoolfellows in the occupation which she was fittest to undertake. "Miss de Sor, let me look at your hand. Ah! I thought so. You have got the thickest wrist among us; you shall draw the corks. If you let the lemonade pop, not a drop of it goes down your throat. Effie, Annis, Priscilla, you are three notoriously lazy girls; it's doing you a true kindness to set you to work. Effie, clear the toilet-table for supper; away with the combs, the brushes, and the looking-glass. Annis, tear the leaves out of your book of exercises, and set them out for plates. No! I'll unpack; nobody touches the baskets but me. Priscilla, you have the prettiest ears in the room. You shall act as sentinel, my dear, and listen at the door. Cecilia, when you have done devouring those tarts with your eyes, take that pair of scissors (Miss de Sor, allow me to apologize for the mean manner in which this school is carried on; the knives and forks are counted and locked up every night)—I say take that pair of scissors, Cecilia, and carve the cake, and don't keep the largest bit for yourself. Are we all ready? Very well. Now take example by me. Talk as much as you like, so long as you don't talk too loud. There is one other thing before we begin. The men always propose toasts on these occasions; let's be like the men. Can any of you make a speech? Ah, it falls on me as usual. I propose the first toast. Down with all schools and teachers—especially the new teacher, who came this half year. Oh, mercy, how it stings!" The fixed gas in the lemonade took the orator, at that moment, by the throat, and effectually checked the flow of her eloquence. It made no difference to the girls. Excepting the ease of feeble stomachs, who cares for eloquence in the presence of a supper-table? There were no feeble stomachs in that bedroom. With what inexhaustible energy Miss Ladd's young ladies ate and drank! How merrily they enjoyed the delightful privilege of talking nonsense! And—alas! alas!—how vainly they tried, in after life, to renew the once unalloyed enjoyment of tarts and lemonade!

In the unintelligible scheme of creation, there appears to be no human happiness—not even the happiness of schoolgirls—which is ever complete. Just as it was drawing to a close, the enjoyment of the feast was interrupted by an alarm from the sentinel at the door.

"Put out the candle!" Priscilla whispered "Somebody on the stairs."

CHAPTER II. BIOGRAPHY IN THE BEDROOM.

The candle was instantly extinguished. In discreet silence the girls stole back to their beds, and listened.

As an aid to the vigilance of the sentinel, the door had been left ajar. Through the narrow opening, a creaking of the broad wooden stairs of the old house became audible. In another moment there was silence. An interval passed, and the creaking was heard again. This time, the sound was distant and diminishing. On a sudden it stopped. The midnight silence was disturbed no more.

What did this mean?

Had one among the many persons in authority under Miss Ladd's roof heard the girls talking, and ascended the stairs to surprise them in the act of violating one of the rules of the house? So far, such a proceeding was by no means uncommon. But was it within the limits of probability that a teacher should alter her opinion of her own duty half-way up the stairs, and deliberately go back to her own room again? The bare idea of such a thing was absurd on the face of it. What more rational explanation could ingenuity discover on the spur of the moment?

Francine was the first to offer a suggestion. She shook and shivered in her bed, and said, "For heaven's sake, light the candle again! It's a Ghost."

"Clear away the supper, you fools, before the ghost can report us to Miss Ladd."

With this excellent advice Emily checked the rising panic. The door was closed, the candle was lit; all traces of the supper disappeared. For five minutes more they listened again. No sound came from the stairs; no teacher, or ghost of a teacher, appeared at the door.

Having eaten her supper, Cecilia's immediate anxieties were at an end; she was at leisure to exert her intelligence for the benefit of her schoolfellows. In her gentle ingratiating way, she offered a composing suggestion. "When we heard the creaking, I don't believe there was anybody on the stairs. In these old houses there are always strange noises at night—and they say the stairs here were made more than two hundred years since."

The girls looked at each other with a sense of relief—but they waited to hear the opinion of the queen. Emily, as usual, justified the confidence placed in her. She discovered an ingenious method of putting Cecilia's suggestion to the test.

"Let's go on talking," she said. "If Cecilia is right, the teachers are all asleep, and we have nothing to fear from them. If she's wrong, we shall sooner or later see one of them at the door. Don't be alarmed, Miss de Sor. Catching us talking at night, in this school, only means a reprimand. Catching us with a light, ends in punishment. Blow out the candle."

Francine's belief in the ghost was too sincerely superstitious to be shaken: she started up in bed. "Oh, don't leave me in the dark! I'll take the punishment, if we are found out."

"On your sacred word of honor?" Emily stipulated.

"Yes—yes."

The queen's sense of humor was tickled.

"There's something funny," she remarked, addressing her subjects, "in a big girl like this coming to a new school and beginning with a punishment. May I ask if you are a foreigner, Miss de Sor?"

"My papa is a Spanish gentleman," Francine answered, with dignity.

"And your mamma?"

"My mamma is English."

"And you have always lived in the West Indies?"

"I have always lived in the Island of St. Domingo."

Emily checked off on her fingers the different points thus far discovered in the character of Mr. de Sor's daughter. "She's ignorant, and superstitious, and foreign, and rich. My dear (forgive the familiarity), you are an interesting girl—and we must really know more of you. Entertain the bedroom. What have you been about all your life? And what in the name of wonder, brings you here? Before you begin I insist on one condition, in the name of all the young ladies in the room. No useful information about the West Indies!"

Francine disappointed her audience.

She was ready enough to make herself an object of interest to her companions; but she was not possessed of the capacity to arrange events in their proper order, necessary to the recital of the simplest narrative. Emily was obliged to help her, by means of questions. In one respect, the result justified the trouble taken to obtain it. A sufficient reason was discovered for the extraordinary appearance of a new pupil, on the day before the school closed for the holidays.

Mr. de Sor's elder brother had left him an estate in St. Domingo, and a fortune in money as well; on the one easy condition that he continued to reside in the island. The question of expense being now beneath the notice of the family, Francine had been sent to England, especially recommended to Miss Ladd as a young lady with grand prospects, sorely in need of a fashionable education. The voyage had been so timed, by the advice of the schoolmistress, as to make the holidays a means of obtaining this object privately. Francine was to be taken to Brighton, where excellent masters could be obtained to assist Miss Ladd. With six weeks before her, she might in some degree make up for lost time; and, when the school opened again, she would avoid the mortification of being put down in the lowest class, along with the children.

The examination of Miss de Sor having produced these results was pursued no further. Her character now appeared in a new, and not very attractive, light. She audaciously took to herself the whole credit of telling her story:

"I think it's my turn now," she said, "to be interested and amused. May I ask you to begin, Miss Emily? All I know of you at present is, that your family name is Brown."

Emily held up her hand for silence.

Was the mysterious creaking on the stairs making itself heard once more? No. The sound that had caught Emily's quick ear came from the beds, on the opposite side of the room, occupied by the three lazy girls. With no new alarm to disturb them, Effie, Annis, and Priscilla had yielded to the composing influences of a good supper and a warm night. They were fast asleep—and the stoutest of the three (softly, as became a young lady) was snoring! The unblemished reputation of the bedroom was dear to Emily, in her capacity of queen. She felt herself humiliated in the presence of the new pupil.

"If that fat girl ever gets a lover," she said indignantly, "I shall consider it my duty to warn the poor man before he marries her. Her ridiculous name is Euphemia. I have christened her (far more appropriately) Boiled Veal. No color in her hair, no color in her eyes, no color in her complexion. In short, no flavor in Euphemia. You naturally object to snoring. Pardon me if I turn my back on you—I am going to throw my slipper at her."

The soft voice of Cecilia—suspiciously drowsy in tone—interposed in the interests of mercy.

"She can't help it, poor thing; and she really isn't loud enough to disturb us."

"She won't disturb you, at any rate! Rouse yourself, Cecilia. We are wide awake on this side of the room—and Francine says it's our turn to amuse her."

A low murmur, dying away gently in a sigh, was the only answer. Sweet Cecilia had yielded to the somnolent influences of the supper and the night. The soft infection of repose seemed to be in some danger of communicating itself to Francine. Her large mouth opened luxuriously in a long-continued yawn.

"Good-night!" said Emily.

Miss de Sor became wide awake in an instant.

"No," she said positively; "you are quite mistaken if you think I am going to sleep. Please exert yourself, Miss Emily—I am waiting to be interested."

Emily appeared to be unwilling to exert herself. She preferred talking of the weather.

"Isn't the wind rising?" she said.

There could be no doubt of it. The leaves in the garden were beginning to rustle, and the pattering of the rain sounded on the windows.

Francine (as her straight chin proclaimed to all students of physiognomy) was an obstinate girl. Determined to carry her point she tried Emily's own system on Emily herself—she put questions.

"Have you been long at this school?"

"More than three years."

"Have you got any brothers and sisters?"

"I am the only child."

"Are your father and mother alive?"

Emily suddenly raised herself in bed.

"Wait a minute," she said; "I think I hear it again."

"The creaking on the stairs?"

"Yes."

Either she was mistaken, or the change for the worse in the weather made it not easy to hear slight noises in the house. The wind was still rising. The passage of it through the great trees in the garden began to sound like the fall of waves on a distant beach. It drove the rain—a heavy downpour by this time—rattling against the windows.

"Almost a storm, isn't it?" Emily said

Francine's last question had not been answered yet. She took the earliest opportunity of repeating it:

"Never mind the weather," she said. "Tell me about your father and mother. Are they both alive?"

Emily's reply only related to one of her parents.

"My mother died before I was old enough to feel my loss."

"And your father?"

Emily referred to another relative—her father's sister. "Since I have grown up," she proceeded, "my good aunt has been a second mother to me. My story is, in one respect, the reverse of yours. You are unexpectedly rich; and I am unexpectedly poor. My aunt's fortune was to have been my fortune, if I outlived her. She has been ruined by the failure of a bank. In her old age, she must live on an income of two hundred a year—and I must get my own living when I leave school."

"Surely your father can help you?" Francine persisted.

"His property is landed property." Her voice faltered, as she referred to him, even in that indirect manner. "It is entailed; his nearest male relative inherits it."

The delicacy which is easily discouraged was not one of the weaknesses in the nature of Francine.

"Do I understand that your father is dead?" she asked.

Our thick-skinned fellow-creatures have the rest of us at their mercy: only give them time, and they carry their point in the end. In sad subdued tones—telling of deeply-rooted reserves of feeling, seldom revealed to strangers—Emily yielded at last.

"Yes," she said, "my father is dead."

"Long ago?"

"Some people might think it long ago. I was very fond of my father. It's nearly four years since he died, and my heart still aches when I think of him. I'm not easily depressed by troubles, Miss de Sor. But his death was sudden—he was in his grave when I first heard of it—and—Oh, he was so good to me; he was so good to me!"

The gay high-spirited little creature who took the lead among them all—who was the life and soul of the school—hid her face in her hands, and burst out crying.

Startled and—to do her justice—ashamed, Francine attempted to make excuses. Emily's generous nature passed over the cruel persistency that had tortured her. "No no; I have nothing to forgive. It isn't your fault. Other girls have not mothers and brothers and sisters—and get reconciled to such a loss as mine. Don't make excuses."

"Yes, but I want you to know that I feel for you," Francine insisted, without the slightest approach to sympathy in face, voice, or manner. "When my uncle died, and left us all the money, papa was much shocked. He trusted to time to help him."

"Time has been long about it with me, Francine. I am afraid there is something perverse in my nature; the hope of meeting again in a better world seems so faint and so far away. No more of it now! Let us talk of that good creature who is asleep on the other side of you. Did I tell you that I must earn my own bread when I leave school? Well, Cecilia has written home and found an employment for me. Not a situation as governess—something quite out of the common way. You shall hear all about it."

In the brief interval that had passed, the weather had begun to change again. The wind was as high as ever; but to judge by the lessening patter on the windows the rain was passing away.

Emily began.

She was too grateful to her friend and school-fellow, and too deeply interested in her story, to notice the air of indifference with which Francine settled herself on her pillow to hear the praises of Cecilia. The most beautiful girl in the school was not an object of interest to a young lady with an obstinate chin and unfortunately-placed eyes. Pouring warm from the speaker's heart the story ran smoothly on, to the monotonous accompaniment of the moaning wind. By fine degrees Francine's eyes closed, opened and closed again. Toward the latter part of the narrative Emily's memory became, for the moment only, confused between two events. She stopped to consider—noticed Francine's silence, in an interval when she might have said a word of encouragement—and looked closer at her. Miss de Sor was asleep.

"She might have told me she was tired," Emily said to herself quietly. "Well! the best thing I can do is to put out the light and follow her example."

As she took up the extinguisher, the bedroom door was suddenly opened from the outer side. A tall woman, robed in a black dressing-gown, stood on the threshold, looking at Emily.

CHAPTER III. THE LATE MR. BROWN.

The woman's lean, long-fingered hand pointed to the candle.

"Don't put it out." Saying those words, she looked round the room, and satisfied herself that the other girls were asleep.

Emily laid down the extinguisher. "You mean to report us, of course," she said. "I am the only one awake, Miss Jethro; lay the blame on me."

"I have no intention of reporting you. But I have something to say."

She paused, and pushed her thick black hair (already streaked with gray) back from her temples. Her eyes, large and dark and dim, rested on Emily with a sorrowful interest. "When your young friends wake to-morrow morning," she went on, "you can tell them that the new teacher, whom nobody likes, has left the school."

For once, even quick-witted Emily was bewildered. "Going away," she said, "when you have only been here since Easter!"

Miss Jethro advanced, not noticing Emily's expression of surprise. "I am not very strong at the best of times," she continued, "may I sit down on your bed?" Remarkable on other occasions for her cold composure, her voice trembled as she made that request—a strange request surely, when there were chairs at her disposal.

Emily made room for her with the dazed look of a girl in a dream. "I beg your pardon, Miss Jethro, one of the things I can't endure is being puzzled. If you don't mean to report us, why did you come in and catch me with the light?"

Miss Jethro's explanation was far from relieving the perplexity which her conduct had caused.

"I have been mean enough," she answered, "to listen at the door, and I heard you talking of your father. I want to hear more about him. That is why I came in."

"You knew my father!" Emily exclaimed.

"I believe I knew him. But his name is so common—there are so many thousands of 'James Browns' in England—that I am in fear of making a mistake. I heard you say that he died nearly four years since. Can you mention any particulars which might help to enlighten me? If you think I am taking a liberty—"

Emily stopped her. "I would help you if I could," she said. "But I was in poor health at the time; and I was staying with friends far away in Scotland, to try change of air. The news of my father's death brought on a relapse. Weeks passed before I was strong enough to travel—weeks and weeks before I saw his grave! I can only tell you what I know from my aunt. He died of heart-complaint."

Miss Jethro started.

Emily looked at her for the first time, with eyes that betrayed a feeling of distrust. "What have I said to startle you?" she asked.

"Nothing! I am nervous in stormy weather—don't notice me." She went on abruptly with her inquiries. "Will you tell me the date of your father's death?"

"The date was the thirtieth of September, nearly four years since."

She waited, after that reply.

Miss Jethro was silent.

"And this," Emily continued, "is the thirtieth of June, eighteen hundred and eighty-one. You can now judge for yourself. Did you know my father?"

Miss Jethro answered mechanically, using the same words.

"I did know your father."

Emily's feeling of distrust was not set at rest. "I never heard him speak of you," she said.

In her younger days the teacher must have been a handsome woman. Her grandly-formed features still suggested the idea of imperial beauty—perhaps Jewish in its origin. When Emily said, "I never heard him speak of you," the color flew into her pallid cheeks: her dim eyes became alive again with a momentary light. She left her seat on the bed, and, turning away, mastered the emotion that shook her.

"How hot the night is!" she said: and sighed, and resumed the subject with a steady countenance. "I am not surprised that your father never mentioned me—to you." She spoke quietly, but her face was paler than ever. She sat down again on the bed. "Is there anything I can do for you," she asked, "before I go away? Oh, I only mean some trifling service that would lay you under no obligation, and would not oblige you to keep up your acquaintance with me."

Her eyes—the dim black eyes that must once have been irresistibly beautiful—looked at Emily so sadly that the generous girl reproached herself for having doubted her father's friend. "Are you thinking of him," she said gently, "when you ask if you can be of service to me?"

Miss Jethro made no direct reply. "You were fond of your father?" she added, in a whisper. "You told your schoolfellow that your heart still aches when you speak of him."

"I only told her the truth," Emily answered simply.

Miss Jethro shuddered—on that hot night!—shuddered as if a chill had struck her.

Emily held out her hand; the kind feeling that had been roused in her glittered prettily in her eyes. "I am afraid I have not done you justice," she said. "Will you forgive me and shake hands?"

Miss Jethro rose, and drew back. "Look at the light!" she exclaimed.

The candle was all burned out. Emily still offered her hand—and still Miss Jethro refused to see it.

"There is just light enough left," she said, "to show me my way to the door. Good-night—and good-by."

Emily caught at her dress, and stopped her. "Why won't you shake hands with me?" she asked.

The wick of the candle fell over in the socket, and left them in the dark. Emily resolutely held the teacher's dress. With or without light, she was still bent on making Miss Jethro explain herself.

They had throughout spoken in guarded tones, fearing to disturb the sleeping girls. The sudden darkness had its inevitable effect. Their voices sank to whispers now. "My father's friend," Emily pleaded, "is surely my friend?"

"Drop the subject."

"Why?"

"You can never be my friend."

"Why not?"

"Let me go!"

Emily's sense of self-respect forbade her to persist any longer. "I beg your pardon for having kept you here against your will," she said—and dropped her hold on the dress.

Miss Jethro instantly yielded on her side. "I am sorry to have been obstinate," she answered. "If you do despise me, it is after all no more than I have deserved." Her hot breath beat on Emily's face: the unhappy woman must have bent over the bed as she made her confession. "I am not a fit person for you to associate with."

"I don't believe it!"

Miss Jethro sighed bitterly. "Young and warm hearted—I was once like you!" She controlled that outburst of despair. Her next words were spoken in steadier tones. "You will have it—you shall have it!" she said. "Some one (in this house or out of it; I don't know which) has betrayed me to the mistress of the school. A wretch in my situation suspects everybody, and worse still, does it without reason or excuse. I heard you girls talking when you ought to have been asleep. You all dislike me. How did I know it mightn't be one of you? Absurd, to a person with a well-balanced mind! I went halfway up the stairs, and felt ashamed of myself, and went back to my room. If I could only have got some rest! Ah, well, it was not to be done. My own vile suspicions kept me awake; I left my bed again. You know what I heard on the other side of that door, and why I was interested in hearing it. Your father never told me he had a daughter. 'Miss Brown,' at this school, was any 'Miss Brown,' to me. I had no idea of who you really were until to-night. I'm wandering. What does all this matter to you? Miss Ladd has been merciful; she lets me go without exposing me. You can guess what has happened. No? Not even yet? Is it innocence or kindness that makes you so slow to understand? My dear, I have obtained admission to this respectable house by means of false references, and I have been discovered. Now you know why you must not be the friend of such a woman as I am! Once more, good-night—and good-by."

Emily shrank from that miserable farewell.

"Bid me good-night," she said, "but don't bid me good-by. Let me see you again."

"Never!"

The sound of the softly-closed door was just audible in the darkness. She had spoken—she had gone—never to be seen by Emily again.

Miserable, interesting, unfathomable creature—the problem that night of Emily's waking thoughts: the phantom of her dreams. "Bad? or good?" she asked herself. "False; for she listened at the door. True; for she told me the tale of her own disgrace. A friend of my father; and she never knew that he had a daughter. Refined, accomplished, lady-like; and she stoops to use a false reference. Who is to reconcile such contradictions as these?"

Dawn looked in at the window—dawn of the memorable day which was, for Emily, the beginning of a new life. The years were before her; and the years in their course reveal baffling mysteries of life and death.

Francine was awakened the next morning by one of the housemaids, bringing up her breakfast on a tray. Astonished at this concession to laziness, in an institution devoted to the practice of all virtues, she looked round. The bedroom was deserted.

"The other young ladies are as busy as bees, miss," the housemaid explained. "They were up and dressed two hours ago: and the breakfast has been cleared away long since. It's Miss Emily's fault. She wouldn't allow them to wake you; she said you could be of no possible use downstairs, and you had better be treated like a visitor. Miss Cecilia was so distressed at your missing your breakfast that she spoke to the housekeeper, and I was sent up to you. Please to excuse it if the tea's cold. This is Grand Day, and we are all topsy-turvy in consequence."

Inquiring what "Grand Day" meant, and why it produced this extraordinary result in a ladies' school, Francine discovered that the first day of the vacation was devoted to the distribution of prizes, in the presence of parents, guardians and friends. An Entertainment was added, comprising those merciless tests of human endurance called Recitations; light refreshments and musical performances being distributed at intervals, to encourage the exhausted audience. The local newspaper sent a reporter to describe the proceedings, and some of Miss Ladd's young ladies enjoyed the intoxicating luxury of seeing their names in print.

"It begins at three o'clock," the housemaid went on, "and, what with practicing and rehearsing, and ornamenting the schoolroom, there's a hubbub fit to make a person's head spin. Besides which," said the girl, lowering her voice, and approaching a little nearer to Francine, "we have all been taken by surprise. The first thing in the morning Miss Jethro left us, without saying good-by to anybody."

"Who is Miss Jethro?"

"The new teacher, miss. We none of us liked her, and we all suspect there's something wrong. Miss Ladd and the clergyman had a long talk together yesterday (in private, you know), and they sent for Miss Jethro—which looks bad, doesn't it? Is there anything more I can do for you, miss? It's a beautiful day after the rain. If I was you, I should go and enjoy myself in the garden."

Having finished her breakfast, Francine decided on profiting by this sensible suggestion.

The servant who showed her the way to the garden was not favorably impressed by the new pupil: Francine's temper asserted itself a little too plainly in her face. To a girl possessing a high opinion of her own importance it was not very agreeable to feel herself excluded, as an illiterate stranger, from the one absorbing interest of her schoolfellows. "Will the time ever come," she wondered bitterly, "when I shall win a prize, and sing and play before all the company? How I should enjoy making the girls envy me!"

A broad lawn, overshadowed at one end by fine old trees—flower beds and shrubberies, and winding paths prettily and invitingly laid out—made the garden a welcome refuge on that fine summer morning. The novelty of the scene, after her experience in the West Indies, the delicious breezes cooled by the rain of the night, exerted their cheering influence even on the sullen disposition of Francine. She smiled, in spite of herself, as she followed the pleasant paths, and heard the birds singing their summer songs over her head.

Wandering among the trees, which occupied a considerable extent of ground, she passed into an open space beyond, and discovered an old fish-pond, overgrown by aquatic plants. Driblets of water trickled from a dilapidated fountain in the middle. On the further side of the pond the ground sloped downward toward the south, and revealed, over a low paling, a pretty view of a village and its church, backed by fir woods mounting the heathy sides of a range of hills beyond. A fanciful little wooden building, imitating the form of a Swiss cottage, was placed so as to command the prospect. Near it, in the shadow of the building, stood a rustic chair and table—with a color-box on one, and a portfolio on the other.

10

Fluttering over the grass, at the mercy of the capricious breeze, was a neglected sheet of drawing-paper. Francine ran round the pond, and picked up the paper just as it was on the point of being tilted into the water. It contained a sketch in water colors of the village and the woods, and Francine had looked at the view itself with indifference—the picture of the view interested her. Ordinary visitors to Galleries of Art, which admit students, show the same strange perversity. The work of the copyist commands their whole attention; they take no interest in the original picture.

Looking up from the sketch, Francine was startled. She discovered a man, at the window of the Swiss summer-house, watching her.

"When you have done with that drawing," he said quietly, "please let me have it back again."

He was tall and thin and dark. His finely-shaped intelligent face—hidden, as to the lower part of it, by a curly black beard—would have been absolutely handsome, even in the eyes of a schoolgirl, but for the deep furrows that marked it prematurely between the eyebrows, and at the sides of the mouth. In the same way, an underlying mockery impaired the attraction of his otherwise refined and gentle manner. Among his fellow-creatures, children and dogs were the only critics who appreciated his merits without discovering the defects which lessened the favorable appreciation of him by men and women. He dressed neatly, but his morning coat was badly made, and his picturesque felt hat was too old. In short, there seemed to be no good quality about him which was not perversely associated with a drawback of some kind. He was one of those harmless and luckless men, possessed of excellent qualities, who fail nevertheless to achieve popularity in their social sphere.

Francine handed his sketch to him, through the window; doubtful whether the words that he had addressed to her were spoken in jest or in earnest.

"I only presumed to touch your drawing," she said, "because it was in danger."

"What danger?" he inquired.

Francine pointed to the pond. "If I had not been in time to pick it up, it would have been blown into the water."

"Do you think it was worth picking up?"

Putting that question, he looked first at the sketch—then at the view which it represented—then back again at the sketch. The corners of his mouth turned upward with a humorous expression of scorn. "Madam Nature," he said, "I beg your pardon." With those words, he composedly tore his work of art into small pieces, and scattered them out of the window.

"What a pity!" said Francine.

He joined her on the ground outside the cottage. "Why is it a pity?" he asked.

"Such a nice drawing."

"It isn't a nice drawing."

"You're not very polite, sir."

He looked at her—and sighed as if he pitied so young a woman for having a temper so ready to take offense. In his flattest contradictions he always preserved the character of a politely-positive man.

"Put it in plain words, miss," he replied. "I have offended the predominant sense in your nature—your sense of self-esteem. You don't like to be told, even indirectly, that you know nothing of Art. In these days, everybody knows everything—and thinks nothing worth knowing after all. But beware how you presume on an appearance of indifference, which is nothing but conceit in disguise. The ruling passion of civilized humanity is, Conceit. You may try the regard of your dearest friend in any other way, and be forgiven. Ruffle the smooth surface of your friend's self-esteem—and there will be an acknowledged coolness between you which will last for life. Excuse me for giving you the benefit of my trumpery experience. This sort of smart talk is my form of conceit. Can I be of use to you in some better way? Are you looking for one of our young ladies?"

Francine began to feel a certain reluctant interest in him when he spoke of "our young ladies." She asked if he belonged to the school.

The corners of his mouth turned up again. "I'm one of the masters," he said. "Are you going to belong to the school, too?"

Francine bent her head, with a gravity and condescension intended to keep him at his proper distance. Far from being discouraged, he permitted his curiosity to take additional liberties. "Are you to have the misfortune of being one of my pupils?" he asked.

"I don't know who you are."

"You won't be much wiser when you do know. My name is Alban Morris."

Francine corrected herself. "I mean, I don't know what you teach."

Alban Morris pointed to the fragments of his sketch from Nature. "I am a bad artist," he said. "Some bad artists become Royal Academicians. Some take to drink. Some get a pension. And some—I am one of them—find refuge in schools. Drawing is an 'Extra' at this school. Will you take my advice? Spare your good father's pocket; say you don't want to learn to draw."

He was so gravely in earnest that Francine burst out laughing. "You are a strange man," she said.

"Wrong again, miss. I am only an unhappy man."

The furrows in his face deepened, the latent humor died out of his eyes. He turned to the summer-house window, and took up a pipe and tobacco pouch, left on the ledge.

"I lost my only friend last year," he said. "Since the death of my dog, my pipe is the one companion I have left. Naturally I am not allowed to enjoy the honest fellow's society in the presence of ladies. They have their own taste in perfumes. Their clothes and their letters reek with the foetid secretion of the musk deer. The clean vegetable smell of tobacco is unendurable to them. Allow me to retire—and let me thank you for the trouble you took to save my drawing."

The tone of indifference in which he expressed his gratitude piqued Francine. She resented it by drawing her own conclusion from what he had said of the ladies and the musk deer. "I was wrong in admiring your drawing," she remarked; "and wrong again in thinking you a strange man. Am I wrong, for the third time, in believing that you dislike women?"

"I am sorry to say you are right," Alban Morris answered gravely.

"Is there not even one exception?"

The instant the words passed her lips, she saw that there was some secretly sensitive feeling in him which she had hurt. His black brows gathered into a frown, his piercing eyes looked at her with angry surprise. It was over in a moment. He raised his shabby hat, and made her a bow.

"There is a sore place still left in me," he said; "and you have innocently hit it. Good-morning."

Before she could speak again, he had turned the corner of the summer-house, and was lost to view in a shrubbery on the westward side of the grounds.

CHAPTER V. DISCOVERIES IN THE GARDEN.

Left by herself, Miss de Sor turned back again by way of the trees.

So far, her interview with the drawing-master had helped to pass the time. Some girls might have found it no easy task to arrive at a true view of the character of Alban Morris. Francine's essentially superficial observation set him down as "a little mad," and left him there, judged and dismissed to her own entire satisfaction.

Arriving at the lawn, she discovered Emily pacing backward and forward, with her head down and her hands behind her, deep in thought. Francine's high opinion of herself would have carried her past any of the other girls, unless they had made special advances to her. She stopped and looked at Emily.

It is the sad fate of little women in general to grow too fat and to be born with short legs. Emily's slim finely-strung figure spoke for itself as to the first of these misfortunes, and asserted its happy freedom from the second, if she only walked across a room. Nature had built her, from head to foot, on a skeleton-scaffolding in perfect proportion. Tall or short matters little to the result, in women who possess the first and foremost advantage of beginning well in their bones. When they live to old age, they often astonish thoughtless men, who walk behind them in the street. "I give you my honor, she was as easy and upright as a young girl; and when you got in front of her and looked—white hair, and seventy years of age."

Francine approached Emily, moved by a rare impulse in her nature—the impulse to be sociable. "You look out of spirits," she began. "Surely you don't regret leaving school?"

In her present mood, Emily took the opportunity (in the popular phrase) of snubbing Francine. "You have guessed wrong; I do regret," she answered. "I have found in Cecilia my dearest friend at school. And school brought with it the change in my life which has helped me to bear the loss of my father. If you must know what I was thinking of just now, I was thinking of my aunt. She has not answered my last letter—and I'm beginning to be afraid she is ill."

"I'm very sorry," said Francine.

"Why? You don't know my aunt; and you have only known me since yesterday afternoon. Why are you sorry?"

Francine remained silent. Without realizing it, she was beginning to feel the dominant influence that Emily exercised over the weaker natures that came in contact with her. To find herself irresistibly attracted by a stranger at a new school—an unfortunate little creature, whose destiny was to earn her own living—filled the narrow mind of Miss de Sor with perplexity. Having waited in vain for a reply, Emily turned away, and resumed the train of thought which her schoolfellow had interrupted.

By an association of ideas, of which she was not herself aware, she now passed from thinking of her aunt to thinking of Miss Jethro. The interview of the previous night had dwelt on her mind at intervals, in the hours of the new day.

Acting on instinct rather than on reason, she had kept that remarkable incident in her school life a secret from every one. No discoveries had been made by other persons. In speaking to her staff of teachers, Miss Ladd had alluded to the affair in the most cautious terms. "Circumstances of a private nature have obliged the lady to retire from my school. When we meet after the holidays, another teacher will be in her place." There, Miss Ladd's explanation had begun and ended. Inquiries addressed to the servants had led to no result. Miss Jethro's luggage was to be forwarded to the London terminus of the railway—and Miss Jethro herself had baffled investigation by leaving the school on foot. Emily's interest in the lost teacher was not the transitory interest of curiosity; her father's mysterious friend was a person whom she honestly desired to see again. Perplexed by the difficulty of finding a means of tracing Miss Jethro, she reached the shady limit of the trees, and turned to walk back again. Approaching the place at which she and Francine had met, an idea occurred to her. It was just possible that Miss Jethro might not be unknown to her aunt.

Still meditating on the cold reception that she had encountered, and still feeling the influence which mastered her in spite of herself, Francine interpreted Emily's return as an implied expression of regret. She advanced with a constrained smile, and spoke first.

"How are the young ladies getting on in the schoolroom?" she asked, by way of renewing the conversation.

Emily's face assumed a look of surprise which said plainly, Can't you take a hint and leave me to myself?

Francine was constitutionally impenetrable to reproof of this sort; her thick skin was not even tickled. "Why are you not helping them," she went on; "you who have the clearest head among us and take the lead in everything?"

It may be a humiliating confession to make, yet it is surely true that we are all accessible to flattery. Different tastes appreciate different methods of burning incense—but the perfume is more or less agreeable to all varieties of noses. Francine's method had its tranquilizing effect on Emily. She answered indulgently, "Miss de Sor, I have nothing to do with it."

"Nothing to do with it? No prizes to win before you leave school?"

"I won all the prizes years ago."

"But there are recitations. Surely you recite?"

Harmless words in themselves, pursuing the same smooth course of flattery as before—but with what a different result! Emily's face reddened with anger the moment they were spoken. Having already irritated Alban Morris, unlucky Francine, by a second mischievous interposition of accident, had succeeded in making Emily smart next. "Who has told you," she burst out; "I insist on knowing!"

"Nobody has told me anything!" Francine declared piteously.

"Nobody has told you how I have been insulted?"

"No, indeed! Oh, Miss Brown, who could insult you?"

In a man, the sense of injury does sometimes submit to the discipline of silence. In a woman—never. Suddenly reminded of her past wrongs (by the pardonable error of a polite schoolfellow), Emily committed the startling inconsistency of appealing to the sympathies of Francine!

"Would you believe it? I have been forbidden to recite—I, the head girl of the school. Oh, not to-day! It happened a month ago—when we were all in consultation, making our arrangements. Miss Ladd asked me if I had decided on a piece to recite. I said, 'I have not only decided, I have learned the piece.' 'And what may it be?' 'The dagger-scene in Macbeth.' There was a howl—I can call it by no other name—a howl of indignation. A man's soliloquy, and, worse still, a murdering man's soliloquy, recited by one of Miss Ladd's young ladies, before an audience of parents and guardians! That was the tone they took with me. I was as firm as a rock. The dagger-scene or nothing. The result is—nothing! An insult to Shakespeare, and an insult to Me. I felt it—I feel it still. I was prepared for any sacrifice in the cause of the drama. If Miss Ladd had met me in a proper spirit, do you know what I would have done? I would have played Macbeth in costume. Just hear me, and judge for yourself. I begin with a dreadful vacancy in my eyes, and a hollow moaning in my voice: 'Is this a dagger that I see before me—?'"

Reciting with her face toward the trees, Emily started, dropped the character of Macbeth, and instantly became herself again: herself, with a rising color and an angry brightening of the eyes. "Excuse me, I can't trust my memory: I must get the play." With that abrupt apology, she walked away rapidly in the direction of the house.

In some surprise, Francine turned, and looked at the trees. She discovered—in full retreat, on his side—the eccentric drawing-master, Alban Morris.

Did he, too, admire the dagger-scene? And was he modestly desirous of hearing it recited, without showing himself? In that case, why should Emily (whose besetting weakness was certainly not want of confidence in her own resources) leave the garden the moment she caught sight of him? Francine consulted her instincts. She had just arrived at a conclusion which expressed itself outwardly by a malicious smile, when gentle Cecilia appeared on the lawn—a lovable object in a broad straw hat and a white dress, with a nosegay in her bosom—smiling, and fanning herself.

"It's so hot in the schoolroom," she said, "and some of the girls, poor things, are so ill-tempered at rehearsal—I have made my escape. I hope you got your breakfast, Miss de Sor. What have you been doing here, all by yourself?"

"I have been making an interesting discovery," Francine replied.

"An interesting discovery in our garden? What can it be?"

"The drawing-master, my dear, is in love with Emily. Perhaps she doesn't care about him. Or, perhaps, I have been an innocent obstacle in the way of an appointment between them."

Cecilia had breakfasted to her heart's content on her favorite dish—buttered eggs. She was in such good spirits that she was inclined to be coquettish, even when there was no man present to fascinate. "We are not allowed to talk about love in this school," she said—and hid her face behind her fan. "Besides, if it came to Miss Ladd's ears, poor Mr. Morris might lose his situation."

"But isn't it true?" asked Francine.

"It may be true, my dear; but nobody knows. Emily hasn't breathed a word about it to any of us. And Mr. Morris keeps his own secret. Now and then we catch him looking at her—and we draw our own conclusions."

"Did you meet Emily on your way here?"

"Yes, and she passed without speaking to me."

"Thinking perhaps of Mr. Morris."

Cecilia shook her head. "Thinking, Francine, of the new life before her—and regretting, I am afraid, that she ever confided her hopes and wishes to me. Did she tell you last night what her prospects are when she leaves school?"

"She told me you had been very kind in helping her. I daresay I should have heard more, if I had not fallen asleep. What is she going to do?"

"To live in a dull house, far away in the north," Cecilia answered; "with only old people in it. She will have to write and translate for a great scholar, who is studying mysterious inscriptions—hieroglyphics, I think they are called—found among the ruins of Central America. It's really no laughing matter, Francine! Emily made a joke of it, too. 'I'll take anything but a situation as a governess,' she said; 'the children who have Me to teach them would be to be pitied indeed!' She begged and prayed me to help her to get an honest living. What could I do? I could only write home to papa. He is a member of Parliament: and everybody who wants a place seems to think he is bound to find it for them. As it happened, he had heard from an old friend of his (a certain Sir Jervis Redwood), who was in search of a secretary. Being in favor of letting the women compete for employment with the men, Sir Jervis was willing to try, what he calls, 'a female.' Isn't that a horrid way of speaking of us? and Miss Ladd says it's ungrammatical, besides. Papa had written back to say he knew of no lady whom he could recommend. When he got my letter speaking of Emily, he kindly wrote again. In the interval, Sir Jervis had received two applications for the vacant place. They were both from old ladies—and he declined to employ them."

"Because they were old," Francine suggested maliciously.

"You shall hear him give his own reasons, my dear. Papa sent me an extract from his letter. It made me rather angry; and (perhaps for that reason) I think I can repeat it word for word:—'We are four old people in this house, and we don't want a fifth. Let us have a young one to cheer us. If your daughter's friend likes the terms, and is not encumbered with a sweetheart, I will send for her when the school breaks up at midsummer.' Coarse and selfish—isn't it? However, Emily didn't agree with me, when I showed her the extract. She accepted the place, very much to her aunt's surprise and regret, when that excellent person heard of it. Now that the time has come (though Emily won't acknowledge it), I believe she secretly shrinks, poor dear, from the prospect."

"Very likely," Francine agreed—without even a pretense of sympathy. "But tell me, who are the four old people?"

15

"First, Sir Jervis himself—seventy, last birthday. Next, his unmarried sister—nearly eighty. Next, his man-servant, Mr. Rook—well past sixty. And last, his man-servant's wife, who considers herself young, being only a little over forty. That is the household. Mrs. Rook is coming to-day to attend Emily on the journey to the North; and I am not at all sure that Emily will like her."

"A disagreeable woman, I suppose?"

"No—not exactly that. Rather odd and flighty. The fact is, Mrs. Rook has had her troubles; and perhaps they have a little unsettled her. She and her husband used to keep the village inn, close to our park: we know all about them at home. I am sure I pity these poor people. What are you looking at, Francine?"

Feeling no sort of interest in Mr. and Mrs. Rook, Francine was studying her schoolfellow's lovely face in search of defects. She had already discovered that Cecilia's eyes were placed too widely apart, and that her chin wanted size and character.

"I was admiring your complexion, dear," she answered coolly. "Well, and why do you pity the Rooks?"

Simple Cecilia smiled, and went on with her story.

"They are obliged to go out to service in their old age, through a misfortune for which they are in no way to blame. Their customers deserted the inn, and Mr. Rook became bankrupt. The inn got what they call a bad name—in a very dreadful way. There was a murder committed in the house."

"A murder?" cried Francine. "Oh, this is exciting! You provoking girl, why didn't you tell me about it before?"

"I didn't think of it," said Cecilia placidly.

"Do go on! Were you at home when it happened?"

"I was here, at school."

"You saw the newspapers, I suppose?"

"Miss Ladd doesn't allow us to read newspapers. I did hear of it, however, in letters from home. Not that there was much in the letters. They said it was too horrible to be described. The poor murdered gentleman—"

Francine was unaffectedly shocked. "A gentleman!" she exclaimed. "How dreadful!"

"The poor man was a stranger in our part of the country," Cecilia resumed; "and the police were puzzled about the motive for a murder. His pocketbook was missing; but his watch and his rings were found on the body. I remember the initials on his linen because they were the same as my mother's initial before she was married—'J. B.' Really, Francine, that's all I know about it."

"Surely you know whether the murderer was discovered?"

"Oh, yes—of course I know that! The government offered a reward; and clever people were sent from London to help the county police. Nothing came of it. The murderer has never been discovered, from that time to this."

"When did it happen?"

"It happened in the autumn."

"The autumn of last year?"

"No! no! Nearly four years since."

CHAPTER VI. ON THE WAY TO THE VILLAGE.

Alban Morris—discovered by Emily in concealment among the trees—was not content with retiring to another part of the grounds. He pursued his retreat, careless in what

16

direction it might take him, to a footpath across the fields, which led to the highroad and the railway station.

Miss Ladd's drawing-master was in that state of nervous irritability which seeks relief in rapidity of motion. Public opinion in the neighborhood (especially public opinion among the women) had long since decided that his manners were offensive, and his temper incurably bad. The men who happened to pass him on the footpath said "Good-morning" grudgingly. The women took no notice of him—with one exception. She was young and saucy, and seeing him walking at the top of his speed on the way to the railway station, she called after him, "Don't be in a hurry, sir! You're in plenty of time for the London train."

To her astonishment he suddenly stopped. His reputation for rudeness was so well established that she moved away to a safe distance, before she ventured to look at him again. He took no notice of her—he seemed to be considering with himself. The frolicsome young woman had done him a service: she had suggested an idea.

"Suppose I go to London?" he thought. "Why not?—the school is breaking up for the holidays—and she is going away like the rest of them." He looked round in the direction of the schoolhouse. "If I go back to wish her good-by, she will keep out of my way, and part with me at the last moment like a stranger. After my experience of women, to be in love again—in love with a girl who is young enough to be my daughter—what a fool, what a driveling, degraded fool I must be!"

Hot tears rose in his eyes. He dashed them away savagely, and went on again faster than ever—resolved to pack up at once at his lodgings in the village, and to take his departure by the next train.

At the point where the footpath led into the road, he came to a standstill for the second time.

The cause was once more a person of the sex associated in his mind with a bitter sense of injury. On this occasion the person was only a miserable little child, crying over the fragments of a broken jug.

Alban Morris looked at her with his grimly humorous smile. "So you've broken a jug?" he remarked.

"And spilt father's beer," the child answered. Her frail little body shook with terror. "Mother'll beat me when I go home," she said.

"What does mother do when you bring the jug back safe and sound?" Alban asked.

"Gives me bren-butter."

"Very well. Now listen to me. Mother shall give you bread and butter again this time."

The child stared at him with the tears suspended in her eyes. He went on talking to her as seriously as ever.

"You understand what I have just said to you?"

"Yes, sir."

"Have you got a pocket-handkerchief?"

"No, sir."

"Then dry your eyes with mine."

He tossed his handkerchief to her with one hand, and picked up a fragment of the broken jug with the other. "This will do for a pattern," he said to himself. The child stared at the handkerchief—stared at Alban—took courage—and rubbed vigorously at her eyes. The instinct, which is worth all the reason that ever pretended to enlighten mankind—the instinct that never deceives—told this little ignorant creature that she had found a friend. She returned the handkerchief in grave silence. Alban took her up in his arms.

"Your eyes are dry, and your face is fit to be seen," he said. "Will you give me a kiss?" The child gave him a resolute kiss, with a smack in it. "Now come and get another jug," he said, as he put her down. Her red round eyes opened wide in alarm. "Have you got money enough?" she asked. Alban slapped his pocket. "Yes, I have," he answered. "That's a good thing," said the child; "come along."

They went together hand in hand to the village, and bought the new jug, and had it filled at the beer-shop. The thirsty father was at the upper end of the fields, where they were making a drain. Alban carried the jug until they were within sight of the laborer. "You haven't far to go," he said. "Mind you don't drop it again—What's the matter now?"

"I'm frightened."

"Why?"

"Oh, give me the jug."

She almost snatched it out of his hand. If she let the precious minutes slip away, there might be another beating in store for her at the drain: her father was not of an indulgent disposition when his children were late in bringing his beer. On the point of hurrying away, without a word of farewell, she remembered the laws of politeness as taught at the infant school—and dropped her little curtsey—and said, "Thank you, sir." That bitter sense of injury was still in Alban's mind as he looked after her. "What a pity she should grow up to be a woman!" he said to himself.

The adventure of the broken jug had delayed his return to his lodgings by more than half an hour. When he reached the road once more, the cheap up-train from the North had stopped at the station. He heard the ringing of the bell as it resumed the journey to London. One of the passengers (judging by the handbag that she carried) had not stopped at the village.

As she advanced toward him along the road, he remarked that she was a small wiry active woman—dressed in bright colors, combined with a deplorable want of taste. Her aquiline nose seemed to be her most striking feature as she came nearer. It might have been fairly proportioned to the rest of her face, in her younger days, before her cheeks had lost flesh and roundness. Being probably near-sighted, she kept her eyes half-closed; there were cunning little wrinkles at the corners of them. In spite of appearances, she was unwilling to present any outward acknowledgment of the march of time. Her hair was palpably dyed— her hat was jauntily set on her head, and ornamented with a gay feather. She walked with a light tripping step, swinging her bag, and holding her head up smartly. Her manner, like her dress, said as plainly as words could speak, "No matter how long I may have lived, I mean to be young and charming to the end of my days." To Alban's surprise she stopped and addressed him.

"Oh, I beg your pardon. Could you tell me if I am in the right road to Miss Ladd's school?" She spoke with nervous rapidity of articulation, and with a singularly unpleasant smile. It parted her thin lips just widely enough to show her suspiciously beautiful teeth; and it opened her keen gray eyes in the strangest manner. The higher lid rose so as to disclose, for a moment, the upper part of the eyeball, and to give her the appearance—not of a woman bent on making herself agreeable, but of a woman staring in a panic of terror. Careless to conceal the unfavorable impression that she had produced on him, Alban answered roughly, "Straight on," and tried to pass her.

She stopped him with a peremptory gesture. "I have treated you politely," she said, "and how do you treat me in return? Well! I am not surprised. Men are all brutes by nature—and you are a man. 'Straight on'?" she repeated contemptuously; "I should like to know how far that helps a person in a strange place. Perhaps you know no more where Miss Ladd's school is than I do? or, perhaps, you don't care to take the trouble of addressing me? Just what I should have expected from a person of your sex! Good-morning."

Alban felt the reproof; she had appealed to his most readily-impressible sense—his sense of humor. He rather enjoyed seeing his own prejudice against women grotesquely reflected in this flighty stranger's prejudice against men. As the best excuse for himself that he could make, he gave her all the information that she could possibly want—then tried again to pass on—and again in vain. He had recovered his place in her estimation: she had not done with him yet.

"You know all about the way there," she said "I wonder whether you know anything about the school?"

No change in her voice, no change in her manner, betrayed any special motive for putting this question. Alban was on the point of suggesting that she should go on to the school, and make her inquiries there—when he happened to notice her eyes. She had hitherto looked him straight in the face. She now looked down on the road. It was a trifling change; in all probability it meant nothing—and yet, merely because it was a change, it roused his curiosity. "I ought to know something about the school," he answered. "I am one of the masters."

"Then you're just the man I want. May I ask your name?"

"Alban Morris."

"Thank you. I am Mrs. Rook. I presume you have heard of Sir Jervis Redwood?"

"No."

"Bless my soul! You are a scholar, of course—and you have never heard of one of your own trade. Very extraordinary. You see, I am Sir Jervis's housekeeper; and I am sent here to take one of your young ladies back with me to our place. Don't interrupt me! Don't be a brute again! Sir Jervis is not of a communicative disposition. At least, not to me. A man—that explains it—a man! He is always poring over his books and writings; and Miss Redwood, at her great age, is in bed half the day. Not a thing do I know about this new inmate of ours, except that I am to take her back with me. You would feel some curiosity yourself in my place, wouldn't you? Now do tell me. What sort of girl is Miss Emily Brown?"

The name that he was perpetually thinking of—on this woman's lips! Alban looked at her.

"Well," said Mrs. Rook, "am I to have no answer? Ah, you want leading. So like a man again! Is she pretty?"

Still examining the housekeeper with mingled feelings of interest and distrust, Alban answered ungraciously:

"Yes."

"Good-tempered?"

Alban again said "Yes."

"So much about herself," Mrs. Rook remarked. "About her family now?" She shifted her bag restlessly from one hand to another. "Perhaps you can tell me if Miss Emily's father—" she suddenly corrected herself—"if Miss Emily's parents are living?"

"I don't know."

"You mean you won't tell me."

"I mean exactly what I have said."

"Oh, it doesn't matter," Mrs. Rook rejoined; "I shall find out at the school. The first turning to the left, I think you said—across the fields?"

He was too deeply interested in Emily to let the housekeeper go without putting a question on his side:

"Is Sir Jervis Redwood one of Miss Emily's old friends?" he asked.

"He? What put that into your head? He has never even seen Miss Emily. She's going to our house—ah, the women are getting the upper hand now, and serve the men right, I say!—she's going to our house to be Sir Jervis's secretary. You would like to have the place yourself, wouldn't you? You would like to keep a poor girl from getting her own living? Oh, you may look as fierce as you please—the time's gone by when a man could frighten me. I like her Christian name. I call Emily a nice name enough. But 'Brown'! Good-morning, Mr. Morris; you and I are not cursed with such a contemptibly common name as that! 'Brown'? Oh, Lord!"

She tossed her head scornfully, and walked away, humming a tune.

Alban stood rooted to the spot. The effort of his later life had been to conceal the hopeless passion which had mastered him in spite of himself. Knowing nothing from Emily—who at once pitied and avoided him—of her family circumstances or of her future plans, he had shrunk from making inquiries of others, in the fear that they, too, might find out his secret, and that their contempt might be added to the contempt which he felt for himself. In this position, and with these obstacles in his way, the announcement of Emily's proposed journey—under the care of a stranger, to fill an employment in the house of a stranger—not only took him by surprise, but inspired him with a strong feeling of distrust. He looked after Sir Jervis Redwood's flighty housekeeper, completely forgetting the purpose which had brought him thus far on the way to his lodgings. Before Mrs. Rook was out of sight, Alban Morris was following her back to the school.

CHAPTER VII. "COMING EVENTS CAST THEIR SHADOWS BEFORE."

Miss De Sor and Miss Wyvil were still sitting together under the trees, talking of the murder at the inn.

"And is that really all you can tell me?" said Francine.

"That is all," Cecilia answered.

"Is there no love in it?"

"None that I know of."

"It's the most uninteresting murder that ever was committed. What shall we do with ourselves? I'm tired of being here in the garden. When do the performances in the schoolroom begin?"

"Not for two hours yet."

Francine yawned. "And what part do you take in it?" she asked.

"No part, my dear. I tried once—only to sing a simple little song. When I found myself standing before all the company and saw rows of ladies and gentlemen waiting for me to begin, I was so frightened that Miss Ladd had to make an apology for me. I didn't get over it for the rest of the day. For the first time in my life, I had no appetite for my dinner. Horrible!" said Cecilia, shuddering over the remembrance of it. "I do assure you, I thought I was going to die."

Perfectly unimpressed by this harrowing narrative, Francine turned her head lazily toward the house. The door was thrown open at the same moment. A lithe little person rapidly descended the steps that led to the lawn.

"It's Emily come back again," said Francine.

"And she seems to be rather in a hurry," Cecilia remarked.

Francine's satirical smile showed itself for a moment. Did this appearance of hurry in Emily's movements denote impatience to resume the recital of "the dagger-scene"? She had no book in her hand; she never even looked toward Francine. Sorrow became plainly visible in her face as she approached the two girls.

Cecilia rose in alarm. She had been the first person to whom Emily had confided her domestic anxieties. "Bad news from your aunt?" she asked.

"No, my dear; no news at all." Emily put her arms tenderly round her friend's neck. "The time has come, Cecilia," she said. "We must wish each other good-by."

"Is Mrs. Rook here already?"

"It's you, dear, who are going," Emily answered sadly. "They have sent the governess to fetch you. Miss Ladd is too busy in the schoolroom to see her—and she has told me all about it. Don't be alarmed. There is no bad news from home. Your plans are altered; that's all."

"Altered?" Cecilia repeated. "In what way?"

20

"In a very agreeable way—you are going to travel. Your father wishes you to be in London, in time for the evening mail to France."

Cecilia guessed what had happened. "My sister is not getting well," she said, "and the doctors are sending her to the Continent."

"To the baths at St. Moritz," Emily added. "There is only one difficulty in the way; and you can remove it. Your sister has the good old governess to take care of her, and the courier to relieve her of all trouble on the journey. They were to have started yesterday. You know how fond Julia is of you. At the last moment, she won't hear of going away, unless you go too. The rooms are waiting at St. Moritz; and your father is annoyed (the governess says) by the delay that has taken place already."

She paused. Cecilia was silent. "Surely you don't hesitate?" Emily said.

"I am too happy to go wherever Julia goes," Cecilia answered warmly; "I was thinking of you, dear." Her tender nature, shrinking from the hard necessities of life, shrank from the cruelly-close prospect of parting. "I thought we were to have had some hours together yet," she said. "Why are we hurried in this way? There is no second train to London, from our station, till late in the afternoon."

"There is the express," Emily reminded her; "and there is time to catch it, if you drive at once to the town." She took Cecilia's hand and pressed it to her bosom. "Thank you again and again, dear, for all you have done for me. Whether we meet again or not, as long as I live I shall love you. Don't cry!" She made a faint attempt to resume her customary gayety, for Cecilia's sake. "Try to be as hard-hearted as I am. Think of your sister—don't think of me. Only kiss me."

Cecilia's tears fell fast. "Oh, my love, I am so anxious about you! I am so afraid that you will not be happy with that selfish old man—in that dreary house. Give it up, Emily! I have got plenty of money for both of us; come abroad with me. Why not? You always got on well with Julia, when you came to see us in the holidays. Oh, my darling! my darling! What shall I do without you?"

All that longed for love in Emily's nature had clung round her school-friend since her father's death. Turning deadly pale under the struggle to control herself, she made the effort—and bore the pain of it without letting a cry or a tear escape her. "Our ways in life lie far apart," she said gently. "There is the hope of meeting again, dear—if there is nothing more."

The clasp of Cecilia's arm tightened round her. She tried to release herself; but her resolution had reached its limits. Her hands dropped, trembling. She could still try to speak cheerfully, and that was all.

"There is not the least reason, Cecilia, to be anxious about my prospects. I mean to be Sir Jervis Redwood's favorite before I have been a week in his service."

She stopped, and pointed to the house. The governess was approaching them. "One more kiss, darling. We shall not forget the happy hours we have spent together; we shall constantly write to each other." She broke down at last. "Oh, Cecilia! Cecilia! leave me for God's sake—I can't bear it any longer!"

The governess parted them. Emily dropped into the chair that her friend had left. Even her hopeful nature sank under the burden of life at that moment.

A hard voice, speaking close at her side, startled her.

"Would you rather be Me," the voice asked, "without a creature to care for you?"

Emily raised her head. Francine, the unnoticed witness of the parting interview, was standing by her, idly picking the leaves from a rose which had dropped out of Cecilia's nosegay.

Had she felt her own isolated position? She had felt it resentfully.

Emily looked at her, with a heart softened by sorrow. There was no answering kindness in the eyes of Miss de Sor—there was only a dogged endurance, sad to see in a creature so young.

"You and Cecilia are going to write to each other," she said. "I suppose there is some comfort in that. When I left the island they were glad to get rid of me. They said, 'Telegraph when you are safe at Miss Ladd's school.' You see, we are so rich, the expense of telegraphing to the West Indies is nothing to us. Besides, a telegram has an advantage over a letter—it doesn't take long to read. I daresay I shall write home. But they are in no hurry; and I am in no hurry. The school's breaking up; you are going your way, and I am going mine—and who cares what becomes of me? Only an ugly old schoolmistress, who is paid for caring. I wonder why I am saying all this? Because I like you? I don't know that I like you any better than you like me. When I wanted to be friends with you, you treated me coolly; I don't want to force myself on you. I don't particularly care about you. May I write to you from Brighton?"

Under all this bitterness—the first exhibition of Francine's temper, at its worst, which had taken place since she joined the school—Emily saw, or thought she saw, distress that was too proud, or too shy, to show itself. "How can you ask the question?" she answered cordially.

Francine was incapable of meeting the sympathy offered to her, even half way. "Never mind how," she said. "Yes or no is all I want from you."

"Oh, Francine! Francine! what are you made of! Flesh and blood? or stone and iron? Write to me of course—and I will write back again."

"Thank you. Are you going to stay here under the trees?"

"Yes."

"All by yourself?"

"All by myself."

"With nothing to do?"

"I can think of Cecilia."

Francine eyed her with steady attention for a moment.

"Didn't you tell me last night that you were very poor?" she asked.

"I did."

"So poor that you are obliged to earn your own living?"

"Yes."

Francine looked at her again.

"I daresay you won't believe me," she said. "I wish I was you."

She turned away irritably, and walked back to the house.

Were there really longings for kindness and love under the surface of this girl's perverse nature? Or was there nothing to be hoped from a better knowledge of her?—In place of tender remembrances of Cecilia, these were the perplexing and unwelcome thoughts which the more potent personality of Francine forced upon Emily's mind.

She rose impatiently, and looked at her watch. When would it be her turn to leave the school, and begin the new life?

Still undecided what to do next, her interest was excited by the appearance of one of the servants on the lawn. The woman approached her, and presented a visiting-card; bearing on it the name of Sir Jervis Redwood. Beneath the name, there was a line written in pencil: "Mrs. Rook, to wait on Miss Emily Brown." The way to the new life was open before her at last!

Looking again at the commonplace announcement contained in the line of writing, she was not quite satisfied. Was it claiming a deference toward herself, to which she was not entitled, to expect a letter either from Sir Jervis, or from Miss Redwood; giving her some information as to the journey which she was about to undertake, and expressing with some little politeness the wish to make her comfortable in her future home? At any rate, her employer had done her one service: he had reminded her that her station in life was not what it had been in the days when her father was living, and when her aunt was in affluent circumstances.

She looked up from the card. The servant had gone. Alban Morris was waiting at a little distance—waiting silently until she noticed him.

CHAPTER VIII. MASTER AND PUPIL.

Emily's impulse was to avoid the drawing-master for the second time. The moment afterward, a kinder feeling prevailed. The farewell interview with Cecilia had left influences which pleaded for Alban Morris. It was the day of parting good wishes and general separations: he had only perhaps come to say good-by. She advanced to offer her hand, when he stopped her by pointing to Sir Jervis Redwood's card.

"May I say a word, Miss Emily, about that woman?" he asked

"Do you mean Mrs. Rook?"

"Yes. You know, of course, why she comes here?"

"She comes here by appointment, to take me to Sir Jervis Redwood's house. Are you acquainted with her?"

"She is a perfect stranger to me. I met her by accident on her way here. If Mrs. Rook had been content with asking me to direct her to the school, I should not be troubling you at this moment. But she forced her conversation on me. And she said something which I think you ought to know. Have you heard of Sir Jervis Redwood's housekeeper before to-day?"

"I have only heard what my friend—Miss Cecilia Wyvil—has told me."

"Did Miss Cecilia tell you that Mrs. Rook was acquainted with your father or with any members of your family?"

"Certainly not!"

Alban reflected. "It was natural enough," he resumed, "that Mrs. Rook should feel some curiosity about You. What reason had she for putting a question to me about your father—and putting it in a very strange manner?"

Emily's interest was instantly excited. She led the way back to the seats in the shade. "Tell me, Mr. Morris, exactly what the woman said." As she spoke, she signed to him to be seated.

Alban observed the natural grace of her action when she set him the example of taking a chair, and the little heightening of her color caused by anxiety to hear what he had still to tell her. Forgetting the restraint that he had hitherto imposed on himself, he enjoyed the luxury of silently admiring her. Her manner betrayed none of the conscious confusion which would have shown itself, if her heart had been secretly inclined toward him. She saw the man looking at her. In simple perplexity she looked at the man.

"Are you hesitating on my account?" she asked. "Did Mrs. Rook say something of my father which I mustn't hear?"

"No, no! nothing of the sort!"

"You seem to be confused."

Her innocent indifference tried his patience sorely. His memory went back to the past time—recalled the ill-placed passion of his youth, and the cruel injury inflicted on him—his pride was roused. Was he making himself ridiculous? The vehement throbbing of his heart almost suffocated him. And there she sat, wondering at his odd behavior. "Even this girl is as cold-blooded as the rest of her sex!" That angry thought gave him back his self-control. He made his excuses with the easy politeness of a man of the world.

"I beg your pardon, Miss Emily; I was considering how to put what I have to say in the fewest and plainest words. Let me try if I can do it. If Mrs. Rook had merely asked me whether your father and mother were living, I should have attributed the question to the

23

commonplace curiosity of a gossiping woman, and have thought no more of it. What she actually did say was this: 'Perhaps you can tell me if Miss Emily's father—' There she checked herself, and suddenly altered the question in this way: 'If Miss Emily's parents are living?' I may be making mountains out of molehills; but I thought at the time (and think still) that she had some special interest in inquiring after your father, and, not wishing me to notice it for reasons of her own, changed the form of the question so as to include your mother. Does this strike you as a far-fetched conclusion?"

"Whatever it may be," Emily said, "it is my conclusion, too. How did you answer her?"

"Quite easily. I could give her no information—and I said so."

"Let me offer you the information, Mr. Morris, before we say anything more. I have lost both my parents."

Alban's momentary outbreak of irritability was at an end. He was earnest and yet gentle, again; he forgave her for not understanding how dear and how delightful to him she was. "Will it distress you," he said, "if I ask how long it is since your father died?"

"Nearly four years," she replied. "He was the most generous of men; Mrs. Rook's interest in him may surely have been a grateful interest. He may have been kind to her in past years—and she may remember him thankfully. Don't you think so?"

Alban was unable to agree with her. "If Mrs. Rook's interest in your father was the harmless interest that you have suggested," he said, "why should she have checked herself in that unaccountable manner, when she first asked me if he was living? The more I think of it now, the less sure I feel that she knows anything at all of your family history. It may help me to decide, if you will tell me at what time the death of your mother took place."

"So long ago," Emily replied, "that I can't even remember her death. I was an infant at the time."

"And yet Mrs. Rook asked me if your 'parents' were living! One of two things," Alban concluded. "Either there is some mystery in this matter, which we cannot hope to penetrate at present—or Mrs. Rook may have been speaking at random; on the chance of discovering whether you are related to some 'Mr. Brown' whom she once knew."

"Besides," Emily added, "it's only fair to remember what a common family name mine is, and how easily people may make mistakes. I should like to know if my dear lost father was really in her mind when she spoke to you. Do you think I could find it out?"

"If Mrs. Rook has any reasons for concealment, I believe you would have no chance of finding it out—unless, indeed, you could take her by surprise."

"In what way, Mr. Morris?"

"Only one way occurs to me just now," he said. "Do you happen to have a miniature or a photograph of your father?"

Emily held out a handsome locket, with a monogram in diamonds, attached to her watch chain. "I have his photograph here," she rejoined; "given to me by my dear old aunt, in the days of her prosperity. Shall I show it to Mrs. Rook?"

"Yes—if she happens, by good luck, to offer you an opportunity."

Impatient to try the experiment, Emily rose as he spoke. "I mustn't keep Mrs. Rook waiting," she said.

Alban stopped her, on the point of leaving him. The confusion and hesitation which she had already noticed began to show themselves in his manner once more.

"Miss Emily, may I ask you a favor before you go? I am only one of the masters employed in the school; but I don't think—let me say, I hope I am not guilty of presumption—if I offer to be of some small service to one of my pupils—"

There his embarrassment mastered him. He despised himself not only for yielding to his own weakness, but for faltering like a fool in the expression of a simple request. The next words died away on his lips.

This time, Emily understood him.

The subtle penetration which had long since led her to the discovery of his secret—overpowered, thus far, by the absorbing interest of the moment—now recovered its activity. In an instant, she remembered that Alban's motive for cautioning her, in her coming intercourse with Mrs. Rook, was not the merely friendly motive which might have actuated him, in the case of one of the other girls. At the same time, her quickness of apprehension warned her not to risk encouraging this persistent lover, by betraying any embarrassment on her side. He was evidently anxious to be present (in her interests) at the interview with Mrs. Rook. Why not? Could he reproach her with raising false hope, if she accepted his services, under circumstances of doubt and difficulty which he had himself been the first to point out? He could do nothing of the sort. Without waiting until he had recovered himself, she answered him (to all appearances) as composedly as if he had spoken to her in the plainest terms.

"After all that you have told me," she said, "I shall indeed feel obliged if you will be present when I see Mrs. Rook."

The eager brightening of his eyes, the flush of happiness that made him look young on a sudden, were signs not to be mistaken. The sooner they were in the presence of a third person (Emily privately concluded) the better it might be for both of them. She led the way rapidly to the house.

CHAPTER IX. MRS. ROOK AND THE LOCKET.

As mistress of a prosperous school, bearing a widely-extended reputation, Miss Ladd prided herself on the liberality of her household arrangements. At breakfast and dinner, not only the solid comforts but the elegant luxuries of the table, were set before the young ladies "Other schools may, and no doubt do, offer to pupils the affectionate care to which they have been accustomed under the parents' roof," Miss Ladd used to say. "At my school, that care extends to their meals, and provides them with a cuisine which, I flatter myself, equals the most successful efforts of the cooks at home." Fathers, mothers, and friends, when they paid visits to this excellent lady, brought away with them the most gratifying recollections of her hospitality. The men, in particular, seldom failed to recognize in their hostess the rarest virtue that a single lady can possess—the virtue of putting wine on the table which may be gratefully remembered by her guests the next morning.

An agreeable surprise awaited Mrs. Rook when she entered the house of bountiful Miss Ladd.

Luncheon was ready for Sir Jervis Redwood's confidential emissary in the waiting-room. Detained at the final rehearsals of music and recitation, Miss Ladd was worthily represented by cold chicken and ham, a fruit tart, and a pint decanter of generous sherry. "Your mistress is a perfect lady!" Mrs. Rook said to the servant, with a burst of enthusiasm. "I can carve for myself, thank you; and I don't care how long Miss Emily keeps me waiting."

As they ascended the steps leading into the house, Alban asked Emily if he might look again at her locket.

"Shall I open it for you?" she suggested.

"No: I only want to look at the outside of it."

He examined the side on which the monogram appeared, inlaid with diamonds. An inscription was engraved beneath.

"May I read it?" he said.

"Certainly!"

The inscription ran thus: "In loving memory of my father. Died 30th September, 1877."

"Can you arrange the locket," Alban asked, "so that the side on which the diamonds appear hangs outward?"

She understood him. The diamonds might attract Mrs. Rook's notice; and in that case, she might ask to see the locket of her own accord. "You are beginning to be of use to me, already," Emily said, as they turned into the corridor which led to the waiting-room.

They found Sir Jervis's housekeeper luxuriously recumbent in the easiest chair in the room. Of the eatable part of the lunch some relics were yet left. In the pint decanter of sherry, not a drop remained. The genial influence of the wine (hastened by the hot weather) was visible in Mrs. Rook's flushed face, and in a special development of her ugly smile. Her widening lips stretched to new lengths; and the white upper line of her eyeballs were more freely and horribly visible than ever.

"And this is the dear young lady?" she said, lifting her hands in over-acted admiration. At the first greetings, Alban perceived that the impression produced was, in Emily's case as in his case, instantly unfavorable.

The servant came in to clear the table. Emily stepped aside for a minute to give some directions about her luggage. In that interval Mrs. Rook's cunning little eyes turned on Alban with an expression of malicious scrutiny.

"You were walking the other way," she whispered, "when I met you." She stopped, and glanced over her shoulder at Emily. "I see what attraction has brought you back to the school. Steal your way into that poor little fool's heart; and then make her miserable for the rest of her life!—No need, miss, to hurry," she said, shifting the polite side of her toward Emily, who returned at the moment. "The visits of the trains to your station here are like the visits of the angels described by the poet, 'few and far between.' Please excuse the quotation. You wouldn't think it to look at me—I'm a great reader."

"Is it a long journey to Sir Jervis Redwood's house?" Emily asked, at a loss what else to say to a woman who was already becoming unendurable to her.

Mrs. Rook looked at the journey from an oppressively cheerful point of view.

"Oh, Miss Emily, you shan't feel the time hang heavy in my company. I can converse on a variety of topics, and if there is one thing more than another that I like, it's amusing a pretty young lady. You think me a strange creature, don't you? It's only my high spirits. Nothing strange about me—unless it's my queer Christian name. You look a little dull, my dear. Shall I begin amusing you before we are on the railway? Shall I tell you how I came by my queer name?"

Thus far, Alban had controlled himself. This last specimen of the housekeeper's audacious familiarity reached the limits of his endurance.

"We don't care to know how you came by your name," he said.

"Rude," Mrs. Rook remarked, composedly. "But nothing surprises me, coming from a man."

She turned to Emily. "My father and mother were a wicked married couple," she continued, "before I was born. They 'got religion,' as the saying is, at a Methodist meeting in a field. When I came into the world—I don't know how you feel, miss; I protest against being brought into the world without asking my leave first—my mother was determined to dedicate me to piety, before I was out of my long clothes. What name do you suppose she had me christened by? She chose it, or made it, herself—the name of 'Righteous'! Righteous Rook! Was there ever a poor baby degraded by such a ridiculous name before? It's needless to say, when I write letters, I sign R. Rook—and leave people to think it's Rosamond, or Rosabelle, or something sweetly pretty of that kind. You should have seen my husband's face when he first heard that his sweetheart's name was 'Righteous'! He was on the point of kissing me, and he stopped. I daresay he felt sick. Perfectly natural under the circumstances."

Alban tried to stop her again. "What time does the train go?" he asked.

Emily entreated him to restrain himself, by a look. Mrs. Rook was still too inveterately amiable to take offense. She opened her traveling-bag briskly, and placed a railway guide in Alban's hands.

"I've heard that the women do the men's work in foreign parts," she said. "But this is England; and I am an Englishwoman. Find out when the train goes, my dear sir, for yourself."

Alban at once consulted the guide. If there proved to be no immediate need of starting for the station, he was determined that Emily should not be condemned to pass the interval in the housekeeper's company. In the meantime, Mrs. Rook was as eager as ever to show her dear young lady what an amusing companion she could be.

"Talking of husbands," she resumed, "don't make the mistake, my dear, that I committed. Beware of letting anybody persuade you to marry an old man. Mr. Rook is old enough to be my father. I bear with him. Of course, I bear with him. At the same time, I have not (as the poet says) 'passed through the ordeal unscathed.' My spirit—I have long since ceased to believe in anything of the sort: I only use the word for want of a better—my spirit, I say, has become embittered. I was once a pious young woman; I do assure you I was nearly as good as my name. Don't let me shock you; I have lost faith and hope; I have become— what's the last new name for a free-thinker? Oh, I keep up with the times, thanks to old Miss Redwood! She takes in the newspapers, and makes me read them to her. What is the new name? Something ending in ic. Bombastic? No, Agnostic?—that's it! I have become an Agnostic. The inevitable result of marrying an old man; if there's any blame it rests on my husband."

"There's more than an hour yet before the train starts," Alban interposed. "I am sure, Miss Emily, you would find it pleasanter to wait in the garden."

"Not at all a bad notion," Mrs. Rook declared. "Here's a man who can make himself useful, for once. Let's go into the garden."

She rose, and led the way to the door. Alban seized the opportunity of whispering to Emily. "Did you notice the empty decanter, when we first came in? That horrid woman is drunk."

Emily pointed significantly to the locket. "Don't let her go. The garden will distract her attention: keep her near me here."

Mrs. Rook gayly opened the door. "Take me to the flower-beds," she said. "I believe in nothing—but I adore flowers."

Mrs. Rook waited at the door, with her eye on Emily. "What do you say, miss?"

"I think we shall be more comfortable if we stay where we are."

"Whatever pleases you, my dear, pleases me." With this reply, the compliant housekeeper— as amiable as ever on the surface—returned to her chair.

Would she notice the locket as she sat down? Emily turned toward the window, so as to let the light fall on the diamonds.

No: Mrs. Rook was absorbed, at the moment, in her own reflections. Miss Emily, having prevented her from seeing the garden, she was maliciously bent on disappointing Miss Emily in return. Sir Jervis's secretary (being young) took a hopeful view no doubt of her future prospects. Mrs. Rook decided on darkening that view in a mischievously-suggestive manner, peculiar to herself.

"You will naturally feel some curiosity about your new home," she began, "and I haven't said a word about it yet. How very thoughtless of me! Inside and out, dear Miss Emily, our house is just a little dull. I say our house, and why not—when the management of it is all thrown on me. We are built of stone; and we are much too long, and are not half high enough. Our situation is on the coldest side of the county, away in the west. We are close to the Cheviot hills; and if you fancy there is anything to see when you look out of window, except sheep, you will find yourself woefully mistaken. As for walks, if you go out on one side of the house you may, or may not, be gored by cattle. On the other side, if the darkness overtakes you, you may, or may not, tumble down a deserted lead mine. But the company, inside the house, makes amends for it all," Mrs. Rook proceeded, enjoying the expression of dismay which was beginning to show itself on Emily's face. "Plenty of excitement for you, my dear, in our small family. Sir Jervis will introduce you to plaster casts of hideous Indian idols; he will keep you writing for him, without mercy, from morning to night; and when he does let you go, old Miss Redwood will find she can't sleep, and will send for the pretty young lady-secretary to read to her. My husband I am sure you will like. He is a respectable man, and bears the highest character. Next to the idols, he's the most hideous object in the house. If you are good enough to encourage him, I don't say that he won't amuse you; he will tell you, for instance, he never in his life hated any human being as he hates his wife. By the way, I must not forget—in the interests of truth, you know—to mention one drawback that does exist in our domestic circle. One of these days we shall have our brains blown out or our throats cut. Sir Jervis's mother left him ten thousand pounds' worth of precious stones all contained in a little cabinet with drawers. He won't let the banker take care of his jewels; he won't sell them; he won't even wear one of the rings on his finger, or one of the pins at his breast. He keeps his cabinet on his dressing-room table; and he says, 'I like to gloat over my jewels, every night, before I go to bed.' Ten thousand pounds' worth of diamonds, rubies, emeralds, sapphires, and what not—at the mercy of the first robber who happens to hear of them. Oh, my dear, he would have no choice, I do assure you, but to use his pistols. We shouldn't quietly submit to be robbed. Sir Jervis inherits the spirit of his ancestors. My husband has the temper of a game cock. I myself, in defense of the property of my employers, am capable of becoming a perfect fiend. And we none of us understand the use of firearms!"

While she was in full enjoyment of this last aggravation of the horrors of the prospect, Emily tried another change of position—and, this time, with success. Greedy admiration suddenly opened Mrs. Rook's little eyes to their utmost width. "My heart alive, miss, what do I see at your watch-chain? How they sparkle! Might I ask for a closer view?"

Emily's fingers trembled; but she succeeded in detaching the locket from the chain. Alban handed it to Mrs. Rook.

She began by admiring the diamonds—with a certain reserve. "Nothing like so large as Sir Jervis's diamonds; but choice specimens no doubt. Might I ask what the value—?"

She stopped. The inscription had attracted her notice: she began to read it aloud: "In loving memory of my father. Died—"

Her face instantly became rigid. The next words were suspended on her lips.

Alban seized the chance of making her betray herself—under pretense of helping her. "Perhaps you find the figures not easy to read," he said. "The date is 'thirtieth September, eighteen hundred and seventy-seven'—nearly four years since."

Not a word, not a movement, escaped Mrs. Rook. She held the locket before her as she had held it from the first. Alban looked at Emily. Her eyes were riveted on the housekeeper: she was barely capable of preserving the appearance of composure. Seeing the necessity of acting for her, he at once said the words which she was unable to say for herself.

"Perhaps, Mrs. Rook, you would like to look at the portrait?" he suggested. "Shall I open the locket for you?"

Without speaking, without looking up, she handed the locket to Alban.

He opened it, and offered it to her. She neither accepted nor refused it: her hands remained hanging over the arms of the chair. He put the locket on her lap.

The portrait produced no marked effect on Mrs. Rook. Had the date prepared her to see it? She sat looking at it—still without moving: still without saying a word. Alban had no mercy on her. "That is the portrait of Miss Emily's father," he said. "Does it represent the same Mr. Brown whom you had in your mind when you asked me if Miss Emily's father was still living?"

That question roused her. She looked up, on the instant; she answered loudly and insolently: "No!"

"And yet," Alban persisted, "you broke down in reading the inscription: and considering what talkative woman you are, the portrait has had a strange effect on you—to say the least of it."

She eyed him steadily while he was speaking—and turned to Emily when he had done. "You mentioned the heat just now, miss. The heat has overcome me; I shall soon get right again."

The insolent futility of that excuse irritated Emily into answering her. "You will get right again perhaps all the sooner," she said, "if we trouble you with no more questions, and leave you to recover by yourself."

The first change of expression which relaxed the iron tensity of the housekeeper's face showed itself when she heard that reply. At last there was a feeling in Mrs. Rook which openly declared itself—a feeling of impatience to see Alban and Emily leave the room.

They left her, without a word more.

CHAPTER X. GUESSES AT THE TRUTH.

"What are we to do next? Oh, Mr. Morris, you must have seen all sorts of people in your time—you know human nature, and I don't. Help me with a word of advice!"

Emily forgot that he was in love with her—forgot everything, but the effect produced by the locket on Mrs. Rook, and the vaguely alarming conclusion to which it pointed. In the fervor of her anxiety she took Alban's arm as familiarly as if he had been her brother. He was gentle, he was considerate; he tried earnestly to compose her. "We can do nothing to any good purpose," he said, "unless we begin by thinking quietly. Pardon me for saying so—you are needlessly exciting yourself."

There was a reason for her excitement, of which he was necessarily ignorant. Her memory of the night interview with Miss Jethro had inevitably intensified the suspicion inspired by the conduct of Mrs. Rook. In less than twenty-four hours, Emily had seen two women shrinking from secret remembrances of her father—which might well be guilty remembrances—innocently excited by herself! How had they injured him? Of what infamy, on their parts, did his beloved and stainless memory remind them? Who could fathom the mystery of it? "What does it mean?" she cried, looking wildly in Alban's compassionate face. "You must have formed some idea of your own. What does it mean?"

"Come, and sit down, Miss Emily. We will try if we can find out what it means, together."

They returned to the shady solitude under the trees. Away, in front of the house, the distant grating of carriage wheels told of the arrival of Miss Ladd's guests, and of the speedy beginning of the ceremonies of the day.

"We must help each other," Alban resumed.

"When we first spoke of Mrs. Rook, you mentioned Miss Cecilia Wyvil as a person who knew something about her. Have you any objection to tell me what you may have heard in that way?"

In complying with his request Emily necessarily repeated what Cecilia had told Francine, when the two girls had met that morning in the garden.

Alban now knew how Emily had obtained employment as Sir Jervis's secretary; how Mr. and Mrs. Rook had been previously known to Cecilia's father as respectable people keeping an inn in his own neighborhood; and, finally, how they had been obliged to begin life again in domestic service, because the terrible event of a murder had given the inn a bad name, and had driven away the customers on whose encouragement their business depended.

Listening in silence, Alban remained silent when Emily's narrative had come to an end.

"Have you nothing to say to me?" she asked.

"I am thinking over what I have just heard," he answered.

Emily noticed a certain formality in his tone and manner, which disagreeably surprised her. He seemed to have made his reply as a mere concession to politeness, while he was thinking of something else which really interested him.

"Have I disappointed you in any way?" she asked.

"On the contrary, you have interested me. I want to be quite sure that I remember exactly what you have said. You mentioned, I think, that your friendship with Miss Cecilia Wyvil began here, at the school?"

"Yes."

"And in speaking of the murder at the village inn, you told me that the crime was committed—I have forgotten how long ago?"

His manner still suggested that he was idly talking about what she had told him, while some more important subject for reflection was in possession of his mind.

"I don't know that I said anything about the time that had passed since the crime was committed," she answered, sharply. "What does the murder matter to us? I think Cecilia told me it happened about four years since. Excuse me for noticing it, Mr. Morris—you seem to have some interests of your own to occupy your attention. Why couldn't you say so plainly when we came out here? I should not have asked you to help me, in that case. Since my poor father's death, I have been used to fight through my troubles by myself."

She rose, and looked at him proudly. The next moment her eyes filled with tears.

In spite of her resistance, Alban took her hand. "Dear Miss Emily," he said, "you distress me: you have not done me justice. Your interests only are in my mind."

Answering her in those terms, he had not spoken as frankly as usual. He had only told her a part of the truth.

Hearing that the woman whom they had just left had been landlady of an inn, and that a murder had been committed under her roof, he was led to ask himself if any explanation might be found, in these circumstances, of the otherwise incomprehensible effect produced on Mrs. Rook by the inscription on the locket.

In the pursuit of this inquiry there had arisen in his mind a monstrous suspicion, which pointed to Mrs. Rook. It impelled him to ascertain the date at which the murder had been committed, and (if the discovery encouraged further investigation) to find out next the manner in which Mr. Brown had died.

Thus far, what progress had he made? He had discovered that the date of Mr. Brown's death, inscribed on the locket, and the date of the crime committed at the inn, approached each other nearly enough to justify further investigation.

In the meantime, had he succeeded in keeping his object concealed from Emily? He had perfectly succeeded. Hearing him declare that her interests only had occupied his mind, the poor girl innocently entreated him to forgive her little outbreak of temper. "If you have any more questions to ask me, Mr. Morris, pray go on. I promise never to think unjustly of you again."

He went on with an uneasy conscience—for it seemed cruel to deceive her, even in the interests of truth—but still he went on.

"Suppose we assume that this woman had injured your father in some way," he said. "Am I right in believing that it was in his character to forgive injuries?"

"Entirely right."

"In that case, his death may have left Mrs. Rook in a position to be called to account, by those who owe a duty to his memory—I mean the surviving members of his family."

"There are but two of us, Mr. Morris. My aunt and myself."

"There are his executors."

"My aunt is his only executor."

"Your father's sister—I presume?"

"Yes."

"He may have left instructions with her, which might be of the greatest use to us."

"I will write to-day, and find out," Emily replied. "I had already planned to consult my aunt," she added, thinking again of Miss Jethro.

"If your aunt has not received any positive instructions," Alban continued, "she may remember some allusion to Mrs. Rook, on your father's part, at the time of his last illness—"

Emily stopped him. "You don't know how my dear father died," she said. "He was struck down—apparently in perfect health—by disease of the heart."

"Struck down in his own house?"

"Yes—in his own house."

Those words closed Alban's lips. The investigation so carefully and so delicately conducted had failed to serve any useful purpose. He had now ascertained the manner of Mr. Brown's death and the place of Mr. Brown's death—and he was as far from confirming his suspicions of Mrs. Rook as ever.

CHAPTER XI. THE DRAWING-MASTER'S CONFESSION.

"Is there nothing else you can suggest?" Emily asked.

"Nothing—at present."

"If my aunt fails us, have we no other hope?"

"I have hope in Mrs. Rook," Alban answered. "I see I surprise you; but I really mean what I say. Sir Jervis's housekeeper is an excitable woman, and she is fond of wine. There is always a weak side in the character of such a person as that. If we wait for our chance, and turn it to the right use when it comes, we may yet succeed in making her betray herself."

Emily listened to him in bewilderment.

"You talk as if I was sure of your help in the future," she said. "Have you forgotten that I leave school to-day, never to return? In half an hour more, I shall be condemned to a long journey in the company of that horrible creature—with a life to look forward to, in the same house with her, among strangers! A miserable prospect, and a hard trial of a girl's courage—is it not, Mr. Morris?"

"You will at least have one person, Miss Emily, who will try with all his heart and soul to encourage you."

"What do you mean?"

"I mean," said Alban, quietly, "that the Midsummer vacation begins to-day; and that the drawing-master is going to spend his holidays in the North."

Emily jumped up from her chair. "You!" she exclaimed. "You are going to Northumberland? With me?"

"Why not?" Alban asked. "The railway is open to all travelers alike, if they have money enough to buy a ticket."

"Mr. Morris! what can you be thinking of? Indeed, indeed, I am not ungrateful. I know you mean kindly—you are a good, generous man. But do remember how completely a girl, in my position, is at the mercy of appearances. You, traveling in the same carriage with me! and that woman putting her own vile interpretation on it, and degrading me in Sir Jervis Redwood's estimation, on the day when I enter his house! Oh, it's worse than thoughtless—it's madness, downright madness."

"You are quite right," Alban gravely agreed, "it is madness. I lost whatever little reason I once possessed, Miss Emily, on the day when I first met you out walking with the young ladies of the school."

Emily turned away in significant silence. Alban followed her.

"You promised just now," he said, "never to think unjustly of me again. I respect and admire you far too sincerely to take a base advantage of this occasion—the only occasion on which I have been permitted to speak with you alone. Wait a little before you condemn a man whom you don't understand. I will say nothing to annoy you—I only ask leave to explain myself. Will you take your chair again?"

She returned unwillingly to her seat. "It can only end," she thought, sadly, "in my disappointing him!"

"I have had the worst possible opinion of women for years past," Alban resumed; "and the only reason I can give for it condemns me out of my own mouth. I have been infamously treated by one woman; and my wounded self-esteem has meanly revenged itself by reviling the whole sex. Wait a little, Miss Emily. My fault has received its fit punishment. I have been thoroughly humiliated—and you have done it."

"Mr. Morris!"

"Take no offense, pray, where no offense is meant. Some few years since it was the great misfortune of my life to meet with a Jilt. You know what I mean?"

"Yes."

"She was my equal by birth (I am a younger son of a country squire), and my superior in rank. I can honestly tell you that I was fool enough to love her with all my heart and soul. She never allowed me to doubt—I may say this without conceit, remembering the miserable end of it—that my feeling for her was returned. Her father and mother (excellent people) approved of the contemplated marriage. She accepted my presents; she allowed all the customary preparations for a wedding to proceed to completion; she had not even mercy enough, or shame enough, to prevent me from publicly degrading myself by waiting for her at the altar, in the presence of a large congregation. The minutes passed—and no bride appeared. The clergyman, waiting like me, was requested to return to the vestry. I was invited to follow him. You foresee the end of the story, of course? She had run away with another man. But can you guess who the man was? Her groom!"

Emily's face reddened with indignation. "She suffered for it? Oh, Mr. Morris, surely she suffered for it?"

"Not at all. She had money enough to reward the groom for marrying her; and she let herself down easily to her husband's level. It was a suitable marriage in every respect. When I last heard of them, they were regularly in the habit of getting drunk together. I am afraid I have disgusted you? We will drop the subject, and resume my precious autobiography at a later date. One showery day in the autumn of last year, you young ladies went out with Miss Ladd for a walk. When you were all trotting back again, under your umbrellas, did you (in particular) notice an ill-tempered fellow standing in the road, and getting a good look at you, on the high footpath above him?"

Emily smiled, in spite of herself. "I don't remember it," she said.

"You wore a brown jacket which fitted you as if you had been born in it—and you had the smartest little straw hat I ever saw on a woman's head. It was the first time I ever noticed such things. I think I could paint a portrait of the boots you wore (mud included), from memory alone. That was the impression you produced on me. After believing, honestly believing, that love was one of the lost illusions of my life—after feeling, honestly feeling, that I would as soon look at the devil as look at a woman—there was the state of mind to which retribution had reduced me; using for his instrument Miss Emily Brown. Oh, don't be afraid of what I may say next! In your presence, and out of your presence, I am man enough to be ashamed of my own folly. I am resisting your influence over me at this moment, with the strongest of all resolutions—the resolution of despair. Let's look at the humorous side of the story again. What do you think I did when the regiment of young ladies had passed by me?"

Emily declined to guess.

"I followed you back to the school; and, on pretense of having a daughter to educate, I got one of Miss Ladd's prospectuses from the porter at the lodge gate. I was in your neighborhood, you must know, on a sketching tour. I went back to my inn, and seriously considered what had happened to me. The result of my cogitations was that I went abroad. Only for a change—not at all because I was trying to weaken the impression you had produced on me! After a while I returned to England. Only because I was tired of traveling—not at all because your influence drew me back! Another interval passed; and luck turned my way, for a wonder. The drawing-master's place became vacant here. Miss Ladd advertised; I produced my testimonials; and took the situation. Only because the salary was a welcome certainty to a poor man—not at all because the new position brought me into personal association with Miss Emily Brown! Do you begin to see why I have troubled you with all this talk about myself? Apply the contemptible system of self-delusion which my confession has revealed, to that holiday arrangement for a tour in the north which has astonished and annoyed you. I am going to travel this afternoon by your train. Only because I feel an intelligent longing to see the northernmost county of England—not at all because I won't let you trust yourself alone with Mrs. Rook! Not at all because I won't leave you to enter Sir Jervis Redwood's service without a friend within reach in case you want him! Mad? Oh, yes—perfectly mad. But, tell me this: What do all sensible people do when they find themselves in the company of a lunatic? They humor him. Let me take your ticket and see your luggage labeled: I only ask leave to be your traveling servant. If you are proud—I shall like you all the better, if you are—pay me wages, and keep me in my proper place in that way."

Some girls, addressed with this reckless intermingling of jest and earnest, would have felt confused, and some would have felt flattered. With a good-tempered resolution, which never passed the limits of modesty and refinement, Emily met Alban Morris on his own ground.

"You have said you respect me," she began; "I am going to prove that I believe you. The least I can do is not to misinterpret you, on my side. Am I to understand, Mr. Morris—you won't think the worse of me, I hope, if I speak plainly—am I to understand that you are in love with me?"

"Yes, Miss Emily—if you please."

He had answered with the quaint gravity which was peculiar to him; but he was already conscious of a sense of discouragement. Her composure was a bad sign—from his point of view.

"My time will come, I daresay," she proceeded. "At present I know nothing of love, by experience; I only know what some of my schoolfellows talk about in secret. Judging by what they tell me, a girl blushes when her lover pleads with her to favor his addresses. Am I blushing?"

"Must I speak plainly, too?" Alban asked.

"If you have no objection," she answered, as composedly as if she had been addressing her grandfather.

"Then, Miss Emily, I must say—you are not blushing."

She went on. "Another token of love—as I am informed—is to tremble. Am I trembling?"

"No."

"Am I too confused to look at you?"

"No."

"Do I walk away with dignity—and then stop, and steal a timid glance at my lover, over my shoulder?"

"I wish you did!"

"A plain answer, Mr. Morris! Yes or No."

"No—of course."

"In one last word, do I give you any sort of encouragement to try again?"

"In one last word, I have made a fool of myself—and you have taken the kindest possible way of telling me so."

This time, she made no attempt to reply in his own tone. The good-humored gayety of her manner disappeared. She was in earnest—truly, sadly in earnest—when she said her next words.

"Is it not best, in your own interests, that we should bid each other good-by?" she asked. "In the time to come—when you only remember how kind you once were to me—we may look forward to meeting again. After all that you have suffered, so bitterly and so undeservedly, don't, pray don't, make me feel that another woman has behaved cruelly to you, and that I—so grieved to distress you—am that heartless creature!"

Never in her life had she been so irresistibly charming as she was at that moment. Her sweet nature showed all its innocent pity for him in her face.

He saw it—he felt it—he was not unworthy of it. In silence, he lifted her hand to his lips. He turned pale as he kissed it.

"Say that you agree with me?" she pleaded.

"I obey you."

As he answered, he pointed to the lawn at their feet. "Look," he said, "at that dead leaf which the air is wafting over the grass. Is it possible that such sympathy as you feel for Me, such love as I feel for You, can waste, wither, and fall to the ground like that leaf? I leave you, Emily—with the firm conviction that there is a time of fulfillment to come in our two lives. Happen what may in the interval—I trust the future."

The words had barely passed his lips when the voice of one of the servants reached them from the house. "Miss Emily, are you in the garden?"

Emily stepped out into the sunshine. The servant hurried to meet her, and placed a telegram in her hand. She looked at it with a sudden misgiving. In her small experience, a telegram was associated with the communication of bad news. She conquered her hesitation—opened it—read it. The color left her face: she shuddered. The telegram dropped on the grass.

"Read it," she said, faintly, as Alban picked it up.

He read these words: "Come to London directly. Miss Letitia is dangerously ill."

"Your aunt?" he asked.

"Yes—my aunt."

BOOK THE SECOND—IN LONDON.

CHAPTER XII. MRS. ELLMOTHER.

The metropolis of Great Britain is, in certain respects, like no other metropolis on the face of the earth. In the population that throngs the streets, the extremes of Wealth and the extremes of Poverty meet, as they meet nowhere else. In the streets themselves, the glory and the shame of architecture—the mansion and the hovel—are neighbors in situation, as they are neighbors nowhere else. London, in its social aspect, is the city of contrasts.

Toward the close of evening Emily left the railway terminus for the place of residence in which loss of fortune had compelled her aunt to take refuge. As she approached her destination, the cab passed—by merely crossing a road—from a spacious and beautiful Park, with its surrounding houses topped by statues and cupolas, to a row of cottages, hard by a stinking ditch miscalled a canal. The city of contrasts: north and south, east and west, the city of social contrasts.

Emily stopped the cab before the garden gate of a cottage, at the further end of the row. The bell was answered by the one servant now in her aunt's employ—Miss Letitia's maid.

Personally, this good creature was one of the ill-fated women whose appearance suggests that Nature intended to make men of them and altered her mind at the last moment. Miss Letitia's maid was tall and gaunt and awkward. The first impression produced by her face was an impression of bones. They rose high on her forehead; they projected on her cheeks; and they reached their boldest development in her jaws. In the cavernous eyes of this unfortunate person rigid obstinacy and rigid goodness looked out together, with equal severity, on all her fellow-creatures alike. Her mistress (whom she had served for a quarter of a century and more) called her "Bony." She accepted this cruelly appropriate nick-name as a mark of affectionate familiarity which honored a servant. No other person was allowed to take liberties with her: to every one but her mistress she was known as Mrs. Ellmother.

"How is my aunt?" Emily asked.

"Bad."

"Why have I not heard of her illness before?"

"Because she's too fond of you to let you be distressed about her. 'Don't tell Emily'; those were her orders, as long as she kept her senses."

"Kept her senses? Good heavens! what do you mean?"

"Fever—that's what I mean."

"I must see her directly; I am not afraid of infection."

"There's no infection to be afraid of. But you mustn't see her, for all that."

"I insist on seeing her."

"Miss Emily, I am disappointing you for your own good. Don't you know me well enough to trust me by this time?"

"I do trust you."

"Then leave my mistress to me—and go and make yourself comfortable in your own room."

Emily's answer was a positive refusal. Mrs. Ellmother, driven to her last resources, raised a new obstacle.

"It's not to be done, I tell you! How can you see Miss Letitia when she can't bear the light in her room? Do you know what color her eyes are? Red, poor soul—red as a boiled lobster."

With every word the woman uttered, Emily's perplexity and distress increased.

"You told me my aunt's illness was fever," she said—"and now you speak of some complaint in her eyes. Stand out of the way, if you please, and let me go to her."

Mrs. Ellmother, still keeping her place, looked through the open door.

"Here's the doctor," she announced. "It seems I can't satisfy you; ask him what's the matter. Come in, doctor." She threw open the door of the parlor, and introduced Emily. "This is the mistress's niece, sir. Please try if you can keep her quiet. I can't." She placed chairs with the hospitable politeness of the old school—and returned to her post at Miss Letitia's bedside.

Doctor Allday was an elderly man, with a cool manner and a ruddy complexion—thoroughly acclimatized to the atmosphere of pain and grief in which it was his destiny to live. He spoke to Emily (without any undue familiarity) as if he had been accustomed to see her for the greater part of her life.

"That's a curious woman," he said, when Mrs. Ellmother closed the door; "the most headstrong person, I think, I ever met with. But devoted to her mistress, and, making allowance for her awkwardness, not a bad nurse. I am afraid I can't give you an encouraging report of your aunt. The rheumatic fever (aggravated by the situation of this house—built on clay, you know, and close to stagnant water) has been latterly complicated by delirium."

"Is that a bad sign, sir?"

"The worst possible sign; it shows that the disease has affected the heart. Yes: she is suffering from inflammation of the eyes, but that is an unimportant symptom. We can keep the pain under by means of cooling lotions and a dark room. I've often heard her speak of you—especially since the illness assumed a serious character. What did you say? Will she know you, when you go into her room? This is about the time when the delirium usually sets in. I'll see if there's a quiet interval."

He opened the door—and came back again.

"By the way," he resumed, "I ought perhaps to explain how it was that I took the liberty of sending you that telegram. Mrs. Ellmother refused to inform you of her mistress's serious illness. That circumstance, according to my view of it, laid the responsibility on the doctor's shoulders. The form taken by your aunt's delirium—I mean the apparent tendency of the words that escape her in that state—seems to excite some incomprehensible feeling in the mind of her crabbed servant. She wouldn't even let me go into the bedroom, if she could possibly help it. Did Mrs. Ellmother give you a warm welcome when you came here?"

"Far from it. My arrival seemed to annoy her."

"Ah—just what I expected. These faithful old servants always end by presuming on their fidelity. Did you ever hear what a witty poet—I forget his name: he lived to be ninety—said of the man who had been his valet for more than half a century? 'For thirty years he was the best of servants; and for thirty years he has been the hardest of masters.' Quite true—I might say the same of my housekeeper. Rather a good story, isn't it?"

The story was completely thrown away on Emily; but one subject interested her now. "My poor aunt has always been fond of me," she said. "Perhaps she might know me, when she recognizes nobody else."

"Not very likely," the doctor answered. "But there's no laying down any rule in cases of this kind. I have sometimes observed that circumstances which have produced a strong impression on patients, when they are in a state of health, give a certain direction to the wandering of their minds, when they are in a state of fever. You will say, 'I am not a circumstance; I don't see how this encourages me to hope'—and you will be quite right. Instead of talking of my medical experience, I shall do better to look at Miss Letitia, and let you know the result. You have got other relations, I suppose? No? Very distressing—very distressing."

Who has not suffered as Emily suffered, when she was left alone? Are there not moments—if we dare to confess the truth—when poor humanity loses its hold on the consolations of religion and the hope of immortality, and feels the cruelty of creation that bids us live, on the condition that we die, and leads the first warm beginnings of love, with merciless certainty, to the cold conclusion of the grave?

"She's quiet, for the time being," Dr. Allday announced, on his return. "Remember, please, that she can't see you in the inflamed state of her eyes, and don't disturb the bed-curtains. The sooner you go to her the better, perhaps—if you have anything to say which depends on her recognizing your voice. I'll call to-morrow morning. Very distressing," he repeated, taking his hat and making his bow—"Very distressing."

Emily crossed the narrow little passage which separated the two rooms, and opened the bed-chamber door. Mrs. Ellmother met her on the threshold. "No," said the obstinate old servant, "you can't come in."

The faint voice of Miss Letitia made itself heard, calling Mrs. Ellmother by her familiar nick-name.

"Bony, who is it?"

"Never mind."

"Who is it?"

"Miss Emily, if you must know."

"Oh! poor dear, why does she come here? Who told her I was ill?"

"The doctor told her."

"Don't come in, Emily. It will only distress you—and it will do me no good. God bless you, my love. Don't come in."

"There!" said Mrs. Ellmother. "Do you hear that? Go back to the sitting-room."

Thus far, the hard necessity of controlling herself had kept Emily silent. She was now able to speak without tears. "Remember the old times, aunt," she pleaded, gently. "Don't keep me out of your room, when I have come here to nurse you!"

"I'm her nurse. Go back to the sitting-room," Mrs. Ellmother repeated.

True love lasts while life lasts. The dying woman relented.

"Bony! Bony! I can't be unkind to Emily. Let her in."

Mrs. Ellmother still insisted on having her way.

"You're contradicting your own orders," she said to her mistress. "You don't know how soon you may begin wandering in your mind again. Think, Miss Letitia—think."

This remonstrance was received in silence. Mrs. Ellmother's great gaunt figure still blocked up the doorway.

"If you force me to it," Emily said, quietly, "I must go to the doctor, and ask him to interfere."

"Do you mean that?" Mrs. Ellmother said, quietly, on her side.

"I do mean it," was the answer.

The old servant suddenly submitted—with a look which took Emily by surprise. She had expected to see anger; the face that now confronted her was a face subdued by sorrow and fear.

"I wash my hands of it," Mrs. Ellmother said. "Go in—and take the consequences."

CHAPTER XIII. MISS LETITIA.

Emily entered the room. The door was immediately closed on her from the outer side. Mrs. Ellmother's heavy steps were heard retreating along the passage. Then the banging of the door that led into the kitchen shook the flimsily-built cottage. Then, there was silence.

The dim light of a lamp hidden away in a corner and screened by a dingy green shade, just revealed the closely-curtained bed, and the table near it bearing medicine-bottles and glasses. The only objects on the chimney-piece were a clock that had been stopped in mercy to the sufferer's irritable nerves, and an open case containing a machine for pouring drops into the eyes. The smell of fumigating pastilles hung heavily on the air. To Emily's excited imagination, the silence was like the silence of death. She approached the bed trembling.

"Won't you speak to me, aunt?"

"Is that you, Emily? Who let you come in?"

"You said I might come in, dear. Are you thirsty? I see some lemonade on the table. Shall I give it to you?"

"No! If you open the bed-curtains, you let in the light. My poor eyes! Why are you here, my dear? Why are you not at the school?"

"It's holiday-time, aunt. Besides, I have left school for good."

"Left school?" Miss Letitia's memory made an effort, as she repeated those words. "You were going somewhere when you left school," she said, "and Cecilia Wyvil had something to do with it. Oh, my love, how cruel of you to go away to a stranger, when you might live here with me!" She paused—her sense of what she had herself just said began to grow confused. "What stranger?" she asked abruptly. "Was it a man? What name? Oh, my mind! Has death got hold of my mind before my body?"

"Hush! hush! I'll tell you the name. Sir Jervis Redwood."

"I don't know him. I don't want to know him. Do you think he means to send for you. Perhaps he has sent for you. I won't allow it! You shan't go!"

"Don't excite yourself, dear! I have refused to go; I mean to stay here with you."

The fevered brain held to its last idea. "Has he sent for you?" she said again, louder than before.

Emily replied once more, in terms carefully chosen with the one purpose of pacifying her. The attempt proved to be useless, and worse—it seemed to make her suspicious. "I won't be deceived!" she said; "I mean to know all about it. He did send for you. Whom did he send?"

"His housekeeper."

"What name?" The tone in which she put the question told of excitement that was rising to its climax. "Don't you know that I'm curious about names?" she burst out. "Why do you provoke me? Who is it?"

"Nobody you know, or need care about, dear aunt. Mrs. Rook."

Instantly on the utterance of that name, there followed an unexpected result. Silence ensued.

Emily waited—hesitated—advanced, to part the curtains, and look in at her aunt. She was stopped by a dreadful sound of laughter—the cheerless laughter that is heard among the mad. It suddenly ended in a dreary sigh.

Afraid to look in, she spoke, hardly knowing what she said. "Is there anything you wish for? Shall I call—?"

Miss Letitia's voice interrupted her. Dull, low, rapidly muttering, it was unlike, shockingly unlike, the familiar voice of her aunt. It said strange words.

"Mrs. Rook? What does Mrs. Rook matter? Or her husband either? Bony, Bony, you're frightened about nothing. Where's the danger of those two people turning up? Do you know how many miles away the village is? Oh, you fool—a hundred miles and more. Never mind the coroner, the coroner must keep in his own district—and the jury too. A risky deception? I call it a pious fraud. And I have a tender conscience, and a cultivated mind. The newspaper? How is our newspaper to find its way to her, I should like to know? You poor old Bony! Upon my word you do me good—you make me laugh."

The cheerless laughter broke out again—and died away again drearily in a sigh.

Accustomed to decide rapidly in the ordinary emergencies of her life, Emily felt herself painfully embarrassed by the position in which she was now placed.

After what she had already heard, could she reconcile it to her sense of duty to her aunt to remain any longer in the room?

In the hopeless self-betrayal of delirium, Miss Letitia had revealed some act of concealment, committed in her past life, and confided to her faithful old servant. Under these circumstances, had Emily made any discoveries which convicted her of taking a base advantage of her position at the bedside? Most assuredly not! The nature of the act of concealment; the causes that had led to it; the person (or persons) affected by it—these were mysteries which left her entirely in the dark. She had found out that her aunt was acquainted with Mrs. Rook, and that was literally all she knew.

Blameless, so far, in the line of conduct that she had pursued, might she still remain in the bed-chamber—on this distinct understanding with herself: that she would instantly return to the sitting-room if she heard anything which could suggest a doubt of Miss Letitia's claim to her affection and respect? After some hesitation, she decided on leaving it to her conscience to answer that question. Does conscience ever say, No—when inclination says, Yes? Emily's conscience sided with her reluctance to leave her aunt.

Throughout the time occupied by these reflections, the silence had remained unbroken. Emily began to feel uneasy. She timidly put her hand through the curtains, and took Miss Letitia's hand. The contact with the burning skin startled her. She turned away to the door, to call the servant—when the sound of her aunt's voice hurried her back to the bed.

"Are you there, Bony?" the voice asked.

Was her mind getting clear again? Emily tried the experiment of making a plain reply. "Your niece is with you," she said. "Shall I call the servant?"

Miss Letitia's mind was still far away from Emily, and from the present time.

"The servant?" she repeated. "All the servants but you, Bony, have been sent away. London's the place for us. No gossiping servants and no curious neighbors in London. Bury the horrid truth in London. Ah, you may well say I look anxious and wretched. I hate deception—and yet, it must be done. Why do you waste time in talking? Why don't you find out where the vile woman lives? Only let me get at her—and I'll make Sara ashamed of herself."

Emily's heart beat fast when she heard the woman's name. "Sara" (as she and her school-fellows knew) was the baptismal name of Miss Jethro. Had her aunt alluded to the disgraced teacher, or to some other woman?

She waited eagerly to hear more. There was nothing to be heard. At this most interesting moment, the silence remained undisturbed.

In the fervor of her anxiety to set her doubts at rest, Emily's faith in her own good resolutions began to waver. The temptation to say something which might set her aunt talking again was too strong to be resisted—if she remained at the bedside. Despairing of herself she rose and turned to the door. In the moment that passed while she crossed the room the very words occurred to her that would suit her purpose. Her cheeks were hot with shame—she hesitated—she looked back at the bed—the words passed her lips.

"Sara is only one of the woman's names," she said. "Do you like her other name?"

The rapidly-muttering tones broke out again instantly—but not in answer to Emily. The sound of a voice had encouraged Miss Letitia to pursue her own confused train of thought, and had stimulated the fast-failing capacity of speech to exert itself once more.

"No! no! He's too cunning for you, and too cunning for me. He doesn't leave letters about; he destroys them all. Did I say he was too cunning for us? It's false. We are too cunning for him. Who found the morsels of his letter in the basket? Who stuck them together? Ah, we know! Don't read it, Bony. 'Dear Miss Jethro'—don't read it again. 'Miss Jethro' in his letter; and 'Sara,' when he talks to himself in the garden. Oh, who would have believed it of him, if we hadn't seen and heard it ourselves!"

There was no more doubt now.

But who was the man, so bitterly and so regretfully alluded to?

No: this time Emily held firmly by the resolution which bound her to respect the helpless position of her aunt. The speediest way of summoning Mrs. Ellmother would be to ring the bell. As she touched the handle a faint cry of suffering from the bed called her back.

"Oh, so thirsty!" murmured the failing voice—"so thirsty!"

She parted the curtains. The shrouded lamplight just showed her the green shade over Miss Letitia's eyes—the hollow cheeks below it—the arms laid helplessly on the bed-clothes. "Oh, aunt, don't you know my voice? Don't you know Emily? Let me kiss you, dear!" Useless to plead with her; useless to kiss her; she only reiterated the words, "So thirsty! so thirsty!" Emily raised the poor tortured body with a patient caution which spared it pain, and put the glass to her aunt's lips. She drank the lemonade to the last drop. Refreshed for the moment, she spoke again—spoke to the visionary servant of her delirious fancy, while she rested in Emily's arms.

"For God's sake, take care how you answer if she questions you. If she knew what we know! Are men ever ashamed? Ha! the vile woman! the vile woman!"

Her voice, sinking gradually, dropped to a whisper. The next few words that escaped her were muttered inarticulately. Little by little, the false energy of fever was wearing itself out. She lay silent and still. To look at her now was to look at the image of death. Once more, Emily kissed her—closed the curtains—and rang the bell. Mrs. Ellmother failed to appear. Emily left the room to call her.

Arrived at the top of the kitchen stairs, she noted a slight change. The door below, which she had heard banged on first entering her aunt's room, now stood open. She called to Mrs. Ellmother. A strange voice answered her. Its accent was soft and courteous; presenting the strongest imaginable contrast to the harsh tones of Miss Letitia's crabbed old maid.

"Is there anything I can do for you, miss?"

The person making this polite inquiry appeared at the foot of the stairs—a plump and comely woman of middle age. She looked up at the young lady with a pleasant smile.

"I beg your pardon," Emily said; "I had no intention of disturbing you. I called to Mrs. Ellmother."

The stranger advanced a little way up the stairs, and answered, "Mrs. Ellmother is not here."

"Do you expect her back soon?"

"Excuse me, miss—I don't expect her back at all."

"Do you mean to say that she has left the house?"

"Yes, miss. She has left the house."

CHAPTER XIV. MRS. MOSEY.

Emily's first act—after the discovery of Mrs. Ellmother's incomprehensible disappearance—was to invite the new servant to follow her into the sitting-room.

"Can you explain this?" she began.

"No, miss."

"May I ask if you have come here by Mrs. Ellmother's invitation?"

"By Mrs. Ellmother's request, miss."

"Can you tell me how she came to make the request?"

"With pleasure, miss. Perhaps—as you find me here, a stranger to yourself, in place of the customary servant—I ought to begin by giving you a reference."

"And, perhaps (if you will be so kind), by mentioning your name," Emily added.

"Thank you for reminding me, miss. My name is Elizabeth Mosey. I am well known to the gentleman who attends Miss Letitia. Dr. Allday will speak to my character and also to my experience as a nurse. If it would be in any way satisfactory to give you a second reference—"

"Quite needless, Mrs. Mosey."

"Permit me to thank you again, miss. I was at home this evening, when Mrs. Ellmother called at my lodgings. Says she, 'I have come here, Elizabeth, to ask a favor of you for old friendship's sake.' Says I, 'My dear, pray command me, whatever it may be.' If this seems rather a hasty answer to make, before I knew what the favor was, might I ask you to bear in mind that Mrs. Ellmother put it to me 'for old friendship's sake'—alluding to my late husband, and to the business which we carried on at that time? Through no fault of ours, we got into difficulties. Persons whom we had trusted proved unworthy. Not to trouble you further, I may say at once, we should have been ruined, if our old friend Mrs. Ellmother had not come forward, and trusted us with the savings of her lifetime. The money was all paid back again, before my husband's death. But I don't consider—and, I think you won't consider—that the obligation was paid back too. Prudent or not prudent, there is nothing Mrs. Ellmother can ask of me that I am not willing to do. If I have put myself in an awkward situation (and I don't deny that it looks so) this is the only excuse, miss, that I can make for my conduct."

Mrs. Mosey was too fluent, and too fond of hearing the sound of her own eminently persuasive voice. Making allowance for these little drawbacks, the impression that she produced was decidedly favorable; and, however rashly she might have acted, her motive was beyond reproach. Having said some kind words to this effect, Emily led her back to the main interest of her narrative.

"Did Mrs. Ellmother give no reason for leaving my aunt, at such a time as this?" she asked.

"The very words I said to her, miss."

"And what did she say, by way of reply?"

"She burst out crying—a thing I have never known her to do before, in an experience of twenty years."

"And she really asked you to take her place here, at a moment's notice?"

"That was just what she did," Mrs. Mosey answered. "I had no need to tell her I was astonished; my lips spoke for me, no doubt. She's a hard woman in speech and manner, I admit. But there's more feeling in her than you would suppose. 'If you are the good friend I take you for,' she says, 'don't ask me for reasons; I am doing what is forced on me, and doing it with a heavy heart.' In my place, miss, would you have insisted on her explaining herself, after that? The one thing I naturally wanted to know was, if I could speak to some lady, in the position of mistress here, before I ventured to intrude. Mrs. Ellmother understood that it was her duty to help me in this particular. Your poor aunt being out of the question she mentioned you."

"How did she speak of me? In an angry way?"

"No, indeed—quite the contrary. She says, 'You will find Miss Emily at the cottage. She is Miss Letitia's niece. Everybody likes her—and everybody is right.'"

"She really said that?"

"Those were her words. And, what is more, she gave me a message for you at parting. 'If Miss Emily is surprised' (that was how she put it) 'give her my duty and good wishes; and tell her to remember what I said, when she took my place at her aunt's bedside.' I don't presume to inquire what this means," said Mrs. Mosey respectfully, ready to hear what it meant, if Emily would only be so good as to tell her. "I deliver the message, miss, as it was delivered to me. After which, Mrs. Ellmother went her way, and I went mine."

"Do you know where she went?"

"No, miss."

"Have you nothing more to tell me?"

"Nothing more; except that she gave me my directions, of course, about the nursing. I took them down in writing—and you will find them in their proper place, with the prescriptions and the medicines."

Acting at once on this hint, Emily led the way to her aunt's room.

Miss Letitia was silent, when the new nurse softly parted the curtains—looked in—and drew them together again. Consulting her watch, Mrs. Mosey compared her written directions with the medicine-bottles on the table, and set one apart to be used at the appointed time. "Nothing, so far, to alarm us," she whispered. "You look sadly pale and tired, miss. Might I advise you to rest a little?"

"If there is any change, Mrs. Mosey—either for the better or the worse—of course you will let me know?"

"Certainly, miss."

Emily returned to the sitting-room: not to rest (after all that she had heard), but to think.

Amid much that was unintelligible, certain plain conclusions presented themselves to her mind.

After what the doctor had already said to Emily, on the subject of delirium generally, Mrs. Ellmother's proceedings became intelligible: they proved that she knew by experience the perilous course taken by her mistress's wandering thoughts, when they expressed themselves in words. This explained the concealment of Miss Letitia's illness from her niece, as well as the reiterated efforts of the old servant to prevent Emily from entering the bedroom.

But the event which had just happened—that is to say, Mrs. Ellmother's sudden departure from the cottage—was not only of serious importance in itself, but pointed to a startling conclusion.

The faithful maid had left the mistress, whom she had loved and served, sinking under a fatal illness—and had put another woman in her place, careless of what that woman might discover by listening at the bedside—rather than confront Emily after she had been within hearing of her aunt while the brain of the suffering woman was deranged by fever. There was the state of the case, in plain words.

In what frame of mind had Mrs. Ellmother adopted this desperate course of action?

To use her own expression, she had deserted Miss Letitia "with a heavy heart." To judge by her own language addressed to Mrs. Mosey, she had left Emily to the mercy of a stranger—animated, nevertheless, by sincere feelings of attachment and respect. That her fears had taken for granted suspicion which Emily had not felt, and discoveries which Emily had (as yet) not made, in no way modified the serious nature of the inference which her conduct justified. The disclosure which this woman dreaded—who could doubt it now?—directly threatened Emily's peace of mind. There was no disguising it: the innocent niece was associated with an act of deception, which had been, until that day, the undetected secret of the aunt and the aunt's maid.

In this conclusion, and in this only, was to be found the rational explanation of Mrs. Ellmother's choice—placed between the alternatives of submitting to discovery by Emily, or of leaving the house.

Poor Miss Letitia's writing-table stood near the window of the sitting-room. Shrinking from the further pursuit of thoughts which might end in disposing her mind to distrust of her dying aunt, Emily looked round in search of some employment sufficiently interesting to absorb her attention. The writing-table reminded her that she owed a letter to Cecilia. That helpful friend had surely the first claim to know why she had failed to keep her engagement with Sir Jervis Redwood.

After mentioning the telegram which had followed Mrs. Rook's arrival at the school, Emily's letter proceeded in these terms:

"As soon as I had in some degree recovered myself, I informed Mrs. Rook of my aunt's serious illness.

"Although she carefully confined herself to commonplace expressions of sympathy, I could see that it was equally a relief to both of us to feel that we were prevented from being traveling companions. Don't suppose that I have taken a capricious dislike to Mrs. Rook—or that you are in any way to blame for the unfavorable impression which she has produced on me. I will make this plain when we meet. In the meanwhile, I need only tell you that I gave her a letter of explanation to present to Sir Jervis Redwood. I also informed him of my address in London: adding a request that he would forward your letter, in case you have written to me before you receive these lines.

"Kind Mr. Alban Morris accompanied me to the railway-station, and arranged with the guard to take special care of me on the journey to London. We used to think him rather a heartless man. We were quite wrong. I don't know what his plans are for spending the summer holidays. Go where he may, I remember his kindness; my best wishes go with him.

"My dear, I must not sadden your enjoyment of your pleasant visit to the Engadine, by writing at any length of the sorrow that I am suffering. You know how I love my aunt, and how gratefully I have always felt her motherly goodness to me. The doctor does not conceal the truth. At her age, there is no hope: my father's last-left relation, my one dearest friend, is dying.

"No! I must not forget that I have another friend—I must find some comfort in thinking of you.

"I do so long in my solitude for a letter from my dear Cecilia. Nobody comes to see me, when I most want sympathy; I am a stranger in this vast city. The members of my mother's family are settled in Australia: they have not even written to me, in all the long years that have passed since her death. You remember how cheerfully I used to look forward to my new life, on leaving school? Good-by, my darling. While I can see your sweet face, in my thoughts, I don't despair—dark as it looks now—of the future that is before me."

Emily had closed and addressed her letter, and was just rising from her chair, when she heard the voice of the new nurse at the door.

CHAPTER XV. EMILY.

"May I say a word?" Mrs. Mosey inquired. She entered the room—pale and trembling. Seeing that ominous change, Emily dropped back into her chair.

"Dead?" she said faintly.

Mrs. Mosey looked at her in vacant surprise.

"I wish to say, miss, that your aunt has frightened me."

Even that vague allusion was enough for Emily.

"You need say no more," she replied. "I know but too well how my aunt's mind is affected by the fever."

Confused and frightened as she was, Mrs. Mosey still found relief in her customary flow of words.

"Many and many a person have I nursed in fever," she announced. "Many and many a person have I heard say strange things. Never yet, miss, in all my experience—!"

"Don't tell me of it!" Emily interposed.

"Oh, but I must tell you! In your own interests, Miss Emily—in your own interests. I won't be inhuman enough to leave you alone in the house to-night; but if this delirium goes on, I must ask you to get another nurse. Shocking suspicions are lying in wait for me in that bedroom, as it were. I can't resist them as I ought, if I go back again, and hear your aunt saying what she has been saying for the last half hour and more. Mrs. Ellmother has expected impossibilities of me; and Mrs. Ellmother must take the consequences. I don't say she didn't warn me—speaking, you will please to understand, in the strictest confidence. 'Elizabeth,' she says, 'you know how wildly people talk in Miss Letitia's present condition. Pay no heed to it,' she says. 'Let it go in at one ear and out at the other,' she says. 'If Miss Emily asks questions—you know nothing about it. If she's frightened—you know nothing about it. If she bursts into fits of crying that are dreadful to see, pity her, poor thing, but take no notice.' All very well, and sounds like speaking out, doesn't it? Nothing of the sort! Mrs. Ellmother warns me to expect this, that, and the other. But there is one horrid thing (which I heard, mind, over and over again at your aunt's bedside) that she does not prepare me for; and that horrid thing is—Murder!"

At that last word, Mrs. Mosey dropped her voice to a whisper—and waited to see what effect she had produced.

Sorely tried already by the cruel perplexities of her position, Emily's courage failed to resist the first sensation of horror, aroused in her by the climax of the nurse's hysterical narrative. Encouraged by her silence, Mrs. Mosey went on. She lifted one hand with theatrical solemnity—and luxuriously terrified herself with her own horrors.

"An inn, Miss Emily; a lonely inn, somewhere in the country; and a comfortless room at the inn, with a makeshift bed at one end of it, and a makeshift bed at the other—I give you my word of honor, that was how your aunt put it. She spoke of two men next; two men asleep (you understand) in the two beds. I think she called them 'gentlemen'; but I can't be sure, and I wouldn't deceive you—you know I wouldn't deceive you, for the world. Miss Letitia muttered and mumbled, poor soul. I own I was getting tired of listening—when she burst out plain again, in that one horrid word—Oh, miss, don't be impatient! don't interrupt me!"

Emily did interrupt, nevertheless. In some degree at least she had recovered herself. "No more of it!" she said—"I won't hear a word more."

But Mrs. Mosey was too resolutely bent on asserting her own importance, by making the most of the alarm that she had suffered, to be repressed by any ordinary method of remonstrance. Without paying the slightest attention to what Emily had said, she went on again more loudly and more excitably than ever.

"Listen, miss—listen! The dreadful part of it is to come; you haven't heard about the two gentlemen yet. One of them was murdered—what do you think of that!—and the other (I heard your aunt say it, in so many words) committed the crime. Did Miss Letitia fancy she was addressing a lot of people when you were nursing her? She called out, like a person making public proclamation, when I was in her room. 'Whoever you are, good people' (she says), 'a hundred pounds reward, if you find the runaway murderer. Search everywhere for a poor weak womanish creature, with rings on his little white hands. There's nothing about him like a man, except his voice—a fine round voice. You'll know him, my friends—the wretch, the monster—you'll know him by his voice.' That was how she put it; I tell you again, that was how she put it. Did you hear her scream? Ah, my dear young lady, so much the better for you! 'O the horrid murder' (she says)—'hush it up!' I'll take my Bible oath before the magistrate," cried Mrs. Mosey, starting out of her chair, "your aunt said, 'Hush it up!'"

Emily crossed the room. The energy of her character was roused at last. She seized the foolish woman by the shoulders, forced her back in the chair, and looked her straight in the face without uttering a word.

For the moment, Mrs. Mosey was petrified. She had fully expected—having reached the end of her terrible story—to find Emily at her feet, entreating her not to carry out her intention of leaving the cottage the next morning; and she had determined, after her sense of her own importance had been sufficiently flattered, to grant the prayer of the helpless young lady. Those were her anticipations—and how had they been fulfilled? She had been treated like a mad woman in a state of revolt!

"How dare you assault me?" she asked piteously. "You ought to be ashamed of yourself. God knows I meant well."

"You are not the first person," Emily answered, quietly releasing her, "who has done wrong with the best intentions."

"I did my duty, miss, when I told you what your aunt said."

"You forgot your duty when you listened to what my aunt said."

"Allow me to explain myself."

"No: not a word more on that subject shall pass between us. Remain here, if you please; I have something to suggest in your own interests. Wait, and compose yourself."

The purpose which had taken a foremost place in Emily's mind rested on the firm foundation of her love and pity for her aunt.

Now that she had regained the power to think, she felt a hateful doubt pressed on her by Mrs. Mosey's disclosures. Having taken for granted that there was a foundation in truth for what she herself had heard in her aunt's room, could she reasonably resist the conclusion that there must be a foundation in truth for what Mrs. Mosey had heard, under similar circumstances?

There was but one way of escaping from this dilemma—and Emily deliberately took it. She turned her back on her own convictions; and persuaded herself that she had been in the wrong, when she had attached importance to anything that her aunt had said, under the influence of delirium. Having adopted this conclusion, she resolved to face the prospect of a night's solitude by the death-bed—rather than permit Mrs. Mosey to have a second

44

opportunity of drawing her own inferences from what she might hear in Miss Letitia's room.

"Do you mean to keep me waiting much longer, miss?"

"Not a moment longer, now you are composed again," Emily answered. "I have been thinking of what has happened; and I fail to see any necessity for putting off your departure until the doctor comes to-morrow morning. There is really no objection to your leaving me to-night."

"I beg your pardon, miss; there is an objection. I have already told you I can't reconcile it to my conscience to leave you here by yourself. I am not an inhuman woman," said Mrs. Mosey, putting her handkerchief to her eyes—smitten with pity for herself.

Emily tried the effect of a conciliatory reply. "I am grateful for your kindness in offering to stay with me," she said.

"Very good of you, I'm sure," Mrs. Mosey answered ironically. "But for all that, you persist in sending me away."

"I persist in thinking that there is no necessity for my keeping you here until to-morrow."

"Oh, have it your own way! I am not reduced to forcing my company on anybody."

Mrs. Mosey put her handkerchief in her pocket, and asserted her dignity. With head erect and slowly-marching steps she walked out of the room. Emily was left in the cottage, alone with her dying aunt.

CHAPTER XVI. MISS JETHRO.

A fortnight after the disappearance of Mrs. Ellmother, and the dismissal of Mrs. Mosey, Doctor Allday entered his consulting-room, punctual to the hour at which he was accustomed to receive patients.

An occasional wrinkling of his eyebrows, accompanied by an intermittent restlessness in his movements, appeared to indicate some disturbance of this worthy man's professional composure. His mind was indeed not at ease. Even the inexcitable old doctor had felt the attraction which had already conquered three such dissimilar people as Alban Morris, Cecilia Wyvil, and Francine de Sor. He was thinking of Emily.

A ring at the door-bell announced the arrival of the first patient.

The servant introduced a tall lady, dressed simply and elegantly in dark apparel. Noticeable features, of a Jewish cast—worn and haggard, but still preserving their grandeur of form— were visible through her veil. She moved with grace and dignity; and she stated her object in consulting Doctor Allday with the ease of a well-bred woman.

"I come to ask your opinion, sir, on the state of my heart," she said; "and I am recommended by a patient, who has consulted you with advantage to herself." She placed a card on the doctor's writing-desk, and added: "I have become acquainted with the lady, by being one of the lodgers in her house."

The doctor recognized the name—and the usual proceedings ensued. After careful examination, he arrived at a favorable conclusion. "I may tell you at once," he said—"there is no reason to be alarmed about the state of your heart."

"I have never felt any alarm about myself," she answered quietly. "A sudden death is an easy death. If one's affairs are settled, it seems, on that account, to be the death to prefer. My object was to settle my affairs—such as they are—if you had considered my life to be in danger. Is there nothing the matter with me?"

"I don't say that," the doctor replied. "The action of your heart is very feeble. Take the medicine that I shall prescribe; pay a little more attention to eating and drinking than ladies usually do; don't run upstairs, and don't fatigue yourself by violent exercise—and I see no reason why you shouldn't live to be an old woman."

"God forbid!" the lady said to herself. She turned away, and looked out of the window with a bitter smile.

Doctor Allday wrote his prescription. "Are you likely to make a long stay in London?" he asked.

"I am here for a little while only. Do you wish to see me again?"

"I should like to see you once more, before you go away—if you can make it convenient. What name shall I put on the prescription?"

"Miss Jethro."

"A remarkable name," the doctor said, in his matter-of-fact way.

Miss Jethro's bitter smile showed itself again.

Without otherwise noticing what Doctor Allday had said, she laid the consultation fee on the table. At the same moment, the footman appeared with a letter. "From Miss Emily Brown," he said. "No answer required."

He held the door open as he delivered the message, seeing that Miss Jethro was about to leave the room. She dismissed him by a gesture; and, returning to the table, pointed to the letter.

"Was your correspondent lately a pupil at Miss Ladd's school?" she inquired.

"My correspondent has just left Miss Ladd," the doctor answered. "Are you a friend of hers?"

"I am acquainted with her."

"You would be doing the poor child a kindness, if you would go and see her. She has no friends in London."

"Pardon me—she has an aunt."

"Her aunt died a week since."

"Are there no other relations?"

"None. A melancholy state of things, isn't it? She would have been absolutely alone in the house, if I had not sent one of my women servants to stay with her for the present. Did you know her father?"

Miss Jethro passed over the question, as if she had not heard it. "Has the young lady dismissed her aunt's servants?" she asked.

"Her aunt kept but one servant, ma'am. The woman has spared Miss Emily the trouble of dismissing her." He briefly alluded to Mrs. Ellmother's desertion of her mistress. "I can't explain it," he said when he had done. "Can you?"

"What makes you think, sir, that I can help you? I have never even heard of the servant—and the mistress was a stranger to me."

At Doctor Allday's age a man is not easily discouraged by reproof, even when it is administered by a handsome woman. "I thought you might have known Miss Emily's father," he persisted.

Miss Jethro rose, and wished him good-morning. "I must not occupy any more of your valuable time," she said.

"Suppose you wait a minute?" the doctor suggested.

Impenetrable as ever, he rang the bell. "Any patients in the waiting-room?" he inquired. "You see I have time to spare," he resumed, when the man had replied in the negative. "I take an interest in this poor girl; and I thought—"

"If you think that I take an interest in her, too," Miss Jethro interposed, "you are perfectly right—I knew her father," she added abruptly; the allusion to Emily having apparently reminded her of the question which she had hitherto declined to notice.

"In that case," Doctor Allday proceeded, "I want a word of advice. Won't you sit down?"

She took a chair in silence. An irregular movement in the lower part of her veil seemed to indicate that she was breathing with difficulty. The doctor observed her with close attention. "Let me see my prescription again," he said. Having added an ingredient, he handed it back with a word of explanation. "Your nerves are more out of order than I supposed. The hardest disease to cure that I know of is—worry."

The hint could hardly have been plainer; but it was lost on Miss Jethro. Whatever her troubles might be, her medical adviser was not made acquainted with them. Quietly folding up the prescription, she reminded him that he had proposed to ask her advice.

"In what way can I be of service to you?" she inquired.

"I am afraid I must try your patience," the doctor acknowledged, "if I am to answer that question plainly."

With these prefatory words, he described the events that had followed Mrs. Mosey's appearance at the cottage. "I am only doing justice to this foolish woman," he continued, "when I tell you that she came here, after she had left Miss Emily, and did her best to set matters right. I went to the poor girl directly—and I felt it my duty, after looking at her aunt, not to leave her alone for that night. When I got home the next morning, whom do you think I found waiting for me? Mrs. Ellmother!"

He stopped—in the expectation that Miss Jethro would express some surprise. Not a word passed her lips.

"Mrs. Ellmother's object was to ask how her mistress was going on," the doctor proceeded. "Every day while Miss Letitia still lived, she came here to make the same inquiry—without a word of explanation. On the day of the funeral, there she was at the church, dressed in deep mourning; and, as I can personally testify, crying bitterly. When the ceremony was over— can you believe it?—she slipped away before Miss Emily or I could speak to her. We have seen nothing more of her, and heard nothing more, from that time to this."

He stopped again, the silent lady still listening without making any remark.

"Have you no opinion to express?" the doctor asked bluntly.

"I am waiting," Miss Jethro answered.

"Waiting—for what?"

"I haven't heard yet, why you want my advice."

Doctor Allday's observation of humanity had hitherto reckoned want of caution among the deficient moral qualities in the natures of women. He set down Miss Jethro as a remarkable exception to a general rule.

"I want you to advise me as to the right course to take with Miss Emily," he said. "She has assured me she attaches no serious importance to her aunt's wanderings, when the poor old lady's fever was at its worst. I don't doubt that she speaks the truth—but I have my own reasons for being afraid that she is deceiving herself. Will you bear this in mind?"

"Yes—if it's necessary."

"In plain words, Miss Jethro, you think I am still wandering from the point. I have got to the point. Yesterday, Miss Emily told me that she hoped to be soon composed enough to examine the papers left by her aunt."

Miss Jethro suddenly turned in her chair, and looked at Doctor Allday.

"Are you beginning to feel interested?" the doctor asked mischievously.

She neither acknowledged nor denied it. "Go on"—was all she said.

"I don't know how you feel," he proceeded; "I am afraid of the discoveries which she may make; and I am strongly tempted to advise her to leave the proposed examination to her aunt's lawyer. Is there anything in your knowledge of Miss Emily's late father, which tells you that I am right?"

"Before I reply," said Miss Jethro, "it may not be amiss to let the young lady speak for herself."

"How is she to do that?" the doctor asked.

Miss Jethro pointed to the writing table. "Look there," she said. "You have not yet opened Miss Emily's letter."

Absorbed in the effort to overcome his patient's reserve, the doctor had forgotten Emily's letter. He opened it immediately.

After reading the first sentence, he looked up with an expression of annoyance. "She has begun the examination of the papers already," he said.

"Then I can be of no further use to you," Miss Jethro rejoined. She made a second attempt to leave the room.

Doctor Allday turned to the next page of the letter. "Stop!" he cried. "She has found something—and here it is."

He held up a small printed Handbill, which had been placed between the first and second pages. "Suppose you look at it?" he said.

"Whether I am interested in it or not?" Miss Jethro asked.

"You may be interested in what Miss Emily says about it in her letter."

"Do you propose to show me her letter?"

"I propose to read it to you."

Miss Jethro took the Handbill without further objection. It was expressed in these words:

"MURDER. 100 POUNDS REWARD.—Whereas a murder was committed on the thirtieth September, 1877, at the Hand-in-Hand Inn, in the village of Zeeland, Hampshire, the above reward will be paid to any person or persons whose exertions shall lead to the arrest and conviction of the suspected murderer. Name not known. Supposed age, between twenty and thirty years. A well-made man, of small stature. Fair complexion, delicate features, clear blue eyes. Hair light, and cut rather short. Clean shaven, with the exception of narrow half-whiskers. Small, white, well-shaped hands. Wore valuable rings on the two last fingers of the left hand. Dressed neatly in a dark-gray tourist-suit. Carried a knapsack, as if on a pedestrian excursion. Remarkably good voice, smooth, full, and persuasive. Ingratiating manners. Apply to the Chief Inspector, Metropolitan Police Office, London."

Miss Jethro laid aside the Handbill without any visible appearance of agitation. The doctor took up Emily's letter, and read as follows:

"You will be as much relieved as I was, my kind friend, when you look at the paper inclosed. I found it loose in a blank book, with cuttings from newspapers, and odd announcements of lost property and other curious things (all huddled together between the leaves), which my aunt no doubt intended to set in order and fix in their proper places. She must have been thinking of her book, poor soul, in her last illness. Here is the origin of those 'terrible words' which frightened stupid Mrs. Mosey! Is it not encouraging to have discovered such a confirmation of my opinion as this? I feel a new interest in looking over the papers that still remain to be examined—"

Before he could get to the end of the sentence Miss Jethro's agitation broke through her reserve.

"Do what you proposed to do!" she burst out vehemently. "Stop her at once from carrying her examination any further! If she hesitates, insist on it!"

At last Doctor Allday had triumphed! "It has been a long time coming," he remarked, in his cool way; "and it's all the more welcome on that account. You dread the discoveries she may make, Miss Jethro, as I do. And you know what those discoveries may be."

"What I do know, or don't know, is of no importance." she answered sharply.

"Excuse me, it is of very serious importance. I have no authority over this poor girl—I am not even an old friend. You tell me to insist. Help me to declare honestly that I know of circumstances which justify me; and I may insist to some purpose."

Miss Jethro lifted her veil for the first time, and eyed him searchingly.

"I believe I can trust you," she said. "Now listen! The one consideration on which I consent to open my lips, is consideration for Miss Emily's tranquillity. Promise me absolute secrecy, on your word of honor."

48

He gave the promise.

"I want to know one thing, first," Miss Jethro proceeded. "Did she tell you—as she once told me—that her father had died of heart-complaint?"

"Yes."

"Did you put any questions to her?"

"I asked how long ago it was."

"And she told you?"

"She told me."

"You wish to know, Doctor Allday, what discoveries Miss Emily may yet make, among her aunt's papers. Judge for yourself, when I tell you that she has been deceived about her father's death."

"Do you mean that he is still living?"

"I mean that she has been deceived—purposely deceived—about the manner of his death."

"Who was the wretch who did it?"

"You are wronging the dead, sir! The truth can only have been concealed out of the purest motives of love and pity. I don't desire to disguise the conclusion at which I have arrived after what I have heard from yourself. The person responsible must be Miss Emily's aunt—and the old servant must have been in her confidence. Remember! You are bound in honor not to repeat to any living creature what I have just said."

The doctor followed Miss Jethro to the door. "You have not yet told me," he said, "how her father died."

"I have no more to tell you."

With those words she left him.

He rang for his servant. To wait until the hour at which he was accustomed to go out, might be to leave Emily's peace of mind at the mercy of an accident. "I am going to the cottage," he said. "If anybody wants me, I shall be back in a quarter of an hour."

On the point of leaving the house, he remembered that Emily would probably expect him to return the Handbill. As he took it up, the first lines caught his eye: he read the date at which the murder had been committed, for the second time. On a sudden the ruddy color left his face.

"Good God!" he cried, "her father was murdered—and that woman was concerned in it."

Following the impulse that urged him, he secured the Handbill in his pocketbook—snatched up the card which his patient had presented as her introduction—and instantly left the house. He called the first cab that passed him, and drove to Miss Jethro's lodgings.

"Gone"—was the servant's answer when he inquired for her. He insisted on speaking to the landlady. "Hardly ten minutes have passed," he said, "since she left my house."

"Hardly ten minutes have passed," the landlady replied, "since that message was brought here by a boy."

The message had been evidently written in great haste: "I am unexpectedly obliged to leave London. A bank note is inclosed in payment of my debt to you. I will send for my luggage." The doctor withdrew.

"Unexpectedly obliged to leave London," he repeated, as he got into the cab again. "Her flight condemns her: not a doubt of it now. As fast as you can!" he shouted to the man; directing him to drive to Emily's cottage.

CHAPTER XVIII. MISS LADD.

Arriving at the cottage, Doctor Allday discovered a gentleman, who was just closing the garden gate behind him.

"Has Miss Emily had a visitor?" he inquired, when the servant admitted him.

"The gentleman left a letter for Miss Emily, sir."

"Did he ask to see her?"

"He asked after Miss Letitia's health. When he heard that she was dead, he seemed to be startled, and went away immediately."

"Did he give his name?"

"No, sir."

The doctor found Emily absorbed over her letter. His anxiety to forestall any possible discovery of the deception which had concealed the terrible story of her father's death, kept Doctor Allday's vigilance on the watch. He doubted the gentleman who had abstained from giving his name; he even distrusted the other unknown person who had written to Emily.

She looked up. Her face relieved him of his misgivings, before she could speak.

"At last, I have heard from my dearest friend," she said. "You remember what I told you about Cecilia? Here is a letter—a long delightful letter—from the Engadine, left at the door by some gentleman unknown. I was questioning the servant when you rang the bell."

"You may question me, if you prefer it. I arrived just as the gentleman was shutting your garden gate."

"Oh, tell me! what was he like?"

"Tall, and thin, and dark. Wore a vile republican-looking felt hat. Had nasty ill-tempered wrinkles between his eyebrows. The sort of man I distrust by instinct."

"Why?"

"Because he doesn't shave."

"Do you mean that he wore a beard?"

"Yes; a curly black beard."

Emily clasped her hands in amazement. "Can it be Alban Morris?" she exclaimed.

The doctor looked at her with a sardonic smile; he thought it likely that he had discovered her sweetheart.

"Who is Mr. Alban Morris?" he asked.

"The drawing-master at Miss Ladd's school."

Doctor Allday dropped the subject: masters at ladies' schools were not persons who interested him. He returned to the purpose which had brought him to the cottage—and produced the Handbill that had been sent to him in Emily's letter.

"I suppose you want to have it back again?" he said.

She took it from him, and looked at it with interest.

"Isn't it strange," she suggested, "that the murderer should have escaped, with such a careful description of him as this circulated all over England?"

She read the description to the doctor.

"'Name not known. Supposed age, between twenty-five and thirty years. A well-made man, of small stature. Fair complexion, delicate features, clear blue eyes. Hair light, and cut rather short. Clean shaven, with the exception of narrow half-whiskers. Small, white, well-shaped hands. Wore valuable rings on the two last fingers of the left hand. Dressed neatly—'"

"That part of the description is useless," the doctor remarked; "he would change his clothes."

"But could he change his voice?" Emily objected. "Listen to this: 'Remarkably good voice, smooth, full, and persuasive.' And here again! 'Ingratiating manners.' Perhaps you will say he could put on an appearance of rudeness?"

"I will say this, my dear. He would be able to disguise himself so effectually that ninety-nine people out of a hundred would fail to identify him, either by his voice or his manner."

"How?"

"Look back at the description: 'Hair cut rather short, clean shaven, with the exception of narrow half-whiskers.' The wretch was safe from pursuit; he had ample time at his disposal—don't you see how he could completely alter the appearance of his head and face?

50

No more, my dear, of this disagreeable subject! Let us get to something interesting. Have you found anything else among your aunt's papers?"

"I have met with a great disappointment," Emily replied. "Did I tell you how I discovered the Handbill?"

"No."

"I found it, with the scrap-book and the newspaper cuttings, under a collection of empty boxes and bottles, in a drawer of the washhand-stand. And I naturally expected to make far more interesting discoveries in this room. My search was over in five minutes. Nothing in the cabinet there, in the corner, but a few books and some china. Nothing in the writing-desk, on that side-table, but a packet of note-paper and some sealing-wax. Nothing here, in the drawers, but tradesmen's receipts, materials for knitting, and old photographs. She must have destroyed all her papers, poor dear, before her last illness; and the Handbill and the other things can only have escaped, because they were left in a place which she never thought of examining. Isn't it provoking?"

With a mind inexpressibly relieved, good Doctor Allday asked permission to return to his patients: leaving Emily to devote herself to her friend's letter.

On his way out, he noticed that the door of the bed-chamber on the opposite side of the passage stood open. Since Miss Letitia's death the room had not been used. Well within view stood the washhand-stand to which Emily had alluded. The doctor advanced to the house door—reflected—hesitated—and looked toward the empty room.

It had struck him that there might be a second drawer which Emily had overlooked. Would he be justified in setting this doubt at rest? If he passed over ordinary scruples it would not be without excuse. Miss Letitia had spoken to him of her affairs, and had asked him to act (in Emily's interest) as co-executor with her lawyer. The rapid progress of the illness had made it impossible for her to execute the necessary codicil. But the doctor had been morally (if not legally) taken into her confidence—and, for that reason, he decided that he had a right in this serious matter to satisfy his own mind.

A glance was enough to show him that no second drawer had been overlooked.

There was no other discovery to detain the doctor. The wardrobe only contained the poor old lady's clothes; the one cupboard was open and empty. On the point of leaving the room, he went back to the washhand-stand. While he had the opportunity, it might not be amiss to make sure that Emily had thoroughly examined those old boxes and bottles, which she had alluded to with some little contempt.

The drawer was of considerable length. When he tried to pull it completely out from the grooves in which it ran, it resisted him. In his present frame of mind, this was a suspicious circumstance in itself. He cleared away the litter so as to make room for the introduction of his hand and arm into the drawer. In another moment his fingers touched a piece of paper, jammed between the inner end of the drawer and the bottom of the flat surface of the washhand-stand. With a little care, he succeeded in extricating the paper. Only pausing to satisfy himself that there was nothing else to be found, and to close the drawer after replacing its contents, he left the cottage.

The cab was waiting for him. On the drive back to his own house, he opened the crumpled paper. It proved to be a letter addressed to Miss Letitia; and it was signed by no less a person than Emily's schoolmistress. Looking back from the end to the beginning, Doctor Allday discovered, in the first sentence, the name of—Miss Jethro.

But for the interview of that morning with his patient he might have doubted the propriety of making himself further acquainted with the letter. As things were, he read it without hesitation.

"DEAR MADAM—I cannot but regard it as providential circumstance that your niece, in writing to you from my house, should have mentioned, among other events of her school life, the arrival of my new teacher, Miss Jethro.

"To say that I was surprised is to express very inadequately what I felt when I read your letter, informing me confidentially that I had employed a woman who was unworthy to associate with the young persons placed under my care. It is impossible for me to suppose that a lady in your position, and possessed of your high principles, would make such a serious accusation as this, without unanswerable reasons for doing so. At the same time I cannot, consistently with my duty as a Christian, suffer my opinion of Miss Jethro to be in any way modified, until proofs are laid before me which it is impossible to dispute.

"Placing the same confidence in your discretion, which you have placed in mine, I now inclose the references and testimonials which Miss Jethro submitted to me, when she presented herself to fill the vacant situation in my school.

"I earnestly request you to lose no time in instituting the confidential inquiries which you have volunteered to make. Whatever the result may be, pray return to me the inclosures which I have trusted to your care, and believe me, dear madam, in much suspense and anxiety, sincerely yours,

"AMELIA LADD."

It is needless to describe, at any length, the impression which these lines produced on the doctor.

If he had heard what Emily had heard at the time of her aunt's last illness, he would have called to mind Miss Letitia's betrayal of her interest in some man unknown, whom she believed to have been beguiled by Miss Jethro—and he would have perceived that the vindictive hatred, thus produced, must have inspired the letter of denunciation which the schoolmistress had acknowledged. He would also have inferred that Miss Letitia's inquiries had proved her accusation to be well founded—if he had known of the new teacher's sudden dismissal from the school. As things were, he was merely confirmed in his bad opinion of Miss Jethro; and he was induced, on reflection, to keep his discovery to himself.

"If poor Miss Emily saw the old lady exhibited in the character of an informer," he thought, "what a blow would be struck at her innocent respect for the memory of her aunt!"

CHAPTER XIX. SIR JERVIS REDWOOD.

In the meantime, Emily, left by herself, had her own correspondence to occupy her attention. Besides the letter from Cecilia (directed to the care of Sir Jervis Redwood), she had received some lines addressed to her by Sir Jervis himself. The two inclosures had been secured in a sealed envelope, directed to the cottage.

If Alban Morris had been indeed the person trusted as messenger by Sir Jervis, the conclusion that followed filled Emily with overpowering emotions of curiosity and surprise. Having no longer the motive of serving and protecting her, Alban must, nevertheless, have taken the journey to Northumberland. He must have gained Sir Jervis Redwood's favor and confidence—and he might even have been a guest at the baronet's country seat—when Cecilia's letter arrived. What did it mean?

Emily looked back at her experience of her last day at school, and recalled her consultation with Alban on the subject of Mrs. Rook. Was he still bent on clearing up his suspicions of Sir Jervis's housekeeper? And, with that end in view, had he followed the woman, on her return to her master's place of abode?

Suddenly, almost irritably, Emily snatched up Sir Jervis's letter. Before the doctor had come in, she had glanced at it, and had thrown it aside in her impatience to read what Cecilia had written. In her present altered frame of mind, she was inclined to think that Sir Jervis might be the more interesting correspondent of the two.

On returning to his letter, she was disappointed at the outset.

In the first place, his handwriting was so abominably bad that she was obliged to guess at his meaning. In the second place, he never hinted at the circumstances under which Cecilia's letter had been confided to the gentleman who had left it at her door.

She would once more have treated the baronet's communication with contempt—but for the discovery that it contained an offer of employment in London, addressed to herself.

Sir Jervis had necessarily been obliged to engage another secretary in Emily's absence. But he was still in want of a person to serve his literary interests in London. He had reason to believe that discoveries made by modern travelers in Central America had been reported from time to time by the English press; and he wished copies to be taken of any notices of this sort which might be found, on referring to the files of newspapers kept in the reading-room of the British Museum. If Emily considered herself capable of contributing in this way to the completeness of his great work on "the ruined cities," she had only to apply to his bookseller in London, who would pay her the customary remuneration and give her every assistance of which she might stand in need. The bookseller's name and address followed (with nothing legible but the two words "Bond Street"), and there was an end of Sir Jervis's proposal.

Emily laid it aside, deferring her answer until she had read Cecilia's letter.

CHAPTER XX. THE REVEREND MILES MIRABEL.

"I am making a little excursion from the Engadine, my dearest of all dear friends. Two charming fellow-travelers take care of me; and we may perhaps get as far as the Lake of Como.

"My sister (already much improved in health) remains at St. Moritz with the old governess. The moment I know what exact course we are going to take, I shall write to Julia to forward any letters which arrive in my absence. My life, in this earthly paradise, will be only complete when I hear from my darling Emily.

"In the meantime, we are staying for the night at some interesting place, the name of which I have unaccountably forgotten; and here I am in my room, writing to you at last—dying to know if Sir Jervis has yet thrown himself at your feet, and offered to make you Lady Redwood with magnificent settlements.

"But you are waiting to hear who my new friends are. My dear, one of them is, next to yourself, the most delightful creature in existence. Society knows her as Lady Janeaway. I love her already, by her Christian name; she is my friend Doris. And she reciprocates my sentiments.

"You will now understand that union of sympathies made us acquainted with each other.

"If there is anything in me to be proud of, I think it must be my admirable appetite. And, if I have a passion, the name of it is Pastry. Here again, Lady Doris reciprocates my sentiments. We sit next to each other at the table d'hote.

"Good heavens, I have forgotten her husband! They have been married rather more than a month. Did I tell you that she is just two years older than I am?

"I declare I am forgetting him again! He is Lord Janeaway. Such a quiet modest man, and so easily amused. He carries with him everywhere a dirty little tin case, with air holes in the cover. He goes softly poking about among bushes and brambles, and under rocks, and behind old wooden houses. When he has caught some hideous insect that makes one shudder, he blushes with pleasure, and looks at his wife and me, and says, with the prettiest lisp: 'This is what I call enjoying the day.' To see the manner in which he obeys Her, is, between ourselves, to feel proud of being a woman.

"Where was I? Oh, at the table d'hote.

53

"Never, Emily—I say it with a solemn sense of the claims of truth—never have I eaten such an infamous, abominable, maddeningly bad dinner, as the dinner they gave us on our first day at the hotel. I ask you if I am not patient; I appeal to your own recollection of occasions when I have exhibited extraordinary self-control. My dear, I held out until they brought the pastry round. I took one bite, and committed the most shocking offense against good manners at table that you can imagine. My handkerchief, my poor innocent handkerchief, received the horrid—please suppose the rest. My hair stands on end, when I think of it. Our neighbors at the table saw me. The coarse men laughed. The sweet young bride, sincerely feeling for me, said, 'Will you allow me to shake hands? I did exactly what you have done the day before yesterday.' Such was the beginning of my friendship with Lady Doris Janeaway.

"We are two resolute women—I mean that she is resolute, and that I follow her—and we have asserted our right of dining to our own satisfaction, by means of an interview with the chief cook.

"This interesting person is an ex-Zouave in the French army. Instead of making excuses, he confessed that the barbarous tastes of the English and American visitors had so discouraged him, that he had lost all pride and pleasure in the exercise of his art. As an example of what he meant, he mentioned his experience of two young Englishmen who could speak no foreign language. The waiters reported that they objected to their breakfasts, and especially to the eggs. Thereupon (to translate the Frenchman's own way of putting it) he exhausted himself in exquisite preparations of eggs. Eggs a la tripe, au gratin, a l'Aurore, a la Dauphine, a la Poulette, a la Tartare, a la Venitienne, a la Bordelaise, and so on, and so on. Still the two young gentlemen were not satisfied. The ex-Zouave, infuriated; wounded in his honor, disgraced as a professor, insisted on an explanation. What, in heaven's name, did they want for breakfast? They wanted boiled eggs; and a fish which they called a Bloaterre. It was impossible, he said, to express his contempt for the English idea of a breakfast, in the presence of ladies. You know how a cat expresses herself in the presence of a dog—and you will understand the allusion. Oh, Emily, what dinners we have had, in our own room, since we spoke to that noble cook!

"Have I any more news to send you? Are you interested, my dear, in eloquent young clergymen?

"On our first appearance at the public table we noticed a remarkable air of depression among the ladies. Had some adventurous gentleman tried to climb a mountain, and failed? Had disastrous political news arrived from England; a defeat of the Conservatives, for instance? Had a revolution in the fashions broken out in Paris, and had all our best dresses become of no earthly value to us? I applied for information to the only lady present who shone on the company with a cheerful face—my friend Doris, of course. '"What day was yesterday?' she asked.

"'Sunday,' I answered.

"'Of all melancholy Sundays,' she continued, the most melancholy in the calendar. Mr. Miles Mirabel preached his farewell sermon, in our temporary chapel upstairs.'

"'And you have not recovered it yet?'

"'We are all heart-broken, Miss Wyvil.'

"This naturally interested me. I asked what sort of sermons Mr. Mirabel preached. Lady Janeaway said: 'Come up to our room after dinner. The subject is too distressing to be discussed in public.'

"She began by making me personally acquainted with the reverend gentleman—that is to say, she showed me the photographic portraits of him. They were two in number. One only presented his face. The other exhibited him at full length, adorned in his surplice. Every lady in the congregation had received the two photographs as a farewell present. 'My portraits,' Lady Doris remarked, 'are the only complete specimens. The others have been irretrievably ruined by tears.'

"You will now expect a personal description of this fascinating man. What the photographs failed to tell me, my friend was so kind as to complete from the resources of her own experience. Here is the result presented to the best of my ability.

"He is young—not yet thirty years of age. His complexion is fair; his features are delicate, his eyes are clear blue. He has pretty hands, and rings prettier still. And such a voice, and such manners! You will say there are plenty of pet parsons who answer to this description. Wait a little—I have kept his chief distinction till the last. His beautiful light hair flows in profusion over his shoulders; and his glossy beard waves, at apostolic length, down to the lower buttons of his waistcoat.

"What do you think of the Reverend Miles Mirabel now?

"The life and adventures of our charming young clergyman, bear eloquent testimony to the saintly patience of his disposition, under trials which would have overwhelmed an ordinary man. (Lady Doris, please notice, quotes in this place the language of his admirers; and I report Lady Doris.)

"He has been clerk in a lawyer's office—unjustly dismissed. He has given readings from Shakespeare—infamously neglected. He has been secretary to a promenade concert company—deceived by a penniless manager. He has been employed in negotiations for making foreign railways—repudiated by an unprincipled Government. He has been translator to a publishing house—declared incapable by envious newspapers and reviews. He has taken refuge in dramatic criticism—dismissed by a corrupt editor. Through all these means of purification for the priestly career, he passed at last into the one sphere that was worthy of him: he entered the Church, under the protection of influential friends. Oh, happy change! From that moment his labors have been blessed. Twice already he has been presented with silver tea-pots filled with sovereigns. Go where he may, precious sympathies environ him; and domestic affection places his knife and fork at innumerable family tables. After a continental career, which will leave undying recollections, he is now recalled to England—at the suggestion of a person of distinction in the Church, who prefers a mild climate. It will now be his valued privilege to represent an absent rector in a country living; remote from cities, secluded in pastoral solitude, among simple breeders of sheep. May the shepherd prove worthy of the flock!

"Here again, my dear, I must give the merit where the merit is due. This memoir of Mr. Mirabel is not of my writing. It formed part of his farewell sermon, preserved in the memory of Lady Doris—and it shows (once more in the language of his admirers) that the truest humility may be found in the character of the most gifted man.

"Let me only add, that you will have opportunities of seeing and hearing this popular preacher, when circumstances permit him to address congregations in the large towns. I am at the end of my news; and I begin to feel—after this long, long letter—that it is time to go to bed. Need I say that I have often spoken of you to Doris, and that she entreats you to be her friend as well as mine, when we meet again in England?

"Good-by, darling, for the present. With fondest love,

"Your CECILIA."

"P.S.—I have formed a new habit. In case of feeling hungry in the night, I keep a box of chocolate under the pillow. You have no idea what a comfort it is. If I ever meet with the man who fulfills my ideal, I shall make it a condition of the marriage settlement, that I am to have chocolate under the pillow."

Without a care to trouble her; abroad or at home, finding inexhaustible varieties of amusement; seeing new places, making new acquaintances—what a disheartening contrast did Cecilia's happy life present to the life of her friend! Who, in Emily's position, could have read that joyously-written letter from Switzerland, and not have lost heart and faith, for the moment at least, as the inevitable result?

A buoyant temperament is of all moral qualities the most precious, in this respect; it is the one force in us—when virtuous resolution proves insufficient—which resists by instinct the stealthy approaches of despair. "I shall only cry," Emily thought, "if I stay at home; better go out."

Observant persons, accustomed to frequent the London parks, can hardly have failed to notice the number of solitary strangers sadly endeavoring to vary their lives by taking a walk. They linger about the flower-beds; they sit for hours on the benches; they look with patient curiosity at other people who have companions; they notice ladies on horseback and children at play, with submissive interest; some of the men find company in a pipe, without appearing to enjoy it; some of the women find a substitute for dinner, in little dry biscuits wrapped in crumpled scraps of paper; they are not sociable; they are hardly ever seen to make acquaintance with each other; perhaps they are shame-faced, or proud, or sullen; perhaps they despair of others, being accustomed to despair of themselves; perhaps they have their reasons for never venturing to encounter curiosity, or their vices which dread detection, or their virtues which suffer hardship with the resignation that is sufficient for itself. The one thing certain is, that these unfortunate people resist discovery. We know that they are strangers in London—and we know no more.

And Emily was one of them.

Among the other forlorn wanderers in the Parks, there appeared latterly a trim little figure in black (with the face protected from notice behind a crape veil), which was beginning to be familiar, day after day, to nursemaids and children, and to rouse curiosity among harmless solitaries meditating on benches, and idle vagabonds strolling over the grass. The woman-servant, whom the considerate doctor had provided, was the one person in Emily's absence left to take care of the house. There was no other creature who could be a companion to the friendless girl. Mrs. Ellmother had never shown herself again since the funeral. Mrs. Mosey could not forget that she had been (no matter how politely) requested to withdraw. To whom could Emily say, "Let us go out for a walk?" She had communicated the news of her aunt's death to Miss Ladd, at Brighton; and had heard from Francine. The worthy schoolmistress had written to her with the truest kindness. "Choose your own time, my poor child, and come and stay with me at Brighton; the sooner the better." Emily shrank—not from accepting the invitation—but from encountering Francine. The hard West Indian heiress looked harder than ever with a pen in her hand. Her letter announced that she was "getting on wretchedly with her studies (which she hated); she found the masters appointed to instruct her ugly and disagreeable (and loathed the sight of them); she had taken a dislike to Miss Ladd (and time only confirmed that unfavorable impression); Brighton was always the same; the sea was always the same; the drives were always the same. Francine felt a presentiment that she should do something desperate, unless Emily joined her, and made Brighton endurable behind the horrid schoolmistress's back." Solitude in London was a privilege and a pleasure, viewed as the alternative to such companionship as this.

Emily wrote gratefully to Miss Ladd, and asked to be excused.

Other days had passed drearily since that time; but the one day that had brought with it Cecilia's letter set past happiness and present sorrow together so vividly and so cruelly that Emily's courage sank. She had forced back the tears, in her lonely home; she had gone out to seek consolation and encouragement under the sunny sky—to find comfort for her sore heart in the radiant summer beauty of flowers and grass, in the sweet breathing of the air, in the happy heavenward soaring of the birds. No! Mother Nature is stepmother to the sick at heart. Soon, too soon, she could hardly see where she went. Again and again she resolutely cleared her eyes, under the shelter of her veil, when passing strangers noticed her; and again and again the tears found their way back. Oh, if the girls at the school were to see her now—the girls who used to say in their moments of sadness, "Let us go to Emily and be cheered"—would they know her again? She sat down to rest and recover herself on the nearest bench. It was unoccupied. No passing footsteps were audible on the remote path to which she had strayed. Solitude at home! Solitude in the Park! Where was Cecilia at that moment? In Italy, among the lakes and mountains, happy in the company of her light-hearted friend.

The lonely interval passed, and persons came near. Two sisters, girls like herself, stopped to rest on the bench.

They were full of their own interests; they hardly looked at the stranger in mourning garments. The younger sister was to be married, and the elder was to be bridesmaid. They talked of their dresses and their presents; they compared the dashing bridegroom of one with the timid lover of the other; they laughed over their own small sallies of wit, over their joyous dreams of the future, over their opinions of the guests invited to the wedding. Too joyfully restless to remain inactive any longer, they jumped up again from the seat. One of them said, "Polly, I'm too happy!" and danced as she walked away. The other cried, "Sally, for shame!" and laughed, as if she had hit on the most irresistible joke that ever was made. Emily rose and went home.

By some mysterious influence which she was unable to trace, the boisterous merriment of the two girls had roused in her a sense of revolt against the life that she was leading. Change, speedy change, to some occupation that would force her to exert herself, presented the one promise of brighter days that she could see. To feel this was to be inevitably reminded of Sir Jervis Redwood. Here was a man, who had never seen her, transformed by the incomprehensible operation of Chance into the friend of whom she stood in need—the friend who pointed the way to a new world of action, the busy world of readers in the library of the Museum.

Early in the new week, Emily had accepted Sir Jervis's proposal, and had so interested the bookseller to whom she had been directed to apply, that he took it on himself to modify the arbitrary instructions of his employer.

"The old gentleman has no mercy on himself, and no mercy on others," he explained, "where his literary labors are concerned. You must spare yourself, Miss Emily. It is not only absurd, it's cruel, to expect you to ransack old newspapers for discoveries in Yucatan, from the time when Stephens published his 'Travels in Central America'—nearly forty years since! Begin with back numbers published within a few years—say five years from the present date—and let us see what your search over that interval will bring forth."

Accepting this friendly advice, Emily began with the newspaper-volume dating from New Year's Day, 1876.

The first hour of her search strengthened the sincere sense of gratitude with which she remembered the bookseller's kindness. To keep her attention steadily fixed on the one subject that interested her employer, and to resist the temptation to read those miscellaneous items of news which especially interest women, put her patience and resolution to a merciless test. Happily for herself, her neighbors on either side were no idlers. To see them so absorbed over their work that they never once looked at her, after the first moment when she took her place between them, was to find exactly the example of which she stood most in need. As the hours wore on, she pursued her weary way, down one column and up another, resigned at least (if not quite reconciled yet) to her task. Her labors ended, for the day, with such encouragement as she might derive from the conviction of having, thus far, honestly pursued a useless search.

57

News was waiting for her when she reached home, which raised her sinking spirits.

On leaving the cottage that morning she had given certain instructions, relating to the modest stranger who had taken charge of her correspondence—in case of his paying a second visit, during her absence at the Museum. The first words spoken by the servant, on opening the door, informed her that the unknown gentleman had called again. This time he had boldly left his card. There was the welcome name that she had expected to see—Alban Morris.

CHAPTER XXII. ALBAN MORRIS.

Having looked at the card, Emily put her first question to the servant.

"Did you tell Mr. Morris what your orders were?" she asked.

"Yes, miss; I said I was to have shown him in, if you had been at home. Perhaps I did wrong; I told him what you told me when you went out this morning—I said you had gone to read at the Museum."

"What makes you think you did wrong?"

"Well, miss, he didn't say anything, but he looked upset."

"Do you mean that he looked angry?"

The servant shook her head. "Not exactly angry—puzzled and put out."

"Did he leave any message?"

"He said he would call later, if you would be so good as to receive him."

In half an hour more, Alban and Emily were together again. The light fell full on her face as she rose to receive him.

"Oh, how you have suffered!"

The words escaped him before he could restrain himself. He looked at her with the tender sympathy, so precious to women, which she had not seen in the face of any human creature since the loss of her aunt. Even the good doctor's efforts to console her had been efforts of professional routine—the inevitable result of his life-long familiarity with sorrow and death. While Alban's eyes rested on her, Emily felt her tears rising. In the fear that he might misinterpret her reception of him, she made an effort to speak with some appearance of composure.

"I lead a lonely life," she said; "and I can well understand that my face shows it. You are one of my very few friends, Mr. Morris"—the tears rose again; it discouraged her to see him standing irresolute, with his hat in his hand, fearful of intruding on her. "Indeed, indeed, you are welcome," she said, very earnestly.

In those sad days her heart was easily touched. She gave him her hand for the second time. He held it gently for a moment. Every day since they had parted she had been in his thoughts; she had become dearer to him than ever. He was too deeply affected to trust himself to answer. That silence pleaded for him as nothing had pleaded for him yet. In her secret self she remembered with wonder how she had received his confession in the school garden. It was a little hard on him, surely, to have forbidden him even to hope.

Conscious of her own weakness—even while giving way to it—she felt the necessity of turning his attention from herself. In some confusion, she pointed to a chair at her side, and spoke of his first visit, when he had left her letters at the door. Having confided to him all that she had discovered, and all that she had guessed, on that occasion, it was by an easy transition that she alluded next to the motive for his journey to the North.

"I thought it might be suspicion of Mrs. Rook," she said. "Was I mistaken?"

"No; you were right."

"They were serious suspicions, I suppose?"

"Certainly! I should not otherwise have devoted my holiday-time to clearing them up."

"May I know what they were?"

"I am sorry to disappoint you," he began.

"But you would rather not answer my question," she interposed.

"I would rather hear you tell me if you have made any other guess."

"One more, Mr. Morris. I guessed that you had become acquainted with Sir Jervis Redwood."

"For the second time, Miss Emily, you have arrived at a sound conclusion. My one hope of finding opportunities for observing Sir Jervis's housekeeper depended on my chance of gaining admission to Sir Jervis's house."

"How did you succeed? Perhaps you provided yourself with a letter of introduction?"

"I knew nobody who could introduce me," Alban replied. "As the event proved, a letter would have been needless. Sir Jervis introduced himself—and, more wonderful still, he invited me to his house at our first interview."

"Sir Jervis introduced himself?" Emily repeated, in amazement. "From Cecilia's description of him, I should have thought he was the last person in the world to do that!"

Alban smiled. "And you would like to know how it happened?" he suggested.

"The very favor I was going to ask of you," she replied.

Instead of at once complying with her wishes, he paused—hesitated—and made a strange request. "Will you forgive my rudeness, if I ask leave to walk up and down the room while I talk? I am a restless man. Walking up and down helps me to express myself freely."

Her f ace brightened for the first time. "How like You that is!" she exclaimed.

Alban looked at her with surprise and delight. She had betrayed an interest in studying his character, which he appreciated at its full value. "I should never have dared to hope," he said, "that you knew me so well already."

"You are forgetting your story," she reminded him.

He moved to the opposite side of the room, where there were fewer impediments in the shape of furniture. With his head down, and his hands crossed behind him, he paced to and fro. Habit made him express himself in his usual quaint way—but he became embarrassed as he went on. Was he disturbed by his recollections? or by the fear of taking Emily into his confidence too freely?

"Different people have different ways of telling a story," he said. "Mine is the methodical way—I begin at the beginning. We will start, if you please, in the railway—we will proceed in a one-horse chaise—and we will stop at a village, situated in a hole. It was the nearest place to Sir Jervis's house, and it was therefore my destination. I picked out the biggest of the cottages—I mean the huts—and asked the woman at the door if she had a bed to let. She evidently thought me either mad or drunk. I wasted no time in persuasion; the right person to plead my cause was asleep in her arms. I began by admiring the baby; and I ended by taking the baby's portrait. From that moment I became a member of the family—the member who had his own way. Besides the room occupied by the husband and wife, there was a sort of kennel in which the husband's brother slept. He was dismissed (with five shillings of mine to comfort him) to find shelter somewhere else; and I was promoted to the vacant place. It is my misfortune to be tall. When I went to bed, I slept with my head on the pillow, and my feet out of the window. Very cool and pleasant in summer weather. The next morning, I set my trap for Sir Jervis."

"Your trap?" Emily repeated, wondering what he meant.

"I went out to sketch from Nature," Alban continued. "Can anybody (with or without a title, I don't care), living in a lonely country house, see a stranger hard at work with a color-box and brushes, and not stop to look at what he is doing? Three days passed, and nothing happened. I was quite patient; the grand open country all round me offered lessons of inestimable value in what we call aerial perspective. On the fourth day, I was absorbed over the hardest of all hard tasks in landscape art, studying the clouds straight from Nature. The magnificent moorland silence was suddenly profaned by a man's voice, speaking (or rather croaking) behind me. 'The worst curse of human life,' the voice said, 'is the detestable necessity of taking exercise. I hate losing my time; I hate fine scenery; I hate fresh air; I hate a pony. Go on, you brute!' Being too deeply engaged with the clouds to look round, I had supposed this pretty speech to be addressed to some second person. Nothing of the sort; the croaking voice had a habit of speaking to itself. In a minute more, there came within my range of view a solitary old man, mounted on a rough pony."

"Was it Sir Jervis?"

Alban hesitated.

"It looked more like the popular notion of the devil," he said.

"Oh, Mr. Morris!"

"I give you my first impression, Miss Emily, for what it is worth. He had his high-peaked hat in his hand, to keep his head cool. His wiry iron-gray hair looked like hair standing on end; his bushy eyebrows curled upward toward his narrow temples; his horrid old globular eyes stared with a wicked brightness; his pointed beard hid his chin; he was covered from his throat to his ankles in a loose black garment, something between a coat and a cloak; and, to complete him, he had a club foot. I don't doubt that Sir Jervis Redwood is the earthly alias which he finds convenient—but I stick to that first impression which appeared to surprise you. 'Ha! an artist; you seem to be the sort of man I want!' In those terms he introduced himself. Observe, if you please, that my trap caught him the moment he came my way. Who wouldn't be an artist?"

"Did he take a liking to you?" Emily inquired.

"Not he! I don't believe he ever took a liking to anybody in his life."

"Then how did you get your invitation to his house?"

"That's the amusing part of it, Miss Emily. Give me a little breathing time, and you shall hear."

CHAPTER XXIII. MISS REDWOOD.

"I got invited to Sir Jervis's house," Alban resumed, "by treating the old savage as unceremoniously as he had treated me. 'That's an idle trade of yours,' he said, looking at my sketch. 'Other ignorant people have made the same remark,' I answered. He rode away, as if he was not used to be spoken to in that manner, and then thought better of it, and came back. 'Do you understand wood engraving?' he asked. 'Yes.' 'And etching?' 'I have practiced etching myself.' 'Are you a Royal Academician?' 'I'm a drawing-master at a ladies' school.' 'Whose school?' 'Miss Ladd's.' 'Damn it, you know the girl who ought to have been my secretary.' I am not quite sure whether you will take it as a compliment—Sir Jervis appeared to view you in the light of a reference to my respectability. At any rate, he went on with his questions. 'How long do you stop in these parts?' 'I haven't made up my mind.' 'Look here; I want to consult you—are you listening?' 'No; I'm sketching.' He burst into a horrid scream. I asked if he felt himself taken ill. 'Ill?' he said—'I'm laughing.' It was a diabolical laugh, in one syllable—not 'ha! ha! ha!' only 'ha!'—and it made him look wonderfully like that eminent person, whom I persist in thinking he resembles. 'You're an impudent dog,' he said; 'where are you living?' He was so delighted when he heard of my uncomfortable position in the kennel-bedroom, that he offered his hospitality on the spot. 'I can't go to you in such a pigstye as that,' he said; 'you must come to me. What's your name?' 'Alban Morris; what's yours?' 'Jervis Redwood. Pack up your traps when you've done your job, and come and try my kennel. There it is, in a corner of your drawing, and devilish like, too.' I packed up my traps, and I tried his kennel. And now you have had enough of Sir Jervis Redwood."

"Not half enough!" Emily answered. "Your story leaves off just at the interesting moment. I want you to take me to Sir Jervis's house."

"And I want you, Miss Emily, to take me to the British Museum. Don't let me startle you! When I called here earlier in the day, I was told that you had gone to the reading-room. Is your reading a secret?"

His manner, when he made that reply, suggested to Emily that there was some foregone conclusion in his mind, which he was putting to the test. She answered without alluding to the impression which he had produced on her.

"My reading is no secret. I am only consulting old newspapers."

He repeated the last words to himself. "Old newspapers?" he said—as if he was not quite sure of having rightly understood her.

She tried to help him by a more definite reply.

"I am looking through old newspapers," she resumed, "beginning with the year eighteen hundred and seventy-six."

"And going back from that time," he asked eagerly; "to earlier dates still?"

"No—just the contrary—advancing from 'seventy-six' to the present time."

He suddenly turned pale—and tried to hide his face from her by looking out of the window. For a moment, his agitation deprived him of his presence of mind. In that moment, she saw that she had alarmed him.

"What have I said to frighten you?" she asked.

He tried to assume a tone of commonplace gallantry. "There are limits even to your power over me," he replied. "Whatever else you may do, you can never frighten me. Are you searching those old newspapers with any particular object in view?"

"Yes."

"May I know what it is?"

"May I know why I frightened you?"

He began to walk up and down the room again—then checked himself abruptly, and appealed to her mercy.

"Don't be hard on me," he pleaded. "I am so fond of you—oh, forgive me! I only mean that it distresses me to have any concealments from you. If I could open my whole heart at this moment, I should be a happier man."

She understood him and believed him. "My curiosity shall never embarrass you again," she answered warmly. "I won't even remember that I wanted to hear how you got on in Sir Jervis's house."

His gratitude seized the opportunity of taking her harmlessly into his confidence. "As Sir Jervis's guest," he said, "my experience is at your service. Only tell me how I can interest you."

She replied, with some hesitation, "I should like to know what happened when you first saw Mrs. Rook." To her surprise and relief, he at once complied with her wishes.

"We met," he said, "on the evening when I first entered the house. Sir Jervis took me into the dining-room—and there sat Miss Redwood, with a large black cat on her lap. Older than her brother, taller than her brother, leaner than her brother—with strange stony eyes, and a skin like parchment—she looked (if I may speak in contradictions) like a living corpse. I was presented, and the corpse revived. The last lingering relics of former good breeding showed themselves faintly in her brow and in her smile. You will hear more of Miss Redwood presently. In the meanwhile, Sir Jervis made me reward his hospitality by professional advice. He wished me to decide whether the artists whom he had employed to illustrate his wonderful book had cheated him by overcharges and bad work—and Mrs. Rook was sent to fetch the engravings from his study upstairs. You remember her petrified appearance, when she first read the inscription on your locket? The same result followed when she found herself face to face with me. I saluted her civilly—she was deaf and blind to my politeness. Her master snatched the illustrations out of her hand, and told her to leave the room. She stood stockstill, staring helplessly. Sir Jervis looked round at his sister; and I followed his example. Miss Redwood was observing the housekeeper too attentively to notice anything else; her brother was obliged to speak to her. 'Try Rook with the bell,' he said. Miss Redwood took a fine old bronze hand-bell from the table at her side, and rang it. At the shrill silvery sound of the bell, Mrs. Rook put her hand to her head as if the ringing had hurt her—turned instantly, and left us. 'Nobody can manage Rook but my sister,' Sir Jervis explained; 'Rook is crazy.' Miss Redwood differed with him. 'No!' she said. Only one word, but there were volumes of contradiction in it. Sir Jervis looked at me slyly; meaning, perhaps, that he thought his sister crazy too. The dinner was brought in at the same moment, and my attention was diverted to Mrs. Rook's husband."

"What was he like?" Emily asked.

"I really can't tell you; he was one of those essentially commonplace persons, whom one never looks at a second time. His dress was shabby, his head was bald, and his hands shook when he waited on us at table—and that is all I remember. Sir Jervis and I feasted on salt fish, mutton, and beer. Miss Redwood had cold broth, with a wine-glass full of rum poured into it by Mr. Rook. 'She's got no stomach,' her brother informed me; 'hot things come up again ten minutes after they have gone down her throat; she lives on that beastly mixture, and calls it broth-grog!' Miss Redwood sipped her elixir of life, and occasionally looked at me with an appearance of interest which I was at a loss to understand. Dinner being over, she rang her antique bell. The shabby old man-servant answered her call. 'Where's your wife?' she inquired. 'Ill, miss.' She took Mr. Rook's arm to go out, and stopped as she passed me. 'Come to my room, if you please, sir, to-morrow at two o'clock,' she said. Sir Jervis explained again: 'She's all to pieces in the morning' (he invariably called his sister 'She'); 'and gets patched up toward the middle of the day. Death has forgotten her, that's about the truth of it.' He lighted his pipe and pondered over the hieroglyphics found among the ruined cities of Yucatan; I lighted my pipe, and read the only book I could find in the dining-room—a dreadful record of shipwrecks and disasters at sea. When the room was full of tobacco-smoke we fell asleep in our chairs—and when we awoke again we got up and went to bed. There is the true story of my first evening at Redwood Hall."

Emily begged him to go on. "You have interested me in Miss Redwood," she said. "You kept your appointment, of course?"

"I kept my appointment in no very pleasant humor. Encouraged by my favorable report of the illustrations which he had submitted to my judgment, Sir Jervis proposed to make me useful to him in a new capacity. 'You have nothing particular to do,' he said, 'suppose you clean my pictures?' I gave him one of my black looks, and made no other reply. My interview with his sister tried my powers of self-command in another way. Miss Redwood declared her purpose in sending for me the moment I entered the room. Without any preliminary remarks—speaking slowly and emphatically, in a wonderfully strong voice for a woman of her age—she said, 'I have a favor to ask of you, sir. I want you to tell me what Mrs. Rook has done.' I was so staggered that I stared at her like a fool. She went on: 'I suspected Mrs. Rook, sir, of having guilty remembrances on her conscience before she had been a week in our service.' Can you imagine my astonishment when I heard that Miss Redwood's view of Mrs. Rook was my view? Finding that I still said nothing, the old lady entered into details: 'We arranged, sir,' (she persisted in calling me 'sir,' with the formal politeness of the old school)—'we arranged, sir, that Mrs. Rook and her husband should occupy the bedroom next to mine, so that I might have her near me in case of my being taken ill in the night. She looked at the door between the two rooms—suspicious! She asked if there was any objection to her changing to another room—suspicious! suspicious! Pray take a seat, sir, and tell me which Mrs. Rook is guilty of—theft or murder?'"

"What a dreadful old woman!" Emily exclaimed. "How did you answer her?"

"I told her, with perfect truth, that I knew nothing of Mrs. Rook's secrets. Miss Redwood's humor took a satirical turn. 'Allow me to ask, sir, whether your eyes were shut, when our housekeeper found herself unexpectedly in your presence?' I referred the old lady to her brother's opinion. 'Sir Jervis believes Mrs. Rook to be crazy,' I reminded her. 'Do you refuse to trust me, sir?' 'I have no information to give you, madam.' She waved her skinny old hand in the direction of the door. I made my bow, and retired. She called me back. 'Old women used to be prophets, sir, in the bygone time,' she said. 'I will venture on a prediction. You will be the means of depriving us of the services of Mr. and Mrs. Rook. If you will be so good as to stay here a day or two longer you will hear that those two people have given us notice to quit. It will be her doing, mind—he is a mere cypher. I wish you good-morning.' Will you believe me, when I tell you that the prophecy was fulfilled?"

"Do you mean that they actually left the house?"

"They would certainly have left the house," Alban answered, "if Sir Jervis had not insisted on receiving the customary month's warning. He asserted his resolution by locking up the old husband in the pantry. His sister's suspicions never entered his head; the housekeeper's conduct (he said) simply proved that she was, what he had always considered her to be, crazy. 'A capital servant, in spite of that drawback,' he remarked; 'and you will see, I shall bring her to her senses.' The impression produced on me was naturally of a very different kind. While I was still uncertain how to entrap Mrs. Rook into confirming my suspicions, she herself had saved me the trouble. She had placed her own guilty interpretation on my appearance in the house—I had driven her away!"

Emily remained true to her resolution not to let her curiosity embarrass Alban again. But the unexpressed question was in her thoughts—"Of what guilt does he suspect Mrs. Rook? And, when he first felt his suspicions, was my father in his mind?"

Alban proceeded.

"I had only to consider next, whether I could hope to make any further discoveries, if I continued to be Sir Jervis's guest. The object of my journey had been gained; and I had no desire to be employed as picture-cleaner. Miss Redwood assisted me in arriving at a decision. I was sent for to speak to her again. The success of her prophecy had raised her spirits. She asked, with ironical humility, if I proposed to honor them by still remaining their guest, after the disturbance that I had provoked. I answered that I proposed to leave by the first train the next morning. 'Will it be convenient for you to travel to some place at a good distance from this part of the world?' she asked. I had my own reasons for going to London, and said so. 'Will you mention that to my brother this evening, just before we sit down to dinner?' she continued. 'And will you tell him plainly that you have no intention of returning to the North? I shall make use of Mrs. Rook's arm, as usual, to help me downstairs—and I will take care that she hears what you say. Without venturing on another prophecy, I will only hint to you that I have my own idea of what will happen; and I should like you to see for yourself, sir, whether my anticipations are realized.' Need I tell you that this strange old woman proved to be right once more? Mr. Rook was released; Mrs. Rook made humble apologies, and laid the whole blame on her husband's temper: and Sir Jervis bade me remark that his method had succeeded in bringing the housekeeper to her senses. Such were the results produced by the announcement of my departure for London— purposely made in Mrs. Rook's hearing. Do you agree with me, that my journey to Northumberland has not been taken in vain?"

Once more, Emily felt the necessity of controlling herself.

Alban had said that he had "reasons of his own for going to London." Could she venture to ask him what those reasons were? She could only persist in restraining her curiosity, and conclude that he would have mentioned his motive, if it had been (as she had at one time supposed) connected with herself. It was a wise decision. No earthly consideration would have induced Alban to answer her, if she had put the question to him.

All doubt of the correctness of his own first impression was now at an end; he was convinced that Mrs. Rook had been an accomplice in the crime committed, in 1877, at the village inn. His object in traveling to London was to consult the newspaper narrative of the murder. He, too, had been one of the readers at the Museum—had examined the back numbers of the newspaper—and had arrived at the conclusion that Emily's father had been the victim of the crime. Unless he found means to prevent it, her course of reading would take her from the year 1876 to the year 1877, and under that date, she would see the fatal report, heading the top of a column, and printed in conspicuous type.

In the meanwhile Emily had broken the silence, before it could lead to embarrassing results, by asking if Alban had seen Mrs. Rook again, on the morning when he left Sir Jervis's house.

"There was nothing to be gained by seeing her," Alban replied. "Now that she and her husband had decided to remain at Redwood Hall, I knew where to find her in case of necessity. As it happened I saw nobody, on the morning of my departure, but Sir Jervis himself. He still held to his idea of having his pictures cleaned for nothing. 'If you can't do it yourself,' he said, 'couldn't you teach my secretary?' He described the lady whom he had engaged in your place as a 'nasty middle-aged woman with a perpetual cold in her head.' At the same time (he remarked) he was a friend to the women, 'because he got them cheap.' I declined to teach the unfortunate secretary the art of picture-cleaning. Finding me determined, Sir Jervis was quite ready to say good-by. But he made use of me to the last. He employed me as postman and saved a stamp. The letter addressed to you arrived at breakfast-time. Sir Jervis said, 'You are going to London; suppose you take it with you?'"

"Did he tell you that there was a letter of his own inclosed in the envelope?"

"No. When he gave me the envelope it was already sealed."

Emily at once handed to him Sir Jervis's letter. "That will tell you who employs me at the Museum, and what my work is," she said.

He looked through the letter, and at once offered—eagerly offered—to help her.

"I have been a student in the reading-room at intervals, for years past," he said. "Let me assist you, and I shall have something to do in my holiday time." He was so anxious to be of use that he interrupted her before she could thank him. "Let us take alternate years," he suggested. "Did you not tell me you were searching the newspapers published in eighteen hundred and seventy-six?"

"Yes."

"Very well. I will take the next year. You will take the year after. And so on."

"You are very kind," she answered—"but I should like to propose an improvement on your plan."

"What improvement?" he asked, rather sharply.

"If you will leave the five years, from 'seventy-six to 'eighty-one, entirely to me," she resumed, "and take the next five years, reckoning backward from 'seventy-six, you will help me to better purpose. Sir Jervis expects me to look for reports of Central American Explorations, through the newspapers of the last forty years; and I have taken the liberty of limiting the heavy task imposed on me. When I report my progress to my employer, I should like to say that I have got through ten years of the examination, instead of five. Do you see any objection to the arrangement I propose?"

He proved to be obstinate—incomprehensibly obstinate.

"Let us try my plan to begin with," he insisted. "While you are looking through 'seventy-six, let me be at work on 'seventy-seven. If you still prefer your own arrangement, after that, I will follow your suggestion with pleasure. Is it agreed?"

Her acute perception—enlightened by his tone as wall as by his words—detected something under the surface already.

"It isn't agreed until I understand you a little better," she quietly replied. "I fancy you have some object of your own in view."

64

She spoke with her usual directness of look and manner. He was evidently disconcerted. "What makes you think so?" he asked.

"My own experience of myself makes me think so," she answered. "If I had some object to gain, I should persist in carrying it out—like you."

"Does that mean, Miss Emily, that you refuse to give way?"

"No, Mr. Morris. I have made myself disagreeable, but I know when to stop. I trust you—and submit."

If he had been less deeply interested in the accomplishment of his merciful design, he might have viewed Emily's sudden submission with some distrust. As it was, his eagerness to prevent her from discovering the narrative of the murder hurried him into an act of indiscretion. He made an excuse to leave her immediately, in the fear that she might change her mind.

"I have inexcusably prolonged my visit," he said. "If I presume on your kindness in this way, how can I hope that you will receive me again? We meet to-morrow in the reading-room."

He hastened away, as if he was afraid to let her say a word in reply.

Emily reflected.

"Is there something he doesn't want me to see, in the news of the year 'seventy-seven?'" The one explanation which suggested itself to her mind assumed that form of expression— and the one method of satisfying her curiosity that seemed likely to succeed, was to search the volume which Alban had reserved for his own reading.

For two days they pursued their task together, seated at opposite desks. On the third day Emily was absent.

Was she ill?

She was at the library in the City, consulting the file of The Times for the year 1877.

CHAPTER XXIV. MR. ROOK.

Emily's first day in the City library proved to be a day wasted.

She began reading the back numbers of the newspaper at haphazard, without any definite idea of what she was looking for. Conscious of the error into which her own impatience had led her, she was at a loss how to retrace the false step that she had taken. But two alternatives presented themselves: either to abandon the hope of making any discovery—or to attempt to penetrate Alban 's motives by means of pure guesswork, pursued in the dark.

How was the problem to be solved? This serious question troubled her all through the evening, and kept her awake when she went to bed. In despair of her capacity to remove the obstacle that stood in her way, she decided on resuming her regular work at the Museum—turned her pillow to get at the cool side of it—and made up her mind to go asleep.

In the case of the wiser animals, the Person submits to Sleep. It is only the superior human being who tries the hopeless experiment of making Sleep submit to the Person. Wakeful on the warm side of the pillow, Emily remained wakeful on the cool side—thinking again and again of the interview with Alban which had ended so strangely.

Little by little, her mind passed the limits which had restrained it thus far. Alban's conduct in keeping his secret, in the matter of the newspapers, now began to associate itself with Alban's conduct in keeping that other secret, which concealed from her his suspicions of Mrs. Rook.

She started up in bed as the next possibility occurred to her.

In speaking of the disaster which had compelled Mr. and Mrs. Rook to close the inn, Cecilia had alluded to an inquest held on the body of the murdered man. Had the inquest been mentioned in the newspapers, at the time? And had Alban seen something in the report, which concerned Mrs. Rook?

Led by the new light that had fallen on her, Emily returned to the library the next morning with a definite idea of what she had to look for. Incapable of giving exact dates, Cecilia had informed her that the crime was committed "in the autumn." The month to choose, in beginning her examination, was therefore the month of August.

No discovery rewarded her. She tried September, next—with the same unsatisfactory results. On Monday the first of October she met with some encouragement at last. At the top of a column appeared a telegraphic summary of all that was then known of the crime. In the number for the Wednesday following, she found a full report of the proceedings at the inquest.

Passing over the preliminary remarks, Emily read the evidence with the closest attention.

The jury having viewed the body, and having visited an outhouse in which the murder had been committed, the first witness called was Mr. Benjamin Rook, landlord of the Hand-in-Hand inn.

On the evening of Sunday, September 30th, 1877, two gentlemen presented themselves at Mr. Rook's house, under circumstances which especially excited his attention.

The youngest of the two was short, and of fair complexion. He carried a knapsack, like a gentleman on a pedestrian excursion; his manners were pleasant; and he was decidedly good-looking. His companion, older, taller, and darker—and a finer man altogether—leaned on his arm and seemed to be exhausted. In every respect they were singularly unlike each other. The younger stranger (excepting little half-whiskers) was clean shaved. The elder wore his whole beard. Not knowing their names, the landlord distinguished them, at the coroner's suggestion, as the fair gentleman, and the dark gentleman.

It was raining when the two arrived at the inn. There were signs in the heavens of a stormy night.

On accosting the landlord, the fair gentleman volunteered the following statement:

Approaching the village, he had been startled by seeing the dark gentleman (a total stranger to him) stretched prostrate on the grass at the roadside—so far as he could judge, in a swoon. Having a flask with brandy in it, he revived the fainting man, and led him to the inn. This statement was confirmed by a laborer, who was on his way to the village at the time.

The dark gentleman endeavored to explain what had happened to him. He had, as he supposed, allowed too long a time to pass (after an early breakfast that morning), without taking food: he could only attribute the fainting fit to that cause. He was not liable to fainting fits. What purpose (if any) had brought him into the neighborhood of Zeeland, he did not state. He had no intention of remaining at the inn, except for refreshment; and he asked for a carriage to take him to the railway station.

The fair gentleman, seeing the signs of bad weather, desired to remain in Mr. Rook's house for the night, and proposed to resume his walking tour the next day.

Excepting the case of supper, which could be easily provided, the landlord had no choice but to disappoint both his guests. In his small way of business, none of his customers wanted to hire a carriage—even if he could have afforded to keep one. As for beds, the few rooms which the inn contained were all engaged; including even the room occupied by himself and his wife. An exhibition of agricultural implements had been opened in the neighborhood, only two days since; and a public competition between rival machines was to be decided on the coming Monday. Not only was the Hand-in-Hand inn crowded, but even the accommodation offered by the nearest town had proved barely sufficient to meet the public demand.

The gentlemen looked at each other and agreed that there was no help for it but to hurry the supper, and walk to the railway station—a distance of between five and six miles—in time to catch the last train.

While the meal was being prepared, the rain held off for a while. The dark man asked his way to the post-office and went out by himself.

He came back in about ten minutes, and sat down afterward to supper with his companion. Neither the landlord, nor any other person in the public room, noticed any change in him on his return. He was a grave, quiet sort of person, and (unlike the other one) not much of a talker.

As the darkness came on, the rain fell again heavily; and the heavens were black.

A flash of lightning startled the gentlemen when they went to the window to look out: the thunderstorm began. It was simply impossible that two strangers to the neighborhood could find their way to the station, through storm and darkness, in time to catch the train. With or without bedrooms, they must remain at the inn for the night. Having already given up their own room to their lodgers, the landlord and landlady had no other place to sleep in than the kitchen. Next to the kitchen, and communicating with it by a door, was an outhouse; used, partly as a scullery, partly as a lumber-room. There was an old truckle-bed among the lumber, on which one of the gentlemen might rest. A mattress on the floor could be provided for the other. After adding a table and a basin, for the purposes of the toilet, the accommodation which Mr. Rook was able to offer came to an end.

The travelers agreed to occupy this makeshift bed-chamber.

The thunderstorm passed away; but the rain continued to fall heavily. Soon after eleven the guests at the inn retired for the night. There was some little discussion between the two travelers, as to which of them should take possession of the truckle-bed. It was put an end to by the fair gentleman, in his own pleasant way. He proposed to "toss up for it"—and he lost. The dark gentleman went to bed first; the fair gentleman followed, after waiting a while. Mr. Rook took his knapsack into the outhouse; and arranged on the table his appliances for the toilet—contained in a leather roll, and including a razor—ready for use in the morning.

Having previously barred the second door of the outhouse, which led into the yard, Mr. Rook fastened the other door, the lock and bolts of which were on the side of the kitchen. He then secured the house door, and the shutters over the lower windows. Returning to the kitchen, he noticed that the time was ten minutes short of midnight. Soon afterward, he and his wife went to bed.

Nothing happened to disturb Mr. and Mrs. Rook during the night.

At a quarter to seven the next morning, he got up; his wife being still asleep. He had been instructed to wake the gentlemen early; and he knocked at their door. Receiving no answer, after repeatedly knocking, he opened the door and stepped into the outhouse.

At this point in his evidence, the witness's recollections appeared to overpower him. "Give me a moment, gentlemen," he said to the jury. "I have had a dreadful fright; and I don't believe I shall get over it for the rest of my life."

The coroner helped him by a question: "What did you see when you opened the door?"

Mr. Rook answered: "I saw the dark man stretched out on his bed—dead, with a frightful wound in his throat. I saw an open razor, stained with smears of blood, at his side."

"Did you notice the door, leading into the yard?"

"It was wide open, sir. When I was able to look round me, the other traveler—I mean the man with the fair complexion, who carried the knapsack—was nowhere to be seen."

"What did you do, after making these discoveries?"

"I closed the yard door. Then I locked the other door, and put the key in my pocket. After that I roused the servant, and sent him to the constable—who lived near to us—while I ran for the doctor, whose house was at the other end of our village. The doctor sent his groom, on horseback, to the police-office in the town. When I returned to the inn, the constable was there—and he and the police took the matter into their own hands."

"You have nothing more to tell us?"

"Nothing more."

CHAPTER XXV. "J. B."

Mr. Rook having completed his evidence, the police authorities were the next witnesses examined.

They had not found the slightest trace of any attempt to break into the house in the night. The murdered man's gold watch and chain were discovered under his pillow. On examining his clothes the money was found in his purse, and the gold studs and sleeve buttons were left in his shirt. But his pocketbook (seen by witnesses who had not yet been examined) was missing. The search for visiting cards and letters had proved to be fruitless. Only the initials, "J. B.," were marked on his linen. He had brought no luggage with him to the inn. Nothing could be found which led to the discovery of his name or of the purpose which had taken him into that part of the country.

The police examined the outhouse next, in search of circumstantial evidence against the missing man.

He must have carried away his knapsack, when he took to flight, but he had been (probably) in too great a hurry to look for his razor—or perhaps too terrified to touch it, if it had attracted his notice. The leather roll, and the other articles used for his toilet, had been taken away. Mr. Rook identified the blood-stained razor. He had noticed overnight the name of the Belgian city, "Liege," engraved on it.

The yard was the next place inspected. Foot-steps were found on the muddy earth up to the wall. But the road on the other side had been recently mended with stones, and the trace of the fugitive was lost. Casts had been taken of the footsteps; and no other means of discovery had been left untried. The authorities in London had also been communicated with by telegraph.

The doctor being called, described a personal peculiarity, which he had noticed at the post-mortem examination, and which might lead to the identification of the murdered man.

As to the cause of death, the witness said it could be stated in two words. The internal jugular vein had been cut through, with such violence, judging by the appearances, that the wound could not have been inflicted, in the act of suicide, by the hand of the deceased person. No other injuries, and no sign of disease, was found on the body. The one cause of death had been Hemorrhage; and the one peculiarity which called for notice had been discovered in the mouth. Two of the front teeth, in the upper jaw, were false. They had been so admirably made to resemble the natural teeth on either side of them, in form and color, that the witness had only hit on the discovery by accidentally touching the inner side of the gum with one of his fingers.

The landlady was examined, when the doctor had retired. Mrs. Rook was able, in answering questions put to her, to give important information, in reference to the missing pocketbook. Before retiring to rest, the two gentlemen had paid the bill—intending to leave the inn the first thing in the morning. The traveler with the knapsack paid his share in money. The other unfortunate gentleman looked into his purse, and found only a shilling and a sixpence in it. He asked Mrs. Rook if she could change a bank-note. She told him it could be done, provided the note was for no considerable sum of money. Upon that he opened his pocketbook (which the witness described minutely) and turned out the contents on the table. After searching among many Bank of England notes, some in one pocket of the book and some in another, he found a note of the value of five pounds. He thereupon settled his bill, and received the change from Mrs. Rook—her husband being in another part of the room, attending to the guests. She noticed a letter in an envelope, and a few cards which looked (to her judgment) like visiting cards, among the bank-notes which he had turned out on the table. When she returned to him with the change, he had just put them back, and was closing the pocketbook. She saw him place it in one of the breast pockets of his coat.

The fellow-traveler who had accompanied him to the inn was present all the time, sitting on the opposite side of the table. He made a remark when he saw the notes produced. He said, "Put all that money back—don't tempt a poor man like me!" It was said laughing, as if by way of a joke.

Mrs. Rook had observed nothing more that night; had slept as soundly as usual; and had been awakened when her husband knocked at the outhouse door, according to instructions received from the gentlemen, overnight.

Three of the guests in the public room corroborated Mrs. Rook's evidence. They were respectable persons, well and widely known in that part of Hampshire. Besides these, there were two strangers staying in the house. They referred the coroner to their employers—eminent manufacturers at Sheffield and Wolverhampton—whose testimony spoke for itself. The last witness called was a grocer in the village, who kept the post-office.

On the evening of the 30th, a dark gentleman, wearing his beard, knocked at the door, and asked for a letter addressed to "J. B., Post-office, Zeeland." The letter had arrived by that morning's post; but, being Sunday evening, the grocer requested that application might be made for it the next morning. The stranger said the letter contained news, which it was of importance to him to receive without delay. Upon this, the grocer made an exception to customary rules and gave him the letter. He read it by the light of the lamp in the passage. It must have been short, for the reading was done in a moment. He seemed to think over it for a while; and then he turned round to go out. There was nothing to notice in his look or in his manner. The witness offered a remark on the weather; and the gentleman said, "Yes, it looks like a bad night"—and so went away.

The postmaster's evidence was of importance in one respect: it suggested the motive which had brought the deceased to Zeeland. The letter addressed to "J. B." was, in all probability, the letter seen by Mrs. Rook among the contents of the pocketbook, spread out on the table.

The inquiry being, so far, at an end, the inquest was adjourned—on the chance of obtaining additional evidence, when the reported proceedings were read by the public.

....

Consulting a later number of the newspaper Emily discovered that the deceased person had been identified by a witness from London.

Henry Forth, gentleman's valet, being examined, made the following statement:

He had read the medical evidence contained in the report of the inquest; and, believing that he could identify the deceased, had been sent by his present master to assist the object of the inquiry. Ten days since, being then out of place, he had answered an advertisement. The next day, he was instructed to call at Tracey's Hotel, London, at six o'clock in the evening, and to ask for Mr. James Brown. Arriving at the hotel he saw the gentleman for a few minutes only. Mr. Brown had a friend with him. After glancing over the valet's references, he said, "I haven't time enough to speak to you this evening. Call here to-morrow morning at nine o'clock." The gentleman who was present laughed, and said, "You won't be up!" Mr. Brown answered, "That won't matter; the man can come to my bedroom, and let me see how he understands his duties, on trial." At nine the next morning, Mr. Brown was reported to be still in bed; and the witness was informed of the number of the room. He knocked at the door. A drowsy voice inside said something, which he interpreted as meaning "Come in." He went in. The toilet-table was on his left hand, and the bed (with the lower curtain drawn) was on his right. He saw on the table a tumbler with a little water in it, and with two false teeth in the water. Mr. Brown started up in bed—looked at him furiously—abused him for daring to enter the room—and shouted to him to "get out." The witness, not accustomed to be treated in that way, felt naturally indignant, and at once withdrew—but not before he had plainly seen the vacant place which the false teeth had been made to fill. Perhaps Mr. Brown had forgotten that he had left his teeth on the table. Or perhaps he (the valet) had misunderstood what had been said to him when he knocked at the door. Either way, it seemed to be plain enough that the gentleman resented the discovery of his false teeth by a stranger.

Having concluded his statement the witness proceeded to identify the remains of the deceased.

He at once recognized the gentleman named James Brown, whom he had twice seen—once in the evening, and again the next morning—at Tracey's Hotel. In answer to further inquiries, he declared that he knew nothing of the family, or of the place of residence, of the deceased. He complained to the proprietor of the hotel of the rude treatment that he had received, and asked if Mr. Tracey knew anything of Mr. James Brown. Mr. Tracey knew nothing of him. On consulting the hotel book it was found that he had given notice to leave, that afternoon.

Before returning to London, the witness produced references which gave him an excellent character. He also left the address of the master who had engaged him three days since.

The last precaution adopted was to have the face of the corpse photographed, before the coffin was closed. On the same day the jury agreed on their verdict: "Willful murder against some person unknown."

....

Two days later, Emily found a last allusion to the crime—extracted from the columns of the South Hampshire Gazette.

A relative of the deceased, seeing the report of the adjourned inquest, had appeared (accompanied by a medical gentleman); had seen the photograph; and had declared the identification by Henry Forth to be correct.

Among other particulars, now communicated for the first time, it was stated that the late Mr. James Brown had been unreasonably sensitive on the subject of his false teeth, and that the one member of his family who knew of his wearing them was the relative who now claimed his remains.

The claim having been established to the satisfaction of the authorities, the corpse was removed by railroad the same day. No further light had been thrown on the murder. The Handbill offering the reward, and describing the suspected man, had failed to prove of any assistance to the investigations of the police.

From that date, no further notice of the crime committed at the Hand-in-Hand inn appeared in the public journals.

....

Emily closed the volume which she had been consulting, and thankfully acknowledged the services of the librarian.

The new reader had excited this gentleman's interest. Noticing how carefully she examined the numbers of the old newspaper, he looked at her, from time to time, wondering whether it was good news or bad of which she was in search. She read steadily and continuously; but she never rewarded his curiosity by any outward sign of the impression that had been produced on her. When she left the room there was nothing to remark in her manner; she looked quietly thoughtful—and that was all.

The librarian smiled—amused by his own folly. Because a stranger's appearance had attracted him, he had taken it for granted that circumstances of romantic interest must be connected with her visit to the library. Far from misleading him, as he supposed, his fancy might have been employed to better purpose, if it had taken a higher flight still—and had associated Emily with the fateful gloom of tragedy, in place of the brighter interest of romance.

There, among the ordinary readers of the day, was a dutiful and affectionate daughter following the dreadful story of the death of her father by murder, and believing it to be the story of a stranger—because she loved and trusted the person whose short-sighted mercy had deceived her. That very discovery, the dread of which had shaken the good doctor's firm nerves, had forced Alban to exclude from his confidence the woman whom he loved, and had driven the faithful old servant from the bedside of her dying mistress—that very discovery Emily had now made, with a face which never changed color, and a heart which beat at ease. Was the deception that had won this cruel victory over truth destined still to triumph in the days which were to come? Yes—if the life of earth is a foretaste of the life of hell. No—if a lie is a lie, be the merciful motive for the falsehood what it may. No—if all deceit contains in it the seed of retribution, to be ripened inexorably in the lapse of time.

CHAPTER XXVI. MOTHER EVE.

The servant received Emily, on her return from the library, with a sly smile. "Here he is again, miss, waiting to see you."

She opened the parlor door, and revealed Alban Morris, as restless as ever, walking up and down the room.

"When I missed you at the Museum, I was afraid you might be ill," he said. "Ought I to have gone away, when my anxiety was relieved? Shall I go away now?"

"You must take a chair, Mr. Morris, and hear what I have to say for myself. When you left me after your last visit, I suppose I felt the force of example. At any rate I, like you, had my suspicions. I have been trying to confirm them—and I have failed."

He paused, with the chair in his hand. "Suspicions of Me?" he asked.

"Certainly! Can you guess how I have been employed for the last two days? No—not even your ingenuity can do that. I have been hard at work, in another reading-room, consulting the same back numbers of the same newspaper, which you have been examining at the British Museum. There is my confession—and now we will have some tea."

She moved to the fireplace, to ring the bell, and failed to see the effect produced on Alban by those lightly-uttered words. The common phrase is the only phrase that can describe it. He was thunderstruck.

"Yes," she resumed, "I have read the report of the inquest. If I know nothing else, I know that the murder at Zeeland can't be the discovery which you are bent on keeping from me. Don't be alarmed for the preservation of your secret! I am too much discouraged to try again."

The servant interrupted them by answering the bell; Alban once more escaped detection. Emily gave her orders with an approach to the old gayety of her school days. "Tea, as soon as possible—and let us have the new cake. Are you too much of a man, Mr. Morris, to like cake?"

In this state of agitation, he was unreasonably irritated by that playful question. "There is one thing I like better than cake," he said; "and that one thing is a plain explanation."

His tone puzzled her. "Have I said anything to offend you?" she asked. "Surely you can make allowance for a girl's curiosity? Oh, you shall have your explanation—and, what is more, you shall have it without reserve!"

She was as good as her word. What she had thought, and what she had planned, when he left her after his last visit, was frankly and fully told. "If you wonder how I discovered the library," she went on, "I must refer you to my aunt's lawyer. He lives in the City—and I wrote to him to help me. I don't consider that my time has been wasted. Mr. Morris, we owe an apology to Mrs. Rook."

Alban's astonishment, when he heard this, forced its way to expression in words. "What can you possibly mean?" he asked.

The tea was brought in before Emily could reply. She filled the cups, and sighed as she looked at the cake. "If Cecilia was here, how she would enjoy it!" With that complimentary tribute to her friend, she handed a slice to Alban. He never even noticed it.

"We have both of us behaved most unkindly to Mrs. Rook," she resumed. "I can excuse your not seeing it; for I should not have seen it either, but for the newspaper. While I was reading, I had an opportunity of thinking over what we said and did, when the poor woman's behavior so needlessly offended us. I was too excited to think, at the time—and, besides, I had been upset, only the night before, by what Miss Jethro said to me."

Alban started. "What has Miss Jethro to do with it?" he asked.

"Nothing at all," Emily answered. "She spoke to me of her own private affairs. A long story—and you wouldn't be interested in it. Let me finish what I had to say. Mrs. Rook was naturally reminded of the murder, when she heard that my name was Brown; and she must certainly have been struck—as I was—by the coincidence of my father's death taking place at the same time when his unfortunate namesake was killed. Doesn't this sufficiently account for her agitation when she looked at the locket? We first took her by surprise: and then we suspected her of Heaven knows what, because the poor creature didn't happen to have her wits about her, and to remember at the right moment what a very common name 'James Brown' is. Don't you see it as I do?"

"I see that you have arrived at a remarkable change of opinion, since we spoke of the subject in the garden at school."

"In my place, you would have changed your opinion too. I shall write to Mrs. Rook by tomorrow's post."

Alban heard her with dismay. "Pray be guided by my advice!" he said earnestly. "Pray don't write that letter!"

"Why not?"

It was too late to recall the words which he had rashly allowed to escape him. How could he reply?

To own that he had not only read what Emily had read, but had carefully copied the whole narrative and considered it at his leisure, appeared to be simply impossible after what he had now heard. Her peace of mind depended absolutely on his discretion. In this serious emergency, silence was a mercy, and silence was a lie. If he remained silent, might the mercy be trusted to atone for the lie? He was too fond of Emily to decide that question fairly, on its own merits. In other words, he shrank from the terrible responsibility of telling her the truth.

"Isn't the imprudence of writing to such a person as Mrs. Rook plain enough to speak for itself?" he suggested cautiously.

"Not to me."

She made that reply rather obstinately. Alban seemed (in her view) to be trying to prevent her from atoning for an act of injustice. Besides, he despised her cake. "I want to know why you object," she said; taking back the neglected slice, and eating it herself.

"I object," Alban answered, "because Mrs. Rook is a coarse presuming woman. She may pervert your letter to some use of her own, which you may have reason to regret."

"Is that all?"

"Isn't it enough?"

"It may be enough for you. When I have done a person an injury, and wish to make an apology, I don't think it necessary to inquire whether the person's manners happen to be vulgar or not."

Alban's patience was still equal to any demands that she could make on it. "I can only offer you advice which is honestly intended for your own good," he gently replied.

"You would have more influence over me, Mr. Morris, if you were a little readier to take me into your confidence. I daresay I am wrong—but I don't like following advice which is given to me in the dark."

It was impossible to offend him. "Very naturally," he said; "I don't blame you."

Her color deepened, and her voice rose. Alban's patient adherence to his own view—so courteously and considerately urged—was beginning to try her temper. "In plain words," she rejoined, "I am to believe that you can't be mistaken in your judgment of another person."

There was a ring at the door of the cottage while she was speaking. But she was too warmly interested in confuting Alban to notice it.

He was quite willing to be confuted. Even when she lost her temper, she was still interesting to him. "I don't expect you to think me infallible," he said. "Perhaps you will remember that I have had some experience. I am unfortunately older than you are."

"Oh if wisdom comes with age," she smartly reminded him, "your friend Miss Redwood is old enough to be your mother—and she suspected Mrs. Rook of murder, because the poor woman looked at a door, and disliked being in the next room to a fidgety old maid."

Alban's manner changed: he shrank from that chance allusion to doubts and fears which he dare not acknowledge. "Let us talk of something else," he said.

She looked at him with a saucy smile. "Have I driven you into a corner at last? And is that your way of getting out of it?"

Even his endurance failed. "Are you trying to provoke me?" he asked. "Are you no better than other women? I wouldn't have believed it of you, Emily."

"Emily?" She repeated the name in a tone of surprise, which reminded him that he had addressed her with familiarity at a most inappropriate time—the time when they were on the point of a quarrel. He felt the implied reproach too keenly to be able to answer her with composure.

"I think of Emily—I love Emily—my one hope is that Emily may love me. Oh, my dear, is there no excuse if I forget to call you 'Miss' when you distress me?"

All that was tender and true in her nature secretly took his part. She would have followed that better impulse, if he had only been calm enough to understand her momentary silence, and to give her time. But the temper of a gentle and generous man, once roused, is slow to subside. Alban abruptly left his chair. "I had better go!" he said.

"As you please," she answered. "Whether you go, Mr. Morris, or whether you stay, I shall write to Mrs. Rook."

The ring at the bell was followed by the appearance of a visitor. Doctor Allday opened the door, just in time to hear Emily's last words. Her vehemence seemed to amuse him.

"Who is Mrs. Rook?" he asked.

"A most respectable person," Emily answered indignantly; "housekeeper to Sir Jervis Redwood. You needn't sneer at her, Doctor Allday! She has not always been in service— she was landlady of the inn at Zeeland."

The doctor, about to put his hat on a chair, paused. The inn at Zeeland reminded him of the Handbill, and of the visit of Miss Jethro.

"Why are you so hot over it?" he inquired

"Because I detest prejudice!" With this assertion of liberal feeling she pointed to Alban, standing quietly apart at the further end of the room. "There is the most prejudiced man living—he hates Mrs. Rook. Would you like to be introduced to him? You're a philosopher; you may do him some good. Doctor Allday—Mr. Alban Morris."

The doctor recognized the man, with the felt hat and the objectionable beard, whose personal appearance had not impressed him favorably.

Although they may hesitate to acknowledge it, there are respectable Englishmen still left, who regard a felt hat and a beard as symbols of republican disaffection to the altar and the throne. Doctor Allday's manner might have expressed this curious form of patriotic feeling, but for the associations which Emily had revived. In his present frame of mind, he was outwardly courteous, because he was inwardly suspicious. Mrs. Rook had been described to him as formerly landlady of the inn at Zeeland. Were there reasons for Mr. Morris's hostile feeling toward this woman which might be referable to the crime committed in her house that might threaten Emily's tranquillity if they were made known? It would not be amiss to see a little more of Mr. Morris, on the first convenient occasion.

"I am glad to make your acquaintance, sir."

"You are very kind, Doctor Allday."

The exchange of polite conventionalities having been accomplished, Alban approached Emily to take his leave, with mingled feelings of regret and anxiety—regret for having allowed himself to speak harshly; anxiety to part with her in kindness.

"Will you forgive me for differing from you?" It was all he could venture to say, in the presence of a stranger.

"Oh, yes!" she said quietly.

"Will you think again, before you decide?"

"Certainly, Mr. Morris. But it won't alter my opinion, if I do."

The doctor, hearing what passed between them, frowned. On what subject had they been differing? And what opinion did Emily decline to alter?

Alban gave it up. He took her hand gently. "Shall I see you at the Museum, to-morrow?" he asked.

She was politely indifferent to the last. "Yes—unless something happens to keep me at home."

The doctor's eyebrows still expressed disapproval. For what object was the meeting proposed? And why at a museum?

"Good-afternoon, Doctor Allday."

"Good-afternoon, sir."

For a moment after Alban's departure, the doctor stood irresolute. Arriving suddenly at a decision, he snatched up his hat, and turned to Emily in a hurry.

"I bring you news, my dear, which will surprise you. Who do you think has just left my house? Mrs. Ellmother! Don't interrupt me. She has made up her mind to go out to service again. Tired of leading an idle life—that's her own account of it—and asks me to act as her reference."

"Did you consent?"

"Consent! If I act as her reference, I shall be asked how she came to leave her last place. A nice dilemma! Either I must own that she deserted her mistress on her deathbed—or tell a lie. When I put it to her in that way, she walked out of the house in dead silence. If she applies to you next, receive her as I did—or decline to see her, which would be better still."

"Why am I to decline to see her?"

"In consequence of her behavior to your aunt, to be sure! No: I have said all I wanted to say—and I have no time to spare for answering idle questions. Good-by."

Socially-speaking, doctors try the patience of their nearest and dearest friends, in this respect—they are almost always in a hurry. Doctor Allday's precipitate departure did not tend to soothe Emily's irritated nerves. She began to find excuses for Mrs. Ellmother in a spirit of pure contradiction. The old servant's behavior might admit of justification: a friendly welcome might persuade her to explain herself. "If she applies to me," Emily determined, "I shall certainly receive her."

Having arrived at this resolution, her mind reverted to Alban.

Some of the sharp things she had said to him, subjected to after-reflection in solitude, failed to justify themselves. Her better sense began to reproach her. She tried to silence that unwelcome monitor by laying the blame on Alban. Why had he been so patient and so good? What harm was there in his calling her "Emily"? If he had told her to call him by his Christian name, she might have done it. How noble he looked, when he got up to go away; he was actually handsome! Women may say what they please and write what they please: their natural instinct is to find their master in a man—especially when they like him. Sinking lower and lower in her own estimation, Emily tried to turn the current of her thoughts in another direction. She took up a book—opened it, looked into it, threw it across the room. If Alban had returned at that moment, resolved on a reconciliation—if he had said, "My dear, I want to see you like yourself again; will you give me a kiss, and make it up"—would he have left her crying, when he went away? She was crying now.

CHAPTER XXVII. MENTOR AND TELEMACHUS.

If Emily's eyes could have followed Alban as her thoughts were following him, she would have seen him stop before he reached the end of the road in which the cottage stood. His heart was full of tenderness and sorrow: the longing to return to her was more than he could resist. It would be easy to wait, within view of the gate, until the doctor's visit came to an end. He had just decided to go back and keep watch—when he heard rapid footsteps approaching. There (devil take him!) was the doctor himself.

"I have something to say to you, Mr. Morris. Which way are you walking?"

"Any way," Alban answered—not very graciously.

"Then let us take the turning that leads to my house. It's not customary for strangers, especially when they happen to be Englishmen, to place confidence in each other. Let me set the example of violating that rule. I want to speak to you about Miss Emily. May I take your arm? Thank you. At my age, girls in general—unless they are my patients—are not objects of interest to me. But that girl at the cottage—I daresay I am in my dotage—I tell you, sir, she has bewitched me! Upon my soul, I could hardly be more anxious about her, if I was her father. And, mind, I am not an affectionate man by nature. Are you anxious about her too?"

"Yes."

"In what way?"

"In what way are you anxious, Doctor Allday?"

The doctor smiled grimly.

"You don't trust me? Well, I have promised to set the example. Keep your mask on, sir— mine is off, come what may of it. But, observe: if you repeat what I am going to say—"

Alban would hear no more. "Whatever you may say, Doctor Allday, is trusted to my honor. If you doubt my honor, be so good as to let go my arm—I am not walking your way."

The doctor's hand tightened its grasp. "That little flourish of temper, my dear sir, is all I want to set me at my ease. I feel I have got hold of the right man. Now answer me this. Have you ever heard of a person named Miss Jethro?"

Alban suddenly came to a standstill.

"All right!" said the doctor. "I couldn't have wished for a more satisfactory reply."

"Wait a minute," Alban interposed. "I know Miss Jethro as a teacher at Miss Ladd's school, who left her situation suddenly—and I know no more."

The doctor's peculiar smile made its appearance again.

"Speaking in the vulgar tone," he said, "you seem to be in a hurry to wash your hands of Miss Jethro."

"I have no reason to feel any interest in her," Alban replied.

"Don't be too sure of that, my friend. I have something to tell you which may alter your opinion. That ex-teacher at the school, sir, knows how the late Mr. Brown met his death, and how his daughter has been deceived about it."

Alban listened with surprise—and with some little doubt, which he thought it wise not to acknowledge.

"The report of the inquest alludes to a 'relative' who claimed the body," he said. "Was that 'relative' the person who deceived Miss Emily? And was the person her aunt?"

"I must leave you to take your own view," Doctor Allday replied. "A promise binds me not to repeat the information that I have received. Setting that aside, we have the same object in view—and we must take care not to get in each other's way. Here is my house. Let us go in, and make a clean breast of it on both sides."

Established in the safe seclusion of his study, the doctor set the example of confession in these plain terms:

"We only differ in opinion on one point," he said. "We both think it likely (from our experience of the women) that the suspected murderer had an accomplice. I say the guilty person is Miss Jethro. You say—Mrs. Rook."

"When you have read my copy of the report," Alban answered, "I think you will arrive at my conclusion. Mrs. Rook might have entered the outhouse in which the two men slept, at any time during the night, while her husband was asleep. The jury believed her when she declared that she never woke till the morning. I don't."

"I am open to conviction, Mr. Morris. Now about the future. Do you mean to go on with your inquiries?"

"Even if I had no other motive than mere curiosity," Alban answered, "I think I should go on. But I have a more urgent purpose in view. All that I have done thus far, has been done in Emily's interests. My object, from the first, has been to preserve her from any association—in the past or in the future—with the woman whom I believe to have been concerned in her father's death. As I have already told you, she is innocently doing all she can, poor thing, to put obstacles in my way."

"Yes, yes," said the doctor; "she means to write to Mrs. Rook—and you have nearly quarreled about it. Trust me to take that matter in hand. I don't regard it as serious. But I am mortally afraid of what you are doing in Emily's interests. I wish you would give it up."

"Why?"

"Because I see a danger. I don't deny that Emily is as innocent of suspicion as ever. But the chances, next time, may be against us. How do you know to what lengths your curiosity may lead you? Or on what shocking discoveries you may not blunder with the best intentions? Some unforeseen accident may open her eyes to the truth, before you can prevent it. I seem to surprise you?"

"You do, indeed, surprise me."

"In the old story, my dear sir, Mentor sometimes surprised Telemachus. I am Mentor—without being, I hope, quite so long-winded as that respectable philosopher. Let me put it in two words. Emily's happiness is precious to you. Take care you are not made the means of wrecking it! Will you consent to a sacrifice, for her sake?"

"I will do anything for her sake."

"Will you give up your inquiries?"

"From this moment I have done with them!"

"Mr. Morris, you are the best friend she has."

"The next best friend to you, doctor."

In that fond persuasion they now parted—too eagerly devoted to Emily to look at the prospect before them in its least hopeful aspect. Both clever men, neither one nor the other asked himself if any human resistance has ever yet obstructed the progress of truth—when truth has once begun to force its way to the light.

For the second time Alban stopped, on his way home. The longing to be reconciled with Emily was not to be resisted. He returned to the cottage, only to find disappointment waiting for him. The servant reported that her young mistress had gone to bed with a bad headache.

Alban waited a day, in the hope that Emily might write to him. No letter arrived. He repeated his visit the next morning. Fortune was still against him. On this occasion, Emily was engaged.

"Engaged with a visitor?" he asked.

"Yes, sir. A young lady named Miss de Sor."

Where had he heard that name before? He remembered immediately that he had heard it at the school. Miss de Sor was the unattractive new pupil, whom the girls called Francine. Alban looked at the parlor window as he left the cottage. It was of serious importance that he should set himself right with Emily. "And mere gossip," he thought contemptuously, "stands in my way!"

If he had been less absorbed in his own interests, he might have remembered that mere gossip is not always to be despised. It has worked fatal mischief in its time.

CHAPTER XXVIII. FRANCINE.

"You're surprised to see me, of course?" Saluting Emily in those terms, Francine looked round the parlor with an air of satirical curiosity. "Dear me, what a little place to live in!"

"What brings you to London?" Emily inquired.

"You ought to know, my dear, without asking. Why did I try to make friends with you at school? And why have I been trying ever since? Because I hate you—I mean because I can't resist you—no! I mean because I hate myself for liking you. Oh, never mind my reasons. I insisted on going to London with Miss Ladd—when that horrid woman announced that she had an appointment with her lawyer. I said, 'I want to see Emily.' 'Emily doesn't like you.' 'I don't care whether she likes me or not; I want to see her.' That's the way we snap at each other, and that's how I always carry my point. Here I am, till my duenna finishes her business and fetches me. What a prospect for You! Have you got any cold meat in the house? I'm not a glutton, like Cecilia—but I'm afraid I shall want some lunch."

"Don't talk in that way, Francine!"

"Do you mean to say you're glad to see me?"

"If you were only a little less hard and bitter, I should always be glad to see you."

"You darling! (excuse my impetuosity). What are you looking at? My new dress? Do you envy me?"

"No; I admire the color—that's all."

Francine rose, and shook out her dress, and showed it from every point of view. "See how it's made: Paris, of course! Money, my dear; money will do anything—except making one learn one's lessons."

"Are you not getting on any better, Francine?"

"Worse, my sweet friend—worse. One of the masters, I am happy to say, has flatly refused to teach me any longer. 'Pupils without brains I am accustomed to,' he said in his broken English; 'but a pupil with no heart is beyond my endurance.' Ha! ha! the mouldy old refugee has an eye for character, though. No heart—there I am, described in two words."

"And proud of it," Emily remarked.

"Yes—proud of it. Stop! let me do myself justice. You consider tears a sign that one has some heart, don't you? I was very near crying last Sunday. A popular preacher did it; no less a person that Mr. Mirabel—you look as if you had heard of him."

"I have heard of him from Cecilia."

"Is she at Brighton? Then there's one fool more in a fashionable watering place. Oh, she's in Switzerland, is she? I don't care where she is; I only care about Mr. Mirabel. We all heard he was at Brighton for his health, and was going to preach. Didn't we cram the church! As to describing him, I give it up. He is the only little man I ever admired—hair as long as mine, and the sort of beard you see in pictures. I wish I had his fair complexion and his white hands. We were all in love with him—or with his voice, which was it?—when he began to read the commandments. I wish I could imitate him when he came to the fifth commandment. He began in his deepest bass voice: 'Honor thy father—' He stopped and looked up to heaven as if he saw the rest of it there. He went on with a tremendous emphasis on the next word. 'And thy mother,' he said (as if that was quite a different thing) in a tearful, fluty, quivering voice which was a compliment to mothers in itself. We all felt it, mothers or not. But the great sensation was when he got into the pulpit. The manner in which he dropped on his knees, and hid his face in his hands, and showed his beautiful rings was, as a young lady said behind me, simply seraphic. We understood his celebrity, from that moment—I wonder whether I can remember the sermon."

"You needn't attempt it on my account," Emily said.

"My dear, don't be obstinate. Wait till you hear him."

"I am quite content to wait."

"Ah, you're just in the right state of mind to be converted; you're in a fair way to become one of his greatest admirers. They say he is so agreeable in private life; I am dying to know him.—Do I hear a ring at the bell? Is somebody else coming to see you?"

The servant brought in a card and a message.

"The person will call again, miss."

Emily looked at the name written on the card.

"Mrs. Ellmother!" she exclaimed.

"What an extraordinary name!" cried Francine. "Who is she?"

"My aunt's old servant."

"Does she want a situation?"

Emily looked at some lines of writing at the back of the card. Doctor Allday had rightly foreseen events. Rejected by the doctor, Mrs. Ellmother had no alternative but to ask Emily to help her.

"If she is out of place," Francine went on, "she may be just the sort of person I am looking for."

"You?" Emily asked, in astonishment.

Francine refused to explain until she got an answer to her question. "Tell me first," she said, "is Mrs. Ellmother engaged?"

"No; she wants an engagement, and she asks me to be her reference."

"Is she sober, honest, middle-aged, clean, steady, good-tempered, industrious?" Francine rattled on. "Has she all the virtues, and none of the vices? Is she not too good-looking, and has she no male followers? In one terrible word—will she satisfy Miss Ladd?"

"What has Miss Ladd to do with it?"

"How stupid you are, Emily! Do put the woman's card down on the table, and listen to me. Haven't I told you that one of my masters has declined to have anything more to do with me? Doesn't that help you to understand how I get on with the rest of them? I am no longer Miss Ladd's pupil, my dear. Thanks to my laziness and my temper, I am to be raised to the dignity of 'a parlor boarder.' In other words, I am to be a young lady who patronizes the school; with a room of my own, and a servant of my own. All provided for by a private arrangement between my father and Miss Ladd, before I left the West Indies. My mother was at the bottom of it, I have not the least doubt. You don't appear to understand me."

"I don't, indeed!"

Francine considered a little. "Perhaps they were fond of you at home," she suggested.

"Say they loved me, Francine—and I loved them."

"Ah, my position is just the reverse of yours. Now they have got rid of me, they don't want me back again at home. I know as well what my mother said to my father, as if I had heard her. 'Francine will never get on at school, at her age. Try her, by all means; but make some other arrangement with Miss Ladd in case of a failure—or she will be returned on our hands like a bad shilling.' There is my mother, my anxious, affectionate mother, hit off to a T."

"She is your mother, Francine; don't forget that."

"Oh, no; I won't forget it. My cat is my kitten's mother—there! there! I won't shock your sensibilities. Let us get back to matter of fact. When I begin my new life, Miss Ladd makes one condition. My maid is to be a model of discretion—an elderly woman, not a skittish young person who will only encourage me. I must submit to the elderly woman, or I shall be sent back to the West Indies after all. How long did Mrs. Ellmother live with your aunt?"

"Twenty-five years, and more.'

"Good heavens, it's a lifetime! Why isn't this amazing creature living with you, now your aunt is dead? Did you send her away?"

"Certainly not."

"Then why did she go?"

"I don't know."

"Do you mean that she went away without a word of explanation?"

"Yes; that is exactly what I mean."

"When did she go? As soon as your aunt was dead?"

"That doesn't matter, Francine."

"In plain English, you won't tell me? I am all on fire with curiosity—and that's how you put me out! My dear, if you have the slightest regard for me, let us have the woman in here when she comes back for her answer. Somebody must satisfy me. I mean to make Mrs. Ellmother explain herself."

"I don't think you will succeed, Francine."

"Wait a little, and you will see. By-the-by, it is understood that my new position at the school gives me the privilege of accepting invitations. Do you know any nice people to whom you can introduce me?"

"I am the last person in the world who has a chance of helping you," Emily answered. "Excepting good Doctor Allday—" On the point of adding the name of Alban Morris, she checked herself without knowing why, and substituted the name of her school-friend. "And not forgetting Cecilia," she resumed, "I know nobody."

"Cecilia's a fool," Francine remarked gravely; "but now I think of it, she may be worth cultivating. Her father is a member of Parliament—and didn't I hear that he has a fine place in the country? You see, Emily, I may expect to be married (with my money), if I can only get into good society. (Don't suppose I am dependent on my father; my marriage portion is provided for in my uncle's will.) Cecilia may really be of some use to me. Why shouldn't I make a friend of her, and get introduced to her father—in the autumn, you know, when the house is full of company? Have you any idea when she is coming back?"

"No."

"Do you think of writing to her?"

"Of course!"

"Give her my kind love; and say I hope she enjoys Switzerland."

"Francine, you are positively shameless! After calling my dearest friend a fool and a glutton, you send her your love for your own selfish ends; and you expect me to help you in deceiving her! I won't do it."

"Keep your temper, my child. We are all selfish, you little goose. The only difference is— some of us own it, and some of us don't. I shall find my own way to Cecilia's good graces quite easily: the way is through her mouth. You mentioned a certain Doctor Allday. Does he give parties? And do the right sort of men go to them? Hush! I think I hear the bell again. Go to the door, and see who it is."

Emily waited, without taking any notice of this suggestion. The servant announced that "the person had called again, to know if there was any answer."

"Show her in here," Emily said.

The servant withdrew, and came back again.

"The person doesn't wish to intrude, miss; it will be quite sufficient if you will send a message by me."

Emily crossed the room to the door.

"Come in, Mrs. Ellmother," she said. "You have been too long away already. Pray come in."

CHAPTER XXIX. "BONY."

Mrs. Ellmother reluctantly entered the room.

Since Emily had seen her last, her personal appearance doubly justified the nickname by which her late mistress had distinguished her. The old servant was worn and wasted; her gown hung loose on her angular body; the big bones of her face stood out, more prominently than ever. She took Emily's offered hand doubtingly. "I hope I see you well, miss," she said—with hardly a vestige left of her former firmness of voice and manner.

"I am afraid you have been suffering from illness," Emily answered gently.

"It's the life I'm leading that wears me down; I want work and change."

Making that reply, she looked round, and discovered Francine observing her with undisguised curiosity. "You have got company with you," she said to Emily. "I had better go away, and come back another time."

Francine stopped her before she could open the door. "You mustn't go away; I wish to speak to you."

"About what, miss?"

The eyes of the two women met—one, near the end of her life, concealing under a rugged surface a nature sensitively affectionate and incorruptibly true: the other, young in years, without the virtues of youth, hard in manner and hard at heart. In silence on either side, they stood face to face; strangers brought together by the force of circumstances, working inexorably toward their hidden end.

Emily introduced Mrs. Ellmother to Francine. "It may be worth your while," she hinted, "to hear what this young lady has to say."

Mrs. Ellmother listened, with little appearance of interest in anything that a stranger might have to say: her eyes rested on the card which contained her written request to Emily. Francine, watching her closely, understood what was passing in her mind. It might be worth while to conciliate the old woman by a little act of attention. Turning to Emily, Francine pointed to the card lying on the table. "You have not attended yet to Mr. Ellmother's request," she said.

Emily at once assured Mrs. Ellmother that the request was granted. "But is it wise," she asked, "to go out to service again, at your age?"

"I have been used to service all my life, Miss Emily—that's one reason. And service may help me to get rid of my own thoughts—that's another. If you can find me a situation somewhere, you will be doing me a good turn."

"Is it useless to suggest that you might come back, and live with me?" Emily ventured to say.

Mrs. Ellmother's head sank on her breast. "Thank you kindly, miss; it is useless."

"Why is it useless?" Francine asked.

Mrs. Ellmother was silent.

"Miss de Sor is speaking to you," Emily reminded her.

"Am I to answer Miss de Sor?"

Attentively observing what passed, and placing her own construction on looks and tones, it suddenly struck Francine that Emily herself might be in Mrs. Ellmother's confidence, and that she might have reasons of her own for assuming ignorance when awkward questions were asked. For the moment at least, Francine decided on keeping her suspicions to herself. "I may perhaps offer you the employment you want," she said to Mrs. Ellmother. "I am staying at Brighton, for the present, with the lady who was Miss Emily's schoolmistress, and I am in need of a maid. Would you be willing to consider it, if I proposed to engage you?"

"Yes, miss."

"In that case, you can hardly object to the customary inquiry. Why did you leave your last place?"

Mrs. Ellmother appealed to Emily. "Did you tell this young lady how long I remained in my last place?"

Melancholy remembrances had been revived in Emily by the turn which the talk had now taken. Francine's cat-like patience, stealthily feeling its way to its end, jarred on her nerves. "Yes," she said; "in justice to you, I have mentioned your long term of service."

Mrs. Ellmother addressed Francine. "You know, miss, that I served my late mistress for over twenty-five years. Will you please remember that—and let it be a reason for not asking me why I left my place."

Francine smiled compassionately. "My good creature, you have mentioned the very reason why I should ask. You live five-and-twenty years with your mistress—and then suddenly leave her—and you expect me to pass over this extraordinary proceeding without inquiry. Take a little time to think."

"I want no time to think. What I had in my mind, when I left Miss Letitia, is something which I refuse to explain, miss, to you, or to anybody."

She recovered some of her old firmness, when she made that reply. Francine saw the necessity of yielding—for the time at least, Emily remained silent, oppressed by remembrance of the doubts and fears which had darkened the last miserable days of her aunt's illness. She began already to regret having made Francine and Mrs. Ellmother known to each other.

"I won't dwell on what appears to be a painful subject," Francine graciously resumed. "I meant no offense. You are not angry, I hope?"

"Sorry, miss. I might have been angry, at one time. That time is over."

It was said sadly and resignedly: Emily heard the answer. Her heart ached as she looked at the old servant, and thought of the contrast between past and present. With what a hearty welcome this broken woman had been used to receive her in the bygone holiday-time! Her eyes moistened. She felt the merciless persistency of Francine, as if it had been an insult offered to herself. "Give it up!" she said sharply.

"Leave me, my dear, to manage my own business," Francine replied. "About your qualifications?" she continued, turning coolly to Mrs. Ellmother. "Can you dress hair?"

"Yes."

"I ought to tell you," Francine insisted, "that I am very particular about my hair."

"My mistress was very particular about her hair," Mrs. Ellmother answered.

"Are you a good needlewoman?"

"As good as ever I was—with the help of my spectacles."

Francine turned to Emily. "See how well we get on together. We are beginning to understand each other already. I am an odd creature, Mrs. Ellmother. Sometimes, I take sudden likings to persons—I have taken a liking to you. Do you begin to think a little better of me than you did? I hope you will produce the right impression on Miss Ladd; you shall have every assistance that I can give. I will beg Miss Ladd, as a favor to me, not to ask you that one forbidden question."

Poor Mrs. Ellmother, puzzled by the sudden appearance of Francine in the character of an eccentric young lady, the creature of genial impulse, thought it right to express her gratitude for the promised interference in her favor. "That's kind of you, miss," she said.

"No, no, only just. I ought to tell you there's one thing Miss Ladd is strict about—sweethearts. Are you quite sure," Francine inquired jocosely, "that you can answer for yourself, in that particular?"

This effort of humor produced its intended effect. Mrs. Ellmother, thrown off her guard, actually smiled. "Lord, miss, what will you say next!"

"My good soul, I will say something next that is more to the purpose. If Miss Ladd asks me why you have so unaccountably refused to be a servant again in this house, I shall take care to say that it is certainly not out of dislike to Miss Emily."

"You need say nothing of the sort," Emily quietly remarked.

"And still less," Francine proceeded, without noticing the interruption—"still less through any disagreeable remembrances of Miss Emily's aunt."

Mrs. Ellmother saw the trap that had been set for her. "It won't do, miss," she said.

"What won't do?"

"Trying to pump me."

Francine burst out laughing. Emily noticed an artificial ring in her gayety which suggested that she was exasperated, rather than amused, by the repulse which had baffled her curiosity once more.

Mrs. Ellmother reminded the merry young lady that the proposed arrangement between them had not been concluded yet. "Am I to understand, miss, that you will keep a place open for me in your service?"

"You are to understand," Francine replied sharply, "that I must have Miss Ladd's approval before I can engage you. Suppose you come to Brighton? I will pay your fare, of course."

"Never mind my fare, miss. Will you give up pumping?"

"Make your mind easy. It's quite useless to attempt pumping you. When will you come?"

Mrs. Ellmother pleaded for a little delay. "I'm altering my gowns," she said. "I get thinner and thinner—don't I, Miss Emily? My work won't be done before Thursday."

"Let us say Friday, then," Francine proposed.

"Friday!" Mrs. Ellmother exclaimed. "You forget that Friday is an unlucky day."

"I forgot that, certainly! How can you be so absurdly superstitious."

"You may call it what you like, miss. I have good reason to think as I do. I was married on a Friday—and a bitter bad marriage it turned out to be. Superstitious, indeed! You don't know what my experience has been. My only sister was one of a party of thirteen at dinner; and she died within the year. If we are to get on together nicely, I'll take that journey on Saturday, if you please."

"Anything to satisfy you," Francine agreed; "there is the address. Come in the middle of the day, and we will give you your dinner. No fear of our being thirteen in number. What will you do, if you have the misfortune to spill the salt?"

"Take a pinch between my finger and thumb, and throw it over my left shoulder," Mrs. Ellmother answered gravely. "Good-day, miss."

"Good-day."

Emily followed the departing visitor out to the hall. She had seen and heard enough to decide her on trying to break off the proposed negotiation—with the one kind purpose of protecting Mrs. Ellmother against the pitiless curiosity of Francine.

"Do you think you and that young lady are likely to get on well together?" she asked.

"I have told you already, Miss Emily, I want to get away from my own home and my own thoughts; I don't care where I go, so long as I do that." Having answered in those words, Mrs. Ellmother opened the door, and waited a while, thinking. "I wonder whether the dead

82

know what is going on in the world they have left?" she said, looking at Emily. "If they do, there's one among them knows my thoughts, and feels for me. Good-by, miss—and don't think worse of me than I deserve."

Emily went back to the parlor. The only resource left was to plead with Francine for mercy to Mrs. Ellmother.

"Do you really mean to give it up?" she asked.

"To give up—what? 'Pumping,' as that obstinate old creature calls it?"

Emily persisted. "Don't worry the poor old soul! However strangely she may have left my aunt and me her motives are kind and good—I am sure of that. Will you let her keep her harmless little secret?"

"Oh, of course!"

"I don't believe you, Francine!"

"Don't you? I am like Cecilia—I am getting hungry. Shall we have some lunch?"

"You hard-hearted creature!"

"Does that mean—no luncheon until I have owned the truth? Suppose you own the truth? I won't tell Mrs. Ellmother that you have betrayed her."

"For the last time, Francine—I know no more of it than you do. If you persist in taking your own view, you as good as tell me I lie; and you will oblige me to leave the room."

Even Francine's obstinacy was compelled to give way, so far as appearances went. Still possessed by the delusion that Emily was deceiving her, she was now animated by a stronger motive than mere curiosity. Her sense of her own importance imperatively urged her to prove that she was not a person who could be deceived with impunity.

"I beg your pardon," she said with humility. "But I must positively have it out with Mrs. Ellmother. She has been more than a match for me—my turn next. I mean to get the better of her; and I shall succeed."

"I have already told you, Francine—you will fail."

"My dear, I am a dunce, and I don't deny it. But let me tell you one thing. I haven't lived all my life in the West Indies, among black servants, without learning something."

"What do you mean?"

"More, my clever friend, than you are likely to guess. In the meantime, don't forget the duties of hospitality. Ring the bell for luncheon."

CHAPTER XXX. LADY DORIS.

The arrival of Miss Ladd, some time before she had been expected, interrupted the two girls at a critical moment. She had hurried over her business in London, eager to pass the rest of the day with her favorite pupil. Emily's affectionate welcome was, in some degree at least, inspired by a sensation of relief. To feel herself in the embrace of the warm-hearted schoolmistress was like finding a refuge from Francine.

When the hour of departure arrived, Miss Ladd invited Emily to Brighton for the second time. "On the last occasion, my dear, you wrote me an excuse; I won't be treated in that way again. If you can't return with us now, come to-morrow." She added in a whisper, "Otherwise, I shall think you include me in your dislike of Francine."

There was no resisting this. It was arranged that Emily should go to Brighton on the next day.

Left by herself, her thoughts might have reverted to Mrs. Ellmother's doubtful prospects, and to Francine's strange allusion to her life in the West Indies, but for the arrival of two letters by the afternoon post. The handwriting on one of them was unknown to her. She opened that one first. It was an answer to the letter of apology which she had persisted in writing to Mrs. Rook. Happily for herself, Alban's influence had not been without its effect, after his departure. She had written kindly—but she had written briefly at the same time.

Mrs. Rook's reply presented a nicely compounded mixture of gratitude and grief. The gratitude was addressed to Emily as a matter of course. The grief related to her "excellent master." Sir Jervis's strength had suddenly failed. His medical attendant, being summoned, had expressed no surprise. "My patient is over seventy years of age," the doctor remarked. "He will sit up late at night, writing his book; and he refuses to take exercise, till headache and giddiness force him to try the fresh air. As the necessary result, he has broken down at last. It may end in paralysis, or it may end in death." Reporting this expression of medical opinion, Mrs. Rook's letter glided imperceptibly from respectful sympathy to modest regard for her own interests in the future. It might be the sad fate of her husband and herself to be thrown on the world again. If necessity brought them to London, would "kind Miss Emily grant her the honor of an interview, and favor a poor unlucky woman with a word of advice?"

"She may pervert your letter to some use of her own, which you may have reason to regret." Did Emily remember Alban's warning words? No: she accepted Mrs. Rook's reply as a gratifying tribute to the justice of her own opinions.

Having proposed to write to Alban, feeling penitently that she had been in the wrong, she was now readier than ever to send him a letter, feeling compassionately that she had been in the right. Besides, it was due to the faithful friend, who was still working for her in the reading room, that he should be informed of Sir Jervis's illness. Whether the old man lived or whether he died, his literary labors were fatally interrupted in either case; and one of the consequences would be the termination of her employment at the Museum. Although the second of the two letters which she had received was addressed to her in Cecilia's handwriting, Emily waited to read it until she had first written to Alban. "He will come to-morrow," she thought; "and we shall both make apologies. I shall regret that I was angry with him and he will regret that he was mistaken in his judgment of Mrs. Rook. We shall be as good friends again as ever."

In this happy frame of mind she opened Cecilia's letter. It was full of good news from first to last.

The invalid sister had made such rapid progress toward recovery that the travelers had arranged to set forth on their journey back to England in a fortnight. "My one regret," Cecilia added, "is the parting with Lady Doris. She and her husband are going to Genoa, where they will embark in Lord Janeaway's yacht for a cruise in the Mediterranean. When we have said that miserable word good-by—oh, Emily, what a hurry I shall be in to get back to you! Those allusions to your lonely life are so dreadful, my dear, that I have destroyed your letter; it is enough to break one's heart only to look at it. When once I get to London, there shall be no more solitude for my poor afflicted friend. Papa will be free from his parliamentary duties in August—and he has promised to have the house full of delightful people to meet you. Who do you think will be one of our guests? He is illustrious; he is fascinating; he deserves a line all to himself, thus:

"The Reverend Miles Mirabel!

"Lady Doris has discovered that the country parsonage, in which this brilliant clergyman submits to exile, is only twelve miles away from our house. She has written to Mr. Mirabel to introduce me, and to mention the date of my return. We will have some fun with the popular preacher—we will both fall in love with him together.

"Is there anybody to whom you would like me to send an invitation? Shall we have Mr. Alban Morris? Now I know how kindly he took care of you at the railway station, your good opinion of him is my opinion. Your letter also mentions a doctor. Is he nice? and do you think he will let me eat pastry, if we have him too? I am so overflowing with hospitality (all for your sake) that I am ready to invite anybody, and everybody, to cheer you and make you happy. Would you like to meet Miss Ladd and the whole school?

"As to our amusements, make your mind easy.

"I have come to a distinct understanding with Papa that we are to have dances every evening—except when we try a little concert as a change. Private theatricals are to follow, when we want another change after the dancing and the music. No early rising; no fixed hour for breakfast; everything that is most exquisitely delicious at dinner—and, to crown all, your room next to mine, for delightful midnight gossipings, when we ought to be in bed. What do you say, darling, to the programme?

"A last piece of news—and I have done.

"I have actually had a proposal of marriage, from a young gentleman who sits opposite me at the table d'hote! When I tell you that he has white eyelashes, and red hands, and such enormous front teeth that he can't shut his mouth, you will not need to be told that I refused him. This vindictive person has abused me ever since, in the most shameful manner. I heard him last night, under my window, trying to set one of his friends against me. 'Keep clear of her, my dear fellow; she's the most heartless creature living.' The friend took my part; he said, 'I don't agree with you; the young lady is a person of great sensibility.' 'Nonsense!' says my amiable lover; 'she eats too much—her sensibility is all stomach.' There's a wretch for you. What a shameful advantage to take of sitting opposite to me at dinner! Good-by, my love, till we meet soon, and are as happy together as the day is long."

Emily kissed the signature. At that moment of all others, Cecilia was such a refreshing contrast to Francine!

Before putting the letter away, she looked again at that part of it which mentioned Lady Doris's introduction of Cecilia to Mr. Mirabel. "I don't feel the slightest interest in Mr. Mirabel," she thought, smiling as the idea occurred to her; "and I need never have known him, but for Lady Doris—who is a perfect stranger to me."

She had just placed the letter in her desk, when a visitor was announced. Doctor Allday presented himself (in a hurry as usual).

"Another patient waiting?" Emily asked mischievously. "No time to spare, again?"

"Not a moment," the old gentleman answered. "Have you heard from Mrs. Ellmother?"

"Yes."

"You don't mean to say you have answered her?"

"I have done better than that, doctor—I have seen her this morning."

"And consented to be her reference, of course?"

"How well you know me!"

Doctor Allday was a philosopher: he kept his temper. "Just what I might have expected," he said. "Eve and the apple! Only forbid a woman to do anything, and she does it directly—be cause you have forbidden her. I'll try the other way with you now, Miss Emily. There was something else that I meant to have forbidden."

"What was it?"

"May I make a special request?"

"Certainly."

"Oh, my dear, write to Mrs. Rook! I beg and entreat of you, write to Mrs. Rook!"

Emily's playful manner suddenly disappeared.

Ignoring the doctor's little outbreak of humor, she waited in grave surprise, until it was his pleasure to explain himself.

Doctor Allday, on his side, ignored the ominous change in Emily; he went on as pleasantly as ever. "Mr. Morris and I have had a long talk about you, my dear. Mr. Morris is a capital fellow; I recommend him as a sweetheart. I also back him in the matter of Mrs. Rook.— What's the matter now? You're as red as a rose. Temper again, eh?"

"Hatred of meanness!" Emily answered indignantly. "I despise a man who plots, behind my back, to get another man to help him. Oh, how I have been mistaken in Alban Morris!"

85

"Oh, how little you know of the best friend you have!" cried the doctor, imitating her. "Girls are all alike; the only man they can understand, is the man who flatters them. Will you oblige me by writing to Mrs. Rook?"

Emily made an attempt to match the doctor, with his own weapons. "Your little joke comes too late," she said satirically. "There is Mrs. Rook's answer. Read it, and—" she checked herself, even in her anger she was incapable of speaking ungenerously to the old man who had so warmly befriended her. "I won't say to you," she resumed, "what I might have said to another person."

"Shall I say it for you?" asked the incorrigible doctor. "'Read it, and be ashamed of yourself'—That was what you had in your mind, isn't it? Anything to please you, my dear." He put on his spectacles, read the letter, and handed it back to Emily with an impenetrable countenance. "What do you think of my new spectacles?" he asked, as he took the glasses off his nose. "In the experience of thirty years, I have had three grateful patients." He put the spectacles back in the case. "This comes from the third. Very gratifying—very gratifying."

Emily's sense of humor was not the uppermost sense in her at that moment. She pointed with a peremptory forefinger to Mrs. Rook's letter. "Have you nothing to say about this?"

The doctor had so little to say about it that he was able to express himself in one word: "Humbug!"

He took his hat—nodded kindly to Emily—and hurried away to feverish pulses waiting to be felt, and to furred tongues that were ashamed to show themselves.

CHAPTER XXXI. MOIRA.

When Alban presented himself the next morning, the hours of the night had exercised their tranquilizing influence over Emily. She remembered sorrowfully how Doctor Allday had disturbed her belief in the man who loved her; no feeling of irritation remained. Alban noticed that her manner was unusually subdued; she received him with her customary grace, but not with her customary smile.

"Are you not well?" he asked.

"I am a little out of spirits," she replied. "A disappointment—that is all."

He waited a moment, apparently in the expectation that she might tell him what the disappointment was. She remained silent, and she looked away from him. Was he in any way answerable for the depression of spirits to which she alluded? The doubt occurred to him—but he said nothing.

"I suppose you have received my letter?" she resumed.

"I have come here to thank you for your letter."

"It was my duty to tell you of Sir Jervis's illness; I deserve no thanks."

"You have written to me so kindly," Alban reminded her; "you have referred to our difference of opinion, the last time I was here, so gently and so forgivingly—"

"If I had written a little later," she interposed, "the tone of my letter might have been less agreeable to you. I happened to send it to the post, before I received a visit from a friend of yours—a friend who had something to say to me after consulting with you."

"Do you mean Doctor Allday?"

"Yes."

"What did he say?"

"What you wished him to say. He did his best; he was as obstinate and unfeeling as you could possibly wish him to be; but he was too late. I have written to Mrs. Rook, and I have received a reply." She spoke sadly, not angrily—and pointed to the letter lying on her desk.

Alban understood: he looked at her in despair. "Is that wretched woman doomed to set us at variance every time we meet!" he exclaimed.

Emily silently held out the letter.

He refused to take it. "The wrong you have done me is not to be set right in that way," he said. "You believe the doctor's visit was arranged between us. I never knew that he intended to call on you; I had no interest in sending him here—and I must not interfere again between you and Mrs. Rook."

"I don't understand you."

"You will understand me when I tell you how my conversation with Doctor Allday ended. I have done with interference; I have done with advice. Whatever my doubts may be, all further effort on my part to justify them—all further inquiries, no matter in what direction—are at an end: I made the sacrifice, for your sake. No! I must repeat what you said to me just now; I deserve no thanks. What I have done, has been done in deference to Doctor Allday—against my own convictions; in spite of my own fears. Ridiculous convictions! ridiculous fears! Men with morbid minds are their own tormentors. It doesn't matter how I suffer, so long as you are at ease. I shall never thwart you or vex you again. Have you a better opinion of me now?"

She made the best of all answers—she gave him her hand.

"May I kiss it?" he asked, as timidly as if he had been a boy addressing his first sweetheart.

She was half inclined to laugh, and half inclined to cry. "Yes, if you like," she said softly.

"Will you let me come and see you again?"

"Gladly—when I return to London."

"You are going away?"

"I am going to Brighton this afternoon, to stay with Miss Ladd."

It was hard to lose her, on the happy day when they understood each other at last. An expression of disappointment passed over his face. He rose, and walked restlessly to the window. "Miss Ladd?" he repeated, turning to Emily as if an idea had struck him. "Did I hear, at the school, that Miss de Sor was to spend the holidays under the care of Miss Ladd?"

"Yes."

"The same young lady," he went on, "who paid you a visit yesterday morning?"

"The same."

That haunting distrust of the future, which he had first betrayed and then affected to ridicule, exercised its depressing influence over his better sense. He was unreasonable enough to feel doubtful of Francine, simply because she was a stranger.

"Miss de Sor is a new friend of yours," he said. "Do you like her?"

It was not an easy question to answer—without entering into particulars which Emily's delicacy of feeling warned her to avoid. "I must know a little more of Miss de Sor," she said, "before I can decide."

Alban's misgivings were naturally encouraged by this evasive reply. He began to regret having left the cottage, on the previous day, when he had heard that Emily was engaged. He might have sent in his card, and might have been admitted. It was an opportunity lost of observing Francine. On the morning of her first day at school, when they had accidentally met at the summer house, she had left a disagreeable impression on his mind. Ought he to allow his opinion to be influenced by this circumstance? or ought he to follow Emily's prudent example, and suspend judgment until he knew a little more of Francine?

"Is any day fixed for your return to London?" he asked.

"Not yet," she said; "I hardly know how long my visit will be."

"In little more than a fortnight," he continued, "I shall return to my classes—they will be dreary classes, without you. Miss de Sor goes back to the school with Miss Ladd, I suppose?"

87

Emily was at a loss to account for the depression in his looks and tones, while he was making these unimportant inquiries. She tried to rouse him by speaking lightly in reply.

"Miss de Sor returns in quite a new character; she is to be a guest instead of a pupil. Do you wish to be better acquainted with her?"

"Yes," he said gravely, "now I know that she is a friend of yours." He returned to his place near her. "A pleasant visit makes the days pass quickly," he resumed. "You may remain at Brighton longer than you anticipate; and we may not meet again for some time to come. If anything happens—"

"Do you mean anything serious?" she asked.

"No, no! I only mean—if I can be of any service. In that case, will you write to me?"

"You know I will!"

She looked at him anxiously. He had completely failed to hide from her the uneasy state of his mind: a man less capable of concealment of feeling never lived. "You are anxious, and out of spirits," she said gently. "Is it my fault?"

"Your fault? oh, don't think that! I have my dull days and my bright days—and just now my barometer is down at dull." His voice faltered, in spite of his efforts to control it; he gave up the struggle, and took his hat to go. "Do you remember, Emily, what I once said to you in the garden at the school? I still believe there is a time of fulfillment to come in our lives." He suddenly checked himself, as if there had been something more in his mind to which he hesitated to give expression—and held out his hand to bid her good-by.

"My memory of what you said in the garden is better than yours," she reminded him. "You said 'Happen what may in the interval, I trust the future.' Do you feel the same trust still?"

He sighed—drew her to him gently—and kissed her on the forehead. Was that his own reply? She was not calm enough to ask him the question: it remained in her thoughts for some time after he had gone.

....

On the same day Emily was at Brighton.

Francine happened to be alone in the drawing-room. Her first proceeding, when Emily was shown in, was to stop the servant.

"Have you taken my letter to the post?"

"Yes, miss."

"It doesn't matter." She dismissed the servant by a gesture, and burst into such effusive hospitality that she actually insisted on kissing Emily. "Do you know what I have been doing?" she said. "I have been writing to Cecilia—directing to the care of her father, at the House of Commons. I stupidly forgot that you would be able to give me the right address in Switzerland. You don't object, I hope, to my making myself agreeable to our dear, beautiful, greedy girl? It is of such importance to me to surround myself with influential friends—and, of course, I have given her your love. Don't look disgusted! Come, and see your room.—Oh, never mind Miss Ladd. You will see her when she wakes. Ill? Is that sort of old woman ever ill? She's only taking her nap after bathing. Bathing in the sea, at her age! How she must frighten the fishes!"

Having seen her own bed-chamber, Emily was next introduced to the room occupied by Francine.

One object that she noticed in it caused her some little surprise—not unmingled with disgust. She discovered on the toilet-table a coarsely caricatured portrait of Mrs. Ellmother. It was a sketch in pencil—wretchedly drawn; but spitefully successful as a likeness. "I didn't know you were an artist," Emily remarked, with an ironical emphasis on the last word. Francine laughed scornfully—crumpled the drawing up in her hand—and threw it into the waste-paper basket.

"You satirical creature!" she burst out gayly. "If you had lived a dull life at St. Domingo, you would have taken to spoiling paper too. I might really have turned out an artist, if I had been clever and industrious like you. As it was, I learned a little drawing—and got tired of

88

it. I tried modeling in wax—and got tired of it. Who do you think was my teacher? One of our slaves."

"A slave!" Emily exclaimed.

"Yes—a mulatto, if you wish me to be particular; the daughter of an English father and a negro mother. In her young time (at least she said so herself) she was quite a beauty, in her particular style. Her master's favorite; he educated her himself. Besides drawing and painting, and modeling in wax, she could sing and play—all the accomplishments thrown away on a slave! When her owner died, my uncle bought her at the sale of the property."

A word of natural compassion escaped Emily—to Francine's surprise.

"Oh, my dear, you needn't pity her! Sappho (that was her name) fetched a high price, even when she was no longer young. She came to us, by inheritance, with the estates and the rest of it; and took a fancy to me, when she found out I didn't get on well with my father and mother. 'I owe it to my father and mother,' she used to say, 'that I am a slave. When I see affectionate daughters, it wrings my heart.' Sappho was a strange compound. A woman with a white side to her character, and a black side. For weeks together, she would be a civilized being. Then she used to relapse, and become as complete a negress as her mother. At the risk of her life she stole away, on those occasions, into the interior of the island, and looked on, in hiding, at the horrid witchcrafts and idolatries of the blacks; they would have murdered a half-blood, prying into their ceremonies, if they had discovered her. I followed her once, so far as I dared. The frightful yellings and drummings in the darkness of the forests frightened me. The blacks suspected her, and it came to my ears. I gave her the warning that saved her life (I don't know what I should have done without Sappho to amuse me!); and, from that time, I do believe the curious creature loved me. You see I can speak generously even of a slave!"

"I wonder you didn't bring her with you to England," Emily said.

"In the first place," Francine answered, "she was my father's property, not mine. In the second place, she's dead. Poisoned, as the other half-bloods supposed, by some enemy among the blacks. She said herself, she was under a spell!"

"What did she mean?"

Francine was not interested enough in the subject to explain. "Stupid superstition, my dear. The negro side of Sappho was uppermost when she was dying—there is the explanation. Be off with you! I hear the old woman on the stairs. Meet her before she can come in here. My bedroom is my only refuge from Miss Ladd."

On the morning of the last day in the week, Emily had a little talk in private with her old schoolmistress. Miss Ladd listened to what she had to say of Mrs. Ellmother, and did her best to relieve Emily's anxieties. "I think you are mistaken, my child, in supposing that Francine is in earnest. It is her great fault that she is hardly ever in earnest. You can trust to my discretion; leave the rest to your aunt's old servant and to me."

Mrs. Ellmother arrived, punctual to the appointed time. She was shown into Miss Ladd's own room. Francine—ostentatiously resolved to take no personal part in the affair—went for a walk. Emily waited to hear the result.

After a long interval, Miss Ladd returned to the drawing-room, and announced that she had sanctioned the engagement of Mrs. Ellmother.

"I have considered your wishes, in this respect," she said. "It is arranged that a week's notice, on either side, shall end the term of service, after the first month. I cannot feel justified in doing more than that. Mrs. Ellmother is such a respectable woman; she is so well known to you, and she was so long in your aunt's service, that I am bound to consider the importance of securing a person who is exactly fitted to attend on such a girl as Francine. In one word, I can trust Mrs. Ellmother."

"When does she enter on her service?" Emily inquired.

"On the day after we return to the school," Miss Ladd replied. "You will be glad to see her, I am sure. I will send her here."

"One word more before you go," Emily said.

"Did you ask her why she left my aunt?"

"My dear child, a woman who has been five-and-twenty years in one place is entitled to keep her own secrets. I understand that she had her reasons, and that she doesn't think it necessary to mention them to anybody. Never trust people by halves—especially when they are people like Mrs. Ellmother."

It was too late now to raise any objections. Emily felt relieved, rather than disappointed, on discovering that Mrs. Ellmother was in a hurry to get back to London by the next train. She had found an opportunity of letting her lodgings; and she was eager to conclude the bargain. "You see I couldn't say Yes," she explained, "till I knew whether I was to get this new place or not—and the person wants to go in tonight."

Emily stopped her at the door. "Promise to write and tell me how you get on with Miss de Sor."

"You say that, miss, as if you didn't feel hopeful about me."

"I say it, because I feel interested about you. Promise to write."

Mrs. Ellmother promised, and hastened away. Emily looked after her from the window, as long as she was in view. "I wish I could feel sure of Francine!" she said to herself.

"In what way?" asked the hard voice of Francine, speaking at the door.

It was not in Emily's nature to shrink from a plain reply. She completed her half-formed thought without a moment's hesitation.

"I wish I could feel sure," she answered, "that you will be kind to Mrs. Ellmother."

"Are you afraid I shall make her life one scene of torment?" Francine inquired. "How can I answer for myself? I can't look into the future."

"For once in your life, can you be in earnest?" Emily said.

"For once in your life, can you take a joke?" Francine replied.

Emily said no more. She privately resolved to shorten her visit to Brighton.

BOOK THE THIRD—NETHERWOODS.

CHAPTER XXXII. IN THE GRAY ROOM.

The house inhabited by Miss Ladd and her pupils had been built, in the early part of the present century, by a wealthy merchant—proud of his money, and eager to distinguish himself as the owner of the largest country seat in the neighborhood.

After his death, Miss Ladd had taken Netherwoods (as the place was called), finding her own house insufficient for the accommodation of the increasing number of her pupils. A lease was granted to her on moderate terms. Netherwoods failed to attract persons of distinction in search of a country residence. The grounds were beautiful; but no landed property—not even a park—was attached to the house. Excepting the few acres on which the building stood, the surrounding land belonged to a retired naval officer of old family, who resented the attempt of a merchant of low birth to assume the position of a gentleman. No matter what proposals might be made to the admiral, he refused them all. The privilege of shooting was not one of the attractions offered to tenants; the country presented no facilities for hunting; and the only stream in the neighborhood was not preserved. In consequence of these drawbacks, the merchant's representatives had to choose between a proposal to use Netherwoods as a lunatic asylum, or to accept as tenant the respectable mistress of a fashionable and prosperous school. They decided in favor of Miss Ladd.

The contemplated change in Francine's position was accomplished, in that vast house, without inconvenience. There were rooms unoccupied, even when the limit assigned to the number of pupils had been reached. On the re-opening of the school, Francine was offered her choice between two rooms on one of the upper stories, and two rooms on the ground floor. She chose these last.

Her sitting-room and bedroom, situated at the back of the house, communicated with each other. The sitting-room, ornamented with a pretty paper of delicate gray, and furnished with curtains of the same color, had been accordingly named, "The Gray Room." It had a French window, which opened on the terrace overlooking the garden and the grounds. Some fine old engravings from the grand landscapes of Claude (part of a collection of prints possessed by Miss Ladd's father) hung on the walls. The carpet was in harmony with the curtains; and the furniture was of light-colored wood, which helped the general effect of subdued brightness that made the charm of the room. "If you are not happy here," Miss Ladd said, "I despair of you." And Francine answered, "Yes, it's very pretty, but I wish it was not so small."

On the twelfth of August the regular routine of the school was resumed. Alban Morris found two strangers in his class, to fill the vacancies left by Emily and Cecilia. Mrs. Ellmother was duly established in her new place. She produced an unfavorable impression in the servants' hall—not (as the handsome chief housemaid explained) because she was ugly and old, but because she was "a person who didn't talk." The prejudice against habitual silence, among the lower order of the people, is almost as inveterate as the prejudice against red hair.

In the evening, on that first day of renewed studies—while the girls were in the grounds, after tea—Francine had at last completed the arrangement of her rooms, and had dismissed Mrs. Ellmother (kept hard at work since the morning) to take a little rest. Standing alone at her window, the West Indian heiress wondered what she had better do next. She glanced at the girls on the lawn, and decided that they were unworthy of serious notice, on the part of a person so specially favored as herself. She turned sidewise, and looked along the length of the terrace. At the far end a tall man was slowly pacing to and fro, with his head down and his hands in his pockets. Francine recognized the rude drawing-master, who had torn up his view of the village, after she had saved it from being blown into the pond.

She stepped out on the terrace, and called to him. He stopped, and looked up.

"Do you want me?" he called back.

"Of course I do!"

She advanced a little to meet him, and offered encouragement under the form of a hard smile. Although his manners might be unpleasant, he had claims on the indulgence of a young lady, who was at a loss how to employ her idle time. In the first place, he was a man. In the second place, he was not as old as the music-master, or as ugly as the dancing-master. In the third place, he was an admirer of Emily; and the opportunity of trying to shake his allegiance by means of a flirtation, in Emily's absence, was too good an opportunity to be lost.

"Do you remember how rude you were to me, on the day when you were sketching in the summer-house?" Francine asked with snappish playfulness. "I expect you to make yourself agreeable this time—I am going to pay you a compliment."

He waited, with exasperating composure, to hear what the proposed compliment might be. The furrow between his eyebrows looked deeper than ever. There were signs of secret trouble in that dark face, so grimly and so resolutely composed. The school, without Emily, presented the severest trial of endurance that he had encountered, since the day when he had been deserted and disgraced by his affianced wife.

"You are an artist," Francine proceeded, "and therefore a person of taste. I want to have your opinion of my sitting-room. Criticism is invited; pray come in."

He seemed to be unwilling to accept the invitation—then altered his mind, and followed Francine. She had visited Emily; she was perhaps in a fair way to become Emily's friend. He remembered that he had already lost an opportunity of studying her character, and—if he saw the necessity—of warning Emily not to encourage the advances of Miss de Sor.

"Very pretty," he remarked, looking round the room—without appearing to care for anything in it, except the prints.

Francine was bent on fascinating him. She raised her eyebrows and lifted her hands, in playful remonstrance. "Do remember it's my room," she said, "and take some little interest in it, for my sake!"

"What do you want me to say?" he asked.

"Come and sit down by me." She made room for him on the sofa. Her one favorite aspiration—the longing to excite envy in others—expressed itself in her next words. "Say something pretty," she answered; "say you would like to have such a room as this."

"I should like to have your prints," he remarked. "Will that do?"

"It wouldn't do—from anybody else. Ah, Mr. Morris, I know why you are not as nice as you might be! You are not happy. The school has lost its one attraction, in losing our dear Emily. You feel it—I know you feel it." She assisted this expression of sympathy to produce the right effect by a sigh. "What would I not give to inspire such devotion as yours! I don't envy Emily; I only wish—" She paused in confusion, and opened her fan. "Isn't it pretty?" she said, with an ostentatious appearance of changing the subject. Alban behaved like a monster; he began to talk of the weather.

"I think this is the hottest day we have had," he said; "no wonder you want your fan. Netherwoods is an airless place at this season of the year."

She controlled her temper. "I do indeed feel the heat," she admitted, with a resignation which gently reproved him; "it is so heavy and oppressive here after Brighton. Perhaps my sad life, far away from home and friends, makes me sensitive to trifles. Do you think so, Mr. Morris?"

The merciless man said he thought it was the situation of the house.

"Miss Ladd took the place in the spring," he continued; "and only discovered the one objection to it some months afterward. We are in the highest part of the valley here—but, you see, it's a valley surrounded by hills; and on three sides the hills are near us. All very well in winter; but in summer I have heard of girls in this school so out of health in the relaxing atmosphere that they have been sent home again."

Francine suddenly showed an interest in what he was saying. If he had cared to observe her closely, he might have noticed it.

"Do you mean that the girls were really ill?" she asked.

"No. They slept badly—lost appetite—started at trifling noises. In short, their nerves were out of order."

"Did they get well again at home, in another air?"

"Not a doubt of it," he answered, beginning to get weary of the subject. "May I look at your books?"

Francine's interest in the influence of different atmospheres on health was not exhausted yet. "Do you know where the girls lived when they were at home?" she inquired.

"I know where one of them lived. She was the best pupil I ever had—and I remember she lived in Yorkshire." He was so weary of the idle curiosity—as it appeared to him—which persisted in asking trifling questions, that he left his seat, and crossed the room. "May I look at your books?" he repeated.

"Oh, yes!"

The conversation was suspended for a while. The lady thought, "I should like to box his ears!" The gentleman thought, "She's only an inquisitive fool after all!" His examination of her books confirmed him in the delusion that there was really nothing in Francine's character which rendered it necessary to caution Emily against the advances of her new friend. Turning away from the book-case, he made the first excuse that occurred to him for putting an end to the interview.

"I must beg you to let me return to my duties, Miss de Sor. I have to correct the young ladies' drawings, before they begin again to-morrow."

Francine's wounded vanity made a last expiring attempt to steal the heart of Emily's lover.

"You remind me that I have a favor to ask," she said. "I don't attend the other classes—but I should so like to join your class! May I?" She looked up at him with a languishing appearance of entreaty which sorely tried Alban's capacity to keep his face in serious order. He acknowledged the compliment paid to him in studiously commonplace terms, and got a little nearer to the open window. Francine's obstinacy was not conquered yet.

"My education has been sadly neglected," she continued; "but I have had some little instruction in drawing. You will not find me so ignorant as some of the other girls." She waited a little, anticipating a few complimentary words. Alban waited also—in silence. "I shall look forward with pleasure to my lessons under such an artist as yourself," she went on, and waited again, and was disappointed again. "Perhaps," she resumed, "I may become your favorite pupil—Who knows?"

"Who indeed!"

It was not much to say, when he spoke at last—but it was enough to encourage Francine. She called him "dear Mr. Morris"; she pleaded for permission to take her first lesson immediately; she clasped her hands—"Please say Yes!"

"I can't say Yes, till you have complied with the rules."

"Are they your rules?"

Her eyes expressed the readiest submission—in that case. He entirely failed to see it: he said they were Miss Ladd's rules—and wished her good-evening.

She watched him, walking away down the terrace. How was he paid? Did he receive a yearly salary, or did he get a little extra money for each new pupil who took drawing lessons? In this last case, Francine saw her opportunity of being even with him "You brute! Catch me attending your class!"

CHAPTER XXXIII. RECOLLECTIONS OF ST. DOMINGO.

The night was oppressively hot. Finding it impossible to sleep, Francine lay quietly in her bed, thinking. The subject of her reflections was a person who occupied the humble position of her new servant.

Mrs. Ellmother looked wretchedly ill. Mrs. Ellmother had told Emily that her object, in returning to domestic service, was to try if change would relieve her from the oppression of her own thoughts. Mrs. Ellmother believed in vulgar superstitions which declared Friday to be an unlucky day; and which recommended throwing a pinch over your left shoulder, if you happened to spill the salt.

In themselves, these were trifling recollections. But they assumed a certain importance, derived from the associations which they called forth.

They reminded Francine, by some mental process which she was at a loss to trace, of Sappho the slave, and of her life at St. Domingo.

She struck a light, and unlocked her writing desk. From one of the drawers she took out an old household account-book.

The first page contained some entries, relating to domestic expenses, in her own handwriting. They recalled one of her efforts to occupy her idle time, by relieving her mother of the cares of housekeeping. For a day or two, she had persevered—and then she had ceased to feel any interest in her new employment. The remainder of the book was completely filled up, in a beautifully clear handwriting, beginning on the second page. A title had been found for the manuscript by Francine. She had written at the top of the page: Sappho's Nonsense.

After reading the first few sentences she rapidly turned over the leaves, and stopped at a blank space near the end of the book. Here again she had added a title. This time it implied a compliment to the writer: the page was headed: Sappho's Sense.

She read this latter part of the manuscript with the closest attention.

"I entreat my kind and dear young mistress not to suppose that I believe in witchcraft—after such an education as I have received. When I wrote down, at your biding, all that I had told you by word of mouth, I cannot imagine what delusion possessed me. You say I have a negro side to my character, which I inherit from my mother. Did you mean this, dear mistress, as a joke? I am almost afraid it is sometimes not far off from the truth.

"Let me be careful, however, to avoid leading you into a mistake. It is really true that the man-slave I spoke of did pine and die, after the spell had been cast on him by my witch-mother's image of wax. But I ought also to have told you that circumstances favored the working of the spell: the fatal end was not brought about by supernatural means.

"The poor wretch was not in good health at the time; and our owner had occasion to employ him in the valley of the island far inland. I have been told, and can well believe, that the climate there is different from the climate on the coast—in which the unfortunate slave had been accustomed to live. The overseer wouldn't believe him when he said the valley air would be his death—and the negroes, who might otherwise have helped him, all avoided a man whom they knew to be under a spell.

"This, you see, accounts for what might appear incredible to civilized persons. If you will do me a favor, you will burn this little book, as soon as you have read what I have written here. If my request is not granted, I can only implore you to let no eyes but your own see these pages. My life might be in danger if the blacks knew what I have now told you, in the interests of truth."

Francine closed the book, and locked it up again in her desk. "Now I know," she said to herself, "what reminded me of St. Domingo."

When Francine rang her bell the next morning, so long a time elapsed without producing an answer that she began to think of sending one of the house-servants to make inquiries. Before she could decide, Mrs. Ellmother presented herself, and offered her apologies.

"It's the first time I have overslept myself, miss, since I was a girl. Please to excuse me, it shan't happen again."

"Do you find that the air here makes you drowsy?" Francine asked.

Mrs. Ellmother shook her head. "I didn't get to sleep," she said, "till morning, and so I was too heavy to be up in time. But air has got nothing to do with it. Gentlefolks may have their whims and fancies. All air is the same to people like me."

"You enjoy good health, Mrs. Ellmother?"

"Why not, miss? I have never had a doctor."

"Oh! That's your opinion of doctors, is it?"

"I won't have anything to do with them—if that's what you mean by my opinion," Mrs. Ellmother answered doggedly. "How will you have your hair done?"

"The same as yesterday. Have you seen anything of Miss Emily? She went back to London the day after you left us."

"I haven't been in London. I'm thankful to say my lodgings are let to a good tenant."

"Then where have you lived, while you were waiting to come here?"

"I had only one place to go to, miss; I went to the village where I was born. A friend found a corner for me. Ah, dear heart, it's a pleasant place, there!"

"A place like this?"

"Lord help you! As little like this as chalk is to cheese. A fine big moor, miss, in Cumberland, without a tree in sight—look where you may. Something like a wind, I can tell you, when it takes to blowing there."

"Have you never been in this part of the country?"

"Not I! When I left the North, my new mistress took me to Canada. Talk about air! If there was anything in it, the people in that air ought to live to be a hundred. I liked Canada."

"And who was your next mistress?"

Thus far, Mrs. Ellmother had been ready enough to talk. Had she failed to hear what Francine had just said to her? or had she some reason for feeling reluctant to answer? In any case, a spirit of taciturnity took sudden possession of her—she was silent.

Francine (as usual) persisted. "Was your next place in service with Miss Emily's aunt?"

"Yes."

"Did the old lady always live in London?"

"No."

"What part of the country did she live in?"

"Kent."

"Among the hop gardens?"

"No."

"In what other part, then?"

"Isle of Thanet."

"Near the sea coast?"

"Yes."

Even Francine could insist no longer: Mrs. Ellmother's reserve had beaten her—for that day at least. "Go into the hall," she said, "and see if there are any letters for me in the rack."

There was a letter bearing the Swiss postmark. Simple Cecilia was flattered and delighted by the charming manner in which Francine had written to her. She looked forward with impatience to the time when their present acquaintance might ripen into friendship. Would "Dear Miss de Sor" waive all ceremony, and consent to be a guest (later in the autumn) at her father's house? Circumstances connected with her sister's health would delay their return to England for a little while. By the end of the month she hoped to be at home again, and to hear if Francine was disengaged. Her address, in England, was Monksmoor Park, Hants.

Having read the letter, Francine drew a moral from it: "There is great use in a fool, when one knows how to manage her."

Having little appetite for her breakfast, she tried the experiment of a walk on the terrace. Alban Morris was right; the air at Netherwoods, in the summer time, was relaxing. The morning mist still hung over the lowest part of the valley, between the village and the hills beyond. A little exercise produced a feeling of fatigue. Francine returned to her room, and trifled with her tea and toast.

Her next proceeding was to open her writing-desk, and look into the old account-book once more. While it lay open on her lap, she recalled what had passed that morning, between Mrs. Ellmother and herself.

The old woman had been born and bred in the North, on an open moor. She had been removed to the keen air of Canada when she left her birthplace. She had been in service after that, on the breezy eastward coast of Kent. Would the change to the climate of Netherwoods produce any effect on Mrs. Ellmother? At her age, and with her seasoned constitution, would she feel it as those school-girls had felt it—especially that one among them, who lived in the bracing air of the North, the air of Yorkshire?

Weary of solitary thinking on one subject, Francine returned to the terrace with a vague idea of finding something to amuse her—that is to say, something she could turn into ridicule— if she joined the girls.

The next morning, Mrs. Ellmother answered her mistress's bell without delay. "You have slept better, this time?" Francine said.

"No, miss. When I did get to sleep I was troubled by dreams. Another bad night—and no mistake!"

"I suspect your mind is not quite at ease," Francine suggested.

"Why do you suspect that, if you please?"

"You talked, when I met you at Miss Emily's, of wanting to get away from your own thoughts. Has the change to this place helped you?"

"It hasn't helped me as I expected. Some people's thoughts stick fast."

"Remorseful thoughts?" Francine inquired.

Mrs. Ellmother held up her forefinger, and shook it with a gesture of reproof. "I thought we agreed, miss, that there was to be no pumping."

The business of the toilet proceeded in silence.

A week passed. During an interval in the labors of the school, Miss Ladd knocked at the door of Francine's room.

"I want to speak to you, my dear, about Mrs. Ellmother. Have you noticed that she doesn't seem to be in good health?"

"She looks rather pale, Miss Ladd."

"It's more serious than that, Francine. The servants tell me that she has hardly any appetite. She herself acknowledges that she sleeps badly. I noticed her yesterday evening in the garden, under the schoolroom window. One of the girls dropped a dictionary. She started at that slight noise, as if it terrified her. Her nerves are seriously out of order. Can you prevail upon her to see the doctor?"

Francine hesitated—and made an excuse. "I think she would be much more likely, Miss Ladd, to listen to you. Do you mind speaking to her?"

"Certainly not!"

Mrs. Ellmother was immediately sent for. "What is your pleasure, miss?" she said to Francine.

Miss Ladd interposed. "It is I who wish to speak to you, Mrs. Ellmother. For some days past, I have been sorry to see you looking ill."

"I never was ill in my life, ma'am."

Miss Ladd gently persisted. "I hear that you have lost your appetite."

"I never was a great eater, ma'am."

It was evidently useless to risk any further allusion to Mrs. Ellmother's symptoms. Miss Ladd tried another method of persuasion. "I daresay I may be mistaken," she said; "but I do really feel anxious about you. To set my mind at rest, will you see the doctor?"

"The doctor! Do you think I'm going to begin taking physic, at my time of life? Lord, ma'am! you amuse me—you do indeed!" She burst into a sudden fit of laughter; the hysterical laughter which is on the verge of tears. With a desperate effort, she controlled herself. "Please, don't make a fool of me again," she said—and left the room.

"What do you think now?" Miss Ladd asked.

Francine appeared to be still on her guard.

"I don't know what to think," she said evasively.

Miss Ladd looked at her in silent surprise, and withdrew.

Left by herself, Francine sat with her elbows on the table and her face in her hands, absorbed in thought. After a long interval, she opened her desk—and hesitated. She took a sheet of note-paper—and paused, as if still in doubt. She snatched up her pen, with a sudden recovery of resolution—and addressed these lines to the wife of her father's agent in London:

"When I was placed under your care, on the night of my arrival from the West Indies, you kindly said I might ask you for any little service which might be within your power. I shall

96

be greatly obliged if you can obtain for me, and send to this place, a supply of artists' modeling wax—sufficient for the product ion of a small image."

CHAPTER XXXIV. IN THE DARK.

A week later, Alban Morris happened to be in Miss Ladd's study, with a report to make on the subject of his drawing-class. Mrs. Ellmother interrupted them for a moment. She entered the room to return a book which Francine had borrowed that morning.

"Has Miss de Sor done with it already?" Miss Ladd asked.

"She won't read it, ma'am. She says the leaves smell of tobacco-smoke."

Miss Ladd turned to Alban, and shook her head with an air of good-humored reproof. "I know who has been reading that book last!" she said.

Alban pleaded guilty, by a look. He was the only master in the school who smoked. As Mrs. Ellmother passed him, on her way out, he noticed the signs of suffering in her wasted face. "That woman is surely in a bad state of health," he said. "Has she seen the doctor?"

"She flatly refuses to consult the doctor," Miss Ladd replied. "If she was a stranger, I should meet the difficulty by telling Miss de Sor (whose servant she is) that Mrs. Ellmother must be sent home. But I cannot act in that peremptory manner toward a person in whom Emily is interested."

From that moment Mrs. Ellmother became a person in whom Alban was interested. Later in the day, he met her in one of the lower corridors of the house, and spoke to her. "I am afraid the air of this place doesn't agree with you," he said.

Mrs. Ellmother's irritable objection to being told (even indirectly) that she looked ill, expressed itself roughly in reply. "I daresay you mean well, sir—but I don't see how it matters to you whether the place agrees with me or not."

"Wait a minute," Alban answered good-humoredly. "I am not quite a stranger to you."

"How do you make that out, if you please?"

"I know a young lady who has a sincere regard for you."

"You don't mean Miss Emily?"

"Yes, I do. I respect and admire Miss Emily; and I have tried, in my poor way, to be of some little service to her."

Mrs. Ellmother's haggard face instantly softened. "Please to forgive me, sir, for forgetting my manners," she said simply. "I have had my health since the day I was born—and I don't like to be told, in my old age, that a new place doesn't agree with me."

Alban accepted this apology in a manner which at once won the heart of the North-countrywoman. He shook hands with her. "You're one of the right sort," she said; "there are not many of them in this house."

Was she alluding to Francine? Alban tried to make the discovery. Polite circumlocution would be evidently thrown away on Mrs. Ellmother. "Is your new mistress one of the right sort?" he asked bluntly.

The old servant's answer was expressed by a frowning look, followed by a plain question. "Do you say that, sir, because you like my new mistress?"

"No."

"Please to shake hands again!" She said it—took his hand with a sudden grip that spoke for itself—and walked away.

Here was an exhibition of character which Alban was just the man to appreciate. "If I had been an old woman," he thought in his dryly humorous way, "I believe I should have been like Mrs. Ellmother. We might have talked of Emily, if she had not left me in such a hurry. When shall I see her again?"

He was destined to see her again, that night—under circumstances which he remembered to the end of his life.

The rules of Netherwoods, in summer time, recalled the young ladies from their evening's recreation in the grounds at nine o'clock. After that hour, Alban was free to smoke his pipe, and to linger among trees and flower-beds before he returned to his hot little rooms in the village. As a relief to the drudgery of teaching the young ladies, he had been using his pencil, when the day's lessons were over, for his own amusement. It was past ten o'clock before he lighted his pipe, and began walking slowly to and fro on the path which led to the summer-house, at the southern limit of the grounds.

In the perfect stillness of the night, the clock of the village church was distinctly audible, striking the hours and the quarters. The moon had not risen; but the mysterious glimmer of starlight trembled on the large open space between the trees and the house.

Alban paused, admiring with an artist's eye the effect of light, so faintly and delicately beautiful, on the broad expanse of the lawn. "Does the man live who could paint that?" he asked himself. His memory recalled the works of the greatest of all landscape painters—the English artists of fifty years since. While recollections of many a noble picture were still passing through his mind, he was startled by the sudden appearance of a bareheaded woman on the terrace steps.

She hurried down to the lawn, staggering as she ran—stopped, and looked back at the house—hastened onward toward the trees—stopped again, looking backward and forward, uncertain which way to turn next—and then advanced once more. He could now hear her heavily gasping for breath. As she came nearer, the starlight showed a panic-stricken face—the face of Mrs. Ellmother.

Alban ran to meet her. She dropped on the grass before he could cross the short distance which separated them. As he raised her in his arms she looked at him wildly, and murmured and muttered in the vain attempt to speak. "Look at me again," he said. "Don't you remember the man who had some talk with you to-day?" She still stared at him vacantly: he tried again. "Don't you remember Miss Emily's friend?"

As the name passed his lips, her mind in some degree recovered its balance. "Yes," she said; "Emily's friend; I'm glad I have met with Emily's friend." She caught at Alban's arm—starting as if her own words had alarmed her. "What am I talking about? Did I say 'Emily'? A servant ought to say 'Miss Emily.' My head swims. Am I going mad?"

Alban led her to one of the garden chairs. "You're only a little frightened," he said. "Rest, and compose yourself."

She looked over her shoulder toward the house. "Not here! I've run away from a she-devil; I want to be out of sight. Further away, Mister—I don't know your name. Tell me your name; I won't trust you, unless you tell me your name!"

"Hush! hush! Call me Alban."

"I never heard of such a name; I won't trust you."

"You won't trust your friend, and Emily's friend? You don't mean that, I'm sure. Call me by my other name—call me 'Morris.'"

"Morris?" she repeated. "Ah, I've heard of people called 'Morris.' Look back! Your eyes are young—do you see her on the terrace?"

"There isn't a living soul to be seen anywhere."

With one hand he raised her as he spoke—and with the other he took up the chair. In a minute more, they were out of sight of the house. He seated her so that she could rest her head against the trunk of a tree.

"What a good fellow!" the poor old creature said, admiring him; "he knows how my head pains me. Don't stand up! You're a tall man. She might see you."

"She can see nothing. Look at the trees behind us. Even the starlight doesn't get through them."

Mrs. Ellmother was not satisfied yet. "You take it coolly," she said. "Do you know who saw us together in the passage to-day? You good Morris, she saw us—she did. Wretch! Cruel, cunning, shameless wretch."

In the shadows that were round them, Alban could just see that she was shaking her clinched fists in the air. He made another attempt to control her. "Don't excite yourself! If she comes into the garden, she might hear you."

The appeal to her fears had its effect.

"That's true," she said, in lowered tones. A sudden distrust of him seized her the next moment. "Who told me I was excited?" she burst out. "It's you who are excited. Deny it if you dare; I begin to suspect you, Mr. Morris; I don't like your conduct. What has become of your pipe? I saw you put your pipe in your coat pocket. You did it when you set me down among the trees where she could see me! You are in league with her—she is coming to meet you here—you know she does not like tobacco-smoke. Are you two going to put me in the madhouse?"

She started to her feet. It occurred to Alban that the speediest way of pacifying her might be by means of the pipe. Mere words would exercise no persuasive influence over that bewildered mind. Instant action, of some kind, would be far more likely to have the right effect. He put his pipe and his tobacco pouch into her hands, and so mastered her attention before he spoke.

"Do you know how to fill a man's pipe for him?" he asked.

"Haven't I filled my husband's pipe hundreds of times?" she answered sharply.

"Very well. Now do it for me."

She took her chair again instantly, and filled the pipe. He lighted it, and seated himself on the grass, quietly smoking. "Do you think I'm in league with her now?" he asked, purposely adopting the rough tone of a man in her own rank of life.

She answered him as she might have answered her husband, in the days of her unhappy marriage.

"Oh, don't gird at me, there's a good man! If I've been off my head for a minute or two, please not to notice me. It's cool and quiet here," the poor woman said gratefully. "Bless God for the darkness; there's something comforting in the darkness—along with a good man like you. Give me a word of advice. You are my friend in need. What am I to do? I daren't go back to the house!"

She was quiet enough now, to suggest the hope that she might be able to give Alban some information "Were you with Miss de Sor," he asked, "before you came out here? What did she do to frighten you?"

There was no answer; Mrs. Ellmother had abruptly risen once more. "Hush!" she whispered. "Don't I hear somebody near us?"

Alban at once went back, along the winding path which they had followed. No creature was visible in the gardens or on the terrace. On returning, he found it impossible to use his eyes to any good purpose in the obscurity among the trees. He waited a while, listening intently. No sound was audible: there was not even air enough to stir the leaves.

As he returned to the place that he had left, the silence was broken by the chimes of the distant church clock, striking the three-quarters past ten.

Even that familiar sound jarred on Mrs. Ellmother's shattered nerves. In her state of mind and body, she was evidently at the mercy of any false alarm which might be raised by her own fears. Relieved of the feeling of distrust which had thus far troubled him, Alban sat down by her again—opened his match-box to relight his pipe—and changed his mind. Mrs. Ellmother had unconsciously warned him to be cautious.

For the first time, he thought it likely that the heat in the house might induce some of the inmates to try the cooler atmosphere in the grounds. If this happened, and if he continued to smoke, curiosity might tempt them to follow the scent of tobacco hanging on the stagnant air.

"Is there nobody near us?" Mrs. Ellmother asked. "Are you sure?"

"Quite sure. Now tell me, did you really mean it, when you said just now that you wanted my advice?"

"Need you ask that, sir? Who else have I got to help me?"

"I am ready and willing to help you—but I can't do it unless I know first what has passed between you and Miss de Sor. Will you trust me?"

"I will!"

"May I depend on you?"

"Try me!"

CHAPTER XXXV. THE TREACHERY OF THE PIPE.

Alban took Mrs. Ellmother at her word. "I am going to venture on a guess," he said. "You have been with Miss de Sor to-night."

"Quite true, Mr. Morris."

"I am going to guess again. Did Miss de Sor ask you to stay with her, when you went into her room?"

"That's it! She rang for me, to see how I was getting on with my needlework—and she was what I call hearty, for the first time since I have been in her service. I didn't think badly of her when she first talked of engaging me; and I've had reason to repent of my opinion ever since. Oh, she showed the cloven foot to-night! 'Sit down,' she says; 'I've nothing to read, and I hate work; let's have a little chat.' She's got a glib tongue of her own. All I could do was to say a word now and then to keep her going. She talked and talked till it was time to light the lamp. She was particular in telling me to put the shade over it. We were half in the dark, and half in the light. She trapped me (Lord knows how!) into talking about foreign parts; I mean the place she lived in before they sent her to England. Have you heard that she comes from the West Indies?"

"Yes; I have heard that. Go on."

"Wait a bit, sir. There's something, by your leave, that I want to know. Do you believe in Witchcraft?"

"I know nothing about it. Did Miss de Sor put that question to you?"

"She did."

"And how did you answer?"

"Neither in one way nor the other. I'm in two minds about that matter of Witchcraft. When I was a girl, there was an old woman in our village, who was a sort of show. People came to see her from all the country round—gentlefolks among them. It was her great age that made her famous. More than a hundred years old, sir! One of our neighbors didn't believe in her age, and she heard of it. She cast a spell on his flock. I tell you, she sent a plague on his sheep, the plague of the Bots. The whole flock died; I remember it well. Some said the sheep would have had the Bots anyhow. Some said it was the spell. Which of them was right? How am I to settle it?"

"Did you mention this to Miss de Sor?"

"I was obliged to mention it. Didn't I tell you, just now, that I can't make up my mind about Witchcraft? 'You don't seem to know whether you believe or disbelieve,' she says. It made me look like a fool. I told her I had my reasons, and then I was obliged to give them."

"And what did she do then?"

"She said, 'I've got a better story of Witchcraft than yours.' And she opened a little book, with a lot of writing in it, and began to read. Her story made my flesh creep. It turns me cold, sir, when I think of it now."

He heard her moaning and shuddering. Strongly as his interest was excited, there was a compassionate reluctance in him to ask her to go on. His merciful scruples proved to be needless. The fascination of beauty it is possible to resist. The fascination of horror fastens its fearful hold on us, struggle against it as we may. Mrs. Ellmother repeated what she had heard, in spite of herself.

"It happened in the West Indies," she said; "and the writing of a woman slave was the writing in the little book. The slave wrote about her mother. Her mother was a black—a Witch in her own country. There was a forest in her own country. The devil taught her Witchcraft in the forest. The serpents and the wild beasts were afraid to touch her. She lived without eating. She was sold for a slave, and sent to the island—an island in the West Indies. An old man lived there; the wickedest man of them all. He filled the black Witch with devilish knowledge. She learned to make the image of wax. The image of wax casts spells. You put pins in the image of wax. At every pin you put, the person under the spell gets nearer and nearer to death. There was a poor black in the island. He offended the Witch. She made his image in wax; she cast spells on him. He couldn't sleep; he couldn't eat; he was such a coward that common noises frightened him. Like Me! Oh, God, like me!"

"Wait a little," Alban interposed. "You are exciting yourself again—wait."

"You're wrong, sir! You think it ended when she finished her story, and shut up her book; there's worse to come than anything you've heard yet. I don't know what I did to offend her. She looked at me and spoke to me, as if I was the dirt under her feet. 'If you're too stupid to understand what I have been reading,' she says, 'get up and go to the glass. Look at yourself, and remember what happened to the slave who was under the spell. You're getting paler and paler, and thinner and thinner; you're pining away just as he did. Shall I tell you why?' She snatched off the shade from the lamp, and put her hand under the table, and brought out an image of wax. My image! She pointed to three pins in it. 'One,' she says, 'for no sleep. One for no appetite. One for broken nerves.' I asked her what I had done to make such a bitter enemy of her. She says, 'Remember what I asked of you when we talked of your being my servant. Choose which you will do? Die by inches' (I swear she said it as I hope to be saved); 'die by inches, or tell me——'"

There—in the full frenzy of the agitation that possessed her—there, Mrs. Ellmother suddenly stopped.

Alban's first impression was that she might have fainted. He looked closer, and could just see her shadowy figure still seated in the chair. He asked if she was ill. No.

"Then why don't you go on?"

"I have done," she answered.

"Do you think you can put me off," he rejoined sternly, "with such an excuse as that? What did Miss de Sor ask you to tell her? You promised to trust me. Be as good as your word."

In the days of her health and strength, she would have set him at defiance. All she could do now was to appeal to his mercy.

"Make some allowance for me," she said. "I have been terribly upset. What has become of my courage? What has broken me down in this way? Spare me, sir."

He refused to listen. "This vile attempt to practice on your fears may be repeated," he reminded her. "More cruel advantage may be taken of the nervous derangement from which you are suffering in the climate of this place. You little know me, if you think I will allow that to go on."

She made a last effort to plead with him. "Oh sir, is this behaving like the good kind man I thought you were? You say you are Miss Emily's friend? Don't press me—for Miss Emily's sake!"

"Emily!" Alban exclaimed. "Is she concerned in this?"

There was a change to tenderness in his voice, which persuaded Mrs. Ellmother that she had found her way to the weak side of him. Her one effort now was to strengthen the impression which she believed herself to have produced. "Miss Emily is concerned in it," she confessed.

"In what way?"

"Never mind in what way."

"But I do mind."

"I tell you, sir, Miss Emily must never know it to her dying day!"

The first suspicion of the truth crossed Alban's mind.

"I understand you at last," he said. "What Miss Emily must never know—is what Miss de Sor wanted you to tell her. Oh, it's useless to contradict me! Her motive in trying to frighten you is as plain to me now as if she had confessed it. Are you sure you didn't betray yourself, when she showed the image of wax?"

"I should have died first!" The reply had hardly escaped her before she regretted it. "What makes you want to be so sure about it?" she said. "It looks as if you knew—"

"I do know."

"What!"

The kindest thing that he could do now was to speak out. "Your secret is no secret to me," he said.

Rage and fear shook her together. For the moment she was like the Mrs. Ellmother of former days. "You lie!" she cried.

"I speak the truth."

"I won't believe you! I daren't believe you!"

"Listen to me. In Emily's interests, listen to me. I have read of the murder at Zeeland—"

"That's nothing! The man was a namesake of her father."

"The man was her father himself. Keep your seat! There is nothing to be alarmed about. I know that Emily is ignorant of the horrid death that her father died. I know that you and your late mistress have kept the discovery from her to this day. I know the love and pity which plead your excuse for deceiving her, and the circumstances that favored the deception. My good creature, Emily's peace of mind is as sacred to me as it is to you! I love her as I love my own life—and better. Are you calmer, now?"

He heard her crying: it was the best relief that could come to her. After waiting a while to let the tears have their way, he helped her to rise. There was no more to be said now. The one thing to do was to take her back to the house.

"I can give you a word of advice," he said, "before we part for the night. You must leave Miss de Sor's service at once. Your health will be a sufficient excuse. Give her warning immediately."

Mrs. Ellmother hung back, when he offered her his arm. The bare prospect of seeing Francine again was revolting to her. On Alban's assurance that the notice to leave could be given in writing, she made no further resistance. The village clock struck eleven as they ascended the terrace steps.

A minute later, another person left the grounds by the path which led to the house. Alban's precaution had been taken too late. The smell of tobacco-smoke had guided Francine, when she was at a loss which way to turn next in search of Mrs. Ellmother. For the last quarter of an hour she had been listening, hidden among the trees.

CHAPTER XXXVI. CHANGE OF AIR.

The inmates of Netherwoods rose early, and went to bed early. When Alban and Mrs. Ellmother arrived at the back door of the house, they found it locked.

102

The only light visible, along the whole length of the building, glimmered through the Venetian blind of the window-entrance to Francine's sitting-room. Alban proposed to get admission to the house by that way. In her horror of again encountering Francine, Mrs. Ellmother positively refused to follow him when he turned away from the door. "They can't be all asleep yet," she said—and rang the bell.

One person was still out of bed—and that person was the mistress of the house. They recognized her voice in the customary question: "Who's there?" The door having been opened, good Miss Ladd looked backward and forward between Alban and Mrs. Ellmother, with the bewildered air of a lady who doubted the evidence of her own eyes. The next moment, her sense of humor overpowered her. She burst out laughing.

"Close the door, Mr. Morris," she said, "and be so good as to tell me what this means. Have you been giving a lesson in drawing by starlight?"

Mrs. Ellmother moved, so that the light of the lamp in Miss Ladd's hand fell on her face. "I am faint and giddy," she said; "let me go to my bed."

Miss Ladd instantly followed her. "Pray forgive me! I didn't see you were ill, when I spoke," she gently explained. "What can I do for you?"

"Thank you kindly, ma'am. I want nothing but peace and quiet. I wish you good-night."

Alban followed Miss Ladd to her study, on the front side of the house. He had just mentioned the circumstances under which he and Mrs. Ellmother had met, when they were interrupted by a tap at the door. Francine had got back to her room unperceived, by way of the French window. She now presented herself, with an elaborate apology, and with the nearest approach to a penitent expression of which her face was capable.

"I am ashamed, Miss Ladd, to intrude on you at this time of night. My only excuse is, that I am anxious about Mrs. Ellmother. I heard you just now in the hall. If she is really ill, I am the unfortunate cause of it."

"In what way, Miss de Sor?"

"I am sorry to say I frightened her—while we were talking in my room—quite unintentionally. She rushed to the door and ran out. I supposed she had gone to her bedroom; I had no idea she was in the grounds."

In this false statement there was mingled a grain of truth. It was true that Francine believed Mrs. Ellmother to have taken refuge in her room—for she had examined the room. Finding it empty, and failing to discover the fugitive in other parts of the house, she had become alarmed, and had tried the grounds next—with the formidable result which has been already related. Concealing this circumstance, she had lied in such a skillfully artless manner that Alban (having no suspicion of what had really happened to sharpen his wits) was as completely deceived as Miss Ladd. Proceeding to further explanation—and remembering that she was in Alban's presence—Francine was careful to keep herself within the strict limit of truth. Confessing that she had frightened her servant by a description of sorcery, as it was practiced among the slaves on her father's estate, she only lied again, in declaring that Mrs. Ellmother had supposed she was in earnest, when she was guilty of no more serious offense than playing a practical joke.

In this case, Alban was necessarily in a position to detect the falsehood. But it was so evidently in Francine's interests to present her conduct in the most favorable light, that the discovery failed to excite his suspicion. He waited in silence, while Miss Ladd administered a severe reproof. Francine having left the room, as penitently as she had entered it (with her handkerchief over her tearless eyes), he was at liberty, with certain reserves, to return to what had passed between Mrs. Ellmother and himself.

"The fright which the poor old woman has suffered," he said, "has led to one good result. I have found her ready at last to acknowledge that she is ill, and inclined to believe that the change to Netherwoods has had something to do with it. I have advised her to take the course which you suggested, by leaving this house. Is it possible to dispense with the usual delay, when she gives notice to leave Miss de Sor's service?"

"She need feel no anxiety, poor soul, on that account," Miss Ladd replied. "In any case, I had arranged that a week's notice on either side should be enough. As it is, I will speak to Francine myself. The least she can do, to express her regret, is to place no difficulties in Mrs. Ellmother's way."

The next day was Sunday.

Miss Ladd broke through her rule of attending to secular affairs on week days only; and, after consulting with Mrs. Ellmother, arranged with Francine that her servant should be at liberty to leave Netherwoods (health permitting) on the next day. But one difficulty remained. Mrs. Ellmother was in no condition to take the long journey to her birthplace in Cumberland; and her own lodgings in London had been let.

Under these circumstances, what was the best arrangement that could be made for her? Miss Ladd wisely and kindly wrote to Emily on the subject, and asked for a speedy reply.

Later in the day, Alban was sent for to see Mrs. Ellmother. He found her anxiously waiting to hear what had passed, on the previous night, between Miss Ladd and himself. "Were you careful, sir, to say nothing about Miss Emily?"

"I was especially careful; I never alluded to her in any way."

"Has Miss de Sor spoken to you?"

"I have not given her the opportunity."

"She's an obstinate one—she might try."

"If she does, she shall hear my opinion of her in plain words." The talk between them turned next on Alban's discovery of the secret, of which Mrs. Ellmother had believed herself to be the sole depositary since Miss Letitia's death. Without alarming her by any needless allusion to Doctor Allday or to Miss Jethro, he answered her inquiries (so far as he was himself concerned) without reserve. Her curiosity once satisfied, she showed no disposition to pursue the topic. She pointed to Miss Ladd's cat, fast asleep by the side of an empty saucer.

"Is it a sin, Mr. Morris, to wish I was Tom? He doesn't trouble himself about his life that is past or his life that is to come. If I could only empty my saucer and go to sleep, I shouldn't be thinking of the number of people in this world, like myself, who would be better out of it than in it. Miss Ladd has got me my liberty tomorrow; and I don't even know where to go, when I leave this place."

"Suppose you follow Tom's example?" Alban suggested. "Enjoy to-day (in that comfortable chair) and let to-morrow take care of itself."

To-morrow arrived, and justified Alban's system of philosophy. Emily answered Miss Ladd's letter, to excellent purpose, by telegraph.

"I leave London to-day with Cecilia" (the message announced) "for Monksmoor Park, Hants. Will Mrs. Ellmother take care of the cottage in my absence? I shall be away for a month, at least. All is prepared for her if she consents."

Mrs. Ellmother gladly accepted this proposal. In the interval of Emily's absence, she could easily arrange to return to her own lodgings. With words of sincere gratitude she took leave of Miss Ladd; but no persuasion would induce her to say good-by to Francine. "Do me one more kindness, ma'am; don't tell Miss de Sor when I go away." Ignorant of the provocation which had produced this unforgiving temper of mind, Miss Ladd gently remonstrated. "Miss de Sor received my reproof in a penitent spirit; she expresses sincere sorrow for having thoughtlessly frightened you. Both yesterday and to-day she has made kind inquiries after your health. Come! come! don't bear malice—wish her good-by." Mrs. Ellmother's answer was characteristic. "I'll say good-by by telegraph, when I get to London."

Her last words were addressed to Alban. "If you can find a way of doing it, sir, keep those two apart."

"Do you mean Emily and Miss de Sor?

"Yes."

"What are you afraid of?"

"I don't know."

"Is that quite reasonable, Mrs. Ellmother?"

"I daresay not. I only know that I am afraid."

The pony chaise took her away. Alban's class was not yet ready for him. He waited on the terrace.

Innocent alike of all knowledge of the serious reason for fear which did really exist, Mrs. Ellmother and Alban felt, nevertheless, the same vague distrust of an intimacy between the two girls. Idle, vain, malicious, false—to know that Francine's character presented these faults, without any discoverable merits to set against them, was surely enough to justify a gloomy view of the prospect, if she succeeded in winning the position of Emily's friend. Alban reasoned it out logically in this way—without satisfying himself, and without accounting for the remembrance that haunted him of Mrs. Ellmother's farewell look. "A commonplace man would say we are both in a morbid state of mind," he thought; "and sometimes commonplace men turn out to be right."

He was too deeply preoccupied to notice that he had advanced perilously near Francine's window. She suddenly stepped out of her room, and spoke to him.

"Do you happen to know, Mr. Morris, why Mrs. Ellmother has gone away without bidding me good-by?"

"She was probably afraid, Miss de Sor, that you might make her the victim of another joke." Francine eyed him steadily. "Have you any particular reason for speaking to me in that way?"

"I am not aware that I have answered you rudely—if that is what you mean."

"That is not what I mean. You seem to have taken a dislike to me. I should be glad to know why."

"I dislike cruelty—and you have behaved cruelly to Mrs. Ellmother."

"Meaning to be cruel?" Francine inquired.

"You know as well as I do, Miss de Sor, that I can't answer that question."

Francine looked at him again "Am I to understand that we are enemies?" she asked.

"You are to understand," he replied, "that a person whom Miss Ladd employs to help her in teaching, cannot always presume to express his sentiments in speaking to the young ladies."

"If that means anything, Mr. Morris, it means that we are enemies."

"It means, Miss de Sor, that I am the drawing-master at this school, and that I am called to my class."

Francine returned to her room, relieved of the only doubt that had troubled her. Plainly no suspicion that she had overheard what passed between Mrs. Ellmother and himself existed in Alban's mind. As to the use to be made of her discovery, she felt no difficulty in deciding to wait, and be guided by events. Her curiosity and her self-esteem had been alike gratified—she had got the better of Mrs. Ellmother at last, and with that triumph she was content. While Emily remained her friend, it would be an act of useless cruelty to disclose the terrible truth. There had certainly been a coolness between them at Brighton. But Francine—still influenced by the magnetic attraction which drew her to Emily—did not conceal from herself that she had offered the provocation, and had been therefore the person to blame. "I can set all that right," she thought, "when we meet at Monksmoor Park." She opened her desk and wrote the shortest and sweetest of letters to Cecilia. "I am entirely at the disposal of my charming friend, on any convenient day—may I add, my dear, the sooner the better?"

The pupils of the drawing-class put away their pencils and color-boxes in high good humor: the teacher's vigilant eye for faults had failed him for the first time in their experience. Not one of them had been reproved; they had chattered and giggled and drawn caricatures on the margin of the paper, as freely as if the master had left the room. Alban's wandering attention was indeed beyond the reach of control. His interview with Francine had doubled his sense of responsibility toward Emily—while he was further than ever from seeing how he could interfere, to any useful purpose, in his present position, and with his reasons for writing under reserve.

One of the servants addressed him as he was leaving the schoolroom. The landlady's boy was waiting in the hall, with a message from his lodgings.

"Now then! what is it?" he asked, irritably.

"The lady wants you, sir." With this mysterious answer, the boy presented a visiting card. The name inscribed on it was—"Miss Jethro."

She had arrived by the train, and she was then waiting at Alban's lodgings. "Say I will be with her directly." Having given the message, he stood for a while, with his hat in his hand—literally lost in astonishment. It was simply impossible to guess at Miss Jethro's object: and yet, with the usual perversity of human nature, he was still wondering what she could possibly want with him, up to the final moment when he opened the door of his sitting-room.

She rose and bowed with the same grace of movement, and the same well-bred composure of manner, which Doctor Allday had noticed when she entered his consulting-room. Her dark melancholy eyes rested on Alban with a look of gentle interest. A faint flush of color animated for a moment the faded beauty of her face—passed away again—and left it paler than before.

"I cannot conceal from myself," she began, "that I am intruding on you under embarrassing circumstances."

"May I ask, Miss Jethro, to what circumstances you allude?"

"You forget, Mr. Morris, that I left Miss Ladd's school, in a manner which justified doubt of me in the minds of strangers."

"Speaking as one of those strangers," Alban replied, "I cannot feel that I had any right to form an opinion, on a matter which only concerned Miss Ladd and yourself."

Miss Jethro bowed gravely. "You encourage me to hope," she said. "I think you will place a favorable construction on my visit when I mention my motive. I ask you to receive me, in the interests of Miss Emily Brown."

Stating her purpose in calling on him in those plain terms, she added to the amazement which Alban already felt, by handing to him—as if she was presenting an introduction—a letter marked, "Private," addressed to her by Doctor Allday.

"I may tell you," she premised, "that I had no idea of troubling you, until Doctor Allday suggested it. I wrote to him in the first instance; and there is his reply. Pray read it."

The letter was dated, "Penzance"; and the doctor wrote, as he spoke, without ceremony.

"MADAM—Your letter has been forwarded to me. I am spending my autumn holiday in the far West of Cornwall. However, if I had been at home, it would have made no difference. I should have begged leave to decline holding any further conversation with you, on the subject of Miss Emily Brown, for the following reasons:

"In the first place, though I cannot doubt your sincere interest in the young lady's welfare, I don't like your mysterious way of showing it. In the second place, when I called at your address in London, after you had left my house, I found that you had taken to flight. I place my own interpretation on this circumstance; but as it is not founded on any knowledge of facts, I merely allude to it, and say no more."

Arrived at that point, Alban offered to return the letter. "Do you really mean me to go on reading it?" he asked.

"Yes," she said quietly.

Alban returned to the letter.

"In the third place, I have good reason to believe that you entered Miss Ladd's school as a teacher, under false pretenses. After that discovery, I tell you plainly I hesitate to attach credit to any statement that you may wish to make. At the same time, I must not permit my prejudices (as you will probably call them) to stand in the way of Miss Emily's interests—supposing them to be really depending on any interference of yours. Miss Ladd's drawing-master, Mr. Alban Morris, is even more devoted to Miss Emily's service than I am. Whatever you might have said to me, you can say to him—with this possible advantage, that he may believe you."

There the letter ended. Alban handed it back in silence.

Miss Jethro pointed to the words, "Mr. Alban Morris is even more devoted to Miss Emily's service than I am."

"Is that true?" she asked.

"Quite true."

"I don't complain, Mr. Morris, of the hard things said of me in that letter; you are at liberty to suppose, if you like, that I deserve them. Attribute it to pride, or attribute it to reluctance to make needless demands on your time—I shall not attempt to defend myself. I leave you to decide whether the woman who has shown you that letter—having something important to say to you—is a person who is mean enough to say it under false pretenses."

"Tell me what I can do for you, Miss Jethro: and be assured, beforehand, that I don't doubt your sincerity."

"My purpose in coming here," she answered, "is to induce you to use your influence over Miss Emily Brown—"

"With what object?" Alban asked, interrupting her.

"My object is her own good. Some years since, I happened to become acquainted with a person who has attained some celebrity as a preacher. You have perhaps heard of Mr. Miles Mirabel?"

"I have heard of him."

"I have been in correspondence with him," Miss Jethro proceeded. "He tells me he has been introduced to a young lady, who was formerly one of Miss Ladd's pupils, and who is the daughter of Mr. Wyvil, of Monksmoor Park. He has called on Mr. Wyvil; and he has since received an invitation to stay at Mr. Wyvil's house. The day fixed for the visit is Monday, the fifth of next month."

Alban listened—at a loss to know what interest he was supposed to have in being made acquainted with Mr. Mirabel's engagements. Miss Jethro's next words enlightened him.

"You are perhaps aware," she resumed, "that Miss Emily Brown is Miss Wyvil's intimate friend. She will be one of the guests at Monksmoor Park. If there are any obstacles which you can place in her way—if there is any influence which you can exert, without exciting suspicion of your motive—prevent her, I entreat you, from accepting Miss Wyvil's invitation, until Mr. Mirabel's visit has come to an end."

"Is there anything against Mr. Mirabel?" he asked.

"I say nothing against him."

"Is Miss Emily acquainted with him?"

"No."

"Is he a person with whom it would be disagreeable to her to associate?"

"Quite the contrary."

"And yet you expect me to prevent them from meeting! Be reasonable, Miss Jethro."

"I can only be in earnest, Mr. Morris—more truly, more deeply in earnest than you can suppose. I declare to you that I am speaking in Miss Emily's interests. Do you still refuse to exert yourself for her sake?"

"I am spared the pain of refusal," Alban answered. "The time for interference has gone by. She is, at this moment, on her way to Monksmoor Park."

Miss Jethro attempted to rise—and dropped back into her chair. "Water!" she said faintly. After drinking from the glass to the last drop, she began to revive. Her little traveling-bag was on the floor at her side. She took out a railway guide, and tried to consult it. Her fingers trembled incessantly; she was unable to find the page to which she wished to refer. "Help me," she said, "I must leave this place—by the first train that passes."

"To see Emily?" Alban asked.

"Quite useless! You have said it yourself—the time for interference has gone by. Look at the guide."

"What place shall I look for?"

"Look for Vale Regis."

Alban found the place. The train was due in ten minutes. "Surely you are not fit to travel so soon?" he suggested.

"Fit or not, I must see Mr. Mirabel—I must make the effort to keep them apart by appealing to him."

"With any hope of success?"

"With no hope—and with no interest in the man himself. Still I must try."

"Out of anxiety for Emily's welfare?"

"Out of anxiety for more than that."

"For what?"

"If you can't guess, I daren't tell you."

That strange reply startled Alban. Before he could ask what it meant, Miss Jethro had left him.

In the emergencies of life, a person readier of resource than Alban Morris it would not have been easy to discover. The extraordinary interview that had now come to an end had found its limits. Bewildered and helpless, he stood at the window of his room, and asked himself (as if he had been the weakest man living), "What shall I do?"

BOOK THE FOURTH—THE COUNTRY HOUSE.

CHAPTER XXXVIII. DANCING.

The windows of the long drawing-room at Monksmoor are all thrown open to the conservatory. Distant masses of plants and flowers, mingled in ever-varying forms of beauty, are touched by the melancholy luster of the rising moon. Nearer to the house, the restful shadows are disturbed at intervals, where streams of light fall over them aslant from the lamps in the room. The fountain is playing. In rivalry with its lighter music, the nightingales are singing their song of ecstasy. Sometimes, the laughter of girls is heard—and, sometimes, the melody of a waltz. The younger guests at Monksmoor are dancing.

Emily and Cecilia are dressed alike in white, with flowers in their hair. Francine rivals them by means of a gorgeous contrast of color, and declares that she is rich with the bright emphasis of diamonds and the soft persuasion of pearls.

Miss Plym (from the rectory) is fat and fair and prosperous: she overflows with good spirits; she has a waist which defies tight-lacing, and she dances joyously on large flat feet. Miss Darnaway (officer's daughter with small means) is the exact opposite of Miss Plym. She is thin and tall and faded—poor soul. Destiny has made it her hard lot in life to fill the place of head-nursemaid at home. In her pensive moments, she thinks of the little brothers and sisters, whose patient servant she is, and wonders who comforts them in their tumbles and tells them stories at bedtime, while she is holiday-making at the pleasant country house.

Tender-hearted Cecilia, remembering how few pleasures this young friend has, and knowing how well she dances, never allows her to be without a partner. There are three invaluable young gentlemen present, who are excellent dancers. Members of different families, they are nevertheless fearfully and wonderfully like each other. They present the same rosy complexions and straw-colored mustachios, the same plump cheeks, vacant eyes and low forehead; and they utter, with the same stolid gravity, the same imbecile small talk. On sofas facing each other sit the two remaining guests, who have not joined the elders at the card-table in another room. They are both men. One of them is drowsy and middle-aged—happy in the possession of large landed property: happier still in a capacity for drinking Mr. Wyvil's famous port-wine without gouty results.

The other gentleman—ah, who is the other? He is the confidential adviser and bosom friend of every young lady in the house. Is it necessary to name the Reverend Miles Mirabel?

There he sits enthroned, with room for a fair admirer on either side of him—the clerical sultan of a platonic harem. His persuasive ministry is felt as well as heard: he has an innocent habit of fondling young persons. One of his arms is even long enough to embrace the circumference of Miss Plym—while the other clasps the rigid silken waist of Francine. "I do it everywhere else," he says innocently, "why not here?" Why not indeed—with that delicate complexion and those beautiful blue eyes; with the glorious golden hair that rests on his shoulders, and the glossy beard that flows over his breast? Familiarities, forbidden to mere men, become privileges and condescensions when an angel enters society—and more especially when that angel has enough of mortality in him to be amusing. Mr. Mirabel, on his social side, is an irresistible companion. He is cheerfulness itself; he takes a favorable view of everything; his sweet temper never differs with anybody. "In my humble way," he confesses, "I like to make the world about me brighter." Laughter (harmlessly produced, observe!) is the element in which he lives and breathes. Miss Darnaway's serious face puts him out; he has laid a bet with Emily—not in money, not even in gloves, only in flowers—that he will make Miss Darnaway laugh; and he has won the wager. Emily's flowers are in his button-hole, peeping through the curly interstices of his beard. "Must you leave me?" he asks tenderly, when there is a dancing man at liberty, and it is Francine's turn to claim him. She leaves her seat not very willingly. For a while, the place is vacant; Miss Plym seizes the opportunity of consulting the ladies' bosom friend.

"Dear Mr. Mirabel, do tell me what you think of Miss de Sor?"

Dear Mr. Mirabel bursts into enthusiasm and makes a charming reply. His large experience of young ladies warns him that they will tell each other what he thinks of them, when they retire for the night; and he is careful on these occasions to say something that will bear repetition.

"I see in Miss de Sor," he declares, "the resolution of a man, tempered by the sweetness of a woman. When that interesting creature marries, her husband will be—shall I use the vulgar word?—henpecked. Dear Miss Plym, he will enjoy it; and he will be quite right too; and, if I am asked to the wedding, I shall say, with heartfelt sincerity, Enviable man!"

In the height of her admiration for Mr. Mirabel's wonderful eye for character, Miss Plym is called away to the piano. Cecilia succeeds to her friend's place—and has her waist taken in charge as a matter of course.

"How do you like Miss Plym?" she asks directly.

Mr. Mirabel smiles, and shows the prettiest little pearly teeth. "I was just thinking of her," he confesses pleasantly; "Miss Plym is so nice and plump, so comforting and domestic—such a perfect clergyman's daughter. You love her, don't you? Is she engaged to be married? In that case—between ourselves, dear Miss Wyvil, a clergyman is obliged to be cautious—I may own that I love her too."

Delicious titillations of flattered self-esteem betray themselves in Cecilia's lovely complexion. She is the chosen confidante of this irresistible man; and she would like to express her sense of obligation. But Mr. Mirabel is a master in the art of putting the right words in the right places; and simple Cecilia distrusts herself and her grammar.

At that moment of embarrassment, a friend leaves the dance, and helps Cecilia out of the difficulty.

Emily approaches the sofa-throne, breathless—followed by her partner, entreating her to give him "one turn more." She is not to be tempted; she means to rest. Cecilia sees an act of mercy, suggested by the presence of the disengaged young man. She seizes his arm, and hurries him off to poor Miss Darnaway; sitting forlorn in a corner, and thinking of the nursery at home. In the meanwhile a circumstance occurs. Mr. Mirabel's all-embracing arm shows itself in a new character, when Emily sits by his side.

It becomes, for the first time, an irresolute arm. It advances a little—and hesitates. Emily at once administers an unexpected check; she insists on preserving a free waist, in her own outspoken language. "No, Mr. Mirabel, keep that for the others. You can't imagine how ridiculous you and the young ladies look, and how absurdly unaware of it you all seem to be." For the first time in his life, the reverend and ready-witted man of the world is at a loss for an answer. Why?

For this simple reason. He too has felt the magnetic attraction of the irresistible little creature whom every one likes. Miss Jethro has been doubly defeated. She has failed to keep them apart; and her unexplained misgivings have not been justified by events: Emily and Mr. Mirabel are good friends already. The brilliant clergyman is poor; his interests in life point to a marriage for money; he has fascinated the heiresses of two rich fathers, Mr. Tyvil and Mr. de Sor—and yet he is conscious of an influence (an alien influence, without a balance at its bankers), which has, in some mysterious way, got between him and his interests.

On Emily's side, the attraction felt is of another nature altogether. Among the merry young people at Monksmoor she is her old happy self again; and she finds in Mr. Mirabel the most agreeable and amusing man whom she has ever met. After those dismal night watches by the bed of her dying aunt, and the dreary weeks of solitude that followed, to live in this new world of luxury and gayety is like escaping from the darkness of night, and basking in the fall brightn ess of day. Cecilia declares that she looks, once more, like the joyous queen of the bedroom, in the bygone time at school; and Francine (profaning Shakespeare without knowing it), says, "Emily is herself again!"

"Now that your arm is in its right place, reverend sir," she gayly resumes, "I may admit that there are exceptions to all rules. My waist is at your disposal, in a case of necessity—that is to say, in a case of waltzing."

"The one case of all others," Mirabel answers, with the engaging frankness that has won him so many friends, "which can never happen in my unhappy experience. Waltzing, I blush to own it, means picking me up off the floor, and putting smelling salts to my nostrils. In other words, dear Miss Emily, it is the room that waltzes—not I. I can't look at those whirling couples there, with a steady head. Even the exquisite figure of our young hostess, when it describes flying circles, turns me giddy."

Hearing this allusion to Cecilia, Emily drops to the level of the other girls. She too pays her homage to the Pope of private life. "You promised me your unbiased opinion of Cecilia," she reminds him; "and you haven't given it yet."

The ladies' friend gently remonstrates. "Miss Wyvil's beauty dazzles me. How can I give an unbiased opinion? Besides, I am not thinking of her; I can only think of you."

Emily lifts her eyes, half merrily, half tenderly, and looks at him over the top of her fan. It is her first effort at flirtation. She is tempted to engage in the most interesting of all games to a girl—the game which plays at making love. What has Cecilia told her, in those bedroom gossipings, dear to the hearts of the two friends? Cecilia has whispered, "Mr. Mirabel admires your figure; he calls you 'the Venus of Milo, in a state of perfect abridgment.'" Where is the daughter of Eve, who would not have been flattered by that pretty compliment—who would not have talked soft nonsense in return? "You can only think of Me," Emily repeats coquettishly. "Have you said that to the last young lady who occupied my place, and will you say it again to the next who follows me?"

"Not to one of them! Mere compliments are for the others—not for you."

"What is for me, Mr. Mirabel?"

"What I have just offered you—a confession of the truth."

Emily is startled by the tone in which he replies. He seems to be in earnest; not a vestige is left of the easy gayety of his manner. His face shows an expression of anxiety which she has never seen in it yet. "Do you believe me?" he asks in a whisper.

She tries to change the subject.

"When am I to hear you preach, Mr. Mirabel?"

He persists. "When you believe me," he says.

His eyes add an emphasis to that reply which is not to be mistaken. Emily turns away from him, and notices Francine. She has left the dance, and is looking with marked attention at Emily and Mirabel. "I want to speak to you," she says, and beckons impatiently to Emily. Mirabel whispers, "Don't go!"

Emily rises nevertheless—ready to avail herself of the first excuse for leaving him. Francine meets her half way, and takes her roughly by the arm.

"What is it?" Emily asks.

"Suppose you leave off flirting with Mr. Mirabel, and make yourself of some use."

"In what way?"

"Use your ears—and look at that girl."

She points disdainfully to innocent Miss Plym. The rector's daughter possesses all the virtues, with one exception—the virtue of having an ear for music. When she sings, she is out of tune; and, when she plays, she murders time.

"Who can dance to such music as that?" says Francine. "Finish the waltz for her."

Emily naturally hesitates. "How can I take her place, unless she asks me?"

Francine laughs scornfully. "Say at once, you want to go back to Mr. Mirabel."

"Do you think I should have got up, when you beckoned to me," Emily rejoins, "if I had not wanted to get away from Mr. Mirabel?"

Instead of resenting this sharp retort, Francine suddenly breaks into good humor. "Come along, you little spit-fire; I'll manage it for you."

She leads Emily to the piano, and stops Miss Plym without a word of apology: "It's your turn to dance now. Here's Miss Brown waiting to relieve you."

Cecilia has not been unobservant, in her own quiet way, of what has been going on. Waiting until Francine and Miss Plym are out of hearing, she bends over Emily, and says, "My dear, I really do think Francine is in love with Mr. Mirabel."

"After having only been a week in the same house with him!" Emily exclaims.

"At any rate," said Cecilia, more smartly than usual, "she is jealous of you."

CHAPTER XXXIX. FEIGNING.

The next morning, Mr. Mirabel took two members of the circle at Monksmoor by surprise. One of them was Emily; and one of them was the master of the house.

Seeing Emily alone in the garden before breakfast, he left his room and joined her. "Let me say one word," he pleaded, "before we go to breakfast. I am grieved to think that I was so unfortunate as to offend you, last night."

Emily's look of astonishment answered for her before she could speak. "What can I have said or done," she asked, "to make you think that?"

"Now I breathe again!" he cried, with the boyish gayety of manner which was one of the secrets of his popularity among women. "I really feared that I had spoken thoughtlessly. It is a terrible confession for a clergyman to make—but it is not the less true that I am one of the most indiscreet men living. It is my rock ahead in life that I say the first thing which comes uppermost, without stopping to think. Being well aware of my own defects, I naturally distrust myself."

"Even in the pulpit?" Emily inquired.

He laughed with the readiest appreciation of the satire—although it was directed against himself.

"I like that question," he said; "it tells me we are as good friends again as ever. The fact is, the sight of the congregation, when I get into the pulpit, has the same effect upon me that the sight of the footlights has on an actor. All oratory (though my clerical brethren are shy of confessing it) is acting—without the scenery and the costumes. Did you really mean it, last night, when you said you would like to hear me preach?"

"Indeed, I did."

"How very kind of you. I don't think myself the sermon is worth the sacrifice. (There is another specimen of my indiscreet way of talking!) What I mean is, that you will have to get up early on Sunday morning, and drive twelve miles to the damp and dismal little village, in which I officiate for a man with a rich wife who likes the climate of Italy. My congregation works in the fields all the week, and naturally enough goes to sleep in church on Sunday. I have had to counteract that. Not by preaching! I wouldn't puzzle the poor people with my eloquence for the world. No, no: I tell them little stories out of the Bible—in a nice easy gossiping way. A quarter of an hour is my limit of time; and, I am proud to say, some of them (mostly the women) do to a certain extent keep awake. If you and the other ladies decide to honor me, it is needless to say you shall have one of my grand efforts. What will be the effect on my unfortunate flock remains to be seen. I will have the church brushed up, and luncheon of course at the parsonage. Beans, bacon, and beer—I haven't got anything else in the house. Are you rich? I hope not!"

"I suspect I am quite as poor as you are, Mr. Mirabel."

"I am delighted to hear it. (More of my indiscretion!) Our poverty is another bond between us."

Before he could enlarge on this text, the breakfast bell rang.

He gave Emily his arm, quite satisfied with the result of the morning's talk. In speaking seriously to her on the previous night, he had committed the mistake of speaking too soon. To amend this false step, and to recover his position in Emily's estimation, had been his object in view—and it had been successfully accomplished. At the breakfast-table that morning, the companionable clergyman was more amusing than ever.

The meal being over, the company dispersed as usual—with the one exception of Mirabel. Without any apparent reason, he kept his place at the table. Mr. Wyvil, the most courteous and considerate of men, felt it an attention due to his guest not to leave the room first. All that he could venture to do was to give a little hint. "Have you any plans for the morning?" he asked.

"I have a plan that depends entirely on yourself," Mirabel answered; "and I am afraid of being as indiscreet as usual, if I mention it. Your charming daughter tells me you play on the violin."

Modest Mr. Wyvil looked confused. "I hope you have not been annoyed," he said; "I practice in a distant room so that nobody may hear me."

"My dear sir, I am eager to hear you! Music is my passion; and the violin is my favorite instrument."

Mr. Wyvil led the way to his room, positively blushing with pleasure. Since the death of his wife he had been sadly in want of a little encouragement. His daughters and his friends were careful—over-careful, as he thought—of intruding on him in his hours of practice. And, sad to say, his daughters and his friends were, from a musical point of view, perfectly right.

Literature has hardly paid sufficient attention to a social phenomenon of a singularly perplexing kind. We hear enough, and more than enough, of persons who successfully cultivate the Arts—of the remarkable manner in which fitness for their vocation shows itself in early life, of the obstacles which family prejudice places in their way, and of the unremitting devotion which has led to the achievement of glorious results.

But how many writers have noticed those other incomprehensible persons, members of families innocent for generations past of practicing Art or caring for Art, who have notwithstanding displayed from their earliest years the irresistible desire to cultivate poetry, painting, or music; who have surmounted obstacles, and endured disappointments, in the single-hearted resolution to devote their lives to an intellectual pursuit—being absolutely without the capacity which proves the vocation, and justifies the sacrifice. Here is Nature, "unerring Nature," presented in flat contradiction with herself. Here are men bent on performing feats of running, without having legs; and women, hopelessly barren, living in constant expectation of large families to the end of their days. The musician is not to be found more completely deprived than Mr. Wyvil of natural capacity for playing on an instrument—and, for twenty years past, it had been the pride and delight of his heart to let no day of his life go by without practicing on the violin.

"I am sure I must be tiring you," he said politely—after having played without mercy for an hour and more.

No: the insatiable amateur had his own purpose to gain, and was not exhausted yet. Mr. Wyvil got up to look for some more music. In that interval desultory conversation naturally took place. Mirabel contrived to give it the necessary direction—the direction of Emily.

"The most delightful girl I have met with for many a long year past!" Mr. Wyvil declared warmly. "I don't wonder at my daughter being so fond of her. She leads a solitary life at home, poor thing; and I am honestly glad to see her spirits reviving in my house."

"An only child?" Mirabel asked.

In the necessary explanation that followed, Emily's isolated position in the world was revealed in few words. But one more discovery—the most important of all—remained to be made. Had she used a figure of speech in saying that she was as poor as Mirabel himself? or had she told him the shocking truth? He put the question with perfect delicacy—but with unerring directness as well.

Mr. Wyvil, quoting his daughter's authority, described Emily's income as falling short even of two hundred a year. Having made that disheartening reply, he opened another music book. "You know this sonata, of course?" he said. The next moment, the violin was under his chin and the performance began.

While Mirabel was, to all appearance, listening with the utmost attention, he was actually endeavoring to reconcile himself to a serious sacrifice of his own inclinations. If he remained much longer in the same house with Emily, the impression that she had produced on him would be certainly strengthened—and he would be guilty of the folly of making an offer of marriage to a woman who was as poor as himself. The one remedy that could be trusted to preserve him from such infatuation as this, was absence. At the end of the week, he had arranged to return to Vale Regis for his Sunday duty; engaging to join his friends again at Monksmoor on the Monday following. That rash promise, there could be no further doubt about it, must not be fulfilled.

He had arrived at this resolution, when the terrible activity of Mr. Wyvil's bow was suspended by the appearance of a third person in the room.

Cecilia's maid was charged with a neat little three-cornered note from her young lady, to be presented to her master. Wondering why his daughter should write to him, Mr. Wyvil opened the note, and was informed of Cecilia's motive in these words:

"DEAREST PAPA—I hear Mr. Mirabel is with you, and as this is a secret, I must write. Emily has received a very strange letter this morning, which puzzles her and alarms me. When you are quite at liberty, we shall be so much obliged if you will tell us how Emily ought to answer it."

Mr. Wyvil stopped Mirabel, on the point of trying to escape from the music. "A little domestic matter to attend to," he said. "But we will finish the sonata first."

CHAPTER XL. CONSULTING.

Out of the music room, and away from his violin, the sound side of Mr. Wyvil's character was free to assert itself. In his public and in his private capacity, he was an eminently sensible man.

As a member of parliament, he set an example which might have been followed with advantage by many of his colleagues. In the first place he abstained from hastening the downfall of representative institutions by asking questions and making speeches. In the second place, he was able to distinguish between the duty that he owed to his party, and the duty that he owed to his country. When the Legislature acted politically—that is to say, when it dealt with foreign complications, or electoral reforms—he followed his leader. When the Legislature acted socially—that is to say, for the good of the people—he followed his conscience. On the last occasion when the great Russian bugbear provoked a division, he voted submissively with his Conservative allies. But, when the question of opening museums and picture galleries on Sundays arrayed the two parties in hostile camps, he broke into open mutiny, and went over to the Liberals. He consented to help in preventing an extension of the franchise; but he refused to be concerned in obstructing the repeal of taxes on knowledge. "I am doubtful in the first case," he said, "but I am sure in the second." He was asked for an explanation: "Doubtful of what? and sure of what?" To the astonishment of his leader, he answered: "The benefit to the people." The same sound sense appeared in the transactions of his private life. Lazy and dishonest servants found that the gentlest of masters had a side to his character which took them by surprise. And, on certain occasions in the experience of Cecilia and her sister, the most indulgent of fathers proved to be as capable of saying No, as the sternest tyrant who ever ruled a fireside.

Called into council by his daughter and his guest, Mr. Wyvil assisted them by advice which was equally wise and kind—but which afterward proved, under the perverse influence of circumstances, to be advice that he had better not have given.

The letter to Emily which Cecilia had recommended to her father's consideration, had come from Netherwoods, and had been written by Alban Morris.

He assured Emily that he had only decided on writing to her, after some hesitation, in the hope of serving interests which he did not himself understand, but which might prove to be interests worthy of consideration, nevertheless. Having stated his motive in these terms, he proceeded to relate what had passed between Miss Jethro and himself. On the subject of Francine, Alban only ventured to add that she had not produced a favorable impression on him, and that he could not think her likely, on further experience, to prove a desirable friend.

On the last leaf were added some lines, which Emily was at no loss how to answer. She had folded back the page, so that no eyes but her own should see how the poor drawing-master finished his letter: "I wish you all possible happiness, my dear, among your new friends; but don't forget the old friend who thinks of you, and dreams of you, and longs to see you again. The little world I live in is a dreary world, Emily, in your absence. Will you write to me now and then, and encourage me to hope?"

Mr. Wyvil smiled, as he looked at the folded page, which hid the signature.

"I suppose I may take it for granted," he said slyly, "that this gentleman really has your interests at heart? May I know who he is?"

Emily answered the last question readily enough. Mr. Wyvil went on with his inquiries. "About the mysterious lady, with the strange name," he proceeded—"do you know anything of her?"

Emily related what she knew; without revealing the true reason for Miss Jethro's departure from Netherwoods. In after years, it was one of her most treasured remembrances, that she had kept secret the melancholy confession which had startled her, on the last night of her life at school.

Mr. Wyvil looked at Alban's letter again. "Do you know how Miss Jethro became acquainted with Mr. Mirabel?" he asked.

"I didn't even know that they were acquainted."

"Do you think it likely—if Mr. Morris had been talking to you instead of writing to you—that he might have said more than he has said in his letter?"

Cecilia had hitherto remained a model of discretion. Seeing Emily hesitate, temptation overcame her. "Not a doubt of it, papa!" she declared confidently.

"Is Cecilia right?" Mr. Wyvil inquired.

Reminded in this way of her influence over Alban, Emily could only make one honest reply. She admitted that Cecilia was right.

Mr. Wyvil thereupon advised her not to express any opinion, until she was in a better position to judge for herself. "When you write to Mr. Morris," he continued, "say that you will wait to tell him what you think of Miss Jethro, until you see him again."

"I have no prospect at present of seeing him again," Emily said.

"You can see Mr. Morris whenever it suits him to come here," Mr. Wyvil replied. "I will write and ask him to visit us, and you can inclose the invitation in your letter."

"Oh, Mr. Wyvil, how good of you!"

"Oh, papa, the very thing I was going to ask you to do!"

The excellent master of Monksmoor looked unaffectedly surprised. "What are you two young ladies making a fuss about?" he said. "Mr. Morris is a gentleman by profession; and—may I venture to say it, Miss Emily?—a valued friend of yours as well. Who has a better claim to be one of my guests?"

Cecilia stopped her father as he was about to leave the room. "I suppose we mustn't ask Mr. Mirabel what he knows of Miss Jethro?" she said.

"My dear, what can you be thinking of? What right have we to question Mr. Mirabel about Miss Jethro?"

"It's so very unsatisfactory, papa. There must be some reason why Emily and Mr. Mirabel ought not to meet—or why should Miss Jethro have been so very earnest about it?"

"Miss Jethro doesn't intend us to know why, Cecilia. It will perhaps come out in time. Wait for time."

Left together, the girls discussed the course which Alban would probably take, on receiving Mr. Wyvil's invitation.

"He will only be too glad," Cecilia asserted, "to have the opportunity of seeing you again."

"I doubt whether he will care about seeing me again, among strangers," Emily replied. "And you forget that there are obstacles in his way. How is he to leave his class?"

"Quite easily! His class doesn't meet on the Saturday half-holiday. He can be here, if he starts early, in time for luncheon; and he can stay till Monday or Tuesday."

"Who is to take his place at the school?"

"Miss Ladd, to be sure—if you make a point of it. Write to her, as well as to Mr. Morris."

The letters being written—and the order having been given to prepare a room for the expected guest—Emily and Cecilia returned to the drawing-room. They found the elders of the party variously engaged—the men with newspapers, and the ladies with work. Entering the conservatory next, they discovered Cecilia's sister languishing among the flowers in an easy chair. Constitutional laziness, in some young ladies, assumes an invalid character, and presents the interesting spectacle of perpetual convalescence. The doctor declared that the baths at St. Moritz had cured Miss Julia. Miss Julia declined to agree with the doctor.

"Come into the garden with Emily and me," Cecilia said.

"Emily and you don't know what it is to be ill," Julia answered.

The two girls left her, and joined the young people who were amusing themselves in the garden. Francine had taken possession of Mirabel, and had condemned him to hard labor in swinging her. He made an attempt to get away when Emily and Cecilia approached, and was peremptorily recalled to his duty. "Higher!" cried Miss de Sor, in her hardest tones of authority. "I want to swing higher than anybody else!" Mirabel submitted with gentleman-like resignation, and was rewarded by tender encouragement expressed in a look.

"Do you see that?" Cecilia whispered. "He knows how rich she is—I wonder whether he will marry her."

Emily smiled. "I doubt it, while he is in this house," she said. "You are as rich as Francine—and don't forget that you have other attractions as well."

Cecilia shook her head. "Mr. Mirabel is very nice," she admitted; "but I wouldn't marry him. Would you?"

Emily secretly compared Alban with Mirabel. "Not for the world!" she answered.

The next day was the day of Mirabel's departure. His admirers among the ladies followed him out to the door, at which Mr. Wyvil's carriage was waiting. Francine threw a nosegay after the departing guest as he got in. "Mind you come back to us on Monday!" she said. Mirabel bowed and thanked her; but his last look was for Emily, standing apart from the others at the top of the steps. Francine said nothing; her lips closed convulsively—she turned suddenly pale.

CHAPTER XLI. SPEECHIFYING.

On the Monday, a plowboy from Vale Regis arrived at Monksmoor.

In respect of himself, he was a person beneath notice. In respect of his errand, he was sufficiently important to cast a gloom over the household. The faithless Mirabel had broken his engagement, and the plowboy was the herald of misfortune who brought his apology. To his great disappointment (he wrote) he was detained by the affairs of his parish. He could only trust to Mr. Wyvil's indulgence to excuse him, and to communicate his sincere sense of regret (on scented note paper) to the ladies.

Everybody believed in the affairs of the parish—with the exception of Francine. "Mr. Mirabel has made the best excuse he could think of for shortening his visit; and I don't wonder at it," she said, looking significantly at Emily.

Emily was playing with one of the dogs; exercising him in the tricks which he had learned. She balanced a morsel of sugar on his nose—and had no attention to spare for Francine.

116

Cecilia, as the mistress of the house, felt it her duty to interfere. "That is a strange remark to make," she answered. "Do you mean to say that we have driven Mr. Mirabel away from us?"

"I accuse nobody," Francine began with spiteful candor.

"Now she's going to accuse everybody!" Emily interposed, addressing herself facetiously to the dog.

"But when girls are bent on fascinating men, whether they like it or not," Francine proceeded, "men have only one alternative—they must keep out of the way." She looked again at Emily, more pointedly than ever.

Even gentle Cecilia resented this. "Whom do you refer to?" she said sharply.

"My dear!" Emily remonstrated, "need you ask?" She glanced at Francine as she spoke, and then gave the dog his signal. He tossed up the sugar, and caught it in his mouth. His audience applauded him—and so, for that time, the skirmish ended.

Among the letters of the next morning's delivery, arrived Alban's reply. Emily's anticipations proved to be correct. The drawing-master's duties would not permit him to leave Netherwoods; and he, like Mirabel, sent his apologies. His short letter to Emily contained no further allusion to Miss Jethro; it began and ended on the first page.

Had he been disappointed by the tone of reserve in which Emily had written to him, under Mr. Wyvil's advice? Or (as Cecilia suggested) had his detention at the school so bitterly disappointed him that he was too disheartened to write at any length? Emily made no attempt to arrive at a conclusion, either one way or the other. She seemed to be in depressed spirits; and she spoke superstitiously, for the first time in Cecilia's experience of her.

"I don't like this reappearance of Miss Jethro," she said. "If the mystery about that woman is ever cleared up, it will bring trouble and sorrow to me—and I believe, in his own secret heart, Alban Morris thinks so too."

"Write, and ask him," Cecilia suggested.

"He is so kind and so unwilling to distress me," Emily answered, "that he wouldn't acknowledge it, even if I am right."

In the middle of the week, the course of private life at Monksmoor suffered an interruption—due to the parliamentary position of the master of the house.

The insatiable appetite for making and hearing speeches, which represents one of the marked peculiarities of the English race (including their cousins in the United States), had seized on Mr. Wyvil's constituents. There was to be a political meeting at the market hall, in the neighboring town; and the member was expected to make an oration, passing in review contemporary events at home and abroad. "Pray don't think of accompanying me," the good man said to his guests. "The hall is badly ventilated, and the speeches, including my own, will not be worth hearing."

This humane warning was ungratefully disregarded. The gentlemen were all interested in "the objects of the meeting"; and the ladies were firm in the resolution not to be left at home by themselves. They dressed with a view to the large assembly of spectators before whom they were about to appear; and they outtalked the men on political subjects, all the way to the town.

The most delightful of surprises was in store for them, when they reached the market hall. Among the crowd of ordinary gentlemen, waiting under the portico until the proceedings began, appeared one person of distinction, whose title was "Reverend," and whose name was Mirabel.

Francine was the first to discover him. She darted up the steps and held out her hand.

"This is a pleasure!" she cried. "Have you come here to see—" she was about to say Me, but, observing the strangers round her, altered the word to Us. "Please give me your arm," she whispered, before her young friends had arrived within hearing. "I am so frightened in a crowd!"

She held fast by Mirabel, and kept a jealous watch on him. Was it only her fancy? or did she detect a new charm in his smile when he spoke to Emily?

Before it was possible to decide, the time for the meeting had arrived. Mr. Wyvil's friends were of course accommodated with seats on the platform. Francine, still insisting on her claim to Mirabel's arm, got a chair next to him. As she seated herself, she left him free for a moment. In that moment, the infatuated man took an empty chair on the other side of him, and placed it for Emily. He communicated to that hated rival the information which he ought to have reserved for Francine. "The committee insist," he said, "on my proposing one of the Resolutions. I promise not to bore you; mine shall be the shortest speech delivered at the meeting."

The proceedings began.

Among the earlier speakers not one was inspired by a feeling of mercy for the audience. The chairman reveled in words. The mover and seconder of the first Resolution (not having so much as the ghost of an idea to trouble either of them), poured out language in flowing and overflowing streams, like water from a perpetual spring. The heat exhaled by the crowded audience was already becoming insufferable. Cries of "Sit down!" assailed the orator of the moment. The chairman was obliged to interfere. A man at the back of the hall roared out, "Ventilation!" and broke a window with his stick. He was rewarded with three rounds of cheers; and was ironically invited to mount the platform and take the chair.

Under these embarrassing circumstances, Mirabel rose to speak.

He secured silence, at the outset, by a humorous allusion to the prolix speaker who had preceded him. "Look at the clock, gentlemen," he said; "and limit my speech to an interval of ten minutes." The applause which followed was heard, through the broken window, in the street. The boys among the mob outside intercepted the flow of air by climbing on each other's shoulders and looking in at the meeting, through the gaps left by the shattered glass. Having proposed his Resolution with discreet brevity of speech, Mirabel courted popularity on the plan adopted by the late Lord Palmerston in the House of Commons—he told stories, and made jokes, adapted to the intelligence of the dullest people who were listening to him. The charm of his voice and manner completed his success. Punctually at the tenth minute, he sat down amid cries of "Go on." Francine was the first to take his hand, and to express admiration mutely by pressing it. He returned the pressure—but he looked at the wrong lady—the lady on the other side.

Although she made no complaint, he instantly saw that Emily was overcome by the heat. Her lips were white, and her eyes were closing. "Let me take you out," he said, "or you will faint."

Francine started to her feet to follow them. The lower order of the audience, eager for amusement, put their own humorous construction on the young lady's action. They roared with laughter. "Let the parson and his sweetheart be," they called out; "two's company, miss, and three isn't." Mr. Wyvil interposed his authority and rebuked them. A lady seated behind Francine interfered to good purpose by giving her a chair, which placed her out of sight of the audience. Order was restored—and the proceedings were resumed.

On the conclusion of the meeting, Mirabel and Emily were found waiting for their friends at the door. Mr. Wyvil innocently added fuel to the fire that was burning in Francine. He insisted that Mirabel should return to Monksmoor, and offered him a seat in the carriage at Emily's side.

Later in the evening, when they all met at dinner, there appeared a change in Miss de Sor which surprised everybody but Mirabel. She was gay and good-humored, and especially amiable and attentive to Emily—who sat opposite to her at the table. "What did you and Mr. Mirabel talk about while you were away from us?" she asked innocently. "Politics?"

Emily readily adopted Francine's friendly tone. "Would you have talked politics, in my place?" she asked gayly.

"In your place, I should have had the most delightful of companions," Francine rejoined; "I wish I had been overcome by the heat too!"

Mirabel—attentively observing her—acknowledged the compliment by a bow, and left Emily to continue the conversation. In perfect good faith she owned to having led Mirabel to talk of himself. She had heard from Cecilia that his early life had been devoted to various occupations, and she was interested in knowing how circumstances had led him into devoting himself to the Church. Francine listened with the outward appearance of implicit belief, and with the inward conviction that Emily was deliberately deceiving her. When the little narrative was at an end, she was more agreeable than ever. She admired Emily's dress, and she rivaled Cecilia in enjoyment of the good things on the table; she entertained Mirabel with humorous anecdotes of the priests at St. Domingo, and was so interested in the manufacture of violins, ancient and modern, that Mr. Wyvil promised to show her his famous collection of instruments, after dinner. Her overflowing amiability included even poor Miss Darnaway and the absent brothers and sisters. She heard with flattering sympathy, how they had been ill and had got well again; what amusing tricks they played, what alarming accidents happened to them, and how remarkably clever they were— "including, I do assure you, dear Miss de Sor, the baby only ten months old." When the ladies rose to retire, Francine was, socially speaking, the heroine of the evening.

While the violins were in course of exhibition, Mirabel found an opportunity of speaking to Emily, unobserved.

"Have you said, or done, anything to offend Miss de Sor?" he asked.

"Nothing whatever!" Emily declared, startled by the question. "What makes you think I have offended her?"

"I have been trying to find a reason for the change in her," Mirabel answered—"especially the change toward yourself."

"Well?"

"Well—she means mischief."

"Mischief of what sort?"

"Of a sort which may expose her to discovery—unless she disarms suspicion at the outset. That is (as I believe) exactly what she has been doing this evening. I needn't warn you to be on your guard."

All the next day Emily was on the watch for events—and nothing happened. Not the slightest appearance of jealousy betrayed itself in Francine. She made no attempt to attract to herself the attentions of Mirabel; and she showed no hostility to Emily, either by word, look, or manner.

....

The day after, an event occurred at Netherwoods. Alban Morris received an anonymous letter, addressed to him in these terms:

"A certain young lady, in whom you are supposed to be interested, is forgetting you in your absence. If you are not mean enough to allow yourself to be supplanted by another man, join the party at Monksmoor before it is too late."

CHAPTER XLII. COOKING.

The day after the political meeting was a day of departures, at the pleasant country house. Miss Darnaway was recalled to the nursery at home. The old squire who did justice to Mr. Wyvil's port-wine went away next, having guests to entertain at his own house. A far more serious loss followed. The three dancing men had engagements which drew them to new spheres of activity in other drawing-rooms. They said, with the same dreary grace of manner, "Very sorry to go"; they drove to the railway, arrayed in the same perfect traveling suits of neutral tint; and they had but one difference of opinion among them—each firmly believed that he was smoking the best cigar to be got in London.

The morning after these departures would have been a dull morning indeed, but for the presence of Mirabel.

When breakfast was over, the invalid Miss Julia established herself on the sofa with a novel. Her father retired to the other end of the house, and profaned the art of music on music's most expressive instrument. Left with Emily, Cecilia, and Francine, Mirabel made one of his happy suggestions. "We are thrown on our own resources," he said. "Let us distinguish ourselves by inventing some entirely new amusement for the day. You young ladies shall sit in council—and I will be secretary." He turned to Cecilia. "The meeting waits to hear the mistress of the house."

Modest Cecilia appealed to her school friends for help; addressing herself in the first instance (by the secretary's advice) to Francine, as the eldest. They all noticed another change in this variable young person. She was silent and subdued; and she said wearily, "I don't care what we do—shall we go out riding?"

The unanswerable objection to riding as a form of amusement, was that it had been more than once tried already. Something clever and surprising was anticipated from Emily when it came to her turn. She, too, disappointed expectation. "Let us sit under the trees," was all that she could suggest, "and ask Mr. Mirabel to tell us a story."

Mirabel laid down his pen and took it on himself to reject this proposal. "Remember," he remonstrated, "that I have an interest in the diversions of the day. You can't expect me to be amused by my own story. I appeal to Miss Wyvil to invent a pleasure which will include the secretary."

Cecilia blushed and looked uneasy. "I think I have got an idea," she announced, after some hesitation. "May I propose that we all go to the keeper's lodge?" There her courage failed her, and she hesitated again.

Mirabel gravely registered the proposal, as far as it went. "What are we to do when we get to the keeper's lodge?" he inquired.

"We are to ask the keeper's wife," Cecilia proceeded, "to lend us her kitchen."

"To lend us her kitchen," Mirabel repeated.

"And what are we to do in the kitchen?"

Cecilia looked down at her pretty hands crossed on her lap, and answered softly, "Cook our own luncheon."

Here was an entirely new amusement, in the most attractive sense of the words! Here was charming Cecilia's interest in the pleasures of the table so happily inspired, that the grateful meeting offered its tribute of applause—even including Francine. The members of the council were young; their daring digestions contemplated without fear the prospect of eating their own amateur cookery. The one question that troubled them now was what they were to cook.

"I can make an omelet," Cecilia ventured to say.

"If there is any cold chicken to be had," Emily added, "I undertake to follow the omelet with a mayonnaise."

"There are clergymen in the Church of England who are even clever enough to fry potatoes," Mirabel announced—"and I am one of them. What shall we have next? A pudding? Miss de Sor, can you make a pudding?"

Francine exhibited another new side to her character—a diffident and humble side. "I am ashamed to say I don't know how to cook anything," she confessed; "you had better leave me out of it."

But Cecilia was now in her element. Her plan of operations was wide enough even to include Francine. "You shall wash the lettuce, my dear, and stone the olives for Emily's mayonnaise. Don't be discouraged! You shall have a companion; we will send to the rectory for Miss Plym—the very person to chop parsley and shallot for my omelet. Oh, Emily, what a morning we are going to have!" Her lovely blue eyes sparkled with joy; she gave Emily a kiss which Mirabel must have been more or less than man not to have coveted. "I declare," cried Cecilia, completely losing her head, "I'm so excited, I don't know what to do with myself!"

Emily's intimate knowledge of her friend applied the right remedy. "You don't know what to do with yourself?" she repeated. "Have you no sense of duty? Give the cook your orders."

Cecilia instantly recovered her presence of mind. She sat down at the writing-table, and made out a list of eatable productions in the animal and vegetable world, in which every other word was underlined two or three times over. Her serious face was a sight to see, when she rang for the cook, and the two held a privy council in a corner.

On the way to the keeper's lodge, the young mistress of the house headed a procession of servants carrying the raw materials. Francine followed, held in custody by Miss Plym—who took her responsibilities seriously, and clamored for instruction in the art of chopping parsley. Mirabel and Emily were together, far behind; they were the only two members of the company whose minds were not occupied in one way or another by the kitchen.

"This child's play of ours doesn't seem to interest you," Mirabel remarked.

"I am thinking," Emily answered, "of what you said to me about Francine."

"I can say something more," he rejoined. "When I noticed the change in her at dinner, I told you she meant mischief. There is another change to-day, which suggests to my mind that the mischief is done."

"And directed against me?" Emily asked.

Mirabel made no direct reply. It was impossible for him to remind her that she had, no matter how innocently, exposed herself to the jealous hatred of Francine. "Time will tell us, what we don't know now," he replied evasively.

"You seem to have faith in time, Mr. Mirabel."

"The greatest faith. Time is the inveterate enemy of deceit. Sooner or later, every hidden thing is a thing doomed to discovery."

"Without exception?"

"Yes," he answered positively, "without exception."

At that moment Francine stopped and looked back at them. Did she think that Emily and Mirabel had been talking together long enough? Miss Plym—with the parsley still on her mind—advanced to consult Emily's experience. The two walked on together, leaving Mirabel to overtake Francine. He saw, in her first look at him, the effort that it cost her to suppress those emotions which the pride of women is most deeply interested in concealing. Before a word had passed, he regretted that Emily had left them together.

"I wish I had your cheerful disposition," she began, abruptly. "I am out of spirits or out of temper—I don't know which; and I don't know why. Do you ever trouble yourself with thinking of the future?"

"As seldom as possible, Miss de Sor. In such a situation as mine, most people have prospects—I have none."

He spoke gravely, conscious of not feeling at ease on his side. If he had been the most modest man that ever lived, he must have seen in Francine's face that she loved him.

When they had first been presented to each other, she was still under the influence of the meanest instincts in her scheming and selfish nature. She had thought to herself, "With my money to help him, that man's celebrity would do the rest; the best society in England would be glad to receive Mirabel's wife." As the days passed, strong feeling had taken the place of those contemptible aspirations: Mirabel had unconsciously inspired the one passion which was powerful enough to master Francine—sensual passion. Wild hopes rioted in her. Measureless desires which she had never felt before, united themselves with capacities for wickedness, which had been the horrid growth of a few nights—capacities which suggested even viler attempts to rid herself of a supposed rivalry than slandering Emily by means of an anonymous letter. Without waiting for it to be offered, she took Mirabel's arm, and pressed it to her breast as they slowly walked on. The fear of discovery which had troubled her after she had sent her base letter to the post, vanished at that inspiriting moment. She bent her head near enough to him when he spoke to feel his breath on her face.

"There is a strange similarity," she said softly, "between your position and mine. Is there anything cheering in my prospects? I am far away from home—my father and mother wouldn't care if they never saw me again. People talk about my money! What is the use of money to such a lonely wretch as I am? Suppose I write to London, and ask the lawyer if I may give it all away to some deserving person? Why not to you?"

"My dear Miss de Sor—!"

"Is there anything wrong, Mr. Mirabel, in wishing that I could make you a prosperous man?"

"You must not even talk of such a thing!"

"How proud you are!" she said submissively.

"Oh, I can't bear to think of you in that miserable village—a position so unworthy of your talents and your claims! And you tell me I must not talk about it. Would you have said that to Emily, if she was as anxious as I am to see you in your right place in the world?"

"I should have answered her exactly as I have answered you."

"She will never embarrass you, Mr. Mirabel, by being as sincere as I am. Emily can keep her own secrets."

"Is she to blame for doing that?"

"It depends on your feeling for her."

"What feeling do you mean?"

"Suppose you heard she was engaged to be married?" Francine suggested.

Mirabel's manner—studiously cold and formal thus far—altered on a sudden. He looked with unconcealed anxiety at Francine. "Do you say that seriously?" he asked.

"I said 'suppose.' I don't exactly know that she is engaged."

"What do you know?"

"Oh, how interested you are in Emily! She is admired by some people. Are you one of them?"

Mirabel's experience of women warned him to try silence as a means of provoking her into speaking plainly. The experiment succeeded: Francine returned to the question that he had put to her, and abruptly answered it.

"You may believe me or not, as you like—I know of a man who is in love with her. He has had his opportunities; and he has made good use of them. Would you like to know who he is?"

"I should like to know anything which you may wish to tell me." He did his best to make the reply in a tone of commonplace politeness—and he might have succeeded in deceiving a man. The woman's quicker ear told her that he was angry. Francine took the full advantage of that change in her favor.

"I am afraid your good opinion of Emily will be shaken," she quietly resumed, "when I tell you that she has encouraged a man who is only drawing-master at a school. At the same time, a person in her circumstances—I mean she has no money—ought not to be very hard to please. Of course she has never spoken to you of Mr. Alban Morris?"

"Not that I remember."

Only four words—but they satisfied Francine.

The one thing wanting to complete the obstacle which she had now placed in Emily's way, was that Alban Morris should enter on the scene. He might hesitate; but, if he was really fond of Emily, the anonymous letter would sooner or later bring him to Monksmoor. In the meantime, her object was gained. She dropped Mirabel's arm.

122

"Here is the lodge," she said gayly—"I declare Cecilia has got an apron on already! Come, and cook."

CHAPTER XLIII. SOUNDING.

Mirabel left Francine to enter the lodge by herself. His mind was disturbed: he felt the importance of gaining time for reflection before he and Emily met again.

The keeper's garden was at the back of the lodge. Passing through the wicket-gate, he found a little summer-house at a turn in the path. Nobody was there: he went in and sat down.

At intervals, he had even yet encouraged himself to underrate the true importance of the feeling which Emily had awakened in him. There was an end to all self-deception now. After what Francine had said to him, this shallow and frivolous man no longer resisted the all-absorbing influence of love. He shrank under the one terrible question that forced itself on his mind:—Had that jealous girl spoken the truth?

In what process of investigation could he trust, to set this anxiety at rest? To apply openly to Emily would be to take a liberty, which Emily was the last person in the world to permit. In his recent intercourse with her he had felt more strongly than ever the importance of speaking with reserve. He had been scrupulously careful to take no unfair advantage of his opportunity, when he had removed her from the meeting, and when they had walked together, with hardly a creature to observe them, in the lonely outskirts of the town. Emily's gaiety and good humor had not led him astray: he knew that these were bad signs, viewed in the interests of love. His one hope of touching her deeper sympathies was to wait for the help that might yet come from time and chance. With a bitter sigh, he resigned himself to the necessity of being as agreeable and amusing as ever: it was just possible that he might lure her into alluding to Alban Morris, if he began innocently by making her laugh.

As he rose to return to the lodge, the keeper's little terrier, prowling about the garden, looked into the summer-house. Seeing a stranger, the dog showed his teeth and growled. Mirabel shrank back against the wall behind him, trembling in every limb. His eyes stared in terror as the dog came nearer: barking in high triumph over the discovery of a frightened man whom he could bully. Mirabel called out for help. A laborer at work in the garden ran to the place—and stopped with a broad grin of amusement at seeing a grown man terrified by a barking dog. "Well," he said to himself, after Mirabel had passed out under protection, "there goes a coward if ever there was one yet!"

Mirabel waited a minute behind the lodge to recover himself. He had been so completely unnerved that his hair was wet with perspiration. While he used his handkerchief, he shuddered at other recollections than the recollection of the dog. "After that night at the inn," he thought, "the least thing frightens me!"

He was received by the young ladies with cries of derisive welcome. "Oh, for shame! for shame! here are the potatoes already cut, and nobody to fry them!"

Mirabel assumed the mask of cheerfulness—with the desperate resolution of an actor, amusing his audience at a time of domestic distress. He astonished the keeper's wife by showing that he really knew how to use her frying-pan. Cecilia's omelet was tough—but the young ladies ate it. Emily's mayonnaise sauce was almost as liquid as water—they swallowed it nevertheless by the help of spoons. The potatoes followed, crisp and dry and delicious—and Mirabel became more popular than ever. "He is the only one of us," Cecilia sadly acknowledged, "who knows how to cook."

When they all left the lodge for a stroll in the park, Francine attached herself to Cecilia and Miss Plym. She resigned Mirabel to Emily—in the happy belief that she had paved the way for a misunderstanding between them.

The merriment at the luncheon table had revived Emily's good spirits. She had a light-hearted remembrance of the failure of her sauce. Mirabel saw her smiling to herself. "May I ask what amuses you?" he said.

"I was thinking of the debt of gratitude that we owe to Mr. Wyvil," she replied. "If he had not persuaded you to return to Monksmoor, we should never have seen the famous Mr. Mirabel with a frying pan in his hand, and never have tasted the only good dish at our luncheon."

Mirabel tried vainly to adopt his companion's easy tone. Now that he was alone with her, the doubts that Francine had aroused shook the prudent resolution at which he had arrived in the garden. He ran the risk, and told Emily plainly why he had returned to Mr. Wyvil's house.

"Although I am sensible of our host's kindness," he answered, "I should have gone back to my parsonage—but for You."

She declined to understand him seriously. "Then the affairs of your parish are neglected—and I am to blame!" she said.

"Am I the first man who has neglected his duties for your sake?" he asked. "I wonder whether the masters at school had the heart to report you when you neglected your lessons?"

She thought of Alban—and betrayed herself by a heightened color. The moment after, she changed the subject. Mirabel could no longer resist the conclusion that Francine had told him the truth.

"When do you leave us," she inquired.

"To-morrow is Saturday—I must go back as usual."

"And how will your deserted parish receive you?"

He made a desperate effort to be as amusing as usual.

"I am sure of preserving my popularity," he said, "while I have a cask in the cellar, and a few spare sixpences in my pocket. The public spirit of my parishioners asks for nothing but money and beer. Before I went to that wearisome meeting, I told my housekeeper that I was going to make a speech about reform. She didn't know what I meant. I explained that reform might increase the number of British citizens who had the right of voting at elections for parliament. She brightened up directly. 'Ah,' she said, 'I've heard my husband talk about elections. The more there are of them (he says) the more money he'll get for his vote. I'm all for reform.' On my way out of the house, I tried the man who works in my garden on the same subject. He didn't look at the matter from the housekeeper's sanguine point of view. 'I don't deny that parliament once gave me a good dinner for nothing at the public-house,' he admitted. 'But that was years ago—and (you'll excuse me, sir) I hear nothing of another dinner to come. It's a matter of opinion, of course. I don't myself believe in reform.' There are specimens of the state of public spirit in our village!" He paused. Emily was listening—but he had not succeeded in choosing a subject that amused her. He tried a topic more nearly connected with his own interests; the topic of the future.

"Our good friend has asked me to prolong my visit, after Sunday's duties are over," he said. "I hope I shall find you here, next week?"

"Will the affairs of your parish allow you to come back?" Emily asked mischievously.

"The affairs of my parish—if you force me to confess it—were only an excuse."

"An excuse for what?"

"An excuse for keeping away from Monksmoor—in the interests of my own tranquillity. The experiment has failed. While you are here, I can't keep away."

She still declined to understand him seriously. "Must I tell you in plain words that flattery is thrown away on me?" she said.

"Flattery is not offered to you," he answered gravely. "I beg your pardon for having led to the mistake by talking of myself." Having appealed to her indulgence by that act of submission, he ventured on another distant allusion to the man whom he hated and feared. "Shall I meet any friends of yours," he resumed, "when I return on Monday?"

"What do you mean?"

"I only meant to ask if Mr. Wyvil expects any new guests?"

As he put the question, Cecilia's voice was heard behind them, calling to Emily. They both turned round. Mr. Wyvil had joined his daughter and her two friends. He advanced to meet Emily.

"I have some news for you that you little expect," he said. "A telegram has just arrived from Netherwoods. Mr. Alban Morris has got leave of absence, and is coming here to-morrow."

CHAPTER XLIV. COMPETING.

Time at Monksmoor had advanced to the half hour before dinner, on Saturday evening.

Cecilia and Francine, Mr. Wyvil and Mirabel, were loitering in the conservatory. In the drawing-room, Emily had been considerately left alone with Alban. He had missed the early train from Netherwoods; but he had arrived in time to dress for dinner, and to offer the necessary explanations.

If it had been possible for Alban to allude to the anonymous letter, he might have owned that his first impulse had led him to destroy it, and to assert his confidence in Emily by refusing Mr. Wyvil's invitation. But try as he might to forget them, the base words that he had read remained in his memory. Irritating him at the outset, they had ended in rousing his jealousy. Under that delusive influence, he persuaded himself that he had acted, in the first instance, without due consideration. It was surely his interest—it might even be his duty—to go to Mr. Wyvil's house, and judge for himself. After some last wretched moments of hesitation, he had decided on effecting a compromise with his own better sense, by consulting Miss Ladd. That excellent lady did exactly what he had expected her to do. She made arrangements which granted him leave of absence, from the Saturday to the Tuesday following. The excuse which had served him, in telegraphing to Mr. Wyvil, must now be repeated, in accounting for his unexpected appearance to Emily. "I found a person to take charge of my class," he said; "and I gladly availed myself of the opportunity of seeing you again."

After observing him attentively, while he was speaking to her, Emily owned, with her customary frankness, that she had noticed something in his manner which left her not quite at her ease.

"I wonder," she said, "if there is any foundation for a doubt that has troubled me?" To his unutterable relief, she at once explained what the doubt was. "I am afraid I offended you, in replying to your letter about Miss Jethro."

In this case, Alban could enjoy the luxury of speaking unreservedly. He confessed that Emily's letter had disappointed him.

"I expected you to answer me with less reserve," he replied; "and I began to think I had acted rashly in writing to you at all. When there is a better opportunity, I may have a word to say—" He was apparently interrupted by something that he saw in the conservatory. Looking that way, Emily perceived that Mirabel was the object which had attracted Alban's attention. The vile anonymous letter was in his mind again. Without a preliminary word to prepare Emily, he suddenly changed the subject. "How do you like the clergyman?" he asked.

"Very much indeed," she replied, without the slightest embarrassment. "Mr. Mirabel is clever and agreeable—and not at all spoiled by his success. I am sure," she said innocently, "you will like him too."

Alban's face answered her unmistakably in the negative sense—but Emily's attention was drawn the other way by Francine. She joined them at the moment, on the lookout for any signs of an encouraging result which her treachery might already have produced. Alban had been inclined to suspect her when he had received the letter. He rose and bowed as she approached. Something—he was unable to realize what it was—told him, in the moment when they looked at each other, that his suspicion had hit the mark.

In the conservatory the ever-amiable Mirabel had left his friends for a while in search of flowers for Cecilia. She turned to her father when they were alone, and asked him which of the gentlemen was to take her in to dinner—Mr. Mirabel or Mr. Morris?

"Mr. Morris, of course," he answered. "He is the new guest—and he turns out to be more than the equal, socially-speaking, of our other friend. When I showed him his room, I asked if he was related to a man who bore the same name—a fellow student of mine, years and years ago, at college. He is my friend's younger son; one of a ruined family—but persons of high distinction in their day."

Mirabel returned with the flowers, just as dinner was announced.

"You are to take Emily to-day," Cecilia said to him, leading the way out of the conservatory. As they entered the drawing-room, Alban was just offering his arm to Emily. "Papa gives you to me, Mr. Morris," Cecilia explained pleasantly. Alban hesitated, apparently not understanding the allusion. Mirabel interfered with his best grace: "Mr. Wyvil offers you the honor of taking his daughter to the dining-room." Alban's face darkened ominously, as the elegant little clergyman gave his arm to Emily, and followed Mr. Wyvil and Francine out of the room. Cecilia looked at her silent and surly companion, and almost envied her lazy sister, dining—under cover of a convenient headache—in her own room.

Having already made up his mind that Alban Morris required careful handling, Mirabel waited a little before he led the conversation as usual. Between the soup and the fish, he made an interesting confession, addressed to Emily in the strictest confidence.

"I have taken a fancy to your friend Mr. Morris," he said. "First impressions, in my case, decide everything; I like people or dislike them on impulse. That man appeals to my sympathies. Is he a good talker?"

"I should say Yes," Emily answered prettily, "if you were not present."

Mirabel was not to be beaten, even by a woman, in the art of paying compliments. He looked admiringly at Alban (sitting opposite to him), and said: "Let us listen."

This flattering suggestion not only pleased Emily—it artfully served Mirabel's purpose. That is to say, it secured him an opportunity for observation of what was going on at the other side of the table.

Alban's instincts as a gentleman had led him to control his irritation and to regret that he had suffered it to appear. Anxious to please, he presented himself at his best. Gentle Cecilia forgave and forgot the angry look which had startled her. Mr. Wyvil was delighted with the son of his old friend. Emily felt secretly proud of the good opinions which her admirer was gathering; and Francine saw with pleasure that he was asserting his claim to Emily's preference, in the way of all others which would be most likely to discourage his rival. These various impressions—produced while Alban's enemy was ominously silent—began to suffer an imperceptible change, from the moment when Mirabel decided that his time had come to take the lead. A remark made by Alban offered him the chance for which he had been on the watch. He agreed with the remark; he enlarged on the remark; he was brilliant and familiar, and instructive and amusing—and still it was all due to the remark. Alban's temper was once more severely tried. Mirabel's mischievous object had not escaped his penetration. He did his best to put obstacles in the adversary's way—and was baffled, time after time, with the readiest ingenuity. If he interrupted—the sweet-tempered clergyman submitted, and went on. If he differed—modest Mr. Mirabel said, in the most amiable manner, "I daresay I am wrong," and handled the topic from his opponent's point of view. Never had such a perfect Christian sat before at Mr. Wyvil's table: not a hard word,

126

not an impatient look, escaped him. The longer Alban resisted, the more surely he lost ground in the general estimation. Cecilia was disappointed; Emily was grieved; Mr. Wyvil's favorable opinion began to waver; Francine was disgusted. When dinner was over, and the carriage was waiting to take the shepherd back to his flock by moonlight, Mirabel's triumph was complete. He had made Alban the innocent means of publicly exhibiting his perfect temper and perfect politeness, under their best and brightest aspect.

So that day ended. Sunday promised to pass quietly, in the absence of Mirabel. The morning came—and it seemed doubtful whether the promise would be fulfilled.

Francine had passed an uneasy night. No such encouraging result as she had anticipated had hitherto followed the appearance of Alban Morris at Monksmoor. He had clumsily allowed Mirabel to improve his position—while he had himself lost ground—in Emily's estimation. If this first disastrous consequence of the meeting between the two men was permitted to repeat itself on future occasions, Emily and Mirabel would be brought more closely together, and Alban himself would be the unhappy cause of it. Francine rose, on the Sunday morning, before the table was laid for breakfast—resolved to try the effect of a timely word of advice.

Her bedroom was situated in the front of the house. The man she was looking for presently passed within her range of view from the window, on his way to take a morning walk in the park. She followed him immediately.

"Good-morning, Mr. Morris."

He raised his hat and bowed—without speaking, and without looking at her.

"We resemble each other in one particular," she proceeded, graciously; "we both like to breathe the fresh air before breakfast."

He said exactly what common politeness obliged him to say, and no more—he said, "Yes." Some girls might have been discouraged. Francine went on.

"It is no fault of mine, Mr. Morris, that we have not been better friends. For some reason, into which I don't presume to inquire, you seem to distrust me. I really don't know what I have done to deserve it."

"Are you sure of that?" he asked—eying her suddenly and searchingly as he spoke.

Her hard face settled into a rigid look; her eyes met his eyes with a stony defiant stare. Now, for the first time, she knew that he suspected her of having written the anonymous letter. Every evil quality in her nature steadily defied him. A hardened old woman could not have sustained the shock of discovery with a more devilish composure than this girl displayed.

"Perhaps you will explain yourself," she said.

"I have explained myself," he answered.

"Then I must be content," she rejoined, "to remain in the dark. I had intended, out of my regard for Emily, to suggest that you might—with advantage to yourself, and to interests that are very dear to you—be more careful in your behavior to Mr. Mirabel. Are you disposed to listen to me?"

"Do you wish me to answer that question plainly, Miss de Sor?"

"I insist on your answering it plainly."

"Then I am not disposed to listen to you."

"May I know why? or am I to be left in the dark again?"

"You are to be left, if you please, to your own ingenuity."

Francine looked at him, with a malignant smile. "One of these days, Mr. Morris—I will deserve your confidence in my ingenuity." She said it, and went back to the house.

This was the only element of disturbance that troubled the perfect tranquillity of the day. What Francine had proposed to do, with the one idea of making Alban serve her purpose, was accomplished a few hours later by Emily's influence for good over the man who loved her.

They passed the afternoon together uninterruptedly in the distant solitudes of the park. In the course of conversation Emily found an opportunity of discreetly alluding to Mirabel.

"You mustn't be jealous of our clever little friend," she said; "I like him, and admire him; but—"

"But you don't love him?"

She smiled at the eager way in which Alban put the question.

"There is no fear of that," she answered brightly.

"Not even if you discovered that he loves you?"

"Not even then. Are you content at last? Promise me not to be rude to Mr. Mirabel again."

"For his sake?"

"No—for my sake. I don't like to see you place yourself at a disadvantage toward another man; I don't like you to disappoint me."

The happiness of hearing her say those words transfigured him—the manly beauty of his earlier and happier years seemed to have returned to Alban. He took her hand—he was too agitated to speak.

"You are forgetting Mr. Mirabel," she reminded him gently.

"I will be all that is civil and kind to Mr. Mirabel; I will like him and admire him as you do. Oh, Emily, are you a little, only a very little, fond of me?"

"I don't quite know."

"May I try to find out?"

"How?" she asked.

Her fair cheek was very near to him. The softly-rising color on it said, Answer me here—and he answered.

CHAPTER XLV. MISCHIEF—MAKING.

On Monday, Mirabel made his appearance—and the demon of discord returned with him.

Alban had employed the earlier part of the day in making a sketch in the park—intended as a little present for Emily. Presenting himself in the drawing-room, when his work was completed, he found Cecilia and Francine alone. He asked where Emily was.

The question had been addressed to Cecilia. Francine answered it.

"Emily mustn't be disturbed," she said.

"Why not?"

"She is with Mr. Mirabel in the rose garden. I saw them talking together—evidently feeling the deepest interest in what they were saying to each other. Don't interrupt them—you will only be in the way."

Cecilia at once protested against this last assertion. "She is trying to make mischief, Mr. Morris—don't believe her. I am sure they will be glad to see you, if you join them in the garden."

Francine rose, and left the room. She turned, and looked at Alban as she opened the door. "Try it," she said—"and you will find I am right."

"Francine sometimes talks in a very ill-natured way," Cecilia gently remarked. "Do you think she means it, Mr. Morris?'

"I had better not offer an opinion," Alban replied.

"Why?"

"I can't speak impartially; I dislike Miss de Sor."

There was a pause. Alban's sense of self-respect forbade him to try the experiment which Francine had maliciously suggested. His thoughts—less easy to restrain—wandered in the direction of the garden. The attempt to make him jealous had failed; but he was conscious, at the same time, that Emily had disappointed him. After what they had said to each other in the park, she ought to have remembered that women are at the mercy of appearances. If

Mirabel had something of importance to say to her, she might have avoided exposing herself to Francine's spiteful misconstruction: it would have been easy to arrange with Cecilia that a third person should be present at the interview.

While he was absorbed in these reflections, Cecilia—embarrassed by the silence—was trying to find a topic of conversation. Alban roughly pushed his sketch-book away from him, on the table. Was he displeased with Emily? The same question had occurred to Cecilia at the time of the correspondence, on the subject of Miss Jethro. To recall those letters led her, by natural sequence, to another effort of memory. She was reminded of the person who had been the cause of the correspondence: her interest was revived in the mystery of Miss Jethro.

"Has Emily told you that I have seen your letter?" she asked.

He roused himself with a start. "I beg your pardon. What letter are you thinking of?"

"I was thinking of the letter which mentions Miss Jethro's strange visit. Emily was so puzzled and so surprised that she showed it to me—and we both consulted my father. Have you spoken to Emily about Miss Jethro?"

"I have tried—but she seemed to be unwilling to pursue the subject."

"Have you made any discoveries since you wrote to Emily?"

"No. The mystery is as impenetrable as ever."

As he replied in those terms, Mirabel entered the conservatory from the garden, evidently on his way to the drawing-room.

To see the man, whose introduction to Emily it had been Miss Jethro's mysterious object to prevent—at the very moment when he had been speaking of Miss Jethro herself—was, not only a temptation of curiosity, but a direct incentive (in Emily's own interests) to make an effort at discovery. Alban pursued the conversation with Cecilia, in a tone which was loud enough to be heard in the conservatory.

"The one chance of getting any information that I can see," he proceeded, "is to speak to Mr. Mirabel."

"I shall be only too glad, if I can be of any service to Miss Wyvil and Mr. Morris."

With those obliging words, Mirabel made a dramatic entry, and looked at Cecilia with his irresistible smile. Startled by his sudden appearance, she unconsciously assisted Alban's design. Her silence gave him the opportunity of speaking in her place.

"We were talking," he said quietly to Mirabel, "of a lady with whom you are acquainted."

"Indeed! May I ask the lady's name?"

"Miss Jethro."

Mirabel sustained the shock with extraordinary self-possession—so far as any betrayal by sudden movement was concerned. But his color told the truth: it faded to paleness—it revealed, even to Cecilia's eyes, a man overpowered by fright.

Alban offered him a chair. He refused to take it by a gesture. Alban tried an apology next. "I am afraid I have ignorantly revived some painful associations. Pray excuse me."

The apology roused Mirabel: he felt the necessity of offering some explanation. In timid animals, the one defensive capacity which is always ready for action is cunning. Mirabel was too wily to dispute the inference—the inevitable inference—which any one must have drawn, after seeing the effect on him that the name of Miss Jethro had produced. He admitted that "painful associations" had been revived, and deplored the "nervous sensibility" which had permitted it to be seen.

"No blame can possibly attach to you, my dear sir," he continued, in his most amiable manner. "Will it be indiscreet, on my part, if I ask how you first became acquainted with Miss Jethro?"

"I first became acquainted with her at Miss Ladd's school," Alban answered. "She was, for a short time only, one of the teachers; and she left her situation rather suddenly." He paused—but Mirabel made no remark. "After an interval of a few months," he resumed, "I saw Miss Jethro again. She called on me at my lodgings, near Netherwoods."

"Merely to renew your former acquaintance?"

Mirabel made that inquiry with an eager anxiety for the reply which he was quite unable to conceal. Had he any reason to dread what Miss Jethro might have it in her power to say of him to another person? Alban was in no way pledged to secrecy, and he was determined to leave no means untried of throwing light on Miss Jethro's mysterious warning. He repeated the plain narrative of the interview, which he had communicated by letter to Emily. Mirabel listened without making any remark.

"After what I have told you, can you give me no explanation?" Alban asked.

"I am quite unable, Mr. Morris, to help you."

Was he lying? or speaking, the truth? The impression produced on Alban was that he had spoken the truth.

Women are never so ready as men to resign themselves to the disappointment of their hopes. Cecilia, silently listening up to this time, now ventured to speak—animated by her sisterly interest in Emily.

"Can you not tell us," she said to Mirabel, "why Miss Jethro tried to prevent Emily Brown from meeting you here?"

"I know no more of her motive than you do," Mirabel replied.

Alban interposed. "Miss Jethro left me," he said, "with the intention—quite openly expressed—of trying to prevent you from accepting Mr. Wyvil's invitation. Did she make the attempt?"

Mirabel admitted that she had made the attempt. "But," he added, "without mentioning Miss Emily's name. I was asked to postpone my visit, as a favor to herself, because she had her own reasons for wishing it. I had my reasons" (he bowed with gallantry to Cecilia) "for being eager to have the honor of knowing Mr. Wyvil and his daughter; and I refused."

Once more, the doubt arose: was he lying? or speaking the truth? And, once more, Alban could not resist the conclusion that he was speaking the truth.

"There is one thing I should like to know," Mirabel continued, after some hesitation. "Has Miss Emily been informed of this strange affair?"

"Certainly!"

Mirabel seemed to be disposed to continue his inquiries—and suddenly changed his mind. Was he beginning to doubt if Alban had spoken without concealment, in describing Miss Jethro's visit? Was he still afraid of what Miss Jethro might have said of him? In any case, he changed the subject, and made an excuse for leaving the room.

"I am forgetting my errand," he said to Alban. "Miss Emily was anxious to know if you had finished your sketch. I must tell her that you have returned."

He bowed and withdrew.

Alban rose to follow him—and checked himself.

"No," he thought, "I trust Emily!" He sat down again by Cecilia's side.

Mirabel had indeed returned to the rose garden. He found Emily employed as he had left her, in making a crown of roses, to be worn by Cecilia in the evening. But, in one other respect, there was a change. Francine was present.

"Excuse me for sending you on a needless errand," Emily said to Mirabel; "Miss de Sor tells me Mr. Morris has finished his sketch. She left him in the drawing-room—why didn't you bring him here?"

"He was talking with Miss Wyvil."

Mirabel answered absently—with his eyes on Francine. He gave her one of those significant looks, which says to a third person, "Why are you here?" Francine's jealousy declined to understand him. He tried a broader hint, in words.

"Are you going to walk in the garden?" he said.

Francine was impenetrable. "No," she answered, "I am going to stay here with Emily."

Mirabel had no choice but to yield. Imperative anxieties forced him to say, in Francine's presence, what he had hoped to say to Emily privately.

130

"When I joined Miss Wyvil and Mr. Morris," he began, "what do you think they were doing? They were talking of—Miss Jethro."

Emily dropped the rose-crown on her lap. It was easy to see that she had been disagreeably surprised.

"Mr. Morris has told me the curious story of Miss Jethro's visit," Mirabel continued; "but I am in some doubt whether he has spoken to me without reserve. Perhaps he expressed himself more freely when he spoke to you. Miss Jethro may have said something to him which tended to lower me in your estimation?"

"Certainly not, Mr. Mirabel—so far as I know. If I had heard anything of the kind, I should have thought it my duty to tell you. Will it relieve your anxiety, if I go at once to Mr. Morris, and ask him plainly whether he has concealed anything from you or from me?"

Mirabel gratefully kissed her hand. "Your kindness overpowers me," he said—speaking, for once, with true emotion.

Emily immediately returned to the house. As soon as she was out of sight, Francine approached Mirabel, trembling with suppressed rage.

CHAPTER XLVI. PRETENDING.

Miss de Sor began cautiously with an apology. "Excuse me, Mr. Mirabel, for reminding you of my presence."

Mr. Mirabel made no reply.

"I beg to say," Francine proceeded, "that I didn't intentionally see you kiss Emily's hand."

Mirabel stood, looking at the roses which Emily had left on her chair, as completely absorbed in his own thoughts as if he had been alone in the garden.

"Am I not even worth notice?" Francine asked. "Ah, I know to whom I am indebted for your neglect!" She took him familiarly by the arm, and burst into a harsh laugh. "Tell me now, in confidence—do you think Emily is fond of you?"

The impression left by Emily's kindness was still fresh in Mirabel's memory: he was in no humor to submit to the jealous resentment of a woman whom he regarded with perfect indifference. Through the varnish of politeness which overlaid his manner, there rose to the surface the underlying insolence, hidden, on all ordinary occasions, from all human eyes. He answered Francine—mercilessly answered her—at last.

"It is the dearest hope of my life that she may be fond of me," he said.

Francine dropped his arm "And fortune favors your hopes," she added, with an ironical assumption of interest in Mirabel's prospects. "When Mr. Morris leaves us to-morrow, he removes the only obstacle you have to fear. Am I right?"

"No; you are wrong."

"In what way, if you please?"

"In this way. I don't regard Mr. Morris as an obstacle. Emily is too delicate and too kind to hurt his feelings—she is not in love with him. There is no absorbing interest in her mind to divert her thoughts from me. She is idle and happy; she thoroughly enjoys her visit to this house, and I am associated with her enjoyment. There is my chance—!"

He suddenly stopped. Listening to him thus far, unnaturally calm and cold, Francine now showed that she felt the lash of his contempt. A hideous smile passed slowly over her white face. It threatened the vengeance which knows no fear, no pity, no remorse—the vengeance of a jealous woman. Hysterical anger, furious language, Mirabel was prepared for. The smile frightened him.

"Well?" she said scornfully, "why don't you go on?"

A bolder man might still have maintained the audacious position which he had assumed. Mirabel's faint heart shrank from it. He was eager to shelter himself under the first excuse that he could find. His ingenuity, paralyzed by his fears, was unable to invent anything new. He feebly availed himself of the commonplace trick of evasion which he had read of in novels, and seen in action on the stage.

"Is it possible," he asked, with an overacted assumption of surprise, "that you think I am in earnest?"

In the case of any other person, Francine would have instantly seen through that flimsy pretense. But the love which accepts the meanest crumbs of comfort that can be thrown to it—which fawns and grovels and deliberately deceives itself, in its own intensely selfish interests—was the love that burned in Francine's breast. The wretched girl believed Mirabel with such an ecstatic sense of belief that she trembled in every limb, and dropped into the nearest chair.

"I was in earnest," she said faintly. "Didn't you see it?"

He was perfectly shameless; he denied that he had seen it, in the most positive manner. "Upon my honor, I thought you were mystifying me, and I humored the joke."

She sighed, and looking at him with an expression of tender reproach. "I wonder whether I can believe you," she said softly.

"Indeed you may believe me!" he assured her.

She hesitated—for the pleasure of hesitating. "I don't know. Emily is very much admired by some men. Why not by you?"

"For the best of reasons," he answered "She is poor, and I am poor. Those are facts which speak for themselves."

"Yes—but Emily is bent on attracting you. She would marry you to-morrow, if you asked her. Don't attempt to deny it! Besides, you kissed her hand."

"Oh, Miss de Sor!"

"Don't call me 'Miss de Sor'! Call me Francine. I want to know why you kissed her hand."

He humored her with inexhaustible servility. "Allow me to kiss your hand, Francine!—and let me explain that kissing a lady's hand is only a form of thanking her for her kindness. You must own that Emily—"

She interrupted him for the third time. "Emily?" she repeated. "Are you as familiar as that already? Does she call you 'Miles,' when you are by yourselves? Is there any effort at fascination which this charming creature has left untried? She told you no doubt what a lonely life she leads in her poor little home?"

Even Mirabel felt that he must not permit this to pass.

"She has said nothing to me about herself," he answered. "What I know of her, I know from Mr. Wyvil."

"Oh, indeed! You asked Mr. Wyvil about her family, of course? What did he say?"

"He said she lost her mother when she was a child—and he told me her father had died suddenly, a few years since, of heart complaint."

"Well, and what else?—Never mind now! Here is somebody coming."

The person was only one of the servants. Mirabel felt grateful to the man for interrupting them. Animated by sentiments of a precisely opposite nature, Francine spoke to him sharply.

"What do you want here?"

"A message, miss."

"From whom?"

"From Miss Brown."

"For me?"

"No, miss." He turned to Mirabel. "Miss Brown wishes to speak to you, sir, if you are not engaged."

Francine controlled herself until the man was out of hearing.

"Upon my word, this is too shameless!" she declared indignantly. "Emily can't leave you with me for five minutes, without wanting to see you again. If you go to her after all that you have said to me," she cried, threatening Mirabel with her outstretched hand, "you are the meanest of men!"

He was the meanest of men—he carried out his cowardly submission to the last extremity. "Only say what you wish me to do," he replied.

Even Francine expected some little resistance from a creature bearing the outward appearance of a man. "Oh, do you really mean it?" she asked "I want you to disappoint Emily. Will you stay here, and let me make your excuses?"

"I will do anything to please you."

Francine gave him a farewell look. Her admiration made a desperate effort to express itself appropriately in words. "You are not a man," she said, "you are an angel!"

Left by himself, Mirabel sat down to rest. He reviewed his own conduct with perfect complacency. "Not one man in a hundred could have managed that she-devil as I have done," he thought. "How shall I explain matters to Emily?"

Considering this question, he looked by chance at the unfinished crown of roses. "The very thing to help me!" he said—and took out his pocketbook, and wrote these lines on a blank page: "I have had a scene of jealousy with Miss de Sor, which is beyond all description. To spare you a similar infliction, I have done violence to my own feelings. Instead of instantly obeying the message which you have so kindly sent to me, I remain here for a little while—entirely for your sake."

Having torn out the page, and twisted it up among the roses, so that only a corner of the paper appeared in view, Mirabel called to a lad who was at work in the garden, and gave him his directions, accompanied by a shilling. "Take those flowers to the servants' hall, and tell one of the maids to put them in Miss Brown's room. Stop! Which is the way to the fruit garden?"

The lad gave the necessary directions. Mirabel walked away slowly, with his hands in his pockets. His nerves had been shaken; he thought a little fruit might refresh him.

CHAPTER XLVII. DEBATING.

In the meanwhile Emily had been true to her promise to relieve Mirabel's anxieties, on the subject of Miss Jethro. Entering the drawing-room in search of Alban, she found him talking with Cecilia, and heard her own name mentioned as she opened the door.

"Here she is at last!" Cecilia exclaimed. "What in the world has kept you all this time in the rose garden?"

"Has Mr. Mirabel been more interesting than usual?" Alban asked gayly. Whatever sense of annoyance he might have felt in Emily's absence, was forgotten the moment she appeared; all traces of trouble in his face vanished when they looked at each other.

"You shall judge for yourself," Emily replied with a smile. "Mr. Mirabel has been speaking to me of a relative who is very dear to him—his sister."

Cecilia was surprised. "Why has he never spoken to us of his sister?" she asked.

"It's a sad subject to speak of, my dear. His sister lives a life of suffering—she has been for years a prisoner in her room. He writes to her constantly. His letters from Monksmoor have interested her, poor soul. It seems he said something about me—and she has sent a kind message, inviting me to visit her one of these days. Do you understand it now, Cecilia?"

"Of course I do! Tell me—is Mr. Mirabel's sister older or younger than he is?"

"Older."

"Is she married?"

133

"She is a widow."

"Does she live with her brother?" Alban asked.

"Oh, no! She has her own house—far away in Northumberland."

"Is she near Sir Jervis Redwood?"

"I fancy not. Her house is on the coast."

"Any children?" Cecilia inquired.

"No; she is quite alone. Now, Cecilia, I have told you all I know—and I have something to say to Mr. Morris. No, you needn't leave us; it's a subject in which you are interested. A subject," she repeated, turning to Alban, "which you may have noticed is not very agreeable to me."

"Miss Jethro?" Alban guessed.

"Yes; Miss Jethro."

Cecilia's curiosity instantly asserted itself.

"We have tried to get Mr. Mirabel to enlighten us, and tried in vain," she said. "You are a favorite. Have you succeeded?"

"I have made no attempt to succeed," Emily replied. "My only object is to relieve Mr. Mirabel's anxiety, if I can—with your help, Mr. Morris."

"In what way can I help you?"

"You mustn't be angry."

"Do I look angry?"

"You look serious. It is a very simple thing. Mr. Mirabel is afraid that Miss Jethro may have said something disagreeable about him, which you might hesitate to repeat. Is he making himself uneasy without any reason?"

"Without the slightest reason. I have concealed nothing from Mr. Mirabel."

"Thank you for the explanation." She turned to Cecilia. "May I send one of the servants with a message? I may as well put an end to Mr. Mirabel's suspense."

The man was summoned, and was dispatched with the message. Emily would have done well, after this, if she had abstained from speaking further of Miss Jethro. But Mirabel's doubts had, unhappily, inspired a similar feeling of uncertainty in her own mind. She was now disposed to attribute the tone of mystery in Alban's unlucky letter to some possible concealment suggested by regard for herself. "I wonder whether I have any reason to feel uneasy?" she said—half in jest, half in earnest.

"Uneasy about what?" Alban inquired.

"About Miss Jethro, of course! Has she said anything of me which your kindness has concealed?"

Alban seemed to be a little hurt by the doubt which her question implied. "Was that your motive," he asked, "for answering my letter as cautiously as if you had been writing to a stranger?"

"Indeed you are quite wrong!" Emily earnestly assured him. "I was perplexed and startled—and I took Mr. Wyvil's advice, before I wrote to you. Shall we drop the subject?"

Alban would have willingly dropped the subject—but for that unfortunate allusion to Mr. Wyvil. Emily had unconsciously touched him on a sore place. He had already heard from Cecilia of the consultation over his letter, and had disapproved of it. "I think you were wrong to trouble Mr. Wyvil," he said.

The altered tone of his voice suggested to Emily that he would have spoken more severely, if Cecilia had not been in the room. She thought him needlessly ready to complain of a harmless proceeding—and she too returned to the subject, after having proposed to drop it not a minute since!

"You didn't tell me I was to keep your letter a secret," she replied.

Cecilia made matters worse—with the best intentions. "I'm sure, Mr. Morris, my father was only too glad to give Emily his advice."

Alban remained silent—ungraciously silent as Emily thought, after Mr. Wyvil's kindness to him.

"The thing to regret," she remarked, "is that Mr. Morris allowed Miss Jethro to leave him without explaining herself. In his place, I should have insisted on knowing why she wanted to prevent me from meeting Mr. Mirabel in this house."

Cecilia made another unlucky attempt at judicious interference. This time, she tried a gentle remonstrance.

"Remember, Emily, how Mr. Morris was situated. He could hardly be rude to a lady. And I daresay Miss Jethro had good reasons for not wishing to explain herself."

Francine opened the drawing-room door and heard Cecilia's last words.

"Miss Jethro again!" she exclaimed.

"Where is Mr. Mirabel?" Emily asked. "I sent him a message."

"He regrets to say he is otherwise engaged for the present," Francine replied with spiteful politeness. "Don't let me interrupt the conversation. Who is this Miss Jethro, whose name is on everybody's lips?"

Alban could keep silent no longer. "We have done with the subject," he said sharply.

"Because I am here?"

"Because we have said more than enough about Miss Jethro already."

"Speak for yourself, Mr. Morris," Emily answered, resenting the masterful tone which Alban's interference had assumed. "I have not done with Miss Jethro yet, I can assure you."

"My dear, you don't know where she lives," Cecilia reminded her.

"Leave me to discover it!" Emily answered hotly. "Perhaps Mr. Mirabel knows. I shall ask Mr. Mirabel."

"I thought you would find a reason for returning to Mr. Mirabel," Francine remarked.

Before Emily could reply, one of the maids entered the room with a wreath of roses in her hand.

"Mr. Mirabel sends you these flowers, miss," the woman said, addressing Emily. "The boy told me they were to be taken to your room. I thought it was a mistake, and I have brought them to you here."

Francine, who happened to be nearest to the door, took the roses from the girl on pretense of handing them to Emily. Her jealous vigilance detected the one visible morsel of Mirabel's letter, twisted up with the flowers. Had Emily entrapped him into a secret correspondence with her? "A scrap of waste paper among your roses," she said, crumpling it up in her hand as if she meant to throw it away.

But Emily was too quick for her. She caught Francine by the wrist. "Waste paper or not," she said; "it was among my flowers and it belongs to me."

Francine gave up the letter, with a look which might have startled Emily if she had noticed it. She handed the roses to Cecilia. "I was making a wreath for you to wear this evening, my dear—and I left it in the garden. It's not quite finished yet."

Cecilia was delighted. "How lovely it is!" she exclaimed. "And how very kind of you! I'll finish it myself." She turned away to the conservatory.

"I had no idea I was interfering with a letter," said Francine; watching Emily with fiercely-attentive eyes, while she smoothed out the crumpled paper.

Having read what Mirabel had written to her, Emily looked up, and saw that Alban was on the point of following Cecilia into the conservatory. He had noticed something in Francine's face which he was at a loss to understand, but which made her presence in the room absolutely hateful to him. Emily followed and spoke to him.

"I am going back to the rose garden," she said.

"For any particular purpose?" Alban inquired

"For a purpose which, I am afraid, you won't approve of. I mean to ask Mr. Mirabel if he knows Miss Jethro's address."

"I hope he is as ignorant of it as I am," Alban answered gravely.

135

"Are we going to quarrel over Miss Jethro, as we once quarreled over Mrs. Rook?" Emily asked—with the readiest recovery of her good humor. "Come! come! I am sure you are as anxious, in your own private mind, to have this matter cleared up as I am."

"With one difference—that I think of consequences, and you don't." He said it, in his gentlest and kindest manner, and stepped into the conservatory.

"Never mind the consequences," she called after him, "if we can only get at the truth. I hate being deceived!"

"There is no person living who has better reason than you have to say that."

Emily looked round with a start. Alban was out of hearing. It was Francine who had answered her.

"What do you mean?" she said.

Francine hesitated. A ghastly paleness overspread her face.

"Are you ill?" Emily asked.

"No—I am thinking."

After waiting for a moment in silence, Emily moved away toward the door of the drawing-room. Francine suddenly held up her hand.

"Stop!" she cried.

Emily stood still.

"My mind is made up," Francine said.

"Made up—to what?"

"You asked what I meant, just now."

"I did."

"Well, my mind is made up to answer you. Miss Emily Brown, you are leading a sadly frivolous life in this house. I am going to give you something more serious to think about than your flirtation with Mr. Mirabel. Oh, don't be impatient! I am coming to the point. Without knowing it yourself, you have been the victim of deception for years past—cruel deception—wicked deception that puts on the mask of mercy."

"Are you alluding to Miss Jethro?" Emily asked, in astonishment. "I thought you were strangers to each other. Just now, you wanted to know who she was."

"I know nothing about her. I care nothing about her. I am not thinking of Miss Jethro."

"Who are you thinking of?"

"I am thinking," Francine answered, "of your dead father."

CHAPTER XLVIII. INVESTIGATING.

Having revived his sinking energies in the fruit garden, Mirabel seated himself under the shade of a tree, and reflected on the critical position in which he was placed by Francine's jealousy.

If Miss de Sor continued to be Mr. Wyvil's guest, there seemed to be no other choice before Mirabel than to leave Monksmoor—and to trust to a favorable reply to his sister's invitation for the free enjoyment of Emily's society under another roof. Try as he might, he could arrive at no more satisfactory conclusion than this. In his preoccupied state, time passed quickly. Nearly an hour had elapsed before he rose to return to the house.

Entering the hall, he was startled by a cry of terror in a woman's voice, coming from the upper regions. At the same time Mr. Wyvil, passing along the bedroom corridor after leaving the music-room, was confronted by his daughter, hurrying out of Emily's bedchamber in such a state of alarm that she could hardly speak.

"Gone!" she cried, the moment she saw her father.

Mr. Wyvil took her in his arms and tried to compose her. "Who has gone?" he asked.

"Emily! Oh, papa, Emily has left us! She has heard dreadful news—she told me so herself."

"What news? How did she hear it?"

"I don't know how she heard it. I went back to the drawing-room to show her my roses—"

"Was she alone?"

"Yes! She frightened me—she seemed quite wild. She said, 'Let me be by myself; I shall have to go home.' She kissed me—and ran up to her room. Oh, I am such a fool! Anybody else would have taken care not to lose sight of her."

"How long did you leave her by herself?"

"I can't say. I thought I would go and tell you. And then I got anxious about her, and knocked at her door, and looked into the room. Gone! Gone!"

Mr. Wyvil rang the bell and confided Cecilia to the care of her maid. Mirabel had already joined him in the corridor. They went downstairs together and consulted with Alban. He volunteered to make immediate inquiries at the railway station. Mr. Wyvil followed him, as far as the lodge gate which opened on the highroad—while Mirabel went to a second gate, at the opposite extremity of the park.

Mr. Wyvil obtained the first news of Emily. The lodge keeper had seen her pass him, on her way out of the park, in the greatest haste. He had called after her, "Anything wrong, miss?" and had received no reply. Asked what time had elapsed since this had happened, he was too confused to be able to answer with any certainty. He knew that she had taken the road which led to the station—and he knew no more.

Mr. Wyvil and Mirabel met again at the house, and instituted an examination of the servants. No further discoveries were made.

The question which occurred to everybody was suggested by the words which Cecilia had repeated to her father. Emily had said she had "heard dreadful news"—how had that news reached her? The one postal delivery at Monksmoor was in the morning. Had any special messenger arrived, with a letter for Emily? The servants were absolutely certain that no such person had entered the house. The one remaining conclusion suggested that somebody must have communicated the evil tidings by word of mouth. But here again no evidence was to be obtained. No visitor had called during the day, and no new guests had arrived. Investigation was completely baffled.

Alban returned from the railway, with news of the fugitive.

He had reached the station, some time after the departure of the London train. The clerk at the office recognized his description of Emily, and stated that she had taken her ticket for London. The station-master had opened the carriage door for her, and had noticed that the young lady appeared to be very much agitated. This information obtained, Alban had dispatched a telegram to Emily—in Cecilia's name: "Pray send us a few words to relieve our anxiety, and let us know if we can be of any service to you."

This was plainly all that could be done—but Cecilia was not satisfied. If her father had permitted it, she would have followed Emily. Alban comforted her. He apologized to Mr. Wyvil for shortening his visit, and announced his intention of traveling to London by the next train. "We may renew our inquiries to some advantage," he added, after hearing what had happened in his absence, "if we can find out who was the last person who saw her, and spoke to her, before your daughter found her alone in the drawing-room. When I went out of the room, I left her with Miss de Sor."

The maid who waited on Miss de Sor was sent for. Francine had been out, by herself, walking in the park. She was then in her room, changing her dress. On hearing of Emily's sudden departure, she had been (as the maid reported) "much shocked and quite at a loss to understand what it meant."

Joining her friends a few minutes later, Francine presented, so far as personal appearance went, a strong contrast to the pale and anxious faces round her. She looked wonderfully well, after her walk. In other respects, she was in perfect harmony with the prevalent feeling. She expressed herself with the utmost propriety; her sympathy moved poor Cecilia to tears.

"I am sure, Miss de Sor, you will try to help us?" Mr. Wyvil began

"With the greatest pleasure," Francine answered.

"How long were you and Miss Emily Brown together, after Mr. Morris left you?"

"Not more than a quarter of an hour, I should think."

"Did anything remarkable occur in the course of conversation?"

"Nothing whatever."

Alban interfered for the first time. "Did you say anything," he asked, "which agitated or offended Miss Brown?"

"That's rather an extraordinary question," Francine remarked.

"Have you no other answer to give?" Alban inquired.

"I answer—No!" she said, with a sudden outburst of anger.

There, the matter dropped. While she spoke in reply to Mr. Wyvil, Francine had confronted him without embarrassment. When Alban interposed, she never looked at him—except when he provoked her to anger. Did she remember that the man who was questioning her, was also the man who had suspected her of writing the anonymous letter? Alban was on his guard against himself, knowing how he disliked her. But the conviction in his own mind was not to be resisted. In some unimaginable way, Francine was associated with Emily's flight from the house.

The answer to the telegram sent from the railway station had not arrived, when Alban took his departure for London. Cecilia's suspense began to grow unendurable: she looked to Mirabel for comfort, and found none. His office was to console, and his capacity for performing that office was notorious among his admirers; but he failed to present himself to advantage, when Mr. Wyvil's lovely daughter had need of his services. He was, in truth, too sincerely anxious and distressed to be capable of commanding his customary resources of ready-made sentiment and fluently-pious philosophy. Emily's influence had awakened the only earnest and true feeling which had ever ennobled the popular preacher's life.

Toward evening, the long-expected telegram was received at last. What could be said, under the circumstances, it said in these words:

"Safe at home—don't be uneasy about me—will write soon."

With that promise they were, for the time, forced to be content.

BOOK THE FIFTH—THE COTTAGE.

CHAPTER XLIX. EMILY SUFFERS.

Mrs. Ellmother—left in charge of Emily's place of abode, and feeling sensible of her lonely position from time to time—had just thought of trying the cheering influence of a cup of tea, when she heard a cab draw up at the cottage gate. A violent ring at the bell followed. She opened the door—and found Emily on the steps. One look at that dear and familiar face was enough for the old servant.

"God help us," she cried, "what's wrong now?"

Without a word of reply, Emily led the way into the bedchamber which had been the scene of Miss Letitia's death. Mrs. Ellmother hesitated on the threshold.

"Why do you bring me in here?" she asked.

"Why did you try to keep me out?" Emily answered.

"When did I try to keep you out, miss?"

"When I came home from school, to nurse my aunt. Ah, you remember now! Is it true—I ask you here, where your old mistress died—is it true that my aunt deceived me about my father's death? And that you knew it?"

There was dead silence. Mrs. Ellmother trembled horribly—her lips dropped apart—her eyes wandered round the room with a stare of idiotic terror. "Is it her ghost tells you that?" she whispered. "Where is her ghost? The room whirls round and round, miss—and the air sings in my ears."

Emily sprang forward to support her. She staggered to a chair, and lifted her great bony hands in wild entreaty. "Don't frighten me," she said. "Stand back."

Emily obeyed her. She dashed the cold sweat off her forehead. "You were talking about your father's death just now," she burst out, in desperate defiant tones. "Well! we know it and we are sorry for it—your father died suddenly."

"My father died murdered in the inn at Zeeland! All the long way to London, I have tried to doubt it. Oh, me, I know it now!"

Answering in those words, she looked toward the bed. Harrowing remembrances of her aunt's delirious self-betrayal made the room unendurable to her. She ran out. The parlor door was open. Entering the room, she passed by a portrait of her father, which her aunt had hung on the wall over the fireplace. She threw herself on the sofa and burst into a passionate fit of crying. "Oh, my father—my dear, gentle, loving father; my first, best, truest friend—murdered! murdered! Oh, God, where was your justice, where was your mercy, when he died that dreadful death?"

A hand was laid on her shoulder; a voice said to her, "Hush, my child! God knows best."

Emily looked up, and saw that Mrs. Ellmother had followed her. "You poor old soul," she said, suddenly remembering; "I frightened you in the other room."

"I have got over it, my dear. I am old; and I have lived a hard life. A hard life schools a person. I make no complaints." She stopped, and began to shudder again. "Will you believe me if I tell you something?" she asked. "I warned my self-willed mistress. Standing by your father's coffin, I warned her. Hide the truth as you may (I said), a time will come when our child will know what you are keeping from her now. One or both of us may live to see it. I am the one who has lived; no refuge in the grave for me. I want to hear about it—there's no fear of frightening or hurting me now. I want to hear how you found it out. Was it by accident, my dear? or did a person tell you?"

Emily's mind was far away from Mrs. Ellmother. She rose from the sofa, with her hands held fast over her aching heart.

"The one duty of my life," she said—"I am thinking of the one duty of my life. Look! I am calm now; I am resigned to my hard lot. Never, never again, can the dear memory of my father be what it was! From this time, it is the horrid memory of a crime. The crime has gone unpunished; the man has escaped others. He shall not escape Me." She paused, and looked at Mrs. Ellmother absently. "What did you say just now? You want to hear how I know what I know? Naturally! naturally! Sit down here—sit down, my old friend, on the sofa with me—and take your mind back to Netherwoods. Alban Morris—"

Mrs. Ellmother recoiled from Emily in dismay. "Don't tell me he had anything to do with it! The kindest of men; the best of men!"

"The man of all men living who least deserves your good opinion or mine," Emily answered sternly.

"You!" Mrs. Ellmother exclaimed, "you say that!"

"I say it. He—who won on me to like him—he was in the conspiracy to deceive me; and you know it! He heard me talk of the newspaper story of the murder of my father—I say, he heard me talk of it composedly, talk of it carelessly, in the innocent belief that it was the murder of a stranger—and he never opened his lips to prevent that horrid profanation! He never even said, speak of something else; I won't hear you! No more of him! God forbid I should ever see him again. No! Do what I told you. Carry your mind back to Netherwoods. One night you let Francine de Sor frighten you. You ran away from her into the garden. Keep quiet! At your age, must I set you an example of self-control?

"I want to know, Miss Emily, where Francine de Sor is now?"

"She is at the house in the country, which I have left."

"Where does she go next, if you please? Back to Miss Ladd?"

"I suppose so. What interest have you in knowing where she goes next?"

"I won't interrupt you, miss. It's true that I ran away into the garden. I can guess who followed me. How did she find her way to me and Mr. Morris, in the dark?"

"The smell of tobacco guided her—she knew who smoked—she had seen him talking to you, on that very day—she followed the scent—she heard what you two said to each other—and she has repeated it to me. Oh, my old friend, the malice of a revengeful girl has enlightened me, when you, my nurse—and he, my lover—left me in the dark: it has told me how my father died!"

"That's said bitterly, miss!"

"Is it said truly?"

"No. It isn't said truly of myself. God knows you would never have been kept in the dark, if your aunt had listened to me. I begged and prayed—I went down on my knees to her—I warned her, as I told you just now. Must I tell you what a headstrong woman Miss Letitia was? She insisted. She put the choice before me of leaving her at once and forever—or giving in. I wouldn't have given in to any other creature on the face of this earth. I am obstinate, as you have often told me. Well, your aunt's obstinacy beat mine; I was too fond of her to say No. Besides, if you ask me who was to blame in the first place, I tell you it wasn't your aunt; she was frightened into it."

"Who frightened her?"

"Your godfather—the great London surgeon—he who was visiting in our house at the time."

"Sir Richard?"

"Yes—Sir Richard. He said he wouldn't answer for the consequences, in the delicate state of your health, if we told you the truth. Ah, he had it all his own way after that. He went with Miss Letitia to the inquest; he won over the coroner and the newspaper men to his will; he kept your aunt's name out of the papers; he took charge of the coffin; he hired the undertaker and his men, strangers from London; he wrote the certificate—who but he! Everybody was cap in hand to the famous man!"

"Surely, the servants and the neighbors asked questions?"

"Hundreds of questions! What did that matter to Sir Richard? They were like so many children, in his hands. And, mind you, the luck helped him. To begin with, there was the common name. Who was to pick out your poor father among the thousands of James Browns? Then, again, the house and lands went to the male heir, as they called him—the man your father quarreled with in the bygone time. He brought his own establishment with him. Long before you got back from the friends you were staying with—don't you remember it?—we had cleared out of the house; we were miles and miles away; and the old servants were scattered abroad, finding new situations wherever they could. How could you suspect us? We had nothing to fear in that way; but my conscience pricked me. I made another attempt to prevail on Miss Letitia, when you had recovered your health. I said, 'There's no fear of a relapse now; break it to her gently, but tell her the truth.' No! Your aunt was too fond of you. She daunted me with dreadful fits of crying, when I tried to persuade her. And that wasn't the worst of it. She bade me remember what an excitable man your father was—she reminded me that the misery of your mother's death laid him low with brain fever—she said, 'Emily takes after her father; I have heard you say it yourself; she has his constitution, and his sensitive nerves. Don't you know how she loved him—how she talks of him to this day? Who can tell (if we are not careful) what dreadful

140

mischief we may do?' That was how my mistress worked on me. I got infected with her fears; it was as if I had caught an infection of disease. Oh, my dear, blame me if it must be; but don't forget how I have suffered for it since! I was driven away from my dying mistress, in terror of what she might say, while you were watching at her bedside. I have lived in fear of what you might ask me—and have longed to go back to you—and have not had the courage to do it. Look at me now!"

The poor woman tried to take out her handkerchief; her quivering hand helplessly entangled itself in her dress. "I can't even dry my eyes," she said faintly. "Try to forgive me, miss!"

Emily put her arms round the old nurse's neck. "It is you," she said sadly, "who must forgive me."

For a while they were silent. Through the window that was open to the little garden, came the one sound that could be heard—the gentle trembling of leaves in the evening wind.

The silence was harshly broken by the bell at the cottage door. They both started.

Emily's heart beat fast. "Who can it be?" she said.

Mrs. Ellmother rose. "Shall I say you can't see anybody?" she asked, before leaving the room.

"Yes! yes!"

Emily heard the door opened—heard low voices in the passage. There was a momentary interval. Then, Mrs. Ellmother returned. She said nothing. Emily spoke to her.

"Is it a visitor?"

"Yes."

"Have you said I can't see anybody?"

"I couldn't say it."

"Why not?"

"Don't be hard on him, my dear. It's Mr. Alban Morris."

CHAPTER L. MISS LADD ADVISES.

Mrs. Ellmother sat by the dying embers of the kitchen fire; thinking over the events of the day in perplexity and distress.

She had waited at the cottage door for a friendly word with Alban, after he had left Emily. The stern despair in his face warned her to let him go in silence. She had looked into the parlor next. Pale and cold, Emily lay on the sofa—sunk in helpless depression of body and mind. "Don't speak to me," she whispered; "I am quite worn out." It was but too plain that the view of Alban's conduct which she had already expressed, was the view to which she had adhered at the interview between them. They had parted in grief—perhaps in anger—perhaps forever. Mrs. Ellmother lifted Emily in compassionate silence, and carried her upstairs, and waited by her until she slept.

In the still hours of the night, the thoughts of the faithful old servant—dwelling for a while on past and present—advanced, by slow degrees, to consideration of the doubtful future. Measuring, to the best of her ability, the responsibility which had fallen on her, she felt that it was more than she could bear, or ought to bear, alone. To whom could she look for help? The gentlefolks at Monksmoor were strangers to her. Doctor Allday was near at hand—but Emily had said, "Don't send for him; he will torment me with questions—and I want to keep my mind quiet, if I can." But one person was left, to whose ever-ready kindness Mrs. Ellmother could appeal—and that person was Miss Ladd.

It would have been easy to ask the help of the good schoolmistress in comforting and advising the favorite pupil whom she loved. But Mrs. Ellmother had another object in view:

141

she was determined that the cold-blooded cruelty of Emily's treacherous friend should not be allowed to triumph with impunity. If an ignorant old woman could do nothing else, she could tell the plain truth, and could leave Miss Ladd to decide whether such a person as Francine deserved to remain under her care.

To feel justified in taking this step was one thing: to put it all clearly in writing was another. After vainly making the attempt overnight, Mrs. Ellmother tore up her letter, and communicated with Miss Ladd by means of a telegraphic message, in the morning. "Miss Emily is in great distress. I must not leave her. I have something besides to say to you which cannot be put into a letter. Will you please come to us?"

Later in the forenoon, Mrs. Ellmother was called to the door by the arrival of a visitor. The personal appearance of the stranger impressed her favorably. He was a handsome little gentleman; his manners were winning, and his voice was singularly pleasant to hear.

"I have come from Mr. Wyvil's house in the country," he said; "and I bring a letter from his daughter. May I take the opportunity of asking if Miss Emily is well?"

"Far from it, sir, I am sorry to say. She is so poorly that she keeps her bed."

At this reply, the visitor's face revealed such sincere sympathy and regret, that Mrs. Ellmother was interested in him: she added a word more. "My mistress has had a hard trial to bear, sir. I hope there is no bad news for her in the young lady's letter?"

"On the contrary, there is news that she will be glad to hear—Miss Wyvil is coming here this evening. Will you excuse my asking if Miss Emily has had medical advice?"

"She won't hear of seeing the doctor, sir. He's a good friend of hers—and he lives close by. I am unfortunately alone in the house. If I could leave her, I would go at once and ask his advice."

"Let me go!" Mirabel eagerly proposed.

Mrs. Ellmother's face brightened. "That's kindly thought of, sir—if you don't mind the trouble."

"My good lady, nothing is a trouble in your young mistress's service. Give me the doctor's name and address—and tell me what to say to him."

"There's one thing you must be careful of," Mrs. Ellmother answered. "He mustn't come here, as if he had been sent for—she would refuse to see him."

Mirabel understood her. "I will not forget to caution him. Kindly tell Miss Emily I called— my name is Mirabel. I will return to-morrow."

He hastened away on his errand—only to find that he had arrived too late. Doctor Allday had left London; called away to a serious case of illness. He was not expected to get back until late in the afternoon. Mirabel left a message, saying that he would return in the evening.

The next visitor who arrived at the cottage was the trusty friend, in whose generous nature Mrs. Ellmother had wisely placed confidence. Miss Ladd had resolved to answer the telegram in person, the moment she read it.

"If there is bad news," she said, "let me hear it at once. I am not well enough to bear suspense; my busy life at the school is beginning to tell on me."

"There is nothing that need alarm you, ma'am—but there is a great deal to say, before you see Miss Emily. My stupid head turns giddy with thinking of it. I hardly know where to begin."

"Begin with Emily," Miss Ladd suggested.

Mrs. Ellmother took the advice. She described Emily's unexpected arrival on the previous day; and she repeated what had passed between them afterward. Miss Ladd's first impulse, when she had recovered her composure, was to go to Emily without waiting to hear more. Not presuming to stop her, Mrs. Ellmother ventured to put a question "Do you happen to have my telegram about you, ma'am?" Miss Ladd produced it. "Will you please look at the last part of it again?"

142

Miss Ladd read the words: "I have something besides to say to you which cannot be put into a letter." She at once returned to her chair.

"Does what you have still to tell me refer to any person whom I know?" she said.

"It refers, ma'am, to Miss de Sor. I am afraid I shall distress you."

"What did I say, when I came in?" Miss Ladd asked. "Speak out plainly; and try—it's not easy, I know—but try to begin at the beginning."

Mrs. Ellmother looked back through her memory of past events, and began by alluding to the feeling of curiosity which she had excited in Francine, on the day when Emily had made them known to one another. From this she advanced to the narrative of what had taken place at Netherwoods—to the atrocious attempt to frighten her by means of the image of wax—to the discovery made by Francine in the garden at night—and to the circumstances under which that discovery had been communicated to Emily.

Miss Ladd's face reddened with indignation. "Are you sure of all that you have said?" she asked.

"I am quite sure, ma'am. I hope I have not done wrong," Mrs. Ellmother added simply, "in telling you all this?"

"Wrong?" Miss Ladd repeated warmly. "If that wretched girl has no defense to offer, she is a disgrace to my school—and I owe you a debt of gratitude for showing her to me in her true character. She shall return at once to Netherwoods; and she shall answer me to my entire satisfaction—or leave my house. What cruelty! what duplicity! In all my experience of girls, I have never met with the like of it. Let me go to my dear little Emily—and try to forget what I have heard."

Mrs. Ellmother led the good lady to Emily's room—and, returning to the lower part of the house, went out into the garden. The mental effort that she had made had left its result in an aching head, and in an overpowering sense of depression. "A mouthful of fresh air will revive me," she thought.

The front garden and back garden at the cottage communicated with each other. Walking slowly round and round, Mrs. Ellmother heard footsteps on the road outside, which stopped at the gate. She looked through the grating, and discovered Alban Morris.

"Come in, sir!" she said, rejoiced to see him. He obeyed in silence. The full view of his face shocked Mrs. Ellmother. Never in her experience of the friend who had been so kind to her at Netherwoods, had he looked so old and so haggard as he looked now. "Oh, Mr. Alban, I see how she has distressed you! Don't take her at her word. Keep a good heart, sir—young girls are never long together of the same mind."

Alban gave her his hand. "I mustn't speak about it," he said. "Silence helps me to bear my misfortune as becomes a man. I have had some hard blows in my time: they don't seem to have blunted my sense of feeling as I thought they had. Thank God, she doesn't know how she has made me suffer! I want to ask her pardon for having forgotten myself yesterday. I spoke roughly to her, at one time. No: I won't intrude on her; I have said I am sorry, in writing. Do you mind giving it to her? Good-by—and thank you. I mustn't stay longer; Miss Ladd expects me at Netherwoods."

"Miss Ladd is in the house, sir, at this moment."

"Here, in London!"

"Upstairs, with Miss Emily."

"Upstairs? Is Emily ill?"

"She is getting better, sir. Would you like to see Miss Ladd?"

"I should indeed! I have something to say to her—and time is of importance to me. May I wait in the garden?"

"Why not in the parlor, sir?"

"The parlor reminds me of happier days. In time, I may have courage enough to look at the room again. Not now."

"If she doesn't make it up with that good man," Mrs. Ellmother thought, on her way back to the house, "my nurse-child is what I have never believed her to be yet—she's a fool."

In half an hour more, Miss Ladd joined Alban on the little plot of grass behind the cottage. "I bring Emily's reply to your letter," she said. "Read it, before you speak to me."

Alban read it: "Don't suppose you have offended me—and be assured that I feel gratefully the tone in which your note is written. I try to write forbearingly on my side; I wish I could write acceptably as well. It is not to be done. I am as unable as ever to enter into your motives. You are not my relation; you were under no obligation of secrecy: you heard me speak ignorantly of the murder of my father, as if it had been the murder of a stranger; and yet you kept me—deliberately, cruelly kept me—deceived! The remembrance of it burns me like fire. I cannot—oh, Alban, I cannot restore you to the place in my estimation which you have lost! If you wish to help me to bear my trouble, I entreat you not to write to me again."

Alban offered the letter silently to Miss Ladd. She signed to him to keep it.

"I know what Emily has written," she said; "and I have told her, what I now tell you—she is wrong; in every way, wrong. It is the misfortune of her impetuous nature that she rushes to conclusions—and those conclusions once formed, she holds to them with all the strength of her character. In this matter, she has looked at her side of the question exclusively; she is blind to your side."

"Not willfully!" Alban interposed.

Miss Ladd looked at him with admiration. "You defend Emily?" she said.

"I love her," Alban answered.

Miss Ladd felt for him, as Mrs. Ellmother had felt for him. "Trust to time, Mr. Morris," she resumed. "The danger to be afraid of is—the danger of some headlong action, on her part, in the interval. Who can say what the end may be, if she persists in her present way of thinking? There is something monstrous, in a young girl declaring that it is her duty to pursue a murderer, and to bring him to justice! Don't you see it yourself?"

Alban still defended Emily. "It seems to me to be a natural impulse," he said—"natural, and noble."

"Noble!" Miss Ladd exclaimed.

"Yes—for it grows out of the love which has not died with her father's death."

"Then you encourage her?"

"With my whole heart—if she would give me the opportunity!"

"We won't pursue the subject, Mr. Morris. I am told by Mrs. Ellmother that you have something to say to me. What is it?"

"I have to ask you," Alban replied, "to let me resign my situation at Netherwoods."

Miss Ladd was not only surprised; she was also—a very rare thing with her—inclined to be suspicious. After what he had said to Emily, it occurred to her that Alban might be meditating some desperate project, with the hope of recovering his lost place in her favor. "Have you heard of some better employment?" she asked.

"I have heard of no employment. My mind is not in a state to give the necessary attention to my pupils."

"Is that your only reason for wishing to leave me?"

"It is one of my reasons."

"The only one which you think it necessary to mention?"

"Yes."

"I shall be sorry to lose you, Mr. Morris."

"Believe me, Miss Ladd, I am not ungrateful for your kindness."

"Will you let me, in all kindness, say something more?" Miss Ladd answered. "I don't intrude on your secrets—I only hope that you have no rash project in view."

"I don't understand you, Miss Ladd."

"Yes, Mr. Morris—you do."

She shook hands with him—and went back to Emily.

CHAPTER LI. THE DOCTOR SEES.

Alban returned to Netherwoods—to continue his services, until another master could be found to take his place.

By a later train Miss Ladd followed him. Emily was too well aware of the importance of the mistress's presence to the well-being of the school, to permit her to remain at the cottage. It was understood that they were to correspond, and that Emily's room was waiting for her at Netherwoods, whenever she felt inclined to occupy it.

Mrs. Ellmother made the tea, that evening, earlier than usual. Being alone again with Emily, it struck her that she might take advantage of her position to say a word in Alban's favor. She had chosen her time unfortunately. The moment she pronounced the name, Emily checked her by a look, and spoke of another person—that person being Miss Jethro.

Mrs. Ellmother at once entered her protest, in her own downright way. "Whatever you do," she said, "don't go back to that! What does Miss Jethro matter to you?"

"I am more interested in her than you suppose—I happen to know why she left the school."

"Begging your pardon, miss, that's quite impossible!"

"She left the school," Emily persisted, "for a serious reason. Miss Ladd discovered that she had used false references."

"Good Lord! who told you that?"

"You see I know it. I asked Miss Ladd how she got her information. She was bound by a promise never to mention the person's name. I didn't say it to her—but I may say it to you. I am afraid I have an idea of who the person was."

"No," Mrs. Ellmother obstinately asserted, "you can't possibly know who it was! How should you know?"

"Do you wish me to repeat what I heard in that room opposite, when my aunt was dying?"

"Drop it, Miss Emily! For God's sake, drop it!"

"I can't drop it. It's dreadful to me to have suspicions of my aunt—and no better reason for them than what she said in a state of delirium. Tell me, if you love me, was it her wandering fancy? or was it the truth?"

"As I hope to be saved, Miss Emily, I can only guess as you do—I don't rightly know. My mistress trusted me half way, as it were. I'm afraid I have a rough tongue of my own sometimes. I offended her—and from that time she kept her own counsel. What she did, she did in the dark, so far as I was concerned."

"How did you offend her?"

"I shall be obliged to speak of your father if I tell you how?"

"Speak of him."

"He was not to blame—mind that!" Mrs. Ellmother said earnestly. "If I wasn't certain of what I say now you wouldn't get a word out of me. Good harmless man—there's no denying it—he was in love with Miss Jethro! What's the matter?"

Emily was thinking of her memorable conversation with the disgraced teacher on her last night at school. "Nothing" she answered. "Go on."

"If he had not tried to keep it secret from us," Mrs. Ellmother resumed, "your aunt might never have taken it into her head that he was entangled in a love affair of the shameful sort. I don't deny that I helped her in her inquiries; but it was only because I felt sure from the first that the more she discovered the more certainly my master's innocence would show itself. He used to go away and visit Miss Jethro privately. In the time when your aunt

145

trusted me, we never could find out where. She made that discovery afterward for herself (I can't tell you how long afterward); and she spent money in employing mean wretches to pry into Miss Jethro's past life. She had (if you will excuse me for saying it) an old maid's hatred of the handsome young woman, who lured your father away from home, and set up a secret (in a manner of speaking) between her brother and herself. I won't tell you how we looked at letters and other things which he forgot to leave under lock and key. I will only say there was one bit, in a journal he kept, which made me ashamed of myself. I read it out to Miss Letitia; and I told her in so many words, not to count any more on me. No; I haven't got a copy of the words—I can remember them without a copy. 'Even if my religion did not forbid me to peril my soul by leading a life of sin with this woman whom I love'—that was how it began—'the thought of my daughter would keep me pure. No conduct of mine shall ever make me unworthy of my child's affection and respect.' There! I'm making you cry; I won't stay here any longer. All that I had to say has been said. Nobody but Miss Ladd knows for certain whether your aunt was innocent or guilty in the matter of Miss Jethro's disgrace. Please to excuse me; my work's waiting downstairs."

From time to time, as she pursued her domestic labors, Mrs. Ellmother thought of Mirabel. Hours on hours had passed—and the doctor had not appeared. Was he too busy to spare even a few minutes of his time? Or had the handsome little gentleman, after promising so fairly, failed to perform his errand? This last doubt wronged Mirabel. He had engaged to return to the doctor's house; and he kept his word.

Doctor Allday was at home again, and was seeing patients. Introduced in his turn, Mirabel had no reason to complain of his reception. At the same time, after he had stated the object of his visit, something odd began to show itself in the doctor's manner.

He looked at Mirabel with an appearance of uneasy curiosity; and he contrived an excuse for altering the visitor's position in the room, so that the light fell full on Mirabel's face.

"I fancy I must have seen you," the doctor said, "at some former time."

"I am ashamed to say I don't remember it," Mirabel answered.

"Ah, very likely I'm wrong! I'll call on Miss Emily, sir, you may depend on it."

Left in his consulting-room, Doctor Allday failed to ring the bell which summoned the next patient who was waiting for him. He took his diary from the table drawer, and turned to the daily entries for the past month of July.

Arriving at the fifteenth day of the month, he glanced at the first lines of writing: "A visit from a mysterious lady, calling herself Miss Jethro. Our conference led to some very unexpected results."

No: that was not what he was in search of. He looked a little lower down: and read on regularly, from that point, as follows:

"Called on Miss Emily, in great anxiety about the discoveries which she might make among her aunt's papers. Papers all destroyed, thank God—except the Handbill, offering a reward for discovery of the murderer, which she found in the scrap-book. Gave her back the Handbill. Emily much surprised that the wretch should have escaped, with such a careful description of him circulated everywhere. She read the description aloud to me, in her nice clear voice: 'Supposed age between twenty-five and thirty years. A well-made man of small stature. Fai r complexion, delicate features, clear blue eyes. Hair light, and cut rather short. Clean shaven, with the exception of narrow half-whiskers'—and so on. Emily at a loss to understand how the fugitive could disguise himself. Reminded her that he could effectually disguise his head and face (with time to help him) by letting his hair grow long, and cultivating his beard. Emily not convinced, even by this self-evident view of the case. Changed the subject."

The doctor put away his diary, and rang the bell.

"Curious," he thought. "That dandified little clergyman has certainly reminded me of my discussion with Emily, more than two months since. Was it his flowing hair, I wonder? or his splendid beard? Good God! suppose it should turn out—?"

146

He was interrupted by the appearance of his patient. Other ailing people followed. Doctor Allday's mind was professionally occupied for the rest of the evening.

CHAPTER LII. "IF I COULD FIND A FRIEND!"

Shortly after Miss Ladd had taken her departure, a parcel arrived for Emily, bearing the name of a bookseller printed on the label. It was large, and it was heavy. "Reading enough, I should think, to last for a lifetime," Mrs. Ellmother remarked, after carrying the parcel upstairs.

Emily called her back as she was leaving the room. "I want to caution you," she said, "before Miss Wyvil comes. Don't tell her—don't tell anybody—how my father met his death. If other persons are taken into our confidence, they will talk of it. We don't know how near to us the murderer may be. The slightest hint may put him on his guard."

"Oh, miss, are you still thinking of that!"

"I think of nothing else."

"Bad for your mind, Miss Emily—and bad for your body, as your looks show. I wish you would take counsel with some discreet person, before you move in this matter by yourself."

Emily sighed wearily. "In my situation, where is the person whom I can trust?"

"You can trust the good doctor."

"Can I? Perhaps I was wrong when I told you I wouldn't see him. He might be of some use to me."

Mrs. Ellmother made the most of this concession, in the fear that Emily might change her mind. "Doctor Allday may call on you tomorrow," she said.

"Do you mean that you have sent for him?"

"Don't be angry! I did it for the best—and Mr. Mirabel agreed with me."

"Mr. Mirabel! What have you told Mr. Mirabel?"

"Nothing, except that you are ill. When he heard that, he proposed to go for the doctor. He will be here again to-morrow, to ask for news of your health. Will you see him?"

"I don't know yet—I have other things to think of. Bring Miss Wyvil up here when she comes."

"Am I to get the spare room ready for her?"

"No. She is staying with her father at the London house."

Emily made that reply almost with an air of relief. When Cecilia arrived, it was only by an effort that she could show grateful appreciation of the sympathy of her dearest friend. When the visit came to an end, she felt an ungrateful sense of freedom: the restraint was off her mind; she could think again of the one terrible subject that had any interest for her now. Over love, over friendship, over the natural enjoyment of her young life, predominated the blighting resolution which bound her to avenge her father's death. Her dearest remembrances of him—tender remembrances once—now burned in her (to use her own words) like fire. It was no ordinary love that had bound parent and child together in the bygone time. Emily had grown from infancy to girlhood, owing all the brightness of her life—a life without a mother, without brothers, without sisters—to her father alone. To submit to lose this beloved, this only companion, by the cruel stroke of disease was of all trials of resignation the hardest to bear. But to be severed from him by the murderous hand of a man, was more than Emily's fervent nature could passively endure. Before the garden gate had closed on her friend she had returned to her one thought, she was breathing again her one aspiration. The books that she had ordered, with her own purpose in view—books that might supply her want of experience, and might reveal the perils which beset the course that lay before her—were unpacked and spread out on the table. Hour after hour,

147

when the old servant believed that her mistress was in bed, she was absorbed over biographies in English and French, which related the stratagems by means of which famous policemen had captured the worst criminals of their time. From these, she turned to works of fiction, which found their chief topic of interest in dwelling on the discovery of hidden crime. The night passed, and dawn glimmered through the window—and still she opened book after book with sinking courage—and still she gained nothing but the disheartening conviction of her inability to carry out her own plans. Almost every page that she turned over revealed the immovable obstacles set in her way by her sex and her age. Could she mix with the people, or visit the scenes, familiar to the experience of men (in fact and in fiction), who had traced the homicide to his hiding-place, and had marked him among his harmless fellow-creatures with the brand of Cain? No! A young girl following, or attempting to follow, that career, must reckon with insult and outrage—paying their abominable tribute to her youth and her beauty, at every turn. What proportion would the men who might respect her bear to the men who might make her the object of advances, which it was hardly possible to imagine without shuddering. She crept exhausted to her bed, the most helpless, hopeless creature on the wide surface of the earth—a girl self-devoted to the task of a man.

Careful to perform his promise to Mirabel, without delay, the doctor called on Emily early in the morning—before the hour at which he usually entered his consulting-room.

"Well? What's the matter with the pretty young mistress?" he asked, in his most abrupt manner, when Mrs. Ellmother opened the door. "Is it love? or jealousy? or a new dress with a wrinkle in it?"

"You will hear about it, sir, from Miss Emily herself. I am forbidden to say anything."

"But you mean to say something—for all that?"

"Don't joke, Doctor Allday! The state of things here is a great deal too serious for joking. Make up your mind to be surprised—I say no more."

Before the doctor could ask what this meant, Emily opened the parlor door. "Come in!" she said, impatiently.

Doctor Allday's first greeting was strictly professional. "My dear child, I never expected this," he began. "You are looking wretchedly ill." He attempted to feel her pulse. She drew her hand away from him.

"It's my mind that's ill," she answered. "Feeling my pulse won't cure me of anxiety and distress. I want advice; I want help. Dear old doctor, you have always been a good friend to me—be a better friend than ever now."

"What can I do?"

"Promise you will keep secret what I am going to say to you—and listen, pray listen patiently, till I have done."

Doctor Allday promised, and listened. He had been, in some degree at least, prepared for a surprise—but the disclosure which now burst on him was more than his equanimity could sustain. He looked at Emily in silent dismay. She had surprised and shocked him, not only by what she said, but by what she unconsciously suggested. Was it possible that Mirabel's personal appearance had produced on her the same impression which was present in his own mind? His first impulse, when he was composed enough to speak, urged him to put the question cautiously.

"If you happened to meet with the suspected man," he said, "have you any means of identifying him?"

"None whatever, doctor. If you would only think it over—"

He stopped her there; convinced of the danger of encouraging her, and resolved to act on his conviction.

"I have enough to occupy me in my profession," he said. "Ask your other friend to think it over."

"What other friend?"

"Mr. Alban Morris."

148

The moment he pronounced the name, he saw that he had touched on some painful association. "Has Mr. Morris refused to help you?" he inquired.

"I have not asked him to help me."

"Why?"

There was no choice (with such a man as Doctor Allday) between offending him or answering him. Emily adopted the last alternative. On this occasion she had no reason to complain of his silence.

"Your view of Mr. Morris's conduct surprises me," he replied—"surprises me more than I can say," he added; remembering that he too was guilty of having kept her in ignorance of the truth, out of regard—mistaken regard, as it now seemed to be—for her peace of mind.

"Be good to me, and pass it over if I am wrong," Emily said: "I can't dispute with you; I can only tell you what I feel. You have always been so kind to me—may I count on your kindness still?"

Doctor Allday relapsed into silence.

"May I at least ask," she went on, "if you know anything of persons—" She paused, discouraged by the cold expression of inquiry in the old man's eyes as he looked at her.

"What persons?" he said.

"Persons whom I suspect."

"Name them."

Emily named the landlady of the inn at Zeeland: she could now place the right interpretation on Mrs. Rook's conduct, when the locket had been put into her hand at Netherwoods. Doctor Allday answered shortly and stiffly: he had never even seen Mrs. Rook. Emily mentioned Miss Jethro next—and saw at once that she had interested him.

"What do you suspect Miss Jethro of doing?" he asked.

"I suspect her of knowing more of my father's death than she is willing to acknowledge," Emily replied.

The doctor's manner altered for the better. "I agree with you," he said frankly. "But I have some knowledge of that lady. I warn you not to waste time and trouble in trying to discover the weak side of Miss Jethro."

"That was not my experience of her at school," Emily rejoined. "At the same time I don't know what may have happened since those days. I may perhaps have lost the place I once held in her regard."

"How?"

"Through my aunt."

"Through your aunt?"

"I hope and trust I am wrong," Emily continued; "but I fear my aunt had something to do with Miss Jethro's dismissal from the school—and in that case Miss Jethro may have found it out." Her eyes, resting on the doctor, suddenly brightened. "You know something about it!" she exclaimed.

He considered a little—whether he should or should not tell her of the letter addressed by Miss Ladd to Miss Letitia, which he had found at the cottage.

"If I could satisfy you that your fears are well founded," he asked, "would the discovery keep you away from Miss Jethro?"

"I should be ashamed to speak to her—even if we met."

"Very well. I can tell you positively, that your aunt was the person who turned Miss Jethro out of the school. When I get home, I will send you a letter that proves it."

Emily's head sank on her breast. "Why do I only hear of this now?" she said.

"Because I had no reason for letting you know of it, before to-day. If I have done nothing else, I have at least succeeded in keeping you and Miss Jethro apart."

Emily looked at him in alarm. He went on without appearing to notice that he had startled her. "I wish to God I could as easily put a stop to the mad project which you are contemplating."

"The mad project?" Emily repeated. "Oh, Doctor Allday. Do you cruelly leave me to myself, at the time of all others, when I am most in need of your sympathy?"

That appeal moved him. He spoke more gently; he pitied, while he condemned her.

"My poor dear child, I should be cruel indeed, if I encouraged you. You are giving yourself up to an enterprise, so shockingly unsuited to a young girl like you, that I declare I contemplate it with horror. Think, I entreat you, think; and let me hear that you have yielded—not to my poor entreaties—but to your own better sense!" His voice faltered; his eyes moistened. "I shall make a fool of myself," he burst out furiously, "if I stay here any longer. Good-by."

He left her.

She walked to the window, and looked out at the fair morning. No one to feel for her—no one to understand her—nothing nearer that could speak to poor mortality of hope and encouragement than the bright heaven, so far away! She turned from the window. "The sun shines on the murderer," she thought, "as it shines on me."

She sat down at the table, and tried to quiet her mind; to think steadily to some good purpose. Of the few friends that she possessed, every one had declared that she was in the wrong. Had they lost the one loved being of all beings on earth, and lost him by the hand of a homicide—and that homicide free? All that was faithful, all that was devoted in the girl's nature, held her to her desperate resolution as with a hand of iron. If she shrank at that miserable moment, it was not from her design—it was from the sense of her own helplessness. "Oh, if I had been a man!" she said to herself. "Oh, if I could find a friend!"

CHAPTER LIII. THE FRIEND IS FOUND.

Mrs. Ellmother looked into the parlor. "I told you Mr. Mirabel would call again," she announced. "Here he is."

"Has he asked to see me?"

"He leaves it entirely to you."

For a moment, and a moment only, Emily was undecided. "Show him in," she said.

Mirabel's embarrassment was visible the moment he entered the room. For the first time in his life—in the presence of a woman—the popular preacher was shy. He who had taken hundreds of fair hands with sympathetic pressure—he who had offered fluent consolation, abroad and at home, to beauty in distress—was conscious of a rising color, and was absolutely at a loss for words when Emily received him. And yet, though he appeared at disadvantage—and, worse still, though he was aware of it himself—there was nothing contemptible in his look and manner. His silence and confusion revealed a change in him which inspired respect. Love had developed this spoiled darling of foolish congregations, this effeminate pet of drawing-rooms and boudoirs, into the likeness of a Man—and no woman, in Emily's position, could have failed to see that it was love which she herself had inspired.

Equally ill at ease, they both took refuge in the commonplace phrases suggested by the occasion. These exhausted there was a pause. Mirabel alluded to Cecilia, as a means of continuing the conversation.

"Have you seen Miss Wyvil?" he inquired.

"She was here last night; and I expect to see her again to-day before she returns to Monksmoor with her father. Do you go back with them?"

"Yes—if you do."

"I remain in London."

"Then I remain in London, too."

The strong feeling that was in him had forced its way to expression at last. In happier days—when she had persistently refused to let him speak to her seriously—she would have been ready with a light-hearted reply. She was silent now. Mirabel pleaded with her not to misunderstand him, by an honest confession of his motives which presented him under a new aspect. The easy plausible man, who had hardly ever seemed to be in earnest before—meant, seriously meant, what he said now.

"May I try to explain myself?" he asked.

"Certainly, if you wish it."

"Pray, don't suppose me capable," Mirabel said earnestly, "of presuming to pay you an idle compliment. I cannot think of you, alone and in trouble, without feeling anxiety which can only be relieved in one way—I must be near enough to hear of you, day by day. Not by repeating this visit! Unless you wish it, I will not again cross the threshold of your door. Mrs. Ellmother will tell me if your mind is more at ease; Mrs. Ellmother will tell me if there is any new trial of your fortitude. She needn't even mention that I have been speaking to her at the door; and she may be sure, and you may be sure, that I shall ask no inquisitive questions. I can feel for you in your misfortune, without wishing to know what that misfortune is. If I can ever be of the smallest use, think of me as your other servant. Say to Mrs. Ellmother, 'I want him'—and say no more."

Where is the woman who could have resisted such devotion as this—inspired, truly inspired, by herself? Emily's eyes softened as she answered him.

"You little know how your kindness touches me," she said.

"Don't speak of my kindness until you have put me to the proof," he interposed. "Can a friend (such a friend as I am, I mean) be of any use?"

"Of the greatest use if I could feel justified in trying you."

"I entreat you to try me!"

"But, Mr. Mirabel, you don't know what I am thinking of."

"I don't want to know."

"I may be wrong. My friends all say I am wrong."

"I don't care what your friends say; I don't care about any earthly thing but your tranquillity. Does your dog ask whether you are right or wrong? I am your dog. I think of You, and I think of nothing else."

She looked back through the experience of the last few days. Miss Ladd—Mrs. Ellmother—Doctor Allday: not one of them had felt for her, not one of them had spoken to her, as this man had felt and had spoken. She remembered the dreadful sense of solitude and helplessness which had wrung her heart, in the interval before Mirabel came in. Her father himself could hardly have been kinder to her than this friend of a few weeks only. She looked at him through her tears; she could say nothing that was eloquent, nothing even that was adequate. "You are very good to me," was her only acknowledgment of all that he had offered. How poor it seemed to be! and yet how much it meant!

He rose—saying considerately that he would leave her to recover herself, and would wait to hear if he was wanted.

"No," she said; "I must not let you go. In common gratitude I ought to decide before you leave me, and I do decide to take you into my confidence." She hesitated; her color rose a little. "I know how unselfishly you offer me your help," she resumed; "I know you speak to me as a brother might speak to a sister—"

He gently interrupted her. "No," he said; "I can't honestly claim to do that. And—may I venture to remind you?—you know why."

She started. Her eyes rested on him with a momentary expression of reproach.

"Is it quite fair," she asked, "in my situation, to say that?"

"Would it have been quite fair," he rejoined, "to allow you to deceive yourself? Should I deserve to be taken into your confidence, if I encouraged you to trust me, under false pretenses? Not a word more of those hopes on which the happiness of my life depends

151

shall pass my lips, unless you permit it. In my devotion to your interests, I promise to forget myself. My motives may be misinterpreted; my position may be misunderstood. Ignorant people may take me for that other happier man, who is an object of interest to you—"

"Stop, Mr. Mirabel! The person to whom you refer has no such claim on me as you suppose."

"Dare I say how happy I am to hear it? Will you forgive me?"

"I will forgive you if you say no more."

Their eyes met. Completely overcome by the new hope that she had inspired, Mirabel was unable to answer her. His sensitive nerves trembled under emotion, like the nerves of a woman; his delicate complexion faded away slowly into whiteness. Emily was alarmed—he seemed to be on the point of fainting. She ran to the window to open it more widely.

"Pray don't trouble yourself," he said, "I am easily agitated by any sudden sensation—and I am a little overcome at this moment by my own happiness."

"Let me give you a glass of wine."

"Thank you—I don't need it indeed."

"You really feel better?"

"I feel quite well again—and eager to hear how I can serve you."

"It's a long story, Mr. Mirabel—and a dreadful story."

"Dreadful?"

"Yes! Let me tell you first how you can serve me. I am in search of a man who has done me the cruelest wrong that one human creature can inflict on another. But the chances are all against me—I am only a woman; and I don't know how to take even the first step toward discovery."

"You will know, when I guide you."

He reminded her tenderly of what she might expect from him, and was rewarded by a grateful look. Seeing nothing, suspecting nothing, they advanced together nearer and nearer to the end.

"Once or twice," Emily continued, "I spoke to you of my poor father, when we were at Monksmoor—and I must speak of him again. You could have no interest in inquiring about a stranger—and you cannot have heard how he died."

"Pardon me, I heard from Mr. Wyvil how he died."

"You heard what I had told Mr. Wyvil," Emily said: "I was wrong."

"Wrong!" Mirabel exclaimed, in a tone of courteous surprise. "Was it not a sudden death?"

"It was a sudden death."

"Caused by disease of the heart?"

"Caused by no disease. I have been deceived about my father's death—and I have only discovered it a few days since."

At the impending moment of the frightful shock which she was innocently about to inflict on him, she stopped—doubtful whether it would be best to relate how the discovery had been made, or to pass at once to the result. Mirabel supposed that she had paused to control her agitation. He was so immeasurably far away from the faintest suspicion of what was coming that he exerted his ingenuity, in the hope of sparing her.

"I can anticipate the rest," he said. "Your sad loss has been caused by some fatal accident. Let us change the subject; tell me more of that man whom I must help you to find. It will only distress you to dwell on your father's death."

"Distress me?" she repeated. "His death maddens me!"

"Oh, don't say that!"

"Hear me! hear me! My father died murdered, at Zeeland—and the man you must help me to find is the wretch who killed him."

She started to her feet with a cry of terror. Mirabel dropped from his chair senseless to the floor.

CHAPTER LIV. THE END OF THE FAINTING FIT.

Emily recovered her presence of mind. She opened the door, so as to make a draught of air in the room, and called for water. Returning to Mirabel, she loosened his cravat. Mrs. Ellmother came in, just in time to prevent her from committing a common error in the treatment of fainting persons, by raising Mirabel's head. The current of air, and the sprinkling of water over his face, soon produced their customary effect. "He'll come round, directly," Mrs. Ellmother remarked. "Your aunt was sometimes taken with these swoons, miss; and I know something about them. He looks a poor weak creature, in spite of his big beard. Has anything frightened him?"

Emily little knew how correctly that chance guess had hit on the truth!

"Nothing can possibly have frightened him," she replied; "I am afraid he is in bad health. He turned suddenly pale while we were talking; and I thought he was going to be taken ill; he made light of it, and seemed to recover. Unfortunately, I was right; it was the threatening of a fainting fit—he dropped on the floor a minute afterward."

A sigh fluttered over Mirabel's lips. His eyes opened, looked at Mrs. Ellmother in vacant terror, and closed again. Emily whispered to her to leave the room. The old woman smiled satirically as she opened the door—then looked back, with a sudden change of humor. To see the kind young mistress bending over the feeble little clergyman set her—by some strange association of ideas—thinking of Alban Morris. "Ah," she muttered to herself, on her way out, "I call him a Man!"

There was wine in the sideboard—the wine which Emily had once already offered in vain. Mirabel drank it eagerly, this time. He looked round the room, as if he wished to be sure that they were alone. "Have I fallen to a low place in your estimation?" he asked, smiling faintly. "I am afraid you will think poorly enough of your new ally, after this?"

"I only think you should take more care of your health," Emily replied, with sincere interest in his recovery. "Let me leave you to rest on the sofa."

He refused to remain at the cottage—he asked, with a sudden change to fretfulness, if she would let her servant get him a cab. She ventured to doubt whether he was quite strong enough yet to go away by himself. He reiterated, piteously reiterated, his request. A passing cab was stopped directly. Emily accompanied him to the gate. "I know what to do," he said, in a hurried absent way. "Rest and a little tonic medicine will soon set me right." The clammy coldness of his skin made Emily shudder, as they shook hands. "You won't think the worse of me for this?" he asked.

"How can you imagine such a thing!" she answered warmly.

"Will you see me, if I come to-morrow?"

"I shall be anxious to see you."

So they parted. Emily returned to the house, pitying him with all her heart.

BOOK THE SIXTH—HERE AND THERE.

CHAPTER LV. MIRABEL SEES HIS WAY.

Reaching the hotel at which he was accustomed to stay when he was in London, Mirabel locked the door of his room. He looked at the houses on the opposite side of the street. His mind was in such a state of morbid distrust that he lowered the blind over the window. In

153

solitude and obscurity, the miserable wretch sat down in a corner, and covered his face with his hands, and tried to realize what had happened to him.

Nothing had been said at the fatal interview with Emily, which could have given him the slightest warning of what was to come. Her father's name—absolutely unknown to him when he fled from the inn—had only been communicated to the public by the newspaper reports of the adjourned inquest. At the time when those reports appeared, he was in hiding, under circumstances which prevented him from seeing a newspaper. While the murder was still a subject of conversation, he was in France—far out of the track of English travelers—and he remained on the continent until the summer of eighteen hundred and eighty-one. No exercise of discretion, on his part, could have extricated him from the terrible position in which he was now placed. He stood pledged to Emily to discover the man suspected of the murder of her father; and that man was—himself!

What refuge was left open to him?

If he took to flight, his sudden disappearance would be a suspicious circumstance in itself, and would therefore provoke inquiries which might lead to serious results. Supposing that he overlooked the risk thus presented, would he be capable of enduring a separation from Emily, which might be a separation for life? Even in the first horror of discovering his situation, her influence remained unshaken—the animating spirit of the one manly capacity for resistance which raised him above the reach of his own fears. The only prospect before him which he felt himself to be incapable of contemplating, was the prospect of leaving Emily.

Having arrived at this conclusion, his fears urged him to think of providing for his own safety.

The first precaution to adopt was to separate Emily from friends whose advice might be hostile to his interests—perhaps even subversive of his security. To effect this design, he had need of an ally whom he could trust. That ally was at his disposal, far away in the north. At the time when Francine's jealousy began to interfere with all freedom of intercourse between Emily and himself at Monksmoor, he had contemplated making arrangements which might enable them to meet at the house of his invalid sister, Mrs. Delvin. He had spoken of her, and of the bodily affliction which confined her to her room, in terms which had already interested Emily. In the present emergency, he decided on returning to the subject, and on hastening the meeting between the two women which he had first suggested at Mr. Wyvil's country seat.

No time was to be lost in carrying out this intention. He wrote to Mrs. Delvin by that day's post; confiding to her, in the first place, the critical position in which he now found himself. This done, he proceeded as follows:

"To your sound judgment, dearest Agatha, it may appear that I am making myself needlessly uneasy about the future. Two persons only know that I am the man who escaped from the inn at Zeeland. You are one of them, and Miss Jethro is the other. On you I can absolutely rely; and, after my experience of her, I ought to feel sure of Miss Jethro. I admit this; but I cannot get over my distrust of Emily's friends. I fear the cunning old doctor; I doubt Mr. Wyvil; I hate Alban Morris.

"Do me a favor, my dear. Invite Emily to be your guest, and so separate her from these friends. The old servant who attends on her will be included in the invitation, of course. Mrs. Ellmother is, as I believe, devoted to the interests of Mr. Alban Morris: she will be well out of the way of doing mischief, while we have her safe in your northern solitude.

"There is no fear that Emily will refuse your invitation.

"In the first place, she is already interested in you. In the second place, I shall consider the small proprieties of social life; and, instead of traveling with her to your house, I shall follow by a later train. In the third place, I am now the chosen adviser in whom she trusts; and what I tell her to do, she will do. It pains me, really and truly pains me, to be compelled to deceive her—but the other alternative is to reveal myself as the wretch of whom she is in search. Was there ever such a situation? And, oh, Agatha, I am so fond of her! If I fail to persuade her to be my wife, I don't care what becomes of me. I used to think disgrace, and death on the scaffold, the most frightful prospect that a man can contemplate. In my present frame of mind, a life without Emily may just as well end in that way as in any other. When we are together in your old sea-beaten tower, do your best, my dear, to incline the heart of this sweet girl toward me. If she remains in London, how do I know that Mr. Morris may not recover the place he has lost in her good opinion? The bare idea of it turns me cold.

"There is one more point on which I must touch, before I can finish my letter.

"When you last wrote, you told me that Sir Jervis Redwood was not expected to live much longer, and that the establishment would be broken up after his death. Can you find out for me what will become, under the circumstances, of Mr. and Mrs. Rook? So far as I am concerned, I don't doubt that the alteration in my personal appearance, which has protected me for years past, may be trusted to preserve me from recognition by these two people. But it is of the utmost importance, remembering the project to which Emily has devoted herself, that she should not meet with Mrs. Rook. They have been already in correspondence; and Mrs. Rook has expressed an intention (if the opportunity offers itself) of calling at the cottage. Another reason, and a pressing reason, for removing Emily from London! We can easily keep the Rooks out of your house; but I own I should feel more at my ease, if I heard that they had left Northumberland."

With that confession, Mrs. Delvin's brother closed his letter.

CHAPTER LVI. ALBAN SEES HIS WAY.

During the first days of Mirabel's sojourn at his hotel in London, events were in progress at Netherwoods, affecting the interests of the man who was the especial object of his distrust. Not long after Miss Ladd had returned to her school, she heard of an artist who was capable of filling the place to be vacated by Alban Morris. It was then the twenty-third of the month. In four days more the new master would be ready to enter on his duties; and Alban would be at liberty.

On the twenty-fourth, Alban received a telegram which startled him. The person sending the message was Mrs. Ellmother; and the words were: "Meet me at your railway station to-day, at two o'clock."

He found the old woman in the waiting-room; and he met with a rough reception.

"Minutes are precious, Mr. Morris," she said; "you are two minutes late. The next train to London stops here in half an hour—and I must go back by it."

"Good heavens, what brings you here? Is Emily—?"

"Emily is well enough in health—if that's what you mean? As to why I come here, the reason is that it's a deal easier for me (worse luck!) to take this journey than to write a letter. One good turn deserves another. I don't forget how kind you were to me, away there at the school—and I can't, and won't, see what's going on at the cottage, behind your back, without letting you know of it. Oh, you needn't be alarmed about her! I've made an excuse to get away for a few hours—but I haven't left her by herself. Miss Wyvil has come to London again; and Mr. Mirabel spends the best part of his time with her. Excuse me for a moment, will you? I'm so thirsty after the journey, I can hardly speak."

She presented herself at the counter in the waiting-room. "I'll trouble you, young woman, for a glass of ale." She returned to Alban in a better humor. "It's not bad stuff, that! When I have said my say, I'll have a drop more—just to wash the taste of Mr. Mirabel out of my mouth. Wait a bit; I have something to ask you. How much longer are you obliged to stop here, teaching the girls to draw?"

"I leave Netherwoods in three days more," Alban replied.

"That's all right! You may be in time to bring Miss Emily to her senses, yet."

"What do you mean?"

"I mean—if you don't stop it—she will marry the parson."

"I can't believe it, Mrs. Ellmother! I won't believe it!"

"Ah, it's a comfort to him, poor fellow, to say that! Look here, Mr. Morris; this is how it stands. You're in disgrace with Miss Emily—and he profits by it. I was fool enough to take a liking to Mr. Mirabel when I first opened the door to him; I know better now. He got on the blind side of me; and now he has got on the blind side of her. Shall I tell you how? By doing what you would have done if you had had the chance. He's helping her—or pretending to help her, I don't know which—to find the man who murdered poor Mr. Brown. After four years! And when all the police in England (with a reward to encourage them) did their best, and it came to nothing!"

"Never mind that!" Alban said impatiently. "I want to know how Mr. Mirabel is helping her?"

"That's more than I can tell you. You don't suppose they take me into their confidence? All I can do is to pick up a word, here and there, when fine weather tempts them out into the garden. She tells him to suspect Mrs. Rook, and to make inquiries after Miss Jethro. And he has his plans; and he writes them down, which is dead against his doing anything useful, in my opinion. I don't hold with your scribblers. At the same time I wouldn't count too positively, in your place, on his being likely to fail. That little Mirabel—if it wasn't for his beard, I should believe he was a woman, and a sickly woman too; he fainted in our house the other day—that little Mirabel is in earnest. Rather than leave Miss Emily from Saturday to Monday, he has got a parson out of employment to do his Sunday work for him. And, what's more, he has persuaded her (for some reasons of his own) to leave London next week."

"Is she going back to Monksmoor?"

"Not she! Mr. Mirabel has got a sister, a widow lady; she's a cripple, or something of the sort. Her name is Mrs. Delvin. She lives far away in the north country, by the sea; and Miss Emily is going to stay with her."

"Are you sure of that?"

"Sure? I've seen the letter."

"Do you mean the letter of invitation?"

"Yes—I do. Miss Emily herself showed it to me. I'm to go with her—'in attendance on my mistress,' as the lady puts it. This I will say for Mrs. Delvin: her handwriting is a credit to the school that taught her; and the poor bedridden creature words her invitation so nicely, that I myself couldn't have resisted it—and I'm a hard one, as you know. You don't seem to heed me, Mr. Morris."

"I beg your pardon, I was thinking."

"Thinking of what—if I may make so bold?"

"Of going back to London with you, instead of waiting till the new master comes to take my place."

"Don't do that, sir! You would do harm instead of good, if you showed yourself at the cottage now. Besides, it would not be fair to Miss Ladd, to leave her before the other man takes your girls off your hands. Trust me to look after your interests; and don't go near Miss Emily—don't even write to her—unless you have got something to say about the murder, which she will be eager to hear. Make some discovery in that direction, Mr. Morris, while the parson is only trying to do it or pretending to do it—and I'll answer for the result. Look at the clock! In ten minutes more the train will be here. My memory isn't as good as it was; but I do think I have told you all I had to tell."

"You are the best of good friends!" Alban said warmly.

"Never mind about that, sir. If you want to do a friendly thing in return, tell me if you know what has become of Miss de Sor."

"She has returned to Netherwoods."

"Aha! Miss Ladd is as good as her word. Would you mind writing to tell me of it, if Miss de Sor leaves the school again? Good Lord! there she is on the platform with bag and baggage. Don't let her see me, Mr. Morris! If she comes in here, I shall set the marks of my ten finger-nails on that false face of hers, as sure as I am a Christian woman."

Alban placed himself at the door, so as to hide Mrs. Ellmother. There indeed was Francine, accompanied by one of the teachers at the school. She took a seat on the bench outside the booking-office, in a state of sullen indifference—absorbed in herself—noticing nothing. Urged by ungovernable curiosity, Mrs. Ellmother stole on tiptoe to Alban's side to look at her. To a person acquainted with the circumstances there could be no possible doubt of what had happened. Francine had failed to excuse herself, and had been dismissed from Miss Ladd's house.

"I would have traveled to the world's end," Mrs. Ellmother said, "to see that!"

She returned to her place in the waiting-room, perfectly satisfied.

The teacher noticed Alban, on leaving the booking-office after taking the tickets. "I shall be glad," she said, looking toward Francine, "when I have resigned the charge of that young lady to the person who is to receive her in London."

"Is she to be sent back to her parents?" Alban asked.

"We don't know yet. Miss Ladd will write to St. Domingo by the next mail. In the meantime, her father's agent in London—the same person who pays her allowance—takes care of her until he hears from the West Indies."

"Does she consent to this?"

"She doesn't seem to care what becomes of her. Miss Ladd has given her every opportunity of explaining and excusing herself, and has produced no impression. You can see the state she is in. Our good mistress—always hopeful even in the worst cases, as you know—thinks she is feeling ashamed of herself, and is too proud and self-willed to own it. My own idea is, that some secret disappointment is weighing on her mind. Perhaps I am wrong."

No. Miss Ladd was wrong; and the teacher was right.

The passion of revenge, being essentially selfish in its nature, is of all passions the narrowest in its range of view. In gratifying her jealous hatred of Emily, Francine had correctly foreseen consequences, as they might affect the other object of her enmity—Alban Morris. But she had failed to perceive the imminent danger of another result, which in a calmer frame of mind might not have escaped discovery. In triumphing over Emily and Alban, she had been the indirect means of inflicting on herself the bitterest of all disappointments— she had brought Emily and Mirabel together. The first forewarning of this catastrophe had reached her, on hearing that Mirabel would not return to Monksmoor. Her worst fears had been thereafter confirmed by a letter from Cecilia, which had followed her to Netherwoods. From that moment, she, who had made others wretched, paid the penalty in suffering as keen as any that she had inflicted. Completely prostrated; powerless, through ignorance of his address in London, to make a last appeal to Mirabel; she was literally, as had just been said, careless what became of her. When the train approached, she sprang to her feet— advanced to the edge of the platform—and suddenly drew back, shuddering. The teacher looked in terror at Alban. Had the desperate girl meditated throwing herself under the wheels of the engine? The thought had been in both their minds; but neither of them acknowledged it. Francine stepped quietly into the carriage, when the train drew up, and laid her head back in a corner, and closed her eyes. Mrs. Ellmother took her place in another compartment, and beckoned to Alban to speak to her at the window.

"Where can I see you, when you go to London?" she asked.

"At Doctor Allday's house."

"On what day?"

"On Tuesday next."

CHAPTER LVII. APPROACHING THE END.

Alban reached London early enough in the afternoon to find the doctor at his luncheon. "Too late to see Mrs. Ellmother," he announced. "Sit down and have something to eat."

"Has she left any message for me?"

"A message, my good friend, that you won't like to hear. She is off with her mistress, this morning, on a visit to Mr. Mirabel's sister."

"Does he go with them?"

"No; he follows by a later train."

"Has Mrs. Ellmother mentioned the address?"

"There it is, in her own handwriting."

Alban read the address:—"Mrs. Delvin, The Clink, Belford, Northumberland."

"Turn to the back of that bit of paper," the doctor said. "Mrs. Ellmother has written something on it."

She had written these words: "No discoveries made by Mr. Mirabel, up to this time. Sir Jervis Redwood is dead. The Rooks are believed to be in Scotland; and Miss Emily, if need be, is to help the parson to find them. No news of Miss Jethro."

"Now you have got your information," Doctor Allday resumed, "let me have a look at you. You're not in a rage: that's a good sign to begin with."

"I am not the less determined," Alban answered.

"To bring Emily to her senses?" the doctor asked.

"To do what Mirabel has not done—and then to let her choose between us."

"Ay? ay? Your good opinion of her hasn't altered, though she has treated you so badly?"

"My good opinion makes allowance for the state of my poor darling's mind, after the shock that has fallen on her," Alban answered quietly. "She is not my Emily now. She will be my Emily yet. I told her I was convinced of it, in the old days at school—and my conviction is as strong as ever. Have you seen her, since I have been away at Netherwoods?"

"Yes; and she is as angry with me as she is with you."

"For the same reason?"

"No, no. I heard enough to warn me to hold my tongue. I refused to help her—that's all. You are a man, and you may run risks which no young girl ought to encounter. Do you remember when I asked you to drop all further inquiries into the murder, for Emily's sake? The circumstances have altered since that time. Can I be of any use?"

"Of the greatest use, if you can give me Miss Jethro's address."

"Oh! You mean to begin in that way, do you?"

"Yes. You know that Miss Jethro visited me at Netherwoods?"

"Go on."

"She showed me your answer to a letter which she had written to you. Have you got that letter?"

Doctor Allday produced it. The address was at a post-office, in a town on the south coast. Looking up when he had copied it, Alban saw the doctor's eyes fixed on him with an oddly-mingled expression: partly of sympathy, partly of hesitation.

"Have you anything to suggest?" he asked.

"You will get nothing out of Miss Jethro," the doctor answered, "unless—" there he stopped.

"Unless, what?"

"Unless you can frighten her."

"How am I to do that?"

After a little reflection, Doctor Allday returned, without any apparent reason, to the subject of his last visit to Emily.

"There was one thing she said, in the course of our talk," he continued, "which struck me as being sensible: possibly (for we are all more or less conceited), because I agreed with her myself. She suspects Miss Jethro of knowing more about that damnable murder than Miss Jethro is willing to acknowledge. If you want to produce the right effect on her—" he looked hard at Alban and checked himself once more.

"Well? what am I to do?"

"Tell her you have an idea of who the murderer is."

"But I have no idea."

"But I have."

"Good God! what do you mean?"

"Don't mistake me! An impression has been produced on my mind—that's all. Call it a freak or fancy; worth trying perhaps as a bold experiment, and worth nothing more. Come a little nearer. My housekeeper is an excellent woman, but I have once or twice caught her rather too near to that door. I think I'll whisper it."

He did whisper it. In breathless wonder, Alban heard of the doubt which had crossed Doctor Allday's mind, on the evening when Mirabel had called at his house.

"You look as if you didn't believe it," the doctor remarked.

"I'm thinking of Emily. For her sake I hope and trust you are wrong. Ought I to go to her at once? I don't know what to do!"

"Find out first, my good fellow, whether I am right or wrong. You can do it, if you will run the risk with Miss Jethro."

Alban recovered himself. His old friend's advice was clearly the right advice to follow. He examined his railway guide, and then looked at his watch. "If I can find Miss Jethro," he answered, "I'll risk it before the day is out."

The doctor accompanied him to the door. "You will write to me, won't you?"

"Without fail. Thank you—and good-by."

BOOK THE SEVENTH—THE CLINK.

CHAPTER LVIII. A COUNCIL OF TWO.

Early in the last century one of the picturesque race of robbers and murderers, practicing the vices of humanity on the borderlands watered by the river Tweed, built a tower of stone on the coast of Northumberland. He lived joyously in the perpetration of atrocities; and he died penitent, under the direction of his priest. Since that event, he has figured in poems and pictures; and has been greatly admired by modern ladies and gentlemen, whom he would have outraged and robbed if he had been lucky enough to meet with them in the good old times.

His son succeeded him, and failed to profit by the paternal example: that is to say, he made the fatal mistake of fighting for other people instead of fighting for himself.

In the rebellion of Forty-Five, this northern squire sided to serious purpose with Prince Charles and the Highlanders. He lost his head; and his children lost their inheritance. In the lapse of years, the confiscated property fell into the hands of strangers; the last of whom (having a taste for the turf) discovered, in course of time, that he was in want of money. A retired merchant, named Delvin (originally of French extraction), took a liking to the wild situation, and purchased the tower. His wife—already in failing health—had been ordered by the doctors to live a quiet life by the sea. Her husband's death left her a rich and lonely widow; by day and night alike, a prisoner in her room; wasted by disease, and having but two interests which reconciled her to life—writing poetry in the intervals of pain, and paying the debts of a reverend brother who succeeded in the pulpit, and prospered nowhere else.

In the later days of its life, the tower had been greatly improved as a place of residence. The contrast was remarkable between the dreary gray outer walls, and the luxuriously furnished rooms inside, rising by two at a time to the lofty eighth story of the building. Among the scattered populace of the country round, the tower was still known by the odd name given to it in the bygone time—"The Clink." It had been so called (as was supposed) in allusion to the noise made by loose stones, washed backward and forward at certain times of the tide, in hollows of the rock on which the building stood.

On the evening of her arrival at Mrs. Delvin's retreat, Emily retired at an early hour, fatigued by her long journey. Mirabel had an opportunity of speaking with his sister privately in her own room.

"Send me away, Agatha, if I disturb you," he said, "and let me know when I can see you in the morning."

"My dear Miles, have you forgotten that I am never able to sleep in calm weather? My lullaby, for years past, has been the moaning of the great North Sea, under my window. Listen! There is not a sound outside on this peaceful night. It is the right time of the tide, just now—and yet, 'the clink' is not to be heard. Is the moon up?"

Mirabel opened the curtains. "The whole sky is one great abyss of black," he answered. "If I was superstitious, I should think that horrid darkness a bad omen for the future. Are you suffering, Agatha?"

"Not just now. I suppose I look sadly changed for the worse since you saw me last?"

But for the feverish brightness of her eyes, she would have looked like a corpse. Her wrinkled forehead, her hollow cheeks, her white lips told their terrible tale of the suffering of years. The ghastly appearance of her face was heightened by the furnishing of the room. This doomed woman, dying slowly day by day, delighted in bright colors and sumptuous materials. The paper on the walls, the curtains, the carpet presented the hues of the rainbow. She lay on a couch covered with purple silk, under draperies of green velvet to keep her warm. Rich lace hid h er scanty hair, turning prematurely gray; brilliant rings glittered on her bony fingers. The room was in a blaze of light from lamps and candles. Even the wine at her side that kept her alive had been decanted into a bottle of lustrous Venetian glass. "My grave is open," she used to say; "and I want all these beautiful things to keep me from looking at it. I should die at once, if I was left in the dark."

Her brother sat by the couch, thinking "Shall I tell you what is in your mind?" she asked.

Mirabel humored the caprice of the moment. "Tell me!" he said.

"You want to know what I think of Emily," she answered. "Your letter told me you were in love; but I didn't believe your letter. I have always doubted whether you were capable of feeling true love—until I saw Emily. The moment she entered the room, I knew that I had never properly appreciated my brother. You are in love with her, Miles; and you are a better man than I thought you. Does that express my opinion?"

Mirabel took her wasted hand, and kissed it gratefully.

"What a position I am in!" he said. "To love her as I love her; and, if she knew the truth, to be the object of her horror—to be the man whom she would hunt to the scaffold, as an act of duty to the memory of her father!"

"You have left out the worst part of it," Mrs. Delvin reminded him. "You have bound yourself to help her to find the man. Your one hope of persuading her to become your wife rests on your success in finding him. And you are the man. There is your situation! You can't submit to it. How can you escape from it?"

"You are trying to frighten me, Agatha."

"I am trying to encourage you to face your position boldly."

"I am doing my best," Mirabel said, with sullen resignation. "Fortune has favored me so far. I have, really and truly, been unable to satisfy Emily by discovering Miss Jethro. She has left the place at which I saw her last—there is no trace to be found of her—and Emily knows it."

"Don't forget," Mrs. Delvin replied, "that there is a trace to be found of Mrs. Rook, and that Emily expects you to follow it."

Mirabel shuddered. "I am surrounded by dangers, whichever way I look," he said. "Do what I may, it turns out to be wrong. I was wrong, perhaps, when I brought Emily here."

"No!"

"I could easily make an excuse," Mirabel persisted "and take her back to London."

"And for all you know to the contrary," his wiser sister replied, "Mrs. Rook may go to London; and you may take Emily back in time to receive her at the cottage. In every way you are safer in my old tower. And—don't forget—you have got my money to help you, if you want it. In my belief, Miles, you will want it."

"You are the dearest and best of sisters! What do you recommend me to do?"

"What you would have been obliged to do," Mrs. Delvin answered, "if you had remained in London. You must go to Redwood Hall tomorrow, as Emily has arranged it. If Mrs. Rook is not there, you must ask for her address in Scotland. If nobody knows the address, you must still bestir yourself in trying to find it. And, when you do fall in with Mrs. Rook—"

"Well?"

"Take care, wherever it may be, that you see her privately."

Mirabel was alarmed. "Don't keep me in suspense," he burst out. "Tell me what you propose."

"Never mind what I propose, to-night. Before I can tell you what I have in my mind, I must know whether Mrs. Rook is in England or Scotland. Bring me that information to-morrow, and I shall have something to say to you. Hark! The wind is rising, the rain is falling. There is a chance of sleep for me—I shall soon hear the sea. Good-night."

"Good-night, dearest—and thank you again, and again!"

CHAPTER LIX. THE ACCIDENT AT BELFORD.

Early in the morning Mirabel set forth for Redwood Hall, in one of the vehicles which Mrs. Delvin still kept at "The Clink" for the convenience of visitors. He returned soon after noon; having obtained information of the whereabout of Mrs. Rook and her husband. When they had last been heard of, they were at Lasswade, near Edinburgh. Whether they had, or had not, obtained the situation of which they were in search, neither Miss Redwood nor any one else at the Hall could tell.

In half an hour more, another horse was harnessed, and Mirabel was on his way to the railway station at Belford, to follow Mrs. Rook at Emily's urgent request. Before his departure, he had an interview with his sister.

Mrs. Delvin was rich enough to believe implicitly in the power of money. Her method of extricating her brother from the serious difficulties that beset him, was to make it worth the while of Mr. and Mrs. Rook to leave England. Their passage to America would be secretly paid; and they would take with them a letter of credit addressed to a banker in New York. If Mirabel failed to discover them, after they had sailed, Emily could not blame his want of devotion to her interests. He understood this; but he remained desponding and irresolute, even with the money in his hands. The one person who could rouse his courage and animate his hope, was also the one person who must know nothing of what had passed between his sister and himself. He had no choice but to leave Emily, without being cheered by her bright looks, invigorated by her inspiriting words. Mirabel went away on his doubtful errand with a heavy heart.

"The Clink" was so far from the nearest post town, that the few letters, usually addressed to the tower, were delivered by private arrangement with a messenger. The man's punctuality depended on the convenience of his superiors employed at the office. Sometimes he arrived early, and sometimes he arrived late. On this particular morning he presented himself, at half past one o'clock, with a letter for Emily; and when Mrs. Ellmother smartly reproved him for the delay, he coolly attributed it to the hospitality of friends whom he had met on the road.

The letter, directed to Emily at the cottage, had been forwarded from London by the person left in charge. It addressed her as "Honored Miss." She turned at once to the end—and discovered the signature of Mrs. Rook!

"And Mr. Mirabel has gone," Emily exclaimed, "just when his presence is of the greatest importance to us!"

Shrewd Mrs. Ellmother suggested that it might be as well to read the letter first—and then to form an opinion.

Emily read it.

"Lasswade, near Edinburgh, Sept. 26th.

"HONORED MISS—I take up my pen to bespeak your kind sympathy for my husband and myself; two old people thrown on the world again by the death of our excellent master. We are under a month's notice to leave Redwood Hall.

"Hearing of a situation at this place (also that our expenses would be paid if we applied personally), we got leave of absence, and made our application. The lady and her son are either the stingiest people that ever lived—or they have taken a dislike to me and my husband, and they make money a means of getting rid of us easily. Suffice it to say that we have refused to accept starvation wages, and that we are still out of place. It is just possible that you may have heard of something to suit us. So I write at once, knowing that good chances are often lost through needless delay.

"We stop at Belford on our way back, to see some friends of my husband, and we hope to get to Redwood Hall in good time on the 28th. Would you please address me to care of Miss Redwood, in case you know of any good situation for which we could apply. Perhaps we may be driven to try our luck in London. In this case, will you permit me to have the honor of presenting my respects, as I ventured to propose when I wrote to you a little time since.

"I beg to remain, Honored Miss,

"Your humble servant,

"R. ROOK."

Emily handed the letter to Mrs. Ellmother. "Read it," she said, "and tell me what you think."

"I think you had better be careful."

"Careful of Mrs. Rook?"

"Yes—and careful of Mrs. Delvin too."

Emily was astonished. "Are you really speaking seriously?" she said. "Mrs. Delvin is a most interesting person; so patient under her sufferings; so kind, so clever; so interested in all that interests me. I shall take the letter to her at once, and ask her advice."

"Have your own way, miss. I can't tell you why—but I don't like her!"

Mrs. Delvin's devotion to the interests of her guest took even Emily by surprise. After reading Mrs. Rook's letter, she rang the bell on her table in a frenzy of impatience. "My brother must be instantly recalled," she said. "Telegraph to him in your own name, telling him what has happened. He will find the message waiting for him, at the end of his journey."

162

The groom, summoned by the bell, was ordered to saddle the third and last horse left in the stables; to take the telegram to Belford, and to wait there until the answer arrived.

"How far is it to Redwood Hall?" Emily asked, when the man had received his orders.

"Ten miles," Mrs. Delvin answered.

"How can I get there to-day?"

"My dear, you can't get there."

"Pardon me, Mrs. Delvin, I must get there."

"Pardon me. My brother represents you in this matter. Leave it to my brother."

The tone taken by Mirabel's sister was positive, to say the least of it. Emily thought of what her faithful old servant had said, and began to doubt her own discretion in so readily showing the letter. The mistake—if a mistake it was—had however been committed; and, wrong or right, she was not disposed to occupy the subordinate position which Mrs. Delvin had assigned to her.

"If you will look at Mrs. Rook's letter again," Emily replied, "you will see that I ought to answer it. She supposes I am in London."

"Do you propose to tell Mrs. Rook that you are in this house?" Mrs. Delvin asked.

"Certainly."

"You had better consult my brother, before you take any responsibility on yourself."

Emily kept her temper. "Allow me to remind you," she said, "that Mr. Mirabel is not acquainted with Mrs. Rook—and that I am. If I speak to her personally, I can do much to assist the object of our inquiries, before he returns. She is not an easy woman to deal with—"

"And therefore," Mrs. Delvin interposed, "the sort of person who requires careful handling by a man like my brother—a man of the world."

"The sort of person, as I venture to think," Emily persisted, "whom I ought to see with as little loss of time as possible."

Mrs. Delvin waited a while before she replied. In her condition of health, anxiety was not easy to bear. Mrs. Rook's letter and Emily's obstinacy had seriously irritated her. But, like all persons of ability, she was capable, when there was serious occasion for it, of exerting self-control. She really liked and admired Emily; and, as the elder woman and the hostess, she set an example of forbearance and good humor.

"It is out of my power to send you to Redwood Hall at once," she resumed. "The only one of my three horses now at your disposal is the horse which took my brother to the Hall this morning. A distance, there and back, of twenty miles. You are not in too great a hurry, I am sure, to allow the horse time to rest?"

Emily made her excuses with perfect grace and sincerity. "I had no idea the distance was so great," she confessed. "I will wait, dear Mrs. Delvin, as long as you like."

They parted as good friends as ever—with a certain reserve, nevertheless, on either side. Emily's eager nature was depressed and irritated by the prospect of delay. Mrs. Delvin, on the other hand (devoted to her brother's interests), thought hopefully of obstacles which might present themselves with the lapse of time. The horse might prove to be incapable of further exertion for that day. Or the threatening aspect of the weather might end in a storm. But the hours passed—and the sky cleared—and the horse was reported to be fit for work again. Fortune was against the lady of the tower; she had no choice but to submit.

Mrs. Delvin had just sent word to Emily that the carriage would be ready for her in ten minutes, when the coachman who had driven Mirabel to Belford returned. He brought news which agreeably surprised both the ladies. Mirabel had reached the station five minutes too late; the coachman had left him waiting the arrival of the next train to the North. He would now receive the telegraphic message at Belford, and might return immediately by taking the groom's horse. Mrs. Delvin left it to Emily to decide whether she would proceed by herself to Redwood Hall, or wait for Mirabel's return.

163

Under the changed circumstances, Emily would have acted ungraciously if she had persisted in holding to her first intention. She consented to wait.

The sea still remained calm. In the stillness of the moorland solitude on the western side of "The Clink," the rapid steps of a horse were heard at some little distance on the highroad. Emily ran out, followed by careful Mrs. Ellmother, expecting to meet Mirabel.

She was disappointed: it was the groom who had returned. As he pulled up at the house, and dismounted, Emily noticed that the man looked excited.

"Is there anything wrong?" she asked.

"There has been an accident, miss."

"Not to Mr. Mirabel!"

"No, no, miss. An accident to a poor foolish woman, traveling from Lasswade."

Emily looked at Mrs. Ellmother. "It can't be Mrs. Rook!" she said.

"That's the name, miss! She got out before the train had quite stopped, and fell on the platform."

"Was she hurt?"

"Seriously hurt, as I heard. They carried her into a house hard by—and sent for the doctor."

"Was Mr. Mirabel one of the people who helped her?"

"He was on the other side of the platform, miss; waiting for the train from London. I got to the station and gave him the telegram, just as the accident took place. We crossed over to hear more about it. Mr. Mirabel was telling me that he would return to 'The Clink' on my horse—when he heard the woman's name mentioned. Upon that, he changed his mind and went to the house."

"Was he let in?"

"The doctor wouldn't hear of it. He was making his examination; and he said nobody was to be in the room but her husband and the woman of the house."

"Is Mr. Mirabel waiting to see her?"

"Yes, miss. He said he would wait all day, if necessary; and he gave me this bit of a note to take to the mistress."

Emily turned to Mrs. Ellmother. "It's impossible to stay here, not knowing whether Mrs. Rook is going to live or die," she said. "I shall go to Belford—and you will go with me."

The groom interfered. "I beg your pardon, miss. It was Mr. Mirabel's most particular wish that you were not, on any account, to go to Belford."

"Why not?"

"He didn't say."

Emily eyed the note in the man's hand with well-grounded distrust. In all probability, Mirabel's object in writing was to instruct his sister to prevent her guest from going to Belford. The carriage was waiting at the door. With her usual promptness of resolution, Emily decided on taking it for granted that she was free to use as she pleased a carriage which had been already placed at her disposal.

"Tell your mistress," she said to the groom, "that I am going to Belford instead of to Redwood Hall."

In a minute more, she and Mrs. Ellmother were on their way to join Mirabel at the station.

CHAPTER LX. OUTSIDE THE ROOM.

Emily found Mirabel in the waiting room at Belford. Her sudden appearance might well have amazed him; but his face expressed a more serious emotion than surprise—he looked at her as if she had alarmed him.

164

"Didn't you get my message?" he asked. "I told the groom I wished you to wait for my return. I sent a note to my sister, in case he made any mistake."

"The man made no mistake," Emily answered. "I was in too great a hurry to be able to speak with Mrs. Delvin. Did you really suppose I could endure the suspense of waiting till you came back? Do you think I can be of no use—I who know Mrs. Rook?"

"They won't let you see her."

"Why not? You seem to be waiting to see her."

"I am waiting for the return of the rector of Belford. He is at Berwick; and he has been sent for at Mrs. Rook's urgent request."

"Is she dying?"

"She is in fear of death—whether rightly or wrongly, I don't know. There is some internal injury from the fall. I hope to see her when the rector returns. As a brother clergyman, I may with perfect propriety ask him to use his influence in my favor."

"I am glad to find you so eager about it."

"I am always eager in your interests."

"Don't think me ungrateful," Emily replied gently. "I am no stranger to Mrs. Rook; and, if I send in my name, I may be able to see her before the clergyman returns."

She stopped. Mirabel suddenly moved so as to place himself between her and the door. "I must really beg of you to give up that idea," he said; "you don't know what horrid sight you may see—what dreadful agonies of pain this unhappy woman may be suffering."

His manner suggested to Emily that he might be acting under some motive which he was unwilling to acknowledge. "If you have a reason for wishing that I should keep away from Mrs. Rook," she said, "let me hear what it is. Surely we trust each other? I have done my best to set the example, at any rate."

Mirabel seemed to be at a loss for a reply.

While he was hesitating, the station-master passed the door. Emily asked him to direct her to the house in which Mrs. Rook had been received. He led the way to the end of the platform, and pointed to the house. Emily and Mrs. Ellmother immediately left the station. Mirabel accompanied them, still remonstrating, still raising obstacles.

The house door was opened by an old man. He looked reproachfully at Mirabel. "You have been told already," he said, "that no strangers are to see my wife?"

Encouraged by discovering that the man was Mr. Rook, Emily mentioned her name. "Perhaps you may have heard Mrs. Rook speak of me," she added.

"I've heard her speak of you oftentimes."

"What does the doctor say?"

"He thinks she may get over it. She doesn't believe him."

"Will you say that I am anxious to see her, if she feels well enough to receive me?"

Mr. Rook looked at Mrs. Ellmother. "Are there two of you wanting to go upstairs?" he inquired.

"This is my old friend and servant," Emily answered. "She will wait for me down here."

"She can wait in the parlor; the good people of this house are well known to me." He pointed to the parlor door—and then led the way to the first floor. Emily followed him. Mirabel, as obstinate as ever, followed Emily.

Mr. Rook opened a door at the end of the landing; and, turning round to speak to Emily, noticed Mirabel standing behind her. Without making any remarks, the old man pointed significantly down the stairs. His resolution was evidently immovable. Mirabel appealed to Emily to help him.

"She will see me, if you ask her," he said, "Let me wait here?"

The sound of his voice was instantly followed by a cry from the bed-chamber—a cry of terror.

165

Mr. Rook hurried into the room, and closed the door. In less than a minute, he opened it again, with doubt and horror plainly visible in his face. He stepped up to Mirabel—eyed him with the closest scrutiny—and drew back again with a look of relief.

"She's wrong," he said; "you are not the man."

This strange proceeding startled Emily.

"What man do you mean?" she asked.

Mr. Rook took no notice of the question. Still looking at Mirabel, he pointed down the stairs once more. With vacant eyes—moving mechanically, like a sleep-walker in his dream—Mirabel silently obeyed. Mr. Rook turned to Emily.

"Are you easily frightened?" he said

"I don't understand you," Emily replied. "Who is going to frighten me? Why did you speak to Mr. Mirabel in that strange way?"

Mr. Rook looked toward the bedroom door. "Maybe you'll hear why, inside there. If I could have my way, you shouldn't see her—but she's not to be reasoned with. A caution, miss. Don't be too ready to believe what my wife may say to you. She's had a fright." He opened the door. "In my belief," he whispered, "she's off her head."

Emily crossed the threshold. Mr. Rook softly closed the door behind her.

CHAPTER LXI. INSIDE THE ROOM.

A decent elderly woman was seated at the bedside. She rose, and spoke to Emily with a mingling of sorrow and confusion strikingly expressed on her face. "It isn't my fault," she said, "that Mrs. Rook receives you in this manner; I am obliged to humor her."

She drew aside, and showed Mrs. Rook with her head supported by many pillows, and her face strangely hidden from view under a veil. Emily started back in horror. "Is her face injured?" she asked.

Mrs. Rook answered the question herself. Her voice was low and weak; but she still spoke with the same nervous hurry of articulation which had been remarked by Alban Morris, on the day when she asked him to direct her to Netherwoods.

"Not exactly injured," she explained; "but one's appearance is a matter of some anxiety even on one's death-bed. I am disfigured by a thoughtless use of water, to bring me to when I had my fall—and I can't get at my toilet-things to put myself right again. I don't wish to shock you. Please excuse the veil."

Emily remembered the rouge on her cheeks, and the dye on her hair, when they had first seen each other at the school. Vanity—of all human frailties the longest-lived—still held its firmly-rooted place in this woman's nature; superior to torment of conscience, unassailable by terror of death!

The good woman of the house waited a moment before she left the room. "What shall I say," she asked, "if the clergyman comes?"

Mrs. Rook lifted her hand solemnly "Say," she answered, "that a dying sinner is making atonement for sin. Say this young lady is present, by the decree of an all-wise Providence. No mortal creature must disturb us." Her hand dropped back heavily on the bed. "Are we alone?" she asked.

"We are alone," Emily answered. "What made you scream just before I came in?"

"No! I can't allow you to remind me of that," Mrs. Rook protested. "I must compose myself. Be quiet. Let me think."

Recovering her composure, she also recovered that sense of enjoyment in talking of herself, which was one of the marked peculiarities in her character.

"You will excuse me if I exhibit religion," she resumed. "My dear parents were exemplary people; I was most carefully brought up. Are you pious? Let us hope so."

Emily was once more reminded of the past.

The bygone time returned to her memory—the time when she had accepted Sir Jervis Redwood's offer of employment, and when Mrs. Rook had arrived at the school to be her traveling companion to the North. The wretched creature had entirely forgotten her own loose talk, after she had drunk Miss Ladd's good wine to the last drop in the bottle. As she was boasting now of her piety, so she had boasted then of her lost faith and hope, and had mockingly declared her free-thinking opinions to be the result of her ill-assorted marriage. Forgotten—all forgotten, in this later time of pain and fear. Prostrate under the dread of death, her innermost nature—stripped of the concealments of her later life—was revealed to view. The early religious training, at which she had scoffed in the insolence of health and strength, revealed its latent influence—intermitted, but a living influence always from first to last. Mrs. Rook was tenderly mindful of her exemplary parents, and proud of exhibiting religion, on the bed from which she was never to rise again.

"Did I tell you that I am a miserable sinner?" she asked, after an interval of silence.

Emily could endure it no longer. "Say that to the clergyman," she answered—"not to me."

"Oh, but I must say it," Mrs. Rook insisted. "I am a miserable sinner. Let me give you an instance of it," she continued, with a shameless relish of the memory of her own frailties. "I have been a drinker, in my time. Anything was welcome, when the fit was on me, as long as it got into my head. Like other persons in liquor, I sometimes talked of things that had better have been kept secret. We bore that in mind—my old man and I—when we were engaged by Sir Jervis. Miss Redwood wanted to put us in the next bedroom to hers—a risk not to be run. I might have talked of the murder at the inn; and she might have heard me. Please to remark a curious thing. Whatever else I might let out, when I was in my cups, not a word about the pocketbook ever dropped from me. You will ask how I know it. My dear, I should have heard of it from my husband, if I had let that out—and he is as much in the dark as you are. Wonderful are the workings of the human mind, as the poet says; and drink drowns care, as the proverb says. But can drink deliver a person from fear by day, and fear by night? I believe, if I had dropped a word about the pocketbook, it would have sobered me in an instant. Have you any remark to make on this curious circumstance?"

Thus far, Emily had allowed the woman to ramble on, in the hope of getting information which direct inquiry might fail to produce. It was impossible, however, to pass over the allusion to the pocketbook. After giving her time to recover from the exhaustion which her heavy breathing sufficiently revealed, Emily put the question:

"Who did the pocketbook belong to?"

"Wait a little," said Mrs. Rook. "Everything in its right place, is my motto. I mustn't begin with the pocketbook. Why did I begin with it? Do you think this veil on my face confuses me? Suppose I take it off. But you must promise first—solemnly promise you won't look at my face. How can I tell you about the murder (the murder is part of my confession, you know), with this lace tickling my skin? Go away—and stand there with your back to me. Thank you. Now I'll take it off. Ha! the air feels refreshing; I know what I am about. Good heavens, I have forgotten something! I have forgotten him. And after such a fright as he gave me! Did you see him on the landing?"

"Who are you talking of?" Emily asked.

Mrs. Rook's failing voice sank lower still.

"Come closer," she said, "this must be whispered. Who am I talking of?" she repeated. "I am talking of the man who slept in the other bed at the inn; the man who did the deed with his own razor. He was gone when I looked into the outhouse in the gray of the morning. Oh, I have done my duty! I have told Mr. Rook to keep an eye on him downstairs. You haven't an idea how obstinate and stupid my husband is. He says I couldn't know the man,

167

because I didn't see him. Ha! there's such a thing as hearing, when you don't see. I heard—and I knew it again."

Emily turned cold from head to foot.

"What did you know again?" she said.

"His voice," Mrs. Rook answered. "I'll swear to his voice before all the judges in England."

Emily rushed to the bed. She looked at the woman who had said those dreadful words, speechless with horror.

"You're breaking your promise!" cried Mrs. Rook. "You false girl, you're breaking your promise!"

She snatched at the veil, and put it on again. The sight of her face, momentary as it had been, reassured Emily. Her wild eyes, made wilder still by the blurred stains of rouge below them, half washed away—her disheveled hair, with streaks of gray showing through the dye—presented a spectacle which would have been grotesque under other circumstances, but which now reminded Emily of Mr. Rook's last words; warning her not to believe what his wife said, and even declaring his conviction that her intellect was deranged. Emily drew back from the bed, conscious of an overpowering sense of self-reproach. Although it was only for a moment, she had allowed her faith in Mirabel to be shaken by a woman who was out of her mind.

"Try to forgive me," she said. "I didn't willfully break my promise; you frightened me."

Mrs. Rook began to cry. "I was a handsome woman in my time," she murmured. "You would say I was handsome still, if the clumsy fools about me had not spoiled my appearance. Oh, I do feel so weak! Where's my medicine?"

The bottle was on the table. Emily gave her the prescribed dose, and revived her failing strength.

"I am an extraordinary person," she resumed. "My resolution has always been the admiration of every one who knew me. But my mind feels—how shall I express it?—a little vacant. Have mercy on my poor wicked soul! Help me."

"How can I help you?"

"I want to recollect. Something happened in the summer time, when we were talking at Netherwoods. I mean when that impudent master at the school showed his suspicions of me. (Lord! how he frightened me, when he turned up afterward at Sir Jervis's house.) You must have seen yourself he suspected me. How did he show it?"

"He showed you my locket," Emily answered.

"Oh, the horrid reminder of the murder!" Mrs. Rook exclaimed. "I didn't mention it: don't blame Me. You poor innocent, I have something dreadful to tell you."

Emily's horror of the woman forced her to speak. "Don't tell me!" she cried. "I know more than you suppose; I know what I was ignorant of when you saw the locket."

Mrs. Rook took offense at the interruption.

"Clever as you are, there's one thing you don't know," she said. "You asked me, just now, who the pocketbook belonged to. It belonged to your father. What's the matter? Are you crying?"

Emily was thinking of her father. The pocketbook was the last present she had given to him—a present on his birthday. "Is it lost?" she asked sadly.

"No; it's not lost. You will hear more of it directly. Dry your eyes, and expect something interesting—I'm going to talk about love. Love, my dear, means myself. Why shouldn't it? I'm not the only nice-looking woman, married to an old man, who has had a lover."

"Wretch! what has that got to do with it?"

"Everything, you rude girl! My lover was like the rest of them; he would bet on race-horses, and he lost. He owned it to me, on the day when your father came to our inn. He said, 'I must find the money—or be off to America, and say good-by forever.' I was fool enough to be fond of him. It broke my heart to hear him talk in that way. I said, 'If I find the money, and more than the money, will you take me with you wherever you go?' Of course, he said

Yes. I suppose you have heard of the inquest held at our old place by the coroner and jury? Oh, what idiots! They believed I was asleep on the night of the murder. I never closed my eyes—I was so miserable, I was so tempted."

"Tempted? What tempted you?"

"Do you think I had any money to spare? Your father's pocketbook tempted me. I had seen him open it, to pay his bill over-night. It was full of bank-notes. Oh, what an overpowering thing love is! Perhaps you have known it yourself."

Emily's indignation once more got the better of her prudence. "Have you no feeling of decency on your death-bed!" she said.

Mrs. Rook forgot her piety; she was ready with an impudent rejoinder. "You hot-headed little woman, your time will come," she answered. "But you're right—I am wandering from the point; I am not sufficiently sensible of this solemn occasion. By-the-by, do you notice my language? I inherit correct English from my mother—a cultivated person, who married beneath her. My paternal grandfather was a gentleman. Did I tell you that there came a time, on that dreadful night, when I could stay in bed no longer? The pocketbook—I did nothing but think of that devilish pocketbook, full of bank-notes. My husband was fast asleep all the time. I got a chair and stood on it. I looked into the place where the two men were sleeping, through the glass in the top of the door. Your father was awake; he was walking up and down the room. What do you say? Was he agitated? I didn't notice. I don't know whether the other man was asleep or awake. I saw nothing but the pocketbook stuck under the pillow, half in and half out. Your father kept on walking up and down. I thought to myself, 'I'll wait till he gets tired, and then I'll have another look at the pocketbook.' Where's the wine? The doctor said I might have a glass of wine when I wanted it."

Emily found the wine and gave it to her. She shuddered as she accidentally touched Mrs. Rook's hand.

The wine helped the sinking woman.

"I must have got up more than once," she resumed. "And more than once my heart must have failed me. I don't clearly remember what I did, till the gray of the morning came. I think that must have been the last time I looked through the glass in the door."

She began to tremble. She tore the veil off her face. She cried out piteously, "Lord, be merciful to me a sinner! Come here," she said to Emily. "Where are you? No! I daren't tell you what I saw; I daren't tell you what I did. When you're possessed by the devil, there's nothing, nothing, nothing you can't do! Where did I find the courage to unlock the door? Where did I find the courage to go in? Any other woman would have lost her senses, when she found blood on her fingers after taking the pocketbook—"

Emily's head swam; her heart beat furiously—she staggered to the door, and opened it to escape from the room.

"I'm guilty of robbing him; but I'm innocent of his blood!" Mrs. Rook called after her wildly. "The deed was done—the yard door was wide open, and the man was gone—when I looked in for the last time. Come back, come back!"

Emily looked round.

"I can't go near you," she said, faintly.

"Come near enough to see this."

She opened her bed-gown at the throat, and drew up a loop of ribbon over her head. The pocketbook was attached to the ribbon. She held it out.

"Your father's book," she said. "Won't you take your father's book?"

For a moment, and only for a moment, Emily was repelled by the profanation associated with her birthday gift. Then, the loving remembrance of the dear hands that had so often touched that relic, drew the faithful daughter back to the woman whom she abhorred. Her eyes rested tenderly on the book. Before it had lain in that guilty bosom, it had been his book. The beloved memory was all that was left to her now; the beloved memory consecrated it to her hand. She took the book.

"Open it," said Mrs. Rook.

There were two five-pound bank-notes in it.

"His?" Emily asked.

"No; mine—the little I have been able to save toward restoring what I stole."

"Oh!" Emily cried, "is there some good in this woman, after all?"

"There's no good in the woman!" Mrs. Rook answered desperately. "There's nothing but fear—fear of hell now; fear of the pocketbook in the past time. Twice I tried to destroy it—and twice it came back, to remind me of the duty that I owed to my miserable soul. I tried to throw it into the fire. It struck the bar, and fell back into the fender at my feet. I went out, and cast it into the well. It came back again in the first bucket of water that was drawn up. From that moment, I began to save what I could. Restitution! Atonement! I tell you the book found a tongue—and those were the grand words it dinned in my ears, morning and night." She stooped to fetch her breath—stopped, and struck her bosom. "I hid it here, so that no person should see it, and no person take it from me. Superstition? Oh, yes, superstition! Shall tell you something? You may find yourself superstitious, if you are ever cut to the heart as I was. He left me! The man I had disgraced myself for, deserted me on the day when I gave him the stolen money. He suspected it was stolen; he took care of his own cowardly self—and left me to the hard mercy of the law, if the theft was found out. What do you call that, in the way of punishment? Haven't I suffered? Haven't I made atonement? Be a Christian—say you forgive me."

"I do forgive you."

"Say you will pray for me."

"I will."

"Ah! that comforts me! Now you can go."

Emily looked at her imploringly. "Don't send me away, knowing no more of the murder than I knew when I came here! Is there nothing, really nothing, you can tell me?"

Mrs. Rook pointed to the door.

"Haven't I told you already? Go downstairs, and see the wretch who escaped in the dawn of the morning!"

"Gently, ma'am, gently! You're talking too loud," cried a mocking voice from outside.

"It's only the doctor," said Mrs. Rook. She crossed her hands over her bosom with a deep-drawn sigh. "I want no doctor, now. My peace is made with my Maker. I'm ready for death; I'm fit for Heaven. Go away! go away!"

CHAPTER LXII. DOWNSTAIRS.

In a moment more, the doctor came in—a brisk, smiling, self-sufficient man—smartly dressed, with a flower in his button-hole. A stifling odor of musk filled the room, as he drew out his handkerchief with a flourish, and wiped his forehead.

"Plenty of hard work in my line, just now," he said. "Hullo, Mrs. Rook! somebody has been allowing you to excite yourself. I heard you, before I opened the door. Have you been encouraging her to talk?" he asked, turning to Emily, and shaking his finger at her with an air of facetious remonstrance.

Incapable of answering him; forgetful of the ordinary restraints of social intercourse—with the one doubt that preserved her belief in Mirabel, eager for confirmation—Emily signed to this stranger to follow her into a corner of the room, out of hearing. She made no excuses: she took no notice of his look of surprise. One hope was all she could feel, one word was all she could say, after that second assertion of Mirabel's guilt. Indicating Mrs. Rook by a glance at the bed, she whispered the word:

"Mad?"

Flippant and familiar, the doctor imitated her; he too looked at the bed.

"No more mad than you are, miss. As I said just now, my patient has been exciting herself; I daresay she has talked a little wildly in consequence. Hers isn't a brain to give way, I can tell you. But there's somebody else—"

Emily had fled from the room. He had destroyed her last fragment of belief in Mirabel's innocence. She was on the landing trying to console herself, when the doctor joined her.

"Are you acquainted with the gentleman downstairs?" he asked.

"What gentleman?"

"I haven't heard his name; he looks like a clergyman. If you know him—"

"I do know him. I can't answer questions! My mind—"

"Steady your mind, miss! and take your friend home as soon as you can. He hasn't got Mrs. Rook's hard brain; he's in a state of nervous prostration, which may end badly. Do you know where he lives?"

"He is staying with his sister—Mrs. Delvin."

"Mrs. Delvin! she's a friend and patient of mine. Say I'll look in to-morrow morning, and see what I can do for her brother. In the meantime, get him to bed, and to rest; and don't be afraid of giving him brandy."

The doctor returned to the bedroom. Emily heard Mrs. Ellmother's voice below.

"Are you up there, miss?"

"Yes."

Mrs. Ellmother ascended the stairs. "It was an evil hour," she said, "that you insisted on going to this place. Mr. Mirabel—" The sight of Emily's face suspended the next words on her lips. She took the poor young mistress in her motherly arms. "Oh, my child! what has happened to you?"

"Don't ask me now. Give me your arm—let us go downstairs."

"You won't be startled when you see Mr. Mirabel—will you, my dear? I wouldn't let them disturb you; I said nobody should speak to you but myself. The truth is, Mr. Mirabel has had a dreadful fright. What are you looking for?"

"Is there a garden here? Any place where we can breathe the fresh air?"

There was a courtyard at the back of the house. They found their way to it. A bench was placed against one of the walls. They sat down.

"Shall I wait till you're better before I say any more?" Mrs. Ellmother asked. "No? You want to hear about Mr. Mirabel? My dear, he came into the parlor where I was; and Mr. Rook came in too—-and waited, looking at him. Mr. Mirabel sat down in a corner, in a dazed state as I thought. It wasn't for long. He jumped up, and clapped his hand on his heart as if his heart hurt him. 'I must and will know what's going on upstairs,' he says. Mr. Rook pulled him back, and told him to wait till the young lady came down. Mr. Mirabel wouldn't hear of it. 'Your wife's frightening her,' he says; 'your wife's telling her horrible things about me.' He was taken on a sudden with a shivering fit; his eyes rolled, and his teeth chattered. Mr. Rook made matters worse; he lost his temper. 'I'm damned,' he says, 'if I don't begin to think you are the man, after all; I've half a mind to send for the police.' Mr. Mirabel dropped into his chair. His eyes stared, his mouth fell open. I took hold of his hand. Cold—cold as ice. What it all meant I can't say. Oh, miss, you know! Let me tell you the rest of it some other time."

Emily insisted on hearing more. "The end!" she cried. "How did it end?"

"I don't know how it might have ended, if the doctor hadn't come in—to pay his visit, you know, upstairs. He said some learned words. When he came to plain English, he asked if anybody had frightened the gentleman. I said Mr. Rook had frightened him. The doctor says to Mr. Rook, 'Mind what you are about. If you frighten him again, you may have his death to answer for.' That cowed Mr. Rook. He asked what he had better do. 'Give me some brandy for him first,' says the doctor; 'and then get him home at once.' I found the

171

brandy, and went away to the inn to order the carriage. Your ears are quicker than mine, miss—do I hear it now?"

They rose, and went to the house door. The carriage was there.

Still cowed by what the doctor had said, Mr. Rook appeared, carefully leading Mirabel out. He had revived under the action of the stimulant. Passing Emily he raised his eyes to her—trembled—and looked down again. When Mr. Rook opened the door of the carriage he paused, with one of his feet on the step. A momentary impulse inspired him with a false courage, and brought a flush into his ghastly face. He turned to Emily.

"May I speak to you?" he asked.

She started back from him. He looked at Mrs. Ellmother. "Tell her I am innocent," he said. The trembling seized on him again. Mr. Rook was obliged to lift him into the carriage.

Emily caught at Mrs. Ellmother's arm. "You go with him," she said. "I can't."

"How are you to get back, miss?"

She turned away and spoke to the coachman. "I am not very well. I want the fresh air—I'll sit by you."

Mrs. Ellmother remonstrated and protested, in vain. As Emily had determined it should be, so it was.

"Has he said anything?" she asked, when they had arrived at their journey's end.

"He has been like a man frozen up; he hasn't said a word; he hasn't even moved."

"Take him to his sister; and tell her all that you know. Be careful to repeat what the doctor said. I can't face Mrs. Delvin. Be patient, my good old friend; I have no secrets from you. Only wait till to-morrow; and leave me by myself to-night."

Alone in her room, Emily opened her writing-case. Searching among the letters in it, she drew out a printed paper. It was the Handbill describing the man who had escaped from the inn, and offering a reward for the discovery of him.

At the first line of the personal description of the fugitive, the paper dropped from her hand. Burning tears forced their way into her eyes. Feeling for her handkerchief, she touched the pocketbook which she had received from Mrs. Rook. After a little hesitation she took it out. She looked at it. She opened it.

The sight of the bank-notes repelled her; she hid them in one of the pockets of the book. There was a second pocket which she had not yet examined. She pat her hand into it, and, touching something, drew out a letter.

The envelope (already open) was addressed to "James Brown, Esq., Post Office, Zeeland." Would it be inconsistent with her respect for her father's memory to examine the letter? No; a glance would decide whether she ought to read it or not.

It was without date or address; a startling letter to look at—for it only contained three words:

"I say No."

The words were signed in initials:

"S. J."

In the instant when she read the initials, the name occurred to her.

Sara Jethro.

CHAPTER LXIII. THE DEFENSE OF MIRABEL.

The discovery of the letter gave a new direction to Emily's thoughts—and so, for the time at least, relieved her mind from the burden that weighed on it. To what question, on her father's part, had "I say No" been Miss Jethro's brief and stern reply? Neither letter nor envelope offered the slightest hint that might assist inquiry; even the postmark had been so carelessly impressed that it was illegible.

Emily was still pondering over the three mysterious words, when she was interrupted by Mrs. Ellmother's voice at the door.

"I must ask you to let me come in, miss; though I know you wished to be left by yourself till to-morrow. Mrs. Delvin says she must positively see you to-night. It's my belief that she will send for the servants, and have herself carried in here, if you refuse to do what she asks. You needn't be afraid of seeing Mr. Mirabel."

"Where is he?"

"His sister has given up her bedroom to him," Mrs. Ellmother answered. "She thought of your feelings before she sent me here—and had the curtains closed between the sitting-room and the bedroom. I suspect my nasty temper misled me, when I took a dislike to Mrs. Delvin. She's a good creature; I'm sorry you didn't go to her as soon as we got back."

"Did she seem to be angry, when she sent you here?"

"Angry! She was crying when I left her."

Emily hesitated no longer.

She noticed a remarkable change in the invalid's sitting-room—so brilliantly lighted on other occasions—the moment she entered it. The lamps were shaded, and the candles were all extinguished. "My eyes don't bear the light so well as usual," Mrs. Delvin said. "Come and sit near me, Emily; I hope to quiet your mind. I should be grieved if you left my house with a wrong impression of me."

Knowing what she knew, suffering as she must have suffered, the quiet kindness of her tone implied an exercise of self-restraint which appealed irresistibly to Emily's sympathies. "Forgive me," she said, "for having done you an injustice. I am ashamed to think that I shrank from seeing you when I returned from Belford."

"I will endeavor to be worthy of your better opinion of me," Mrs. Delvin replied. "In one respect at least, I may claim to have had your best interests at heart—while we were still personally strangers. I tried to prevail on my poor brother to own the truth, when he discovered the terrible position in which he was placed toward you. He was too conscious of the absence of any proof which might induce you to believe him, if he attempted to defend himself—in one word, he was too timid—to take my advice. He has paid the penalty, and I have paid the penalty, of deceiving you."

Emily started. "In what way have you deceived me?" she asked.

"In the way that was forced on us by our own conduct," Mrs. Delvin said. "We have appeared to help you, without really doing so; we calculated on inducing you to marry my brother, and then (when he could speak with the authority of a husband) on prevailing on you to give up all further inquiries. When you insisted on seeing Mrs. Rook, Miles had the money in his hand to bribe her and her husband to leave England."

"Oh, Mrs. Delvin!"

"I don't attempt to excuse myself. I don't expect you to consider how sorely I was tempted to secure the happiness of my brother's life, by marriage with such a woman as yourself. I don't remind you that I knew—when I put obstacles in your way—that you were blindly devoting yourself to the discovery of an innocent man."

Emily heard her with angry surprise. "Innocent?" she repeated. "Mrs. Rook recognized his voice the instant she heard him speak."

Impenetrable to interruption, Mrs. Delvin went on. "But what I do ask," she persisted, "even after our short acquaintance, is this. Do you suspect me of deliberately scheming to make you the wife of a murderer?"

Emily had never viewed the serious question between them in this light. Warmly, generously, she answered the appeal that had been made to her. "Oh, don't think that of me! I know I spoke thoughtlessly and cruelly to you, just now—"

173

"You spoke impulsively," Mrs. Delvin interposed; "that was all. My one desire before we part—how can I expect you to remain here, after what has happened?—is to tell you the truth. I have no interested object in view; for all hope of your marriage with my brother is now at an end. May I ask if you have heard that he and your father were strangers, when they met at the inn?"

"Yes; I know that."

"If there had been any conversation between them, when they retired to rest, they might have mentioned their names. But your father was preoccupied; and my brother, after a long day's walk, was so tired that he fell asleep as soon as his head was on the pillow. He only woke when the morning dawned. What he saw when he looked toward the opposite bed might have struck with terror the boldest man that ever lived. His first impulse was naturally to alarm the house. When he got on his feet, he saw his own razor—a blood-stained razor on the bed by the side of the corpse. At that discovery, he lost all control over himself. In a panic of terror, he snatched up his knapsack, unfastened the yard door, and fled from the house. Knowing him, as you and I know him, can we wonder at it? Many a man has been hanged for murder, on circumstantial evidence less direct than the evidence against poor Miles. His horror of his own recollections was so overpowering that he forbade me even to mention the inn at Zeeland in my letters, while he was abroad. 'Never tell me (he wrote) who that wretched murdered stranger was, if I only heard of his name, I believe it would haunt me to my dying day. I ought not to trouble you with these details—and yet, I am surely not without excuse. In the absence of any proof, I cannot expect you to believe as I do in my brother's innocence. But I may at least hope to show you that there is some reason for doubt. Will you give him the benefit of that doubt?"

"Willingly!" Emily replied. "Am I right in supposing that you don't despair of proving his innocence, even yet'?"

"I don't quite despair. But my hopes have grown fainter and fainter, as the years have gone on. There is a person associated with his escape from Zeeland; a person named Jethro—"

"You mean Miss Jethro!"

"Yes. Do you know her?"

"I know her—and my father knew her. I have found a letter, addressed to him, which I have no doubt was written by Miss Jethro. It is barely possible that you may understand what it means. Pray look at it."

"I am quite unable to help you," Mrs. Delvin answered, after reading the letter. "All I know of Miss Jethro is that, but for her interposition, my brother might have fallen into the hands of the police. She saved him."

"Knowing him, of course?"

"That is the remarkable part of it: they were perfect strangers to each other."

"But she must have had some motive."

"There is the foundation of my hope for Miles. Miss Jethro declared, when I wrote and put the question to her, that the one motive by which she was actuated was the motive of mercy. I don't believe her. To my mind, it is in the last degree improbable that she would consent to protect a stranger from discovery, who owned to her (as my brother did) that he was a fugitive suspected of murder. She knows something, I am firmly convinced, of that dreadful event at Zeeland—and she has some reason for keeping it secret. Have you any influence over her?"

"Tell me where I can find her."

"I can't tell you. She has removed from the address at which my brother saw her last. He has made every possible inquiry—without result."

As she replied in those discouraging terms, the curtains which divided Mrs. Delvin's bedroom from her sitting-room were drawn aside. An elderly woman-servant approached her mistress's couch.

"Mr. Mirabel is awake, ma'am. He is very low; I can hardly feel his pulse. Shall I give him some more brandy?"

Mrs. Delvin held out her hand to Emily. "Come to me to-morrow morning," she said—and signed to the servant to wheel her couch into the next room. As the curtain closed over them, Emily heard Mirabel's voice. "Where am I?" he said faintly. "Is it all a dream?"

The prospect of his recovery the next morning was gloomy indeed. He had sunk into a state of deplorable weakness, in mind as well as in body. The little memory of events that he still preserved was regarded by him as the memory of a dream. He alluded to Emily, and to his meeting with her unexpectedly. But from that point his recollection failed him. They had talked of something interesting, he said—but he was unable to remember what it was. And they had waited together at a railway station—but for what purpose he could not tell. He sighed and wondered when Emily would marry him—and so fell asleep again, weaker than ever.

Not having any confidence in the doctor at Belford, Mrs. Delvin had sent an urgent message to a physician at Edinburgh, famous for his skill in treating diseases of the nervous system. "I cannot expect him to reach this remote place, without some delay," she said; "I must bear my suspense as well as I can."

"You shall not bear it alone," Emily answered. "I will wait with you till the doctor comes."

Mrs. Delvin lifted her frail wasted hands to Emily's face, drew it a little nearer—and kissed her.

CHAPTER LXIV. ON THE WAY TO LONDON.

The parting words had been spoken. Emily and her companion were on their way to London.

For some little time, they traveled in silence—alone in the railway carriage. After submitting as long as she could to lay an embargo on the use of her tongue, Mrs. Ellmother started the conversation by means of a question: "Do you think Mr. Mirabel will get over it, miss?"

"It's useless to ask me," Emily said. "Even the great man from Edinburgh is not able to decide yet, whether he will recover or not."

"You have taken me into your confidence, Miss Emily, as you promised—and I have got something in my mind in consequence. May I mention it without giving offense?"

"What is it?"

"I wish you had never taken up with Mr. Mirabel."

Emily was silent. Mrs. Ellmother, having a design of her own to accomplish, ventured to speak more plainly. "I often think of Mr. Alban Morris," she proceeded. "I always did like him, and I always shall."

Emily suddenly pulled down her veil. "Don't speak of him!" she said.

"I didn't mean to offend you."

"You don't offend me. You distress me. Oh, how often I have wished—!" She threw herself back in a corner of the carriage and said no more.

Although not remarkable for the possession of delicate tact, Mrs. Ellmother discovered that the best course she could now follow was a course of silence.

Even at the time when she had most implicitly trusted Mirabel, the fear that she might have acted hastily and harshly toward Alban had occasionally troubled Emily's mind. The impression produced by later events had not only intensified this feeling, but had presented the motives of that true friend under an entirely new point of view. If she had been left in ignorance of the manner of her father's death—as Alban had designed to leave her; as she would have been left, but for the treachery of Francine—how happily free she would have been from thoughts which it was now a terror to her to recall. She would have parted from Mirabel, when the visit to the pleasant country house had come to an end, remembering him as an amusing acquaintance and nothing more. He would have been spared, and she would have been spared, the shock that had so cruelly assailed them both. What had she gained by Mrs. Rook's detestable confession? The result had been perpetual disturbance of mind provoked by self-torturing speculations on the subject of the murder. If Mirabel was innocent, who was guilty? The false wife, without pity and without shame—or the brutal husband, who looked capable of any enormity? What was her future to be? How was it all to end? In the despair of that bitter moment—seeing her devoted old servant looking at her with kind compassionate eyes—Emily's troubled spirit sought refuge in impetuous self-betrayal; the very betrayal which she had resolved should not escape her, hardly a minute since!

She bent forward out of her corner, and suddenly drew up her veil. "Do you expect to see Mr. Alban Morris, when we get back?" she asked.

"I should like to see him, miss—if you have no objection."

"Tell him I am ashamed of myself! and say I ask his pardon with all my heart!"

"The Lord be praised!" Mrs. Ellmother burst out—and then, when it was too late, remembered the conventional restraints appropriate to the occasion. "Gracious, what a fool I am!" she said to herself. "Beautiful weather, Miss Emily, isn't it?" she continued, in a desperate hurry to change the subject.

Emily reclined again in her corner of the carriage. She smiled, for the first time since she had become Mrs. Delvin's guest at the tower.

BOOK THE LAST—AT HOME AGAIN.

CHAPTER LXV. CECILIA IN A NEW CHARACTER.

Reaching the cottage at night, Emily found the card of a visitor who had called during the day. It bore the name of "Miss Wyvil," and had a message written on it which strongly excited Emily's curiosity.

"I have seen the telegram which tells your servant that you return to-night. Expect me early to-morrow morning—with news that will deeply interest you."

To what news did Cecilia allude? Emily questioned the woman who had been left in charge of the cottage, and found that she had next to nothing to tell. Miss Wyvil had flushed up, and had looked excited, when she read the telegraphic message—that was all. Emily's impatience was, as usual, not to be concealed. Expert Mrs. Ellmother treated the case in the right way—first with supper, and then with an adjournment to bed. The clock struck twelve, when she put out the young mistress's candle. "Ten hours to pass before Cecilia comes here!" Emily exclaimed. "Not ten minutes," Mrs. Ellmother reminded her, "if you will only go to sleep."

Cecilia arrived before the breakfast-table was cleared; as lovely, as gentle, as affectionate as ever—but looking unusually serious and subdued.

"Out with it at once!" Emily cried. "What have you got to tell me?"

"Perhaps, I had better tell you first," Cecilia said, "that I know what you kept from me when I came here, after you left us at Monksmoor. Don't think, my dear, that I say this by way of complaint. Mr. Alban Morris says you had good reasons for keeping your secret."

"Mr. Alban Morris! Did you get your information from him?"

176

"Yes. Do I surprise you?"

"More than words can tell!"

"Can you bear another surprise? Mr. Morris has seen Miss Jethro, and has discovered that Mr. Mirabel has been wrongly suspected of a dreadful crime. Our amiable little clergyman is guilty of being a coward—and guilty of nothing else. Are you really quiet enough to read about it?"

She produced some leaves of paper filled with writing. "There," she explained, "is Mr. Morris's own account of all that passed between Miss Jethro and himself."

"But how do you come by it?"

"Mr. Morris gave it to me. He said, 'Show it to Emily as soon as possible; and take care to be with her while she reads it.' There is a reason for this—" Cecilia's voice faltered. On the brink of some explanation, she seemed to recoil from it. "I will tell you by-and-by what the reason is," she said.

Emily looked nervously at the manuscript. "Why doesn't he tell me himself what he has discovered? Is he—" The leaves began to flutter in her trembling fingers—"is he angry with me?"

"Oh, Emily, angry with You! Read what he has written and you shall know why he keeps away."

Emily opened the manuscript.

CHAPTER LXVI. ALBAN'S NARRATIVE.

"The information which I have obtained from Miss Jethro has been communicated to me, on the condition that I shall not disclose the place of her residence. 'Let me pass out of notice (she said) as completely as if I had passed out of life; I wish to be forgotten by some, and to be unknown by others.'" With this one stipulation, she left me free to write the present narrative of what passed at the interview between us. I feel that the discoveries which I have made are too important to the persons interested to be trusted to memory.

1. She Receives Me.

"Finding Miss Jethro's place of abode, with far less difficulty than I had anticipated (thanks to favoring circumstances), I stated plainly the object of my visit. She declined to enter into conversation with me on the subject of the murder at Zeeland.

"I was prepared to meet with this rebuke, and to take the necessary measures for obtaining a more satisfactory reception. 'A person is suspected of having committed the murder,' I said; 'and there is reason to believe that you are in a position to say whether the suspicion is justified or not. Do you refuse to answer me, if I put the question?'

"Miss Jethro asked who the person was.

"I mentioned the name—Mr. Miles Mirabel.

"It is not necessary, and it would certainly be not agreeable to me, to describe the effect which this reply produced on Miss Jethro. After giving her time to compose herself, I entered into certain explanations, in order to convince her at the outset of my good faith. The result justified my anticipations. I was at once admitted to her confidence.

"She said, 'I must not hesitate to do an act of justice to an innocent man. But, in such a serious matter as this, you have a right to judge for yourself whether the person who is now speaking to you is a person whom you can trust. You may believe that I tell the truth about others, if I begin—whatever it may cost me—by telling the truth about myself.'"

2. She Speaks of Herself.

"I shall not attempt to place on record the confession of a most unhappy woman. It was the common story of sin bitterly repented, and of vain effort to recover the lost place in social esteem. Too well known a story, surely, to be told again.

"But I may with perfect propriety repeat what Miss Jethro said to me, in allusion to later events in her life which are connected with my own personal experience. She recalled to my memory a visit which she had paid to me at Netherwoods, and a letter addressed to her by Doctor Allday, which I had read at her express request.

"She said, 'You may remember that the letter contained some severe reflections on my conduct. Among other things, the doctor mentions that he called at the lodging I occupied during my visit to London, and found I had taken to flight: also that he had reason to believe I had entered Miss Ladd's service, under false pretenses.'

"I asked if the doctor had wronged her.

"She answered 'No: in one case, he is ignorant; in the other, he is right. On leaving his house, I found myself followed in the street by the man to whom I owe the shame and misery of my past life. My horror of him is not to be described in words. The one way of escaping was offered by an empty cab that passed me. I reached the railway station safely, and went back to my home in the country. Do you blame me?'

"It was impossible to blame her—and I said so.

"She then confessed the deception which she had practiced on Miss Ladd. 'I have a cousin,' she said, 'who was a Miss Jethro like me. Before her marriage she had been employed as a governess. She pitied me; she sympathized with my longing to recover the character that I had lost. With her permission, I made use of the testimonials which she had earned as a teacher—I was betrayed (to this day I don't know by whom)—and I was dismissed from Netherwoods. Now you know that I deceived Miss Ladd, you may reasonably conclude that I am likely to deceive You.'

"I assured her, with perfect sincerity, that I had drawn no such conclusion. Encouraged by my reply, Miss Jethro proceeded as follows."

3. She Speaks of Mirabel.

"'Four years ago, I was living near Cowes, in the Isle of Wight—in a cottage which had been taken for me by a gentleman who was the owner of a yacht. We had just returned from a short cruise, and the vessel was under orders to sail for Cherbourg with the next tide.

"'While I was walking in my garden, I was startled by the sudden appearance Of a man (evidently a gentleman) who was a perfect stranger to me. He was in a pitiable state of terror, and he implored my protection. In reply to my first inquiries, he mentioned the inn at Zeeland, and the dreadful death of a person unknown to him; whom I recognized (partly by the description given, and partly by comparison of dates) as Mr. James Brown. I shall say nothing of the shock inflicted on me: you don't want to know what I felt. What I did (having literally only a minute left for decision) was to hide the fugitive from discovery, and to exert my influence in his favor with the owner of the yacht. I saw nothing more of him. He was put on board, as soon as the police were out of sight, and was safely landed at Cherbourg.'

"I asked what induced her to run the risk of protecting a stranger, who was under suspicion of having committed a murder.

"She said, 'You shall hear my explanation directly. Let us have done with Mr. Mirabel first. We occasionally corresponded, during the long absence on the continent; never alluding, at his express request, to the horrible event at the inn. His last letter reached me, after he had established himself at Vale Regis. Writing of the society in the neighborhood, he informed me of his introduction to Miss Wyvil, and of the invitation that he had received to meet her friend and schoolfellow at Monksmoor. I knew that Miss Emily possessed a Handbill describing personal peculiarities in Mr. Mirabel, not hidden under the changed appearance of his head and face. If she remembered or happened to refer to that description, while she was living in the same house with him, there was a possibility at least of her suspicion being excited. The fear of this took me to you. It was a morbid fear, and, as events turned out, an unfounded fear: but I was unable to control it. Failing to produce any effect on you, I went to Vale Regis, and tried (vainly again) to induce Mr. Mirabel to send an excuse to Monksmoor. He, like you, wanted to know what my motive was. When I tell you that I acted solely in Miss Emily's interests, and that I knew how she had been deceived about her father's death, need I say why I was afraid to acknowledge my motive?'

"I understood that Miss Jethro might well be afraid of the consequences, if she risked any allusion to Mr. Brown's horrible death, and if it afterward chanced to reach his daughter's ears. But this state of feeling implied an extraordinary interest in the preservation of Emily's peace of mind. I asked Miss Jethro how that interest had been excited?

"She answered, 'I can only satisfy you in one way. I must speak of her father now.'"

Emily looked up from the manuscript. She felt Cecilia's arm tenderly caressing her. She heard Cecilia say, "My poor dear, there is one last trial of your courage still to come. I am afraid of what you are going to read, when you turn to the next page. And yet—"

"And yet," Emily replied gently, "it must be done. I have learned my hard lesson of endurance, Cecilia, don't be afraid."

Emily turned to the next page.

4. She Speaks of the Dead.

"For the first time, Miss Jethro appeared to be at a loss how to proceed. I could see that she was suffering. She rose, and opening a drawer in her writing table, took a letter from it.

"She said, 'Will you read this? It was written by Miss Emily's father. Perhaps it may say more for me than I can say for myself?'

"I copy the letter. It was thus expressed:

"'You have declared that our farewell to-day is our farewell forever. For the second time, you have refused to be my wife; and you have done this, to use your own words, in mercy to Me.

"'In mercy to Me, I implore you to reconsider your decision.

"'If you condemn me to live without you—I feel it, I know it—you condemn me to despair which I have not fortitude enough to endure. Look at the passages which I have marked for you in the New Testament. Again and again, I say it; your true repentance has made you worthy of the pardon of God. Are you not worthy of the love, admiration, and respect of man? Think! oh, Sara, think of what our lives might be, and let them be united for time and for eternity.

"'I can write no more. A deadly faintness oppresses me. My mind is in a state unknown to me in past years. I am in such confusion that I sometimes think I hate you. And then I recover from my delusion, and know that man never loved woman as I love you.

"'You will have time to write to me by this evening's post. I shall stop at Zeeland to-morrow, on my way back, and ask for a letter at the post office. I forbid explanations and excuses. I forbid heartless allusions to your duty. Let me have an answer which does not keep me for a moment in suspense.

"'For the last time, I ask you: Do you consent to be my wife? Say, Yes—or say, No.'

"I gave her back the letter—with the one comment on it, which the circumstances permitted me to make:

"'You said No?'

"She bent her head in silence.

"I went on—not willingly, for I would have spared her if it had been possible. I said, 'He died, despairing, by his own hand—and you knew it?'

"She looked up. 'No! To say that I knew it is too much. To say that I feared it is the truth.'

"'Did you love him?'

"She eyed me in stern surprise. 'Have I any right to love? Could I disgrace an honorable man by allowing him to marry me? You look as if you held me responsible for his death.'

179

"'Innocently responsible,' I said.

"She still followed her own train of thought. 'Do you suppose I could for a moment anticipate that he would destroy himself, when I wrote my reply? He was a truly religious man. If he had been in his right mind, he would have shrunk from the idea of suicide as from the idea of a crime.'

"On reflection, I was inclined to agree with her. In his terrible position, it was at least possible that the sight of the razor (placed ready, with the other appliances of the toilet, for his fellow-traveler's use) might have fatally tempted a man whose last hope was crushed, whose mind was tortured by despair. I should have been merciless indeed, if I had held Miss Jethro accountable thus far. But I found it hard to sympathize with the course which she had pursued, in permitting Mr. Brown's death to be attributed to murder without a word of protest. 'Why were you silent?' I said.

"She smiled bitterly.

"'A woman would have known why, without asking,' she replied. 'A woman would have understood that I shrank from a public confession of my shameful past life. A woman would have remembered what reasons I had for pitying the man who loved me, and for accepting any responsibility rather than associate his memory, before the world, with an unworthy passion for a degraded creature, ending in an act of suicide. Even if I had made that cruel sacrifice, would public opinion have believed such a person as I am—against the evidence of a medical man, and the verdict of a jury? No, Mr. Morris! I said nothing, and I was resolved to say nothing, so long as the choice of alternatives was left to me. On the day when Mr. Mirabel implored me to save him, that choice was no longer mine—and you know what I did. And now again when suspicion (after all the long interval that had passed) has followed and found that innocent man, you know what I have done. What more do you ask of me?'

"'Your pardon,' I said, 'for not having understood you—and a last favor. May I repeat what I have heard to the one person of all others who ought to know, and who must know, what you have told me?'

"It was needless to hint more plainly that I was speaking of Emily. Miss Jethro granted my request.

"'It shall be as you please,' she answered. 'Say for me to his daughter, that the grateful remembrance of her is my one refuge from the thoughts that tortured me, when we spoke together on her last night at school. She has made this dead heart of mine feel a reviving breath of life, when I think of her. Never, in our earthly pilgrimage, shall we meet again—I implore her to pity and forget me. Farewell, Mr. Morris; farewell forever.'

"I confess that the tears came into my eyes. When I could see clearly again, I was alone in the room."

CHAPTER LXVII. THE TRUE CONSOLATION.

Emily closed the pages which told her that her father had died by his own hand.

Cecilia still held her tenderly embraced. By slow degrees, her head dropped until it rested on her friend's bosom. Silently she suffered. Silently Cecilia bent forward, and kissed her forehead. The sounds that penetrated to the room were not out of harmony with the time. From a distant house the voices of children were just audible, singing the plaintive melody of a hymn; and, now and then, the breeze blew the first faded leaves of autumn against the window. Neither of the girls knew how long the minutes followed each other uneventfully, before there was a change. Emily raised her head, and looked at Cecilia.

"I have one friend left," she said.

"Not only me, love—oh, I hope not only me!"

"Yes. Only you."

"I want to say something, Emily; but I am afraid of hurting you."

"My dear, do you remember what we once read in a book of history at school? It told of the death of a tortured man, in the old time, who was broken on the wheel. He lived through it long enough to say that the agony, after the first stroke of the club, dulled his capacity for feeling pain when the next blows fell. I fancy pain of the mind must follow the same rule. Nothing you can say will hurt me now."

"I only wanted to ask, Emily, if you were engaged—at one time—to marry Mr. Mirabel. Is it true?"

"False! He pressed me to consent to an engagement—and I said he must not hurry me."

"What made you say that?"

"I thought of Alban Morris."

Vainly Cecilia tried to restrain herself. A cry of joy escaped her.

"Are you glad?" Emily asked. "Why?"

Cecilia made no direct reply. "May I tell you what you wanted to know, a little while since?" she said. "You asked why Mr. Morris left it all to me, instead of speaking to you himself. When I put the same question to him, he told me to read what he had written. 'Not a shadow of suspicion rests on Mr. Mirabel,' he said. 'Emily is free to marry him—and free through Me. Can I tell her that? For her sake, and for mine, it must not be. All that I can do is to leave old remembrances to plead for me. If they fail, I shall know that she will be happier with Mr. Mirabel than with me.' 'And you will submit?' I asked. 'Because I love her,' he answered, 'I must submit.' Oh, how pale you are! Have I distressed you?"

"You have done me good."

"Will you see him?"

Emily pointed to the manuscript. "At such a time as this?" she said.

Cecilia still held to her resolution. "Such a time as this is the right time," she answered. "It is now, when you most want to be comforted, that you ought to see him. Who can quiet your poor aching heart as he can quiet it?" She impulsively snatched at the manuscript and threw it out of sight. "I can't bear to look at it," she said. "Emily! if I have done wrong, will you forgive me? I saw him this morning before I came here. I was afraid of what might happen—I refused to break the dreadful news to you, unless he was somewhere near us. Your good old servant knows where to go. Let me send her—"

Mrs. Ellmother herself opened the door, and stood doubtful on the threshold, hysterically sobbing and laughing at the same time. "I'm everything that's bad!" the good old creature burst out. "I've been listening—I've been lying—I said you wanted him. Turn me out of my situation, if you like. I've got him! Here he is!"

In another moment, Emily was in his arms—and they were alone. On his faithful breast the blessed relief of tears came to her at last: she burst out crying.

"Oh, Alban, can you forgive me?"

He gently raised her head, so that he could see her face.

"My love, let me look at you," he said. "I want to think again of the day when we parted in the garden at school. Do you remember the one conviction that sustained me? I told you, Emily, there was a time of fulfillment to come in our two lives; and I have never wholly lost the dear belief. My own darling, the time has come!"

POSTSCRIPT. GOSSIP IN THE STUDIO.

The winter time had arrived. Alban was clearing his palette, after a hard day's work at the cottage. The servant announced that tea was ready, and that Miss Ladd was waiting to see him in the next room.

Alban ran in, and received the visitor cordially with both hands. "Welcome back to England! I needn't ask if the sea-voyage has done you good. You are looking ten years younger than when you went away."

Miss Ladd smiled. "I shall soon be ten years older again, if I go back to Netherwoods," she replied. "I didn't believe it at the time; but I know better now. Our friend Doctor Allday was right, when he said that my working days were over. I must give up the school to a younger and stronger successor, and make the best I can in retirement of what is left of my life. You and Emily may expect to have me as a near neighbor. Where is Emily?"

"Far away in the North."

"In the North! You don't mean that she has gone back to Mrs. Delvin?"

"She has gone back—with Mrs. Ellmother to take care of her—at my express request. You know what Emily is, when there is an act of mercy to be done. That unhappy man has been sinking (with intervals of partial recovery) for months past. Mrs. Delvin sent word to us that the end was near, and that the one last wish her brother was able to express was the wish to see Emily. He had been for some hours unable to speak when my wife arrived. But he knew her, and smiled faintly. He was just able to lift his hand. She took it, and waited by him, and spoke words of consolation and kindness from time to time. As the night advanced, he sank into sleep, still holding her hand. They only knew that he had passed from sleep to death—passed without a movement or a sigh—when his hand turned cold. Emily remained for a day at the tower to comfort poor Mrs. Delvin—and she comes home, thank God, this evening!"

"I needn't ask if you are happy?" Miss Ladd said.

"Happy? I sing, when I have my bath in the morning. If that isn't happiness (in a man of my age) I don't know what is!"

"And how are you getting on?"

"Famously! I have turned portrait painter, since you were sent away for your health. A portrait of Mr. Wyvil is to decorate the town hall in the place that he represents; and our dear kind-hearted Cecilia has induced a fascinated mayor and corporation to confide the work to my hands."

"Is there no hope yet of that sweet girl being married?" Miss Ladd asked. "We old maids all believe in marriage, Mr. Morris—though some of us don't own it."

"There seems to be a chance," Alban answered. "A young lord has turned up at Monksmoor; a handsome pleasant fellow, and a rising man in politics. He happened to be in the house a few days before Cecilia's birthday; and he asked my advice about the right present to give her. I said, 'Try something new in Tarts.' When he found I was in earnest, what do you think he did? Sent his steam yacht to Rouen for some of the famous pastry! You should have seen Cecilia, when the young lord offered his delicious gift. If I could paint that smile and those eyes, I should be the greatest artist living. I believe she will marry him. Need I say how rich they will be? We shall not envy them—we are rich too. Everything is comparative. The portrait of Mr. Wyvil will put three hundred pounds in my pocket. I have earned a hundred and twenty more by illustrations, since we have been married. And my wife's income (I like to be particular) is only five shillings and tenpence short of two hundred a year. Moral! we are rich as well as happy."

"Without a thought of the future?" Miss Ladd asked slyly.

"Oh, Doctor Allday has taken the future in hand! He revels in the old-fashioned jokes, which used to be addressed to newly-married people, in his time. 'My dear fellow,' he said the other day, 'you may possibly be under a joyful necessity of sending for the doctor, before we are all a year older. In that case, let it be understood that I am Honorary Physician to the family.' The warm-hearted old man talks of getting me another portrait to do. 'The greatest ass in the medical profession (he informed me) has just been made a baronet; and his admiring friends have decided that he is to be painted at full length, with his bandy legs hidden under a gown, and his great globular eyes staring at the spectator—I'll get you the job.' Shall I tell you what he says of Mrs. Rook's recovery?"

Miss Ladd held up her hands in amazement. "Recovery!" she exclaimed.

"And a most remarkable recovery too," Alban informed her. "It is the first case on record of any person getting over such an injury as she has received. Doctor Allday looked grave when he heard of it. 'I begin to believe in the devil,' he said; 'nobody else could have saved Mrs. Rook.' Other people don't take that view. She has been celebrated in all the medical newspapers—and she has been admitted to come excellent almshouse, to live in comfortable idleness to a green old age. The best of it is that she shakes her head, when her wonderful recovery is mentioned. 'It seems such a pity,' she says; 'I was so fit for heaven.' Mr. Rook having got rid of his wife, is in excellent spirits. He is occupied in looking after an imbecile old gentleman; and, when he is asked if he likes the employment, he winks mysteriously and slaps his pocket. Now, Miss Ladd, I think it's my turn to hear some news. What have you got to tell me?"

"I believe I can match your account of Mrs. Rook," Miss Ladd said. "Do you care to hear what has become of Francine?"

Alban, rattling on hitherto in boyish high spirits, suddenly became serious. "I have no doubt Miss de Sor is doing well," he said sternly. "She is too heartless and wicked not to prosper."

"You are getting like your old cynical self again, Mr. Morris—and you are wrong. I called this morning on the agent who had the care of Francine, when I left England. When I mentioned her name, he showed me a telegram, sent to him by her father. 'There's my authority,' he said, 'for letting her leave my house.' The message was short enough to be easily remembered: 'Anything my daughter likes as long as she doesn't come back to us.' In those cruel terms Mr. de Sor wrote of his own child. The agent was just as unfeeling, in his way. He called her the victim of slighted love and clever proselytizing. 'In plain words,' he said, 'the priest of the Catholic chapel close by has converted her; and she is now a novice in a convent of Carmelite nuns in the West of England. Who could have expected it? Who knows how it may end?'"

As Miss Ladd spoke, the bell rang at the cottage gate. "Here she is!" Alban cried, leading the way into the hall. "Emily has come home."

183

Note from the Editor

Odin's Library Classics strives to bring you unedited and unabridged works of classical literature. As such, this is the complete and unabridged version of the original English text unless noted. In some instances, obvious typographical errors have been corrected. This is done to preserve the original text as much as possible. The English language has evolved since the writing and some of the words appear in their original form, or at least the most commonly used form at the time. This is done to protect the original intent of the author. If at any time you are unsure of the meaning of a word, please do your research on the etymology of that word. It is important to preserve the history of the English language.

Taylor Anderson

Printed in Great Britain
by Amazon